Also by Jodi Ellen Malpas

The
FORBIDDEN

Jodi was born and raised in the Midlands town of Northampton, England, where she lives with her two boys and a beagle. She is a self-professed daydreamer, a Converse and mojito addict, and has a terrible weak spot for alpha males. Writing powerful love stories and creating addictive characters has become her passion – a passion she now shares with her devoted readers. She's now a proud number one *New York Times* bestselling author – all six of her published novels having hit the *New York Times* bestsellers list – as well as a *Sunday Times* bestseller and international bestseller. Her work is published in over twenty languages across the world.

To find out more, visit www.jodiellenmalpas.co.uk, or find Jodi on Facebook www.facebook.com/jodi.malpas, and on Twitter @JodiEllenMalpas

The FORBIDDEN

JODI ELLEN MALPAS

First published in Great Britain in 2017 by Orion Books,
an imprint of The Orion Publishing Group Ltd
Carmelite House, 50 Victoria Embankment,
London EC4Y 0DZ

An Hachette UK company

1 3 5 7 9 10 8 6 4 2

A CIP catalogue record for this book is
available from the British Library.

ISBN 978 1 4091 6642 9

Typeset by Input Data Services Ltd, Somerset

Printed in Great Britain by Clays Ltd, St Ives plc

MIX
Paper from
responsible sources
FSC® C104740

www.orionbooks.co.uk

For Jamie

A note from the author

'The forbidden' is exactly that. Not allowed. Prohibited. Banned. At least, that's what society says. But what about your heart?

It took a massive leap of faith for me to put these words on paper. I've always said that I write what my heart tells me to write, not what people *want* me to write. Never has my own motto been so significant in my writing career. I questioned my sense when I came up with the idea of *The Forbidden*. Then I reminded myself of my motto, of my heart's desire, and my heart really wanted to tell this story, despite knowing that it might not be what people expect from me. I couldn't let my fear of the taboo subject matter dictate my writing. So I dived right in – no holding back, no inhibitions, no softly-softly approach.

The Forbidden is controversial. I've no doubt it'll cause debate, and I'm cool with that. As a writer, you accept that what you send out into the world is going to be picked apart, sometimes for the good, sometimes for the bad. This story is about the conflict. The feelings. The questions. It's about the heart ruling the head.

I ask you to go into it with an open mind, and please remember that it is a story. One of passion, of love and of heartache. It's about falling in love with the wrong person at the wrong time. Because it happens. Every single day. But above all of that, it's about being true to yourself and your heart. It's about finding your soul mate and fighting for them. It's about standing by what you believe in. And we all believe in true love.

JEM xxx

Chapter 1

I kick my way through the piles of mail on the wooden floor, balancing a box in my hands as the door slams shut behind me. The vibrations dislodge two years' worth of dust from the picture rails in the empty hallway, the fine particles bursting into the dim light before me and finding their way to my nose. I sneeze – once, twice, three times – dropping the box at my feet to rub away the tickle.

'Damn it,' I sniff, kicking the box to the side and heading down the hall in search of tissues.

Entering the lounge, I weave through the haphazard boxes in search of the one labelled BATHROOM. I don't fancy my chances. Boxes piled five high surround me, all waiting to be unpacked. I don't know where to start.

Circling slowly, I take in my new place – a ground-floor flat in a converted Georgian house on a tree-lined street in west London. The window in the lounge is huge, the ceilings high, the floors original. I wander through to the kitchen, grimacing at the stale smell and the layer of grime on every surface. The place has been empty for two years, and it shows. But it's nothing a day with a pair of rubber gloves and a bottle of cleaner can't sort.

Suddenly excited, envisioning how everything will sparkle after I've attacked it with a bucket load of detergent, I throw the double doors open into the courtyard garden to let in some air, then head to the master bedroom. It's a *massive* space, with a huge en suite and an original ornate fireplace. I smile, backing up into the corridor, and enter the second bedroom, though I have other ideas for this space. I picture my desk beneath the window looking out onto the cute courtyard, and my workbench spanning the back wall scattered with technical drawings and files. It's mine. All mine.

It's taken me a year to find the perfect flat in my price range, but I'm finally here. I finally have my own place, as well as my own studio to work from. I always told myself I'd have my own business and my own home by the time I'm thirty. I beat my target by a whole year. And now I have this weekend to make it feel like home.

As if on cue, there's a bang on the front door. I dash through the flat – *my* flat – and fling the door open, coming face to face with a bottle of Prosecco being thrust at me.

'Welcome home!' Lizzy sings, producing two glasses too.

'Oh, my God, you're a saint!' I lunge forward, seize the goods, and stand aside, welcoming her into my new home. I have the biggest grin on my face.

She beams right back and charges in, her short black hair brushing her chin, her dark eyes gleaming with happiness – happiness for me. 'First we toast, then we clean.'

I agree as I close the door behind her, following her into the cluttered lounge.

'Holy shit, Annie!' she gasps, coming to a stop at the doorway when she spies the mountain of boxes. 'Where did all this stuff come from?'

I push past her and place the glasses on a box, starting to peel back the foil from the bottle of fizz. 'Most of it is work stuff,' I say, popping the cork and starting to pour.

'How many books and pens does one architect need?' she asks, pointing to the opposite side of the lounge, where there's a line of plastic boxes running the length of one wall, all stuffed with various files, textbooks and stationery.

'Most of the books are from uni. Micky's stopping by

tomorrow with a van to take the stuff I don't want to the charity shop.' I hand Lizzy a glass and chink it with mine.

'Cheers,' she says, sipping as she gazes around. 'Where do we start?'

I join her, sipping while looking around at the mess that is my new home. 'I need to get my bedroom sorted so I have somewhere to sleep. I'll tackle the rest over the weekend.'

'Ooh, your boudoir!' She waggles suggestive eyebrows at me, and I roll my eyes.

'This is a man-free zone.' Knocking back another glug of Prosecco, I make tracks to my bedroom. 'Except for Micky,' I add, arriving in the huge space, mentally moving my bed, my wardrobes and my dressing table – which have all been dumped in the middle of the room. I hope Lizzy has stretched in preparation to shift all this hefty stuff.

'Your life is a man-free zone.'

'I'm too busy with work,' I point out, smiling a satisfied smile. I love it. My new business has gone from strength to strength. There's no better feeling than watching the vision in your head come to life, seeing a drawing turn into an actual building. From the age of twelve, I knew exactly what I wanted to do. Dad bought me a rabbit for my birthday, and quite unimpressed with the hutch that it came with, I nagged my father into extending it to make better accommodation for my new friend. He laughed and told me to draw what I wanted. So, I did. I've never looked back. After two years acing my A levels, four years at Bath University, and seven years working at a commercial firm while powering through my three architect exams, I'm now where I always planned on being. Working for myself. Making people's dream projects come to life.

I hold up my glass of fizz. 'How's your job, anyway?'

'I work to live, Annie. I don't live to work. I only think of pedicures, skin and nails when I'm at the salon.' Lizzy joins me on the threshold of my new bedroom. 'And don't change the subject. It's been one year, two months and one week since you got laid.'

'That's very accurate of you.'

Lizzy shrugs. 'It was my twenty-eighth.'

I remember the night all too well, though his name escapes me.

'Tom,' she prompts, as if reading my mind, turning to me. 'Cute rugby player dude. Jason's friend of a friend.'

Cute rugby player dude's thighs invade my mind. I smile, remembering the night I met Lizzy's boyfriend's friend of a friend, Tom. 'He was quite cute, wasn't he?'

'Very! So why didn't you see him again?'

'I don't know.' I shrug. 'There wasn't anything there.'

'There were thighs!'

I laugh. 'You know what I mean. Sparks. Chemistry.'

She scoffs. 'Annie, there's never been sparks for you in the whole time I've known you.'

She's right. When will a man appear and sweep me off my feet? Bamboozle me? Make me think of something other than my career? The only thing that gets my pulse racing is my job.

'Have you sworn off men forever?' Lizzy breaks into my thoughts. 'Because Jason has plenty of friends with friends.'

'I got bored of it all. Dating. The stress. The expectations. Nothing ever . . . clicked for me,' I say dismissively. 'Anyway, I'm too in love with my job and my freedom right now.'

Lizzy laughs, genuinely amused as she wanders into the room, peeking into the en suite. 'Your freedom is being seriously hampered by an eighty-hour working week.'

'Ninety,' I reply, and she frowns. 'I worked ninety hours last week. And I have the freedom to do that.'

'But what about fun stuff?'

'My job is fun,' I retort indignantly. 'I get to design beautiful buildings and watch them come to life.'

'I've hardly seen you recently,' she grumbles.

'I know. It's been crazy.'

'Yes, that posh couple in Chelsea have stolen all your time. How's it going, by the way?'

'Great,' I reply, because it is. But it's one of the toughest projects I've undertaken. It took months of designs and negotiating to finally come to a compromise with the local authorities to build an ultra-modern, eco-efficient home. The hard work was worth every bit of effort. The cube house on the edge of the common has helped me towards the ridiculous deposit I needed for my new home.

'They moved in last Friday.' I make my way to the double doors that lead into the courtyard garden, picturing the small space bursting with green, a cast-iron table and a couple of chairs outside where I can enjoy my morning coffee. 'Isn't this perfect?'

'It's great,' Lizzy says, following. 'Me and Jason seriously need to think about buying rather than renting.'

'Or building.' I waggle a cheeky eyebrow at her. 'I know an amazing architect.'

Lizzy scoffs. 'We couldn't afford you.'

I laugh and make my way inside. 'Are you going to help me make my bed or not?'

'I'm coming!' she sing-songs, shutting the doors behind her.

Three hours later, after a trip to the shop to restock on Prosecco, we've cleaned, polished and washed everything in sight, attacking the bathroom too. The old claw-foot bath is sparkling, and Lizzy unpacked all of my toiletries and cosmetics while I made up my bed. It already feels like home. I peek in the mirror as I pass, seeing my dark hair is a knotted mess on top of my head. I yank the hair-tie out and let it tumble over my shoulders, combing my fingers through to rid it of knots. I blink my pale green eyes a few times, something irritating me, as I lean into the mirror to remove a few specks of dust from my lashes.

'Don't forget we're out next Saturday,' Lizzy reminds me, tying a black sack as she emerges from the bathroom. 'Jason's on a work thing, Nat is escaping John as he's got his kid that night, and Micky is . . . well, he's always free. So I want no excuses that you have to work.'

I wander to my bed and plump my pillows, pulling back the duvet ready to fall into it once Lizzy has left. 'No excuses,' I confirm.

'Great!' She drops the black sack with the pile of others by the door, brushing off her hands. 'And what about your housewarming? We need to christen this place.'

'It's the Saturday after. I've invited a few new clients too.'

'Does that mean no orgy?'

I laugh. 'No orgy.'

'Oh, okay. I'll take care of snacks. You take care of cocktails.'

'Deal.'

She squeals and throws her arms around me. 'It's perfect, Annie. You've worked hard for it.'

'Thanks.' I return her hug, breathing in the scent of the millions of candles we've lit.

'How long have you given yourself off work?' she asks, releasing me and collecting her bag from the floor.

'Just the weekend.'

'Wow, you're pushing the boat out, aren't you?'

I ignore her sarcasm. 'I have to get some drawings finalised for my client's new art gallery. No rest for the wicked.'

'And no play, either,' Lizzy remarks, grinning a little as she pulls her mobile from her bag. 'Great,' she mumbles, looking down at the screen.

'What?'

She shoves it back in her bag and forces a smile. 'Jason's working late again. He was supposed to be picking me up' – she glances down at her watch – 'like, now.'

'You can stay, if you like.'

'Nah, I'll get the Tube. You go to bed.'

She leaves me with a kiss on the cheek and an order to sleep well. I've no doubt I will. In my brand new bed, with brand new sheets and brand new duvet, I'm asleep before my head hits the brand new pillow.

I wake the next morning to hard, relentless banging on my front door. Sitting up, I spend a few disorientated moments blinking sleepily as I look around my unfamiliar surroundings.

Bang, bang, bang!

Then my phone starts screeching from under my pillow, followed by more banging, backed up by someone shouting my name. My palms come up to my face and scrub at my cheeks before I feel for my phone and pull it from under the pillow. Micky's name flashes up at me. Then I register the time. 'Oh, shit!' I scramble from under my covers, stumbling my way out of my bedroom.

Bang, bang, bang!

'Okay, okay!' I yell, leaping over a box and crashing into the door. Swinging it open, I come face to face with a bright-eyed, bushy-tailed Micky. 'Seriously!' I yell, my head drumming with bangs, rings and shouts.

'Morning, treacle!' He lands a kiss on my cheek and pushes his way past me, oohing and swooning as he starts to explore my new abode. 'Nice place!'

I shut the front door and follow him in, frowning at the man-bun he's sporting. 'What's happened to your hair?' I ask, watching as he inspects every nook and cranny.

'You like?' he asks, reaching behind and feeling at the dark blonde bundle. 'It's starting to get in my way when I'm at work.' He kicks a box out of the way and takes a slurp from his Starbucks as he hands me one.

I accept gratefully and head for my bedroom. He's in his work uniform, namely shorts and a T-shirt. He's a personal trainer. A very popular personal trainer. His waiting list consists of women. All women. 'You working today?' I ask, setting my coffee on my bedside table.

Micky follows me in and plonks himself on the edge of my bed. 'Two sessions this afternoon.' He squeezes my thigh as I pass him, and I yelp. 'When are you gonna let me at you?'

'Never!' I laugh. 'I'd rather shove hot pokers in my eyes.'

'A few squats will do you good.'

I scoff at his suggestion and pull on some jeans. 'You have plenty of squatting arses to admire without torturing mine.'

He grins wickedly. 'Speaking of which, I just took on a new client.'

I fasten my jeans. 'Married?' I ask, pulling off my vest and throwing a U2 T-shirt over my head.

'Nope.' He grins. 'You know I limit married clients to five at any one time. That's an hour a day that I have to be professional. Five whole hours a week!'

I laugh out loud. The man is an outrageous flirt, but he's also one of the best PTs in London. Women are lining up to be bent, stretched and manipulated into position by my oldest friend. For more reasons than achieving physical fitness. 'Must be exhausting.'

'It is when they're tempting you constantly through each session. An innocent brush of my thigh here, an arse thrust in my face there.'

'If it's that challenging to keep your mind and eyes from wandering, you should just take on single women. Or men.'

'I need a balance of clients. Besides, the married ones try harder,' he says, and my eyebrows jump up. Micky rolls his eyes. 'In training,' he clarifies.

'So you've never been tempted?'

'Never!' He shakes his head furiously. 'I love my legs too much to risk an angry husband breaking them, thanks.'

Dragging my dark hair into a high ponytail, I chuckle and

slip on my flip-flops. I've known Micky for centuries. We grew up together. Played mummies and daddies together. Romped naked in the paddling pool together. He even hammered a few nails into the rabbit hutch extension when we were twelve. Our parents were, and still are, best friends.

'So how was your first night?' he asks, patting down my bedcovers.

'I don't think I've ever slept for so long.' It's a good sign. 'C'mon. Let's get rid of some of this shit so I can start figuring out where everything's going to go.'

We head into the lounge and I start slapping yellow Post-it notes on everything that I don't want to keep while Micky follows me around, placing it all to one side of the room. 'Hey, I'll have that.' Micky swipes the Post-it off a miniature set of drawers that used to sit on my dressing table in my old bedroom. 'I need somewhere to put my hair-ties.'

I laugh and carry on slapping Post-its on what needs to go. 'Your man-bun looks cute,' I say as Micky fondles his new friend with a smile. Truth be told, Micky could shave his hair off and look cute. The man is just cute full stop. His light brown eyes are constantly laughing and his jaw is constantly peppered with stubble. He's hot, but he's just Micky to me.

'Thanks.' He bats his lashes.

'Hey, we're going out next Saturday for drinks. You coming?'

'Of course,' he replies quickly. 'Lizzy and Nat coming?' He waggles a suggestive eyebrow.

'Don't even dare. Both know you're a tart.' He just can't help himself. Me, Nat and Lizzy are the only women in London who are immune to Micky's charm.

'Ouchy!' he sniggers, getting me in a headlock.

'Get off, you twat!' I wrestle out of his hold and straighten myself out, batting him away when he starts dancing around me, fists held up in front of his face.

'Yoo-hoo!' My mother's voice sails into the room, followed

by the sound of her heels clicking on the wooden floor.

I give Micky a quick jab in the biceps, and he yelps playfully. I follow the echo of Mum's call until I find her shimmying past the boxes lining the corridor, being careful not to catch her pleated skirt on any of them.

'Oh, look at the high ceilings!' she croons. 'And the picture rails!'

I rest my shoulder on the doorframe and watch with a smile as she shuffles towards me. Micky joins me, his chest meeting my back.

'Michael!' she shrieks, picking up her pace to make it to us. 'Give me a hug!' She virtually knocks me off my feet to get her hands on him. 'Let me see your handsome chops.' She squeezes his jaw fiercely, and I laugh. 'Where have you been? I haven't seen you in weeks!'

'Working hard, June.'

Mum smiles at him, releasing his face. 'When are you going to make an honest woman of my Annie?'

Micky looks across to me, just as I roll my eyes. 'As soon as she'll have me.' He grins wickedly, knowing exactly what he's doing, as he always does when my mother goes off at a tangent about our friendship.

Micky doesn't want to date me. He's too busy being a slut, and I'm too busy building my career. Our relationship is purely platonic – something we're both happy with. There's never been anything more than friendship between us. No sparks. No chemistry. Nothing. I often wonder whether any man will ever stir anything within me, because if Micky Letts hasn't, then it's possible no man will. He has women falling at his feet with just a hint of his disarming smile. Me? I feel nothing. I think I'm abnormal.

Mum tucks her bag neatly in the crook of her arm and produces a carrier bag loaded with cleaning supplies. 'I've come to help!'

'Dressed in that?' I ask, taking in her cream blouse, pleated skirt and heeled shoes.

'Always look your best, dear.' She sniffs. 'Your father will be here soon with his tool box. Now, where do we start?'

'I'm out of here,' Micky says, grabbing a box with a yellow sticker on it before dropping a peck on my mother's cheek and marching out of my door, hands full. He blows me a kiss as he passes.

I grin and turn to find my mother armoured up with some yellow rubber gloves and a bottle of cleaner.

'Let's get scrubbing,' she sings excitedly.

Chapter 2

My nails are shot to bits – the result of a week's worth of scrubbing and manual labour in between keeping on top of my clients, my e-mails and my designs. But my new flat is now a *sparkly* new flat. Everything has a home and every room has been painted. All of my reference books have been loaded onto the shelves in my studio, my computer and printer set up, and my desk placed in the window. I bloody love it. And now I am *more* than ready for a night out with the girls to let my hair down.

My iPod is cranked to the max and I'm dancing around my bedroom in my towel, the windows flung open, while I sing at the top of my voice to Madonna's 'Like A Prayer' and sip wine.

After making my eyes all smoky and smudged, slipping on a little black dress and the highest black heels I own, and pinning my hair into a mess of a low bun, I grab my bag and head for the door, hearing Lizzy knocking as I'm on my way.

'Nice.' She nods approvingly when I answer, though she looks a little vacant.

'You okay?' I ask, stepping out.

'Yeah, fine.' She looks effortlessly gorgeous, her black bobbed hair wavy today, and her brown eyes dramatic with heavy eyeliner. Her bright pink shift dress and leather biker jacket is perfectly edgy and perfectly Lizzy. 'You've made quite an effort too,' I observe as I link arms with her and we start down the path together.

'Just threw something on,' she says, waving off my compliment. 'Nat's meeting us there. And whatever you do, tell her you love her hair.'

'Why, what's she done?' I look at Lizzy in horror. Nat's hair is her pride and joy. Thick, blonde, glossy and down to her bum, it's groomed better than the Queen's corgis.

'John's kid got his bubblegum stuck in it.'

'Oh, shit,' I breathe, seeing Nat's face clear as day in my mind's eye. It's angry. Very, *very* angry. She's met the man of her dreams, but the man of her dreams comes with an added extra: a six-year-old boy who is a little bit of a handful. Scrap that. He's a *lot* of a handful. Nat's not exactly maternal. 'How much?' I wince, waiting for it, and then I gasp when Lizzy's cutting gesture saws at her shoulders. 'Oh, no.'

'And I've split up with Jason.'

I stagger to a stop. 'What?'

She shakes her head, tears threatening. 'I don't want to talk about it tonight.'

I snap my mouth shut quickly and, though it pains me, I refrain from pressing. 'Okay.' She needs a girls' night out, and I'm more than happy to oblige. 'Wait. Does Nat know?'

She nods and quickly wipes under her eyes. 'Let's just have fun tonight, please.'

'Done.' I grab her arm and march on, determined to distract her for tonight, my mind racing with what could have happened.

It's a challenge, but I manage not to choke when I clap eyes on Nat's dramatic, unplanned transformation. Her long locks are no more, and the scowl on her face tells me that she hasn't come to terms with it yet.

'Tell her it looks great,' Lizzy mumbles under her breath as we head towards her.

'It looks great!' I shriek, resting my bum on one of the tall stools. Everyone falls silent, Lizzy rolls her eyes and Nat growls at me. 'What?' I ask, shrinking.

'I look about fifty,' Nat mutters.

'No you don't,' Lizzy and I sing in unison, so fucking over the top. She really does look older. Perhaps not quite fifty, but definitely older than her thirty years.

'I love it!' I declare, happy that I sound sincere enough, prompting Nat's hands to go up to her hair and feel the lack of length.

'Really?' she asks, looking for reassurance.

'Yes, makes you look more sophisticated.'

She smiles, grateful, and Lizzy knocks my arm as she passes me, her way of congratulating me on a job well done. 'I'm getting drinks,' she declares. 'Who wants what?'

'Wine!' Nat and I chant.

Lizzy heads for the bar, and I take the opportunity to interrogate Nat. 'What's happened with Lizzy and Jason?' I ask, leaning forward over the table.

'I don't know.' She shrugs nonchalantly, ever the compassionate type. 'She refuses to talk about it.'

'But I thought they were solid.'

'Yeah, me too. Apparently not, eh?'

'You sound so concerned.' I give her a disappointed look, and she just shrugs again. Nat's not exactly the emotional type. She's a loss adjuster for a huge insurance firm. A real tough cookie, and she struggles to separate that from her personal life. Most men are intimidated by her. Most women too, actually. Tall, leggy, blonde and a bit of an emotional retard.

'My hair was massacred,' she snipes, 'so I'm moody.'

Our conversation is cut short – not that it was going anywhere – when Lizzy slides a tray onto the table, loaded with not only wine, but shots too. I look at Nat, who nods her understanding. Lizzy is on a mission to total drunkenness.

We both accept the shots she hands us and throw them back as ordered. Then I ponder who of my friends is in the most turmoil, therefore needing my attention. You'd think this would be an easy decision, but Nat was probably as much in love with her hair as I thought Lizzy was with Jason. I flick my eyes between them; both distracted. Nat is still stroking her new bob, and Lizzy's now daydreaming into her wine glass.

It's no good. I can't hold back. 'What happened?' I ask Lizzy, knocking her knee.

She snaps out of her trance and looks at me, her usually bright eyes dulling. Then they well up, her bottom lip trembling. 'He cheated!' she wails, bursting into tears. 'And it's not the first time, either!'

'Oh my God!' I cry, jumping down from my stool and taking her in a hug. She shakes and blubbers all over me, finally losing the ability to hold it together. 'Why didn't you say anything?'

'When it happened before, I forgave him,' Lizzy sniffs. 'Thought it would just be a one-off, and I knew how you'd all react. I didn't want you to think badly of him, and I didn't want you to think I'm a walkover.'

I look across Lizzy's head at Nat, giving her a guilty look. She returns it, knowing that's exactly what we would have done. *Bastard*, I mouth, and she nods, her lip curling.

Lizzy howls some more, making our tangle of limbs vibrate. 'It's been going on for months,' she sobs. 'Some tart in the office. He's been working late more and more, and I found text messages on his phone.'

Me and Nat scowl at each other, but neither of us say anything, probably because we have no idea what to say, leaving Lizzy to go on and dish the sordid details.

'She's twenty-one!' she howls into my chest. 'Twenty-fucking-one!'

Ouch!

Nat's face is a picture of horror, and I expect mine is too. 'Let's drink,' I suggest, now willing to get plastered on Lizzy's behalf.

One hour later . . . or it could be two – I'm not sure – we are all pretty tipsy, but no one is crying so our inebriated states can only be a good thing. Micky has arrived, and doesn't Lizzy know it. He looks gorgeous, his man-bun perfect. She's all over him like a rash, and it's not a problem for Micky. Though he does keep flicking wary eyes at me, waiting for the warning. It won't come. Not tonight. Besides, Lizzy needs distracting and I'm too tipsy to care. A bit of harmless flirting won't hurt.

Polishing off yet another glass of wine, I look around for Nat. I find her on the dance floor, all by herself, swaying to a bit of Moby. A few drinks inside her and she belongs to any dance floor, no matter where.

I shimmy over to the bar to get more shots, since we're clearly not drunk enough. Ordering four Slippery Nipples with a grin, I bob to the music while I wait for the barman to get our drinks. I slip him a twenty. 'Do you have a tray?' I ask.

'All out,' he calls as he walks away with my money.

I look down at the four shot glasses, pondering what to do. There's a simple solution, but I'm on my way to total drunkenness and it's not coming to me, so I start to negotiate the tiny glasses between my fingers, confident I can manage them all in one go and save myself an extra trip to our table . . . which is twenty feet away. 'Damn,' I mutter, knocking one and spilling the stickiness all over my hand. I start to lick at my fingers, lapping up the creamy concoction, set on minimal waste. Then I take the remainder of the shot and knock it back, reducing my load to three glasses. Far more manageable.

If you're totally sober. Which I'm not. I accept my change when the barman slides it across the counter to me. 'Thanks,' I call, starting to collect the three remaining glasses in my hands.

Another one goes over, and once again I lick the mess from my hand.

'You're not doing very well there, are you?'

The amused voice pulls me around, my lapping tongue around my fingers slowing to a standstill, my eyes widening at the sight of the man standing next to me at the bar.

Holy . . . shit.

I'm not often rendered speechless. Never, in fact. Now is making up for it, and I can't figure out if it's too much alcohol or the awe I'm in. *So* fucking hot! I take in every teeny tiny piece of him, from his shoes – which, it should be noted, are very stylish tan Jeffery West brogues – to the very top of his beautiful head. I say *beautiful*. I'm not sure it's complimentary enough. Classically handsome, maybe? Jaw-dropping? Stunning? Nothing seems adequate. He has scruff. Yummy scruff, which I guess is a result of not shaving for at least five days, and his grey eyes are ridiculously twinkly. Like little stars are popping in their depths. His hair is cut close to his head at the sides, but longer on top and manipulated to the side. Just long enough to hold on to . . .

I gulp down my wonder. The man can dress. Casual. Easy. A lovely fitted shirt, collar open, sleeves rolled up, loose and hanging out of his fitted Armani jeans. Did I mention he had good shoes?

'Need a hand?' he asks, eyeing me with . . . what is that?

A hand? Where would I put that hand? I tilt my head in silent contemplation, now staring at his hands. Big, capable hands, one wrapped around a bottle of beer. Then my eyes are lifting, following that bottle until it reaches his lips. His mouth opens. I catch sight of a sliver of his tongue, and his lips wrap around the bottle, his head tipping back. The throat. Holy shit, the throat. The swallow. The quiet gasp.

The colossal blast that's just happened in my knickers.

I flinch and cross my legs on the spot. I have no fucking clue what's going on inside me, but it's snapped me out of my ridiculous inertness. 'Shots!' I blurt, making a grab for the glasses. 'Hey, I ordered four,' I call to the waiter, scowling across the bar.

The man next to me starts laughing, a deep, sexy low rumble. More blasts. Oh . . . God. *Be quiet!*

'Just how drunk are you?' he asks, and I look at him to see him watching me closely.

'Perfectly sober, thanks,' I say, snatching my eyes away from him quickly before I give them the opportunity to embarrass me again. 'I ordered four.'

'And you've spilt two,' he points out. I look down and see the two empties . . . and it comes back to me. How long was I daydreaming? Or admiring? Or drooling?

'Oh.'

'Not drunk?'

I keep my eyes on the bar. They can't be trusted. 'Like I said, perfectly sober.' I gather up the remaining glasses and make to turn, being sure to maintain my stability. Not that I'm stubborn or anything. I'm not drunk.

'Care to prove it?' he asks, pulling me to a stop. A challenge?

I risk a peek at him out of the corner of my eye and find the most gorgeous smile on his already gorgeous face. Where the hell did he come from?

Prove it? 'How?' I ask, my curiosity getting the better of me.

'Take the shots to your friends.' He nods past me, and I look over to see my friends all now gathered around the tall table, Micky's arms flying in the air dramatically, the girls laughing. I manage to note that Dishy Man here knows who I'm with. How long has he been here? There's no *way* he would have slipped under any of the girls' Hot-Man Radar. 'Then come back to see me, if you want,' he adds quietly.

If I want? Do I want? I have another quick peek up at him. He's still smiling. It's a dangerous smile. Very dangerous. He's too handsome to be harmless.

I slink off, shamelessly adopting a mild sway of my arse as I go, resisting the urge to see if he's watching me. He *is* watching me. I just know it, and it's got me all hot and bothered.

Lizzy is on me like a pouncing tiger when I arrive back at the table. 'Who in God's name is that?' she asks, eyes wide with excitement as she takes a shot.

'I don't know,' I reply, downing the last shot myself instead of giving it up to any of my friends, all the while feeling the magnetic pull of the man behind me, my body tightening with the strain it's taking not to turn and seek him out again.

'Annie, I know you're pretty much immune to men, but this is taking the piss. He's watching you.'

Immune? I'm not sure I'd say *immune*. I've just never felt anything close to special. So why the hell am I tingling all over and trembling like a fool? I don't feel very immune now. 'He can watch.'

She gapes at me. 'Well, if you won't talk to him, then I will, since I'm single now.' Pushing past me, she slaps a smile on her face and heads towards the bar, and *my* man.

I have no idea what comes over me, but the next moment my hand has shot out and I've seized Lizzy's wrist, yanking her to a stop. I squeeze my eyes shut, annoyed with myself. 'Just hold on one minute.' I breathe in deeply and turn to her. 'A rebound fuck with a stranger isn't the way forward.'

She's holding back a grin that will probably split her face if it escapes. She has me. For the first time – probably *ever* – a man has caught my attention. I shouldn't read too much into it. I expect this particular man has caught every woman's attention, the unholy, good-looking son of a bitch.

Leaning into me, Lizzy pushes her mouth to my ear, just as my eyes fall on him again. He's still watching me. Intently, almost challengingly. 'He looks like a hard fucker,' Lizzy whispers, giggling as she breaks away, giving me a coy look. 'Do womankind a favour and get laid.' She nods past me. 'By him.'

'I'm just going to talk to him,' I protest, leaving my friend behind and giving in to the pull luring me back to him. I drink in air and start a steady pace towards him, dropping my bottom lip from between my teeth when I realise I'm biting it.

He maintains a serious face, watching me as he leans on the bar casually. 'I believe I saw a slight stagger,' he says, raising his eyebrows.

He's just too fucking handsome for his own good. And, undoubtedly, my good too. 'Sober,' I mouth, leaning next to him at the bar.

Keeping his eyes on mine, he calls to the barman. 'Two tequilas, please.'

'Tequila,' I muse, looking over my shoulder when the salt and lemon land behind me. 'Is that my challenge?'

'Crying off?' he goads, reaching into his pocket and pulling out some notes.

'Never,' I scoff, turning to the bar. I don't know what his game is, but I want to play. With him. 'You're asking me to prove I'm sober by doing a shot?' I narrow my eyes on him, teasing. 'Or is your plan to get me drunk and take advantage of me?'

He smiles to himself as he pays the barman. 'You don't look like the kind of woman who could be taken advantage of.'

'What kind of woman do I look like, then?' I challenge quietly.

He turns to me, watching me for a few moments. 'I don't know, but I think I'd like to find out.'

I hold his gaze for a few seconds, no retort coming to me. I think I want him to find out too, just as much as I want to find out what kind of man *he* is. My eyes drop from his sparkling greys, down his tall, lean frame to his feet.

Oh . . . fuck . . .

'Let's play,' he says, moving in closer and pulling one of the glasses forward. I don't mean to, but I yank my arm away abruptly when he brushes against me, startled by the tiny stabs of pleasure that pitter-patter all over my skin. The fleeting touch tells me he would feel as good as he looks, and – give me strength – he smells divine, all manly and earthy and fucking edible.

The sudden lapse in movement and talking from both of us becomes slightly awkward. I can feel him looking down at me.

'What do I have to do?' I ask again quietly, almost on a breathy gasp.

He clears his throat. 'You're not drunk?'

'Not even the slightest bit.' I raise my nose in the air.

'Good. Then you'll smash this challenge first time.' He places a finger on the brim of one of the shot glasses. 'Brace your palms on the edge of the bar,' he orders, firmly but softly. I look at him, finding a serious face. 'Go on.'

Frowning, I place my hands on the edge of the bar. 'Okay?'

He takes my hips. He takes my fucking hips! I freeze from top to toe and swallow hard, waiting. My insides are quickly furling, my mind in chaos. 'Move back a bit,' he says, pulling at them a little until I step back.

Oh, Jesus. I'm on fire. I have a strange man bending me over a bar in public, and Annie I'm-immune-to-men Ryan isn't fighting him off. It's like he has me under a spell. What gives? I dare not look behind me. I'm not stupid enough to think Lizzy isn't currently watching a man manipulate my body to where he wants it.

'You feel tense,' he observes, releasing me and moving back to my side.

I don't deny it; neither do I confirm it. His big hands felt so good resting on my hips, so much so I have to resist not claiming them and putting them back where they were. 'What now?' I ask, evidently struggling for air, damn me.

'Now.' He picks up his beer and grins. 'I get to gloat that I had you bent over a bar within five minutes of meeting you.' He takes a swig, still grinning, and I hear the roar of a man down the bar laughing his head off.

Oh, the fucker! Part of me admires him. Another part of me wants to slap him stupid; I don't care how beautiful he is. And another part of me wants to rip his clothes from his body and ravish the sly bastard.

I cannot *believe* I fell for it! How many women has he played like a fiddle? I drop my head, shaking it to myself.

I knew that smile was dangerous. A man who can bend a woman to his will so easily *and* so soon couldn't be anything less than lethal. And the fact that he got me with his wicked game means hats off to him. I can't possibly take that away from him, and since I'm lacking in the dignity department right now, I decide not to slap him. Nor will I chuck a drink over his head, or fire a load of verbal abuse at him.

I'll do what he least expects.

I push myself up and turn to face him, unable to stop myself from smiling at his half-grin. Holding his gaze, I slowly lick the back of my hand, blindly take the salt off the bar, sprinkle a bit and take one of the shots of tequila. But as I'm taking my hand to my mouth to lick the salt up, he seizes my wrist and takes the shot from my other hand. My heartbeat accelerates, our eyes glued to each other as he moves into me and slowly brings my hand to his mouth. I watch, gripped, as he lazily licks up the salt from the back of my hand, eyes on mine, and then knocks the tequila back. *Kill me now, for I will certainly die a happy woman.* His tongue on my skin. His eyes boring into mine. His hold of my wrist. I must look like a statue – unable to talk, move or think clearly.

'There's one more tequila,' he says, cocking his head towards the bar but keeping me in his sights. 'And it's yours.'

Oh good Lord. My heart is speeding up by the second as I watch him lick the back of his hand and sprinkle some salt. Then he offers it to me. I stare at his hand, and then slowly look up at him. I could get lost in those glittery grey eyes.

'I taste good,' he whispers.

I've no doubt. It takes everything in me and more to take his hand and bring it to my mouth, and when my tongue slips free, I close my eyes and brace myself. I taste no salt. I taste *him*. And it might well be the most intoxicating taste I've ever experienced. I swallow, keeping hold of his hand while I take the tequila and throw it back, not even wincing as it burns its way down my throat.

He nods approvingly. 'Told you,' he murmurs, pulling his hand away.

I fight my way back to life, looking away from him before I self-combust. 'It was nice playing with you,' I breathe, turning away. I need the ladies'. Quickly.

'Whoa!' He slips his hand around my wrist and stills me. My whole body locks up again. After being clued in to his pathetic man-game of getting me bent over the bar, all bodily reactions to him should have been halted in their annoying tracks. Then he licked me. And I licked him. The tingles engulfing me are so fierce I'm having to refrain from brushing them off. 'Don't go just yet,' he says gently.

I look up at him, cocking my head, trying to wrestle some sensibility through my cloud of lust. I haven't been with a man in a long, *long* while. About one year, two months and two weeks, to be precise. Jason's friend of a friend.

'And what are you planning on doing with me if I stay?' I ask, taking a quick scan of his hand in search of a ring, just to be sure. No ring. How a woman hasn't staked a claim on him yet is beyond me.

'I plan on talking to you,' he says softly, watching me with a hint of curiosity.

'As opposed to licking me?'

'You didn't like my game?' he asks evenly, seriously, something lingering behind his eyes. Something tempting. Something that makes me a little . . . cautious. And a lot *hot*.

His grasp, still circling my wrist, gives me a moment's pause. The heat of our combined skin isn't to be ignored. I'm intrigued by him, if only because he's captured my attention and kept it, even after his sly stunt. Talk. He wants to talk.

I gently pull my arm away and he releases me slowly, never removing his eyes from mine. Then he blindly pulls a bar stool forward, indicating for me to take a seat. 'Drink? Or have you had enough?'

I rest my bum on the stool and flick him a tired look, but I really don't think I should be drinking any more. Especially not now, when I should probably keep my wits about me. 'I'll have a water, please.'

He signals the barman over, ordering my water and another beer. I look across to my friends, and find none of them looking this way. Except Micky. He cocks his head in question, and I nod my reassurance. I'm fine. Totally fine.

The man with no name lowers to a stool before me, one foot resting on the floor, the other on a footrest, his elbow propped on the bar. His shirt crinkles around his midriff a little. It looks like there could be abs beneath that crisp white material. And his bent arm is hinting at some pretty solid biceps.

'What's your name?' he asks, pulling my eyes back up to his face. He still looks serious, a distinct contrast from the cocky grin that was fixed to his face when I first clapped eyes on him.

'Annie,' I answer. 'Yours?'

'Jack.' He presents me with his hand, still watching me as I decide whether I should touch him again. It's definitely not a good idea. If anything, I should be retreating, moving away, possibly even leaving right this minute. There are intentions in his serious eyes that I can read perfectly; intentions that should frighten me – so why I reach forward and place my hand gently in his is beyond my ability to analyse right now. I'm rapt. En-thralled. It's a revelation, and I quite like it.

As soon as contact is made, skin on skin, he seizes my hand quickly, shocking me. My eyes fly up to his, expecting to find a cheeky grin, but he's still looking at me seriously. 'Gotcha,' he murmurs, squeezing his big palm around mine. I lose my breath. My heart gallops. My skin heats. Holy shit, he certainly has.

He starts to slowly shake my hand, up and down, taking a long time about it too. I swallow repeatedly, my throat as dry as a bone as he controls my movements.

Gotcha?

His lips slowly curve, as if he knows my thoughts, and I'm faced with that sparkly-eyed smile again. 'I licked it, so it's mine,' he says around his smile.

His declaration has me shaking my head in wonder as he lowers my held hand to my bare leg, taking advantage of his position and dragging his fingers down my thigh as he pulls away. I jerk on my stool and make a grab for my water.

'Do you lick many women?' I ask, and immediately kick myself for it. That's none of my business, and I honestly don't want to know.

His face is suddenly serious. 'Licking women in bars isn't usually my thing.'

'What about bending them over bars?'

A mild smile ghosts his lips, as if he's reading my thoughts. 'I don't know what came over me,' he admits on a mild laugh, bringing his hand to his jaw and stroking over his bristle. I'm glad, because I don't know what came over me either. 'What do you do, Annie?'

'I'm an architect,' I answer swiftly. *Talk. Just talk.* 'Mainly domestic projects, but I'm slowly moving my business into the commercial sector.'

'You have your own firm?' he asks, and I nod. 'That's impressive for someone in her . . .' Jack fades off, cocking his head in question.

I smile at his cute ploy to extract my age. 'I'm twenty-nine.'

'Wow, that really is impressive. Congratulations. I like seeing people succeeding.'

'Thank you.'

'Are you mar—'

'No.' I laugh.

'Taken?'

I'm not so quick to answer this time. I don't know why. Probably because my answer will open the path to . . . what? 'No.'

There's relief in his eyes. There's definitely relief. 'You're a good-time girl?' he asks, a suggestive edge to his tone.

'Well, I don't usually let strange men bend me over bars and lick me, if that's what you're getting at.'

'I'm honoured.' Jack smiles, satisfied. 'So what do you usually do for fun? I mean, when I'm not around to bend and lick you.'

I match his smile and take a sip of water to moisten my increasingly dry mouth. 'I work hard. I have good friends. I have my good times with them.'

'Through choice or because of a bad experience?'

'We're getting a bit personal, aren't we?' I cock him a questioning look, and he smiles on a shrug.

'Just trying to figure you out.'

His jean-clad knee brushes mine, and I whip my leg away on a skip of my pathetic heart. He won't need to figure out anything. I'm happy to tell him. 'I have no interest in men right now.' I don't know why, but I find myself biting my lip and watching closely for his reaction.

He nods slowly. 'That could change,' he muses – out of the blue, shocking me.

My back straightens, my breath hitching a little. 'How d'you mean?' I ask quietly, trying to weave interest through my words. I try. All that's woven through every word I'm speaking to this man is intrigue. And desire.

'I mean,' he starts, leaning in a bit, 'you've clearly never been consumed by a man.' He pauses, giving me a moment to agree, but I don't. I'm fixated on him. 'But one day a man will come along and he'll swallow you up, Annie. Blindside you.' There's suggestion in his words that I'm finding hard not to be curious about. And I'm still just staring at him.

My pulse pounds in my ears as he pulls away and turns back towards the bar, calling the barman over. I don't hear what he orders. My surroundings have been reduced to a blur of activity, the loud sounds of the bar now a distant white noise. There's a magnetic appeal to Jack – not just his looks, but his persona, his voice . . . his words.

'Here.' He takes my limp hand and removes the water, handing me a shot glass. The contact wrenches me from my trance, and I glance around, finding the world is still happening around me. Chinking glasses with me, he smiles that lovely smile – the one that had me hooked the moment I saw him. 'Here's to being blindsided,' he says, raising his glass.

He knocks his drink back, then slams the glass on the bar and wipes his mouth with the back of his hand. My eyes follow every single movement as I try to read between the lines, try to unravel his words and form any sense out of them. Of course, they make perfect sense as they are, but something is telling me there's more to it. Maybe the slight harshness of his tone. Maybe the way he's looking at me.

'Drink up.' His fingertip meets the bottom of my glass and encourages it up to my lips, and he watches me as I slowly tip the liquid down my throat, caught in a massive state of conflict.

I want him.

For the first time in my life, I really, *really* want a man. I can feel . . . something.

'What do *you* do, Jack?' I ask, following my instinct to find out more about this man who's got me all hot and bothered.

'I have many talents.'

I hold back my grin. 'Such as?'

'Oh, the list is endless. How long have you got?'

Forever! I quickly snap my mind back into line. *Really, Annie? Get a grip!* 'You're cute,' I quip, and then wince at my poorly chosen reply. Jack's far from cute; this tall, well-formed, strapping hunk of a man.

Jack glances away for a fleeting moment, laughing to himself. 'You're quite cute yourself.' His eyes return to mine, twinkling madly. 'How are you single?'

I should ask him the same question. 'Because I want to be. Because relationships require hard work that I'd rather invest elsewhere.'

Jack nods, staring deeply into my eyes. 'Invest in yourself?'

'Yes,' I answer honestly, even if it makes me sound selfish. Maybe my outlook will change one day, when the right man comes along. Who knows. But at this point in my life, there is no man, and I'm quite content with that. 'I've made promises to myself that I plan to keep.'

He breathes in deeply, his fingers fiddling with the label of his beer bottle. 'I admire you. Your own happiness is important, and you're clearly happy.'

I sit back a little, assessing his disposition. 'Aren't you happy?'

'Right now I'm deliriously happy.'

I smile and Jack grins cheekily, reaching forward and placing a palm on my knee, squeezing gently. My smile drops in a second, my eyes darting down to his hand touching my bare flesh. Heat spreads through me like cracking glass, and water ripples up the side of my highball. My shakes get so bad I'm forced to place my drink on the bar and hold on to it in an attempt to disguise my trembling.

My eyes flick up to Jack's, finding that his smile has dropped and his amusement has disappeared. Slowly, he peels his hand away from my leg. Good Lord. My world just spun out of control while he had hold of me. In those few blissful seconds, I forgot my name, my job and my ambitions. Suddenly my only motivation was Jack – to touch him, talk to him, listen to him. This stranger removed me from my real life and put me somewhere else. Somewhere distracting. Somewhere consuming.

Consuming. Nothing's ever consumed me, except work. I've only spent a few minutes with Jack, and already I feel a little addicted to the intensity that leaks from him. This is alien ... and frightening. It's caught me so completely off guard.

My heartbeat kick-starts again, and I shake myself back to life. *My* life. My *real* life. 'It was nice talking to you, Jack. I really must go,' I breathe, slipping down from my stool. I need to escape him now, because my mind is in a muddle and I'm scared of the reaction I'm having to him. I do the polite thing and offer my hand.

He nods, slowly and understandingly. 'Undoubtedly the wisest decision you'll make, for both of us.'

He takes my hand and, I swear, explosions happen. The stupid type that people read of in books, the ones where you roll your eyes because it's so ridiculous to think that two people could have such a powerful connection. Blindsided.

'Here.' He opens my fingers and places something in my palm. 'Something to remember me by.'

I look down and see a Budweiser bottle top. 'Why would I want to remember you?' I ask, glancing up at him.

'Because this night will go down in history.' He smiles as he forces my hand into a fist, locking the bottle top tightly inside my grasp.

He's right. There's no way I'll ever forget my encounter with Jack. 'And what do you have to remember me by?'

He reaches forward and ghosts a finger down my cheek, robbing me of cognitive thought. 'I have this,' he murmurs, taking his touch to his temple and tapping lightly. 'Stored away up here.'

My knees go weak, my blood's on fire. I don't need a bottle top because I too have his face stored in a safe place in my mind. Jack leans into me and takes the tops of my arms, holding me in place. When his chest meets mine, my knees actually give, and I whimper, my forehead falling onto his shoulder. Oh my God, who is this man?

His lips meet my ear and he spends a few incredible moments breathing into it before he speaks. 'If I ever lay eyes on you again, Annie, I can't promise I'll do what's best and walk away next time.'

He breaks away and leaves, signalling to his friend, a fair-haired man, who follows. He gives me a questioning look as he passes me, taking in my obvious condition. Which is what? Thunderstruck? It's the only way to describe it. I feel like I've been tackled from the side without warning, winding me.

My lungs begin to burn, and I realise I'm holding my breath. It all comes rushing out, so fast and so much of it, I lose my stability and make a grab for the bar.

'Hey, you okay?' Lizzy appears by my side, her eyes travelling between me and Jack as he leaves the bar.

'Yes,' I squeak, and the shakes set in, an aftermath of my encounter with the most handsome and intense man I've ever come across.

'Well, wasn't he just the finest piece of arse you've ever seen,' Lizzy says, grinning at me, before slowly losing her chirpy face and replacing it with a worried frown. 'Hey, you sure you're okay?'

Jesus, I need to snap out of it. 'Yes, fine.' I shake myself back to life and swipe up my water, chugging it down at an epic rate.

'So where's he gone?' she asks.

'He was a cocky twat,' I mutter indignantly, lying through my teeth. It's the only way to go. Telling Lizzy that my body burned with want, not only every time Jack touched me, but with every word he spoke too, would be a mistake.

'He could have been the rebound screw I need,' Lizzy sighs in dismay.

'You don't mean that.'

'I do. What a waste. You'll regret this.'

'Maybe,' I muse, casting my eyes to the bar entrance, seeing no sign of him. He's gone, and it's beyond me why that's making my stomach sink. 'Anyway, are you okay?' I divert, a sensible move. I need to forget the last half-hour ever happened. The best decision I've ever made? What, walking away? And what did he mean, for both of us?

'Perfectly fine,' Lizzy says, taking my arm and starting to walk us back to the table.

I look at her. 'Micky *definitely* shouldn't be your rebound fuck.'

'We're just flirting.'

I don't miss the look that passes between them as we approach, but I'm too side-tracked to give the situation the concern it deserves, still tingling from top to toe. I look to the door again, his last words playing on repeat in my mind.

If I ever lay eyes on you again, Annie, I can't promise I'll do what's best and walk away next time.

Chapter 3

The night ends with no further wobbles from me, but lots from my friends. Everyone is totalled, but having only drunk water since my enthralling encounter with one prime example of an unholy delicious man, I've maintained a sensible level of tipsiness. I've been knocked sideways, and it's taken the rest of the evening to gather myself.

Lizzy has harped on endlessly about my failure to bed said man; Micky has flirted outrageously with Lizzy, and she with him; and Nat has worn away the wood of the dance floor.

It's time for taxis.

'It's been the best night ever!' Nat sings as I herd them like sheep to the line of cabs. She throws her arms into the air and swishes her hair. 'And I fucking love my new hair! Do you love my new hair?' She looks to Micky, who now has a wilting Lizzy in a headlock.

'I fucking love your new hair,' he agrees, hiccupping.

'I think it makes you look older,' Lizzy chimes in on a slur.

'Sophisticated!' Nat screeches indignantly. 'Eh, Annie?'

'Sophisticated,' I confirm on a laugh. 'In you get!' I order, pulling open the door of a waiting cab and guiding them in one by one. Surprisingly, no one trips up the step, but they do all land in their seats with a thud. The taxi man looks at me, his years of experience telling him that I'm the one he needs to communicate with.

'Evening,' I say as I bend to get in, but as I lift my foot from the kerb something catches my attention across the road. I straighten my body to look over the roof of the cab as heat creeps through my veins, making my blood pound its way to my heart until it's racing. *If I ever lay eyes on you again, Annie, I can't promise I'll do what's best and walk away next time.*

He's standing on the other side of the road, his hands resting lightly in his jeans pockets. And he's staring across at me, intensity in his grey eyes shining bright, even from across the street. My stomach begins to fill with butterflies.

'C'mon, Annie!' Micky yells, reaching for my hand that's resting on the door. 'Get in!'

The rest of the group starts chanting, possibly telling me to get in the cab too, but I can't hear them. Nor can I hear the rush of traffic as it zooms by; the cars passing between me and Jack are just a blur.

I don't know what to do. Get in the cab – the sensible option – or shut the door and send my friends on their way – the stupid option. I'm not stupid. Never have been.

He looks like a statue, frozen into position. He's waiting for me to decide, our eyes never unlocking. Then he nods, so very mildly I nearly miss it. He can see my inner conflict. He's silently willing me to remain where I am, because despite what he said, *I* could be the one to walk away. To make the decision for both of us.

The choice is down to me. Whether it's the right decision for both of us is unknown. But right and wrong aren't featuring in my mind. It's too consumed by *him*.

I shift my grip on the door, ready to shut it. 'I'll see you tomorrow, guys,' I say, not looking at them.

'Huh?' they all call in unison, but I ignore them and turn to the cabbie, reeling off their addresses. But my eyes remain focused on Jack across the road. I slam the door, hearing my friends' confused mumbles, but the driver pulls away before they can protest further. There's no question that any one of them would leave me alone on a night out, but the alcohol is in my favour tonight. I look to the back of the cab as it drives off, seeing Lizzy looking out of the back window, her confusion evident. Then her eyes flick to the other side of the road and her mouth drops open. I just catch the sight of her straight lips before the cab takes a corner.

My phone rings two seconds later. I don't answer it, but I do send a text, telling her that I'm fine and I know what I'm doing. It's a lie. I haven't the faintest idea what I'm doing.

I look up through my lashes to Jack. There's a road between us – him standing on one kerb, me on the other, cars whizzing on by between us. And when he steps into the road, having a quick check for traffic, I start backing up as he comes closer, until my back's pressed into a brick wall. My breathing is shot to bits and my body is trembling like a flame in the breeze.

When he reaches me, both of his palms land on the wall on either side of my head. I'm staring at his neck, afraid to lift my eyes to his face now that he's this close. 'Why didn't I carry on walking home?' he asks, his frustration clear and present. 'Why the fuck didn't I just carry on walking?'

Because you felt it too, I scream in my head, feeling dizzy from the intoxicating smell of him – his closeness, the light skim of his groin across my dress.

His hard stare drills holes into me as his face slowly lowers towards mine. I hold my breath and let him brush his lips lightly over mine, our eyes still open and locked. My breath stutters, as does his. Then he pulls away a few inches, his tongue running across his bottom lip, as if tasting what he's just had. His chest forces against mine from his deep inhale. 'Tell me to go,' he whispers, the demand licking its way from the base to the top of my spine. 'Tell me.'

'Go.'

'Not a fucking chance.' He swoops in and takes my mouth as if he owns it – deeply, passionately and with an unfathomable conviction. I'm immediately lost in a haze of want and lust as he grinds into me. Our tongues duel, our bodies press together, and it's beyond any level of pleasure I thought possible.

I bring my arms up to circle his neck, holding him while we kiss like we might never get the opportunity to do this again. One of his big palms slides onto the back of my thigh and tugs, bringing my leg to his waist. I'm inhaling his groans, swallowing them down into the deepest parts of me, whimpering each time he circles his hips into mine, forcing me harder to the wall.

Holy fucking shit, I'm lost.

'I need more than this,' he says desperately, working his lips to my ear and licking the shell slowly, panting hard. 'I need you naked. I need to be inside you. I need you fucking now. Where do you live?'

His question gives me a moment's pause. I'm as desperate for all of that as he is, but I still have a tiny scrap of sense within me somewhere. No way am I taking him to my place. I still have to be wise.

This isn't me. I'm not reckless, but right now, halting this is impossible. It might be the spontaneity; it might be how illicit this feels; it might be the thrill factor, the danger and the unknown. Or it might just be something as simple as intoxicating chemistry. I don't know, but I want more.

'Your place,' I counter, nuzzling into his neck, feeling him shake his head.

'I can't wait that long.' He pulls away from me, leaving me a shaky mess held against the wall. 'Hotel.'

I nod, thinking that's best all round. Mutual ground. He wastes no time, sliding his hand to my lower back and putting some weight behind it. I manage to prise myself from the bricks with his support, but my legs are still quivering beyond my control as we walk urgently down the street. I look at him discreetly out of the corner of my eye, finding him focused forward, his jaw tense. And I definitely detect his trembling beyond mine. We're both wound up like tightly coiled springs, dying to let loose on each other. It's new to me – odd and thrilling.

The walk to the nearest hotel is excruciatingly long. Jack approaches the reception desk and asks for a room, and though the lady eyes me knowingly, I don't even blush.

He gets a room card, marches me to the lift and virtually tosses me inside. He doesn't even wait for the doors to close. He's on me again, kissing me brutally, pinning me against the back wall and making sure I feel what's concealed behind the fly of his jeans. He rolls us, now *his* back against the wall, our mouths going at it like starved lions. The small space is drenched in moans, groans, whimpers and cries of passion.

When the doors open we practically fall out, our mouths still glued as he walks me backwards down the corridor, having a quick check for the right room before he fumbles with the card and kicks the door open. He breaks our kiss and pushes me inside. I stumble back, dazed, disoriented . . . wanting like I've never wanted before.

He starts to unfasten his shirt as he prowls towards me, and once he's worked his way through his buttons, he shrugs it off.

And I gulp down my awe as I take in the smooth planes of his torso, the perfection of his body making me giddy. He can't be real. Is he real? Am I here?

The way he's looking at me – the hunger, the resolve. I've never felt so wanted and, weirdly, needed. It's a satisfying revelation. But there's an alien feeling too, one that I should probably devote a little more time towards analysing. How much I need *him* right now. A stranger.

His hands move to the button of his fly as he comes to a stop before me, just a few feet away. The waistband of his boxers is peeking above his jeans, taut material spanning a taut stomach. My eyes fix on his fingers as he lazily reveals more of himself to me, torturing me, his shallow breathing matching my own. Why so slow now? Why is he dragging this out? I flick desperate eyes to his and find him watching me closely. Then his jeans hit the floor. Followed by his boxers.

The muscles in my legs threaten to give up on me as I stare at him before me, stark naked and beyond stunning. This isn't me. I don't bend to a man's will, but this man has had me bending from the second he found me at the bar. I'm unsure whether I loathe the notion, or love it. What I do know, though, is there is nothing I can do about it. Neither do I want to. A night of dirty, raw fucking is currently standing before me, with illicit promises shining from his grey eyes, and I'm going in feet first.

As soon as I find my feet.

Kicking away his shoes, jeans and boxers, he takes my hands delicately, like he's sensed I need a moment of gentleness and reassurance.

'Ready, Annie?' he asks softly. 'Because I sure as hell am.'

He doesn't wait for my answer. He must see the certainty in my eyes. Moving into me, pressing me against the window behind me, the side of his coarse face resting against my cheek, he grips the hem of my dress and pulls it up between us. My arms lift with it as my mind searches frantically for some poise, anything to match his calm, measured actions. I have nothing.

He's taking it slowly now, savouring every moment, every movement, every sound. My dress is gone, but he's still pressed against me, moving his hands around to my back. I feel the clasp of my bra release and then he steps away, pulling the straps down my arms, his eyes falling down my body.

He swallows.

Hard.

He blinks.

Slowly.

He growls under his breath.

Then he drops my bra to the floor and his eyes to my skimpy black knickers. The sight of his big, naked body before me distracts me from any shyness. The power of his presence distracts me from any restraint I should be working hard to find.

My fingers reach for the sides of my knickers and push them down my thighs, revealing myself in my entirety to him.

And I wait.

And wait.

I wait so long for him to make his move, wondering where my mind has gone. It's lost, fallen into a pit of recklessness. All I can do is admire what's before me.

'Ever experienced this before?' he asks quietly. 'The chemistry, the need?'

'No.' My answer is easy and it's the truth.

'Me neither.' He steps forward and cages me against the window, picking up on the crazy, passionate kiss he started in the street and continued in the lift. My mind swims with pleasure.

He's naked. I'm naked. We're touching everywhere that two people can touch, his erection wedged against my lower stomach, pulsing in time with my body. He moans around my lips, his hands sliding down to my bum and onto my thighs, squeezing constantly. I lock his wide shoulders in my arms and let him at me.

A swift tug hauls me up to his waist on a whimper, his cock poised and ready to enter me. The glass behind me is becoming slippery, my back sliding across the smooth surface as a result of my dampening skin.

'Open up to me,' he orders, feeling the constriction of my thighs.

Without a moment's thought I relax, letting him hold me against the window with his body. 'Condom,' I breathe into his mouth, managing to locate a shred of sense through my hunger.

'I don't have one.' He continues to kiss me, and my heart sinks. 'Jesus, this wasn't part of my plan for this evening, Annie,' he declares. 'You?'

I lap my tongue around his, digging my nails into his shoulders. 'I don't have one. We should stop.'

'Are you on the pill?'

'Yes, but that doesn't make this right.' I continue to kiss him, speaking into his mouth. 'We should stop.'

'I know.' He takes my hands from his shoulders and pushes them up the glass, releasing my mouth briefly to bite my lip before plunging his tongue deep again, exploring far and wide. 'We need to stop.'

'We do,' I confirm through my pleasure, letting him thread his fingers with mine above my head, his lips kissing their way across my cheek and into my neck.

'Tell me to stop,' he demands weakly and with zero conviction, sucking and biting at my flesh.

'Oh God!' I breathe, slamming my head against the glass behind me, my thighs tightening around his waist again. 'Jack, you need to stop.'

'I will. You want me to?'

'No!'

He swivels his hips and enters me on a ragged shout of satisfaction, his teeth clamped lightly around the flesh of my neck. My whole world explodes into a haze of powerful pleasure as I scream to the ceiling, a long, despairing, satisfied scream. He's still now, but breathing erratically, his long, thick length fully inside of me. The fullness twists my mind, warmth fills my veins and boils my bloodstream, and the rightness prevents me from fighting him off. His grip on my hands above my head is now solid and my legs are wrapped around him like ivy.

'My heart is hammering,' he confesses, his hips shaking with the strain to keep still. 'It's beating so fucking hard, and it feels so fucking good. Where did you come from, Annie?'

I'd ask him the same question if it wasn't for my inability to talk. So I push my face into his instead, closing my eyes and relishing the feel of our bodies connected so completely.

Strangers.

Two complete strangers. It defies reason that our join-ing could be this intoxicating. This whole situation defies *me*. Taking my chin to my shoulder, I look behind me, out of the window. The city below is alive with lights, people going about their business. And I'm up high above them all, pinned against this window with a stranger's cock buried inside me.

'Are you okay?' His soft question prompts me to ask myself the very same thing, because I think the mind I've lost has gone forever.

And I'm totally okay with it.

I grind down in answer, making him jerk on a whimper. So I go again, building up the friction as much as I can without Jack moving.

'Jesus,' he mumbles, dragging his face from my neck.

His grey eyes land on me. Sparks erupt. More desire floods me. My world starts to spin out of control. He watches me as he draws back, slow, sure and careful, and when he pauses, only the tip of his cock inside me, I pull in breath and hold it, bracing myself.

He pounds forward, and I cry out. Jack grunts and the mo-mentum is set – no more waiting, no more conscience, no more doubts. He thrusts hard, hitting me again and again, adding the odd deep grind here and there so as to never let me guess what's coming next. My cries of pleasure are on a loop, our sweat is mingling, and his hands around mine are locked tightly, keep-ing my arms ramrod straight above my head. It's insane. It's crazy, raw, carnal fucking, and it's making me wonder amid the intoxicating feelings if one night of this passion and these feel-ings will be enough. I'm vehemently holding back, not wanting this to end just yet. I can only hope Jack feels the same.

'Fuck!' he shouts, releasing my hands and cupping my arse, peeling me away from the window and turning. He carries me across the room and holds me with one arm under my bum as he swipes the contents of the desk from the surface, then lowers me onto the hard wood, coming down with me so as not to break our connection. I yelp, squirming across the polished wood as he jacks me forward and rises to standing, taking hold of my thighs. My hands go above my head and grip the edge of the desk.

His teeth clench as he withdraws, his head dropping back but his eyes remaining on mine. He yanks me up and down the desk, our sweaty skin slapping, our shouts and cries of pleasure loud and chaotic.

Yet I still hold back on letting the looming orgasm claim me.

The desk is creaking under the force, and just when I think it might give under the strain, his arm slides under my back and pulls me up. The front of my body crashes with his, and my shout is loud. I cling to him as he takes reverse steps and then falls to his back on the bed with me straddling him. 'Fuck me, Annie,' he demands, his voice like gravel, full of hunger and sex. 'Fuck me hard.'

I don't delay. I've had my order. My hips kick in and I rock back and forth, my palms braced into the hardness of his chest. His fingers claw into my thighs, his face strained. 'Oh shit,' he groans, his hips now flexing up and meeting my rhythm.

The sight of him, the effect I'm having on him, it's addictive. I'm spent but energised, my body doing things without thought. Then I'm moving again. His stomach muscles tense and he sits up, edging us to the side of the bed with me on his lap. He guides my legs behind his back so I'm wrapped around him, and his hands find my hips, lifting and then pulling me back down precisely on an exhale of shaky breath.

I yelp, the new position sending him so deep. My head goes limp, but I refuse to lose his gaze as he guides me ferociously, slamming me down onto his lap repeatedly. I don't know how much longer I'll be able to fight off my release. He's challenging me on so many levels. 'Jack,' I gasp, my head falling forward, our foreheads meeting.

He senses my struggle and flips me around, taking me to my back and re-entering quickly. I scream. He roars. I'm in pieces, almost frightened by the potential of the orgasm that's going to strike me. It's going to be powerful. He comes down to his forearms, my thighs clamp around his waist, and he takes us on that final stretch towards explosion.

He nods, and I nod right back. He looks in pain as he takes the last few strokes, his face twisting, as I'm sure mine is. The veins in his neck bulge, his cock swells, and I'm shoved over the edge, screaming as the nerves in my clitoris explode.

My world goes blank, my body lax, and Jack collapses on top of me, pinning me to the mattress as we both splutter and gasp for breath. And as if it's instinctive, my arms come up around his back and hold him to me, pulling his heavy body closer while we ride the waves of pleasure ripping through our bodies. His chest is rolling atop mine and his skin's wet under my hands on his back.

Opening my eyes, I look up to the ceiling of the hotel room, my hearing fuzzy with the sounds of our breathlessness. Jack is breathtaking in more ways than one.

The silence is comfortable; neither of us is in a rush to break it, and I begin to wonder if he's doing what I'm doing right now. Is he trying to fathom what just happened? Is he quietly trying to wrap his mind around the extreme madness of the incredible moment we just shared? My thoughts begin to race as I absentmindedly trace small circles across his back.

I'm interrupted when he chuckles softly, squirming above me. Despite myself, I smile. 'You ticklish?'

He lifts his torso on a shudder and looks down at me. His eyes. God, his eyes are sparkling madly. 'Not usually. But your touch seems to do things to me.'

I hold back from telling him that the feeling is mutual,

though I sense he sees it in my eyes when he reaches up to my face and draws a perfect line down my cheek to my chin, smiling as he does. He looks thoughtful, and I'm desperate to know what his thoughts are. 'Architect Annie,' he murmurs, casting his gaze to mine. 'I'm glad I didn't carry on walking home.' He dips and pushes a sweet kiss onto my lips, stealing my breath once again. 'You've been a welcome distraction from real life.'

I fall into the pace of his kiss, and gladly let him distract me from life as I know it too.

Just for tonight.

Chapter 4

The texture of the sheets beneath me is unfamiliar. So is the smell of the cotton. I feel my muscles pull as I go to roll over, and I moan, aching everywhere, as I blink my eyes open sleepily. I frown, then quickly wince as I move again, trying to sit up. Where the hell am I?

A deep, sleepy inhale penetrates my confusion, and I glance down, seeing the full, naked length of a man's body. I study the expanse of his lean muscles, working my way up to his stunning face.

'Oh my God,' I whisper. Such a gorgeous face, rough with scruff, his lashes long. His lips are slightly parted, and one perfect, thick arm extends above his head, draped across the white pillow.

Jack.

Flashbacks.

So many flashbacks. Against the window, on the desk, sitting on the edge of the bed, me straddling him, Jack above me. Him gazing down at me. His light chuckles as I stroked his back. His words. His kisses. And then the explosive sex all over again – in the shower, against the bathroom door, back in this bed. I reach up and feel my damp hair, then clench my thighs, wincing at the soreness.

No condom.

What the hell have I done? He's a stranger. A complete stranger. The fact that he seemed like anything *but* a stranger the whole time we were exploring each other is forgotten now.

The connection is lost amid a sea of regret.

A quick glance at the bedside clock tells me it's 4.15. The sun is on its way up.

I shuffle as quietly as a mouse to the edge of the bed and search the floor in the dim light for my dress, finding it by the window. I tiptoe across the carpet, tense from top to toe, which isn't helping my achy muscles. Jesus, I feel like I've been hit by a fucking bus. I make quick work of wriggling into my dress, slipping my feet into my heels and swiping up my underwear and bag.

Then, like I might be struck down by lightning if I make even the tiniest of sounds, I slip out of the room – the room Jack paid for so we could fuck – cringing as I ease the door closed. I run down the corridor to the lift like a madwoman and hit the call button, and when the doors to the lift open, I'm hit with more flashbacks. I'm pressed against the back wall, he's kissing me with a crazy passion, and my face is pure ecstasy.

I slam a lid on those thoughts and dive in the lift.

I fucked a fucking stranger.

I let myself into my flat and put myself straight in the shower. The hot water cleaning away the evidence of my careless encounter is only a mild comfort. I can't wash my mind of the reminders. Doubt I ever will. My muscles protest my every move as I soap my body over and over, letting the water pound down harshly, hotter than I'd usually tolerate it.

Against the window. His huge, hard body touching me everywhere.

I shake my head and soap harder, concentrating on my obsessive need to scrub myself until I bleed. I feel dirty. Ashamed of myself for being so careless. But worse, I feel overcome by the connection we shared, the feelings still lingering, like he could be standing here in the shower with me now.

On the desk. The look in his grey eyes.

I bunch the sponge in my fist and grit my teeth, throwing it to the shower floor before grabbing the shampoo and squirting some in my hand. My fingers go into my hair and lather, hard, fast and furious.

Hard, fast and furious. The feel of him taking me so powerfully.

I shout and let my back fall against the wall, my hurt muscles folding and taking me down to the shower floor. I just sit there and relive every single crazy, intense second I had with Jack as I stare up at the showerhead pouring water down on me. I can only hope that once I've lived the whole scene from beginning to end, my mind will relent and be fulfilled enough to let me forget about him. Forget about the man who momentarily steered me off course from real life.

I recognise these sheets. The feel, the smell. I roll over, hissing as I go. The aches just seem to be getting worse. My phone tells me it's 9.30. After torturing myself in my shower with hot water and memories, I clambered into bed and drifted off to sleep, though my dreams gave me no respite. I saw his grey eyes, heard his velvet voice, felt his soft lips and that body made for sinful things. Just a one-night stand. It was just a one-night stand.

A loud crash sounds from the kitchen, and I bolt upright.

'Hello?' I jump out of bed and throw on a T-shirt.

'Damn!' Micky's curse calms me a little, but it also makes me wonder. What's he doing here this early on a Sunday? I make tracks to the kitchen and find him kneeling on the floor, sweeping up coffee grounds. In his boxers.

'What are you doing?' I ask, stepping over the mess to grab him the dustpan.

'This is why I do Starbucks,' he grumbles, looking up at me. His man-bun is no more, his shoulder-length blonde hair a messy mop. He narrows a suspicious eye on me from his crouched position, humming to himself. 'What time did you get in, you dirty stop-out?'

I start to back away, stray coffee crunching under my feet as I go. 'Um . . .' I gulp and look over my shoulder, feeling and looking all kinds of guilty. 'Who's that on the couch?' I blurt incredulously, seeing movement coming from under a pile of blankets in the lounge. I swing around to find Micky now looking as guilty as I expect I was a moment ago.

'Ah . . . well . . . you see . . .' He stands and points the dustpan brush at me, thinking hard.

'I gave you a spare key for emergencies.' I snap, annoyed. 'Getting your leg over isn't an emergency.'

'I came here to make sure you got home safely!' he fires back, puffy-chested. 'So what time did you get in?'

I do a quick calculation in my head. I piled them all in a taxi at 12.30. It would have taken half an hour to get here. Micky and Lizzy were so drunk; I can't imagine they were at it for . . .

My thoughts halt right there. 'Lizzy!' I screech, swinging around. Her head pops up from beneath the blankets, her hair a crazy mess, her eyes squinting.

'Hey,' she croaks, before quickly diving back under the covers to hide.

I grit my teeth and slowly turn back towards my slag of a friend, scowling hard at him. He looks sheepish. He should. 'You arsehole.'

'You didn't care so much last night,' he protests, throwing his half-naked body back to the kitchen floor and sweeping up some more grounds. 'Because you were too busy being bent over a bar.' He tosses me a disgusted look and I wilt on the spot, evading his accusing eyes. 'Are you gonna tell me what time you got in or what?'

'Two,' I lie, stomping over to the cupboard and yanking it open, pulling down a mug – the biggest I can find.

'I was awake at two.'

'Three, then. I can't remember. And I don't think you're in any position to pass judgement,' I point out huffily, flicking the kettle on.

'I'm a bloke, Annie. I can take care of myself. You didn't have a clue who he was.'

'I'm back in one piece, aren't I? And I didn't see you rushing to stop me. Oh no! Because you were too intent on getting your end away with Lizzy. Bloody Lizzy!'

'Yes?' Her head reappears from beneath the blankets, her eyes blinking back the sleep.

'Nothing!' we both shout, making her slink back under, her tail between her legs.

'She's just split up with Jason! A flirt, yes, but—'

'We were pissed.' Micky levels an annoyed look on me. I match it as I pass him and shut the kitchen door, my hand curled tightly around the handle of my empty coffee mug. I'm shaking, and now that I've stopped shouting, I'm hurting again. Everywhere. Aching like a bitch.

Micky's annoyed look becomes concerned as his gaze skates up and down my body. 'Are you okay?'

I fall apart. I slam the mug down on the counter and cover my face with my hands and blubber like a dramatic female. I never cry. Not ever. Not even when I know it would be appropriate for me to shed a tear, like at the end of the soppiest movies, or when my mum got all emotional when I left for university.

I. Just. Do. Not. Cry.

'Whoa!' Micky's on me in a flash, his strong arms circling my shoulders and cuddling me. I don't think he's ever had to do this, except maybe once when we were fifteen and my rabbit died. 'What's happened, Annie? Tell me.'

'Nothing,' I sob, shaking my head into him. I don't know what's wrong with me. This is utterly ridiculous, but I can't shake the flashbacks, nor can I forget the incredible feelings

Jack evoked. It's crazy, and it's so fucking frustrating.

Micky kisses my head a few times before pulling me out of his chest and looking down at my tear-stained cheeks. 'Did he do something to you?'

'No,' I assure him. 'It was just . . .' I pause, not sure how to word it. 'Intense. I don't know. Some stupid connection. Chemistry. Whatever you want to call it.' I brush my face off, sniff back my stupid, uncalled-for emotion and laugh. 'Jesus, we seriously packed some alcohol away last night, didn't we?'

Micky laughs quietly and thumbs over his shoulder to the kitchen door, where Lizzy is beyond. 'We definitely did.'

I roll my eyes. I know that face. That's his *why-the-fuck-did-I-do-that?* face. I only hope Lizzy is as regretful as Micky and there's no awkwardness between us all. 'I need coffee,' I sigh, holding up my mug. 'Please make me coffee.'

'I'll make you coffee,' he agrees, taking the mug and patting my arse as I turn to open the door.

I head for the couch and my hidden friend, landing on the edge and squishing her feet, though she doesn't murmur a sound or move a muscle. 'You know, you'll still be on *my* couch in *my* flat with Micky in the kitchen, no matter how long you hide under there.'

Quiet.

I poke the sheets, where I expect her head to be.

No movement.

Rolling my eyes, I grab the blanket and yank it back, exposing Lizzy . . . who is stark naked.

'Hey!' she yells, reclaiming the blanket and pulling it back.

'Sorry!' I chuckle. 'But it's nothing I haven't seen before, and now it's nothing Micky hasn't seen before.'

She arranges the material beneath her chin, peeking at me out of the corner of her eye as she faffs and fiddles, making a long-arse job of it. 'Are you mad at me?' She pouts.

I shake my head, reclining. How can I be? She's grieving. 'You're a silly twat.'

'I know.' Her agreement is easy. 'So.' She cocks her head. 'What happened?'

I don't look at her, afraid she might see the entire illicit encounter in my eyes. 'I had a drink with him.'

'Potential?'

'No.' I laugh, but it fades as I fall into thought.

Micky walks in and hands me my giant mug, giving me a look. I shrug and take my coffee as he hands Lizzy hers.

'Ladies,' he says, trotting back off to the kitchen. I fear the worst when Lizzy's eyes follow his arse all the way. I can't blame her. He has a great arse. And back. And stomach. And legs. 'Then why the tears?' she asks, returning her attention to me.

'I'm tired,' I mumble. 'Hung-over, hungry and in need of caffeine.' I slurp my coffee ravenously, hearing my phone ringing from my room. The thought of engaging my muscles to get up from the couch is enough of a reason to stay put. So I let it ring off. Ten seconds later, Lizzy's fishing through her bag to find hers. She looks at the screen and tosses it across the couch to me, and I catch Nat's name glowing threateningly up at me. I look at Lizzy. She looks smug. 'I might have mentioned a man when we dropped her home in the cab.'

Great. 'Why are you looking at me like that?' I ask moodily. 'Don't you think she's gonna want *your* dirt?' I point to the kitchen and Lizzy dives beneath the blankets again.

'Hello.' I sound bright and chirpy.

'Spill it, Ryan. And where the fuck is Lizzy?'

'Nothing to spill,' I reply robotically, deciding that I'm never going to speak of it again. Never. 'I had a drink with him.' That's it, and when Micky looks through to me and smiles, I know my secret will be safe with him. 'And Lizzy stayed on my couch.'

'With?'

'No one.' I lie again. I can't drop Micky in it now. Nat won't be impressed.

'Where's Micky?'

'Home, I guess.' I'm on a roll, but just when I think I might have got him off the hook and saved him a lecture from Nat, he trips on nothing and sends his coffee flying.

'Bastard!' he yells, jumping around the kitchen. 'Mother-fucker, that's fucking hot!'

I slump on the couch. 'Home, you guess?' Nat asks tiredly. 'I'm on my way over. Seriously! What the fuck have you lot been up to?'

'Bring Starbucks!' I yell, just as she hangs up.

We slob about all day. Spread all over my lounge, we watch trash television and eat hangover food. It's a clean sweep of hurting heads. As I sit on the couch, wedged at the end, my feet dangling over Micky's shoulders where he's sitting on the floor below me, I become more and more frustrated by my inability to empty my head of the events from last night. I don't know how many times I go over it. Over and over, again and again, until I decide I need some air.

I slip out of my flat quietly into my courtyard garden, breath-ing some sense into myself. Or at least trying to. I ponder what time he might have woken up. I wonder what he might have thought. I wonder if he was relieved that I was gone, or whether he was disappointed. The questions drive me positively mad.

A one-night stand. That's all. I know how they work. But with a man I'd talked to for half an hour? And in a hotel? And without protection? I must have lost my mind. But something about Jack made it easy to lose. He stripped me of sense. Had me surrendering to him. It's so unlike me, and what's more, all this fucking picking things to pieces is unlike me too.

I look up to the sky. I left that hotel room for a reason. Prob-lem is, I don't know what that reason was. I was out of there like a shot, my instinct kicking in and backing me up. It would be easy to accept if there was nothing there for me – no spark, no connection, no chemistry. But there *was* a spark. There *was* chemistry. There was a deep, inexplicable connection. And it scared me. It's the only explanation for me running.

'Get . . . a . . . fucking . . . grip . . . woman,' I say slowly, slapping the ball of my palm into my forehead. Leaving before he woke was the best decision. No morning awkwardness. No wondering what comes next. Simple. So why my mind is trying to make this a tattered mess of complication is beyond me.

I need to stop with this silly obsessing, because no man that gifted and gorgeous can be good for a woman. *That's* why I ran.

I make my way back into my flat and nip to the loo to check my face, brushing at my cheeks. I still look flushed. Fucked, even. Shaking my head, I go to grab my bag from the bed to get my phone, my searching fingers faltering when I lay my hand on something else. I pull out my hand and stare at the Budweiser bottle top lying in the centre of my palm.

Something to remember him by.

Last night really will go down in history. *My* history. It was a night to remember, and I'm sad that that's now all I have to remember him by. Memories. And a bottle cap.

Chapter 5

The week has flown by, work swallowing up all my time, but I've managed to catch up with Micky for lunch, and Lizzy for dinner. Micky was how I expected him to be: blasé about the weekend's events between him and Lizzy. I met Lizzy the next day hoping to find the same reaction. She rolled her eyes at the mention of it, her regret clear. 'Trust me, it was a mindless screw with a mate,' she said. 'I've already forgotten about it.'

I wish I could convince myself to do the same about Jack. Forget about it. But his damn face just keeps popping into my mind, along with every other gorgeous piece of him. It's like he's branded himself on my brain. I'm being tormented daily by him and memories of that night – a night that I have no hope of forgetting. Reliving it all is both frustrating and thrilling. My body still aches, now more deliciously, rather than the initial deep wince-worthy ache. Soon, all physical evidence of my encounter with Jack will be gone. Yet I know the memories will still be as fresh as they were the next morning. It's Friday, for God's sake! Nearly a whole week. When will he fuck off out of my head?

'I love this,' Colin Pine says, looking over the revised drawing of the front elevation of his new gallery. He's a studious man, his life revolving around art, creating it and filling his creative mind with as much information as he can get. His nose is constantly buried in some kind of textbook, magazine or cultural article. 'And you think the planning department will pass it?' he asks, looking at me as he pushes his spectacles up his nose.

I put my coffee down and smile. 'The regulations stipulate the frontage being in keeping with the street and area.' I point to the drawing and to the sash windows. 'We're not really changing all that much on the front, and given the building is currently derelict, anything is an improvement.'

Colin laughs. 'You'd think the council would be thankful someone is finally renovating the place, instead of enforcing their red tape. It's an eyesore.'

'I agree, and that's probably why they've passed these plans.'

He looks at me, shocked. 'They've passed them?'

I smile. 'After the two rejected submissions, I went down to the offices to pin the planning officer down. These right here are a yes.'

'Finally!' he chants, clapping his hands.

'And this roof in the back will be what sets it apart from all other galleries.'

'I agree.' He sighs, shaking his head in despair. 'But the cost, Annie.'

I smile to myself. I knew the potential cost would be an issue. Which is why I've been digging. 'I have a proposal.'

'Which is what?'

'I know of these guys based in France, and I made a quick call. They have estimated roughly half the price of the British manufacturer, keeping us right on track with the budget.' My excitement is hardly containable. 'My only concern is getting it from France to Dover intact.'

'A good haulage firm will do the job, right?'

'I hope so, because if it's damaged when it arrives on site, the schedule will go down the pan and your contractors won't be happy about it. Neither will you, I expect, since we're working to a tight schedule for your launch evening.'

'But half the price?'

'Subject to final measurements, which I'm sure are quite accurate. So yes.'

'Then it's a no-brainer.'

'Fabulous!'

Colin stands and collects his briefcase. 'I'll leave it in your capable hands, Annie. Just let me know what you need and when. And I could do with a copy of those drawings to send to my contractors so they can give me a final quote. It'll be helpful if you give me the details of this French company too, so they can liaise with them.'

'I'll sort it this evening.'

'Or you could just bring them along to the meeting on Monday morning? I'm due at the auction house at ten, so what do you say we meet at the bistro around the corner at nine thirty?'

'Sure.' Gathering up my things, I offer my hand and receive a solid shake. 'I'll see you tomorrow night, then?'

Colin frowns. 'What's happening tomorrow night?'

'I invited you to my housewarming?' I smile, throwing my bag over my shoulder. 'But don't worry if you've forgotten.'

'Damn, I have a dinner arrangement with the contractor who'll be undertaking the work here.' He thumbs over his shoulder. 'Something informal before we kick things off on Monday at the meeting. I'll sneak away as soon as I can.'

'Hey, bring them along. I can do informal before Monday too.'

'Yes, that's a great idea!'

'That's that sorted then. I'll see you tomorrow.' I smile and get on my way.

Bringing the tablespoon to my lips, I slurp the concoction loudly and roll the liquid around my mouth. 'More rum,' I declare to myself, tipping the bottle over the bowl and stirring it as it glugs out. I lift the spoon and slurp again, this time wincing. Strong. Perfect! I transfer the bowl of punch onto the big table and lick at my sticky fingers before collecting glasses from the cupboard and lining them up for easy access. I want everything in sight so I don't have to be running around all night playing hostess at my housewarming. I want to enjoy myself and get drunk enough to stamp out the lingering memories of Jack. I need tonight – my friends, alcohol and some laughs.

There's a knock on the door and I run to let the gang in, but when I swing it open, I find only Lizzy. No one else, just Lizzy. 'Where's everyone?'

'On their way.' She pushes her way in and heads for the kitchen. 'I wanted to talk to you before they all get here.'

'Why? What's up?' Has something happened with Jason? I follow her and crack open a bottle of wine, pouring us both a glass.

'*You*, Annie. You're what's up! You've been weird this week. Quiet. What gives?'

I clam up, my eyes darting. I can't deny I've been off sorts. Even Micky passed comment at lunch, and when I responded to Nat's text message with a one-word answer yesterday, she was on the phone asking me what was up too. 'My head is full, that's all,' I say lamely, sipping my wine.

'Of what?' Lizzy sounds suspicious and curious. I like neither.

'Work. Things to do around this place.'

'Bollocks,' she spits, insulted. 'You've not been the same since Saturday night. What happened? And please don't insult me by saying it was just a pleasant drink.'

'It was a pleasant drink,' I mumble on a shrug.

'Annie!'

'Okay!' I slam my glass down in frustration. 'I fucked him. Or he fucked me. It was unbelievably good. *He* was unbelievably good, but aside from his capabilities, there was . . .' I fade off, a string of shocked gasps coming from my friend. 'Something.'

'"Something"?' she asks quietly. 'What do you mean?'

'I don't know,' I grate, reclaiming my wine and taking a long slug. 'Chemistry. A connection. Something I haven't experienced before.'

'Oh shit,' she breathes.

'That doesn't help.'

'I can't believe you kept this from me, Annie!'

'Well, with you and Jason—'

'Bollocks to me and Jason. He's a cheating dick. How was it left? Did you give him your number? Arrange a date?'

I cringe all over my kitchen. 'I sneaked out when he was asleep.'

'What?' Lizzy screeches, slamming her own glass down. 'Are you fucking shitting me?'

'No. I wish I was.' I surprise myself with my willing answer, and the fact that yes, I regret walking out and leaving no line of possible contact. 'I can't stop thinking about him, Lizzy. It's driving me fucking loopy.'

'Wow. That good, huh?'

I collapse to my arse on a chair, exhausted after my confession. 'It's crazy, isn't it?' I wonder for the millionth time whether Jack has thought about *me*. I want to believe he's as tummy-tied as I am, reliving the night, obsessing about the connection we had and what it might mean.

'Have you looked him up?'

I laugh. 'I've hardly got much to go on. His name's Jack and . . . well, his name's Jack.'

'Do you *want* to find him?'

Now *that's* the operative question. Right now it's all in my head. Safe and secure in my mind, where I can relive the perfection day and night forever . . . even if it's slowly driving me mad. I shouldn't do anything stupid, like risk ruining that. Like finding him and discovering that he's actually a dick. Like realising that drink clouded my judgement. Like discovering that he is nothing like I remember. But what if he is? What if the sparks fly again and the constant butterflies in my tummy erupt?

Lizzy stands up and my eyes rise with her, until I find her face.

She's smiling knowingly. 'Tonight we get pissed. Tomorrow we hit Google and see if we can find the man who's knocked my mate's knees bandy.'

Screw it. He's clearly not going to fuck off out of my head. 'Fine.'

I head for the door when I hear the doorbell ring, finding Micky, Nat and a scattering of other people behind them. They all wave bottles at me, their tickets for entry. I laugh, swing the door wide open and let them all trample through my flat as they sing their hellos. Just as Nat passes, I snatch her elbow. 'Where's John?' I ask, doing another quick check of the sea of heads to make sure I've not missed him.

'He's not here.'

'Oh?' I release her arm when she shakes off her light blazer.

'Annie, I'm just not made to deal with kids.' She rolls her eyes. 'And bubblegum. I owe it to my hair to make a stand.'

I give her a sympathetic face to hide my own eye-roll. 'There's a bottle open in the fridge.'

'Fab!' She's off down the hall quickly. 'Now we're all single!' she sings, crashing into the kitchen and demanding alcohol. I smile and follow her, letting Lizzy kiss me on the cheek as I pass her.

'Okay?' she asks tentatively, wiping away the pink lipstick she's just smeared on my cheek.

'Perfect.' I chink our glasses and throw back the first of many wines.

An hour later, Micky is playing DJ and everyone is shouting requests at him. The drink is flowing and the chatter is lively, laughter filling my new home. I smile as I stand in the court-yard watching all of my friends mingle and drink. Nat comes from the kitchen, her eyes scanning the crowd. She spots me and waves an arm in the air. 'More guests at the door!' she calls, pointing through the kitchen to the hallway before she makes a beeline for Micky, delighted at the sight of shots.

I rush to the door and swing it open, finding Colin. 'Hey!' I sing, standing aside. 'Welcome, come in.'

'Hi, Annie!' Colin chimes happily, walking into my hallway and taking me in a friendly hug. 'Thanks for the invite.'

I let him release me, and an attractive lady in a silver dress quickly approaches me, holding up a bottle of wine, tapping the side with a long red fingernail. 'I brought you this, since we're technically gatecrashing.'

Colin laughs. 'Annie, this is Stephanie.'

I accept the bottle. 'Nice to meet you, Stephanie.'

'And this is her husband, Jack.' Colin nods past me. 'My contractor.'

I turn back towards the door, frowning, my brain slow to catch on.

Jack? Contractor?

Husband?

My blood runs cold and the bottle of wine slips through my fingers, shattering at my feet as I stare into familiar, intense grey eyes.

Chapter 6

'*Jack*,' I barely whisper, my mouth dry, my hand squeezing the door handle to try to steady my trembling.

'Oh no!' Stephanie cries, appearing at my side. 'Are you okay?' She bends and starts collecting the broken pieces of glass. 'Oh my, there's wine everywhere!'

I just stare. And so does he. I know Stephanie is talking, but I can't make out a word she's saying, hearing only Jack's voice through the flashbacks currently bombarding me, more vivid and real than any time before.

I blink rapidly, my breathing coming in short, fast bursts. I need to pull myself together. Quickly. Ripping my eyes away from Jack's, I drop to my haunches and start carelessly collecting pieces of glass, my mind in chaos.

He's here? Oh, my God, he's here! And he's *married*? I start to sweat.

'I'm so sorry,' I mumble to the floor, feeling a sharp stab of pain bolt through my finger. Dropping all of the shards I've clumsily gathered, I suck in air and look blankly down at blood trickling from the cut. Tears flood my eyes, a mixture of pain and desperation as Stephanie grabs my arm.

'You've cut yourself,' she says, pulling me to my feet. 'Let me see.'

I'm trembling in her hold. She must feel it. 'I'm sorry,' I mumble mindlessly, looking up at her.

She looks straight into my eyes, and I look away quickly, fearful of what she might read in them. 'Here, Jack, take Annie to clean up in the bathroom while I clear this mess up.'

'No, it's fine!' I blurt out, yanking my hand away fast, my panic rising. 'Honestly, it's just a silly nick. I need to mop this up.'

'I'll wipe up,' Colin offers. 'You get a bandage.'

'Come.' Jack's voice hits me from the side, and then his hand claims my wrist.

I jolt like a frightened animal, jumping back a few steps. Then I do something so utterly stupid. I look at him, finding grey eyes full of concern.

He tilts his head, saying so much before he breathes a word. 'Where's the bathroom?' he asks.

I point down the corridor, losing the ability to talk. Before I can even think to protest, Jack has his hand against the small of my back, pushing me towards my bedroom. His touch is like fire against my back, burning through the material of my dress.

We're going to be alone. What will he say? What will I say? He's married? He's here, in my house with his fucking wife! And he's Colin's contractor! My stomach churns.

He doesn't close my bedroom door behind us, choosing to only push it shut a little. Then he's leading the way across my room, pulling me along behind him urgently. After a quick check over his shoulder, he pulls the bathroom door closed behind us, and though I'm a wreck on the inside, I manage to appreciate how suspicious the closed doors might look if his wife comes to find us. I step forward to push it open again, but Jack intercepts me, blocking my way with his tall, well-built body. More flashbacks, except his body is naked.

I refuse to look up at him. I'm a big fat mess on the inside – confused, hurt and angry – but a lust and desire that I'm all too familiar with is dominating me. And I'm terrified by it. It wasn't the alcohol that night. It wasn't my imagination. It was real, and I'm feeling it all again now. When I really shouldn't be.

He doesn't speak, leaving the silence drenched with unspoken words and penetrated with potent craving. I knew I should have stayed away! I *sensed* there was a reason I should have stayed away. Oh my God, he's married! I checked for a ring that night. He wasn't wearing a ring!

'I need to go.' I push past him, but he seizes me and holds me in place, his breathing wild and laboured.

'You're Colin's architect?' he asks, his voice rich and smooth even though it carries reasonable worry.

'Yes,' I answer, short and sharp, not following it up with any of the questions that I should be firing at him.

Pretend I don't know him. Pretend I've never clapped eyes on him before in my life. It's the only way. 'Why didn't you tell me you're married?' The question just falls right out.

His hands squeeze my shoulders. 'I couldn't,' he says simply. 'I physically couldn't utter the fucking words to you, because at that moment in time, Annie, I was wishing I wasn't, more than I've ever wished it before.'

Wished it before? I shake my head before I can let that question hold me here any longer. 'I really must go.'

'No,' he grates, shaking me a little.

My anxiety rockets. I can only pretend nothing happened between us if he lets me, and his attitude right now is telling me he's not prepared to. Or maybe he's worried I'll say something to his wife. His *wife*! His wife who's currently sweeping up broken glass in my hallway.

Anger bubbles up from my toes, and I brave looking at him. His handsome face is like a sucker punch to my turning stomach. I feel sick. 'I won't say anything if that's what you're worried about.'

'You were gone,' he whispers, taking my arm and pulling me towards the sink.

He flips the tap on and forces my hand under the running water. There's no pain. I can't feel a damn thing through my shock.

'I woke up and you were just gone,' he says. 'Why?'

His audacity astounds me. Like I have to justify my actions to him? 'It's fucking irrelevant now, don't you think?' I seethe, wrenching my hand from the sink and grabbing a hand towel to wrap it in.

I'm so stupid! I bet he's out most weekends enticing women back to hotels with those sinfully good looks, the right words, his twinkling eyes and a bit of charming banter. He's clearly got away with it too, because his wife obviously trusts him. She didn't think twice about sending him into a room alone with me. What an arsehole! I'm suddenly so mad with myself for wasting a whole week going over every tiny detail of our encounter, picking it to pieces and trying to make sense of it. How many women has he blindsided?

He moves in closer and bends a little, his scent invading my nose. I hold my breath to avoid it. To stop myself from relishing it.

'There was nothing irrelevant about that night, Annie. I've thought of nothing else since.' His hand comes up and cups my cheek, his thumb circling lightly over my skin.

My whole body relaxes, the feel of him touching me so tenderly cutting through my anger, and I release my breath, getting a strong hit of his manly smell. It sends me woozy.

'There was something there between us,' he whispers. 'Fucking hell, something that's possessed me. I can't get you out of my head, Annie. I've been back to that bar every damn fucking night looking for you.' His face comes close, his breath warming my cheeks as I close my eyes and fall into a trance. 'You felt it too, didn't you? It wasn't just sex. Tell me you felt it too.' He brushes his scruff lightly across my cheek and I moan, despite myself, suddenly catapulted back into that hotel room. 'I thought I'd never see you again.'

I swallow, trying not to let the confirmation that he's thought about it too run away with me. It's a moot point now. But his touch. It's like fire, pulling the memories to the front of my mind, making me relive them all relentlessly.

'That night,' he breathes. 'With you curled into my side, I had no worries. No problems. I felt nothing beyond you, and it was fucking perfect, Annie.'

I swallow and squeeze my eyes shut. 'Perfect until I found out that you're married.' The words hurt, and though I'm willing myself to step back, to remove myself from his touch because I know I shouldn't be loving the feel of him, I don't. I remain where I am, unwilling and unable to rob myself of the amazing feelings that I've dreamed about experiencing again.

'You kept it,' Jack says softly, pulling my eyes open. He picks up the bottle cap from the shelf above my sink and fiddles with it for a few seconds, studying it moving between the tips of his fingers. I say nothing, watching as he looks back to me. 'You couldn't forget either.'

We stare at each other for a few moments as he blindly puts the bottle cap back. Then he moves closer to me, pushing his body into mine. Explosions. And his mouth drops lazily towards mine. In my head, I'm screaming, demanding I push him away. But my heart is fluttering and my body is coming to life again. His lips. His touch. His voice. His face. His kisses. Soft kisses turning into hard kisses. Just one more of those consuming kisses. One more. *Please, one more.* His lips gently brush mine, and I go lax against him.

'Jack!'

I'm snapped from my recklessness when her voice slams into the bathroom, and I fly back, as does Jack, just as the door opens and his wife appears. 'Is it bad?' she asks, approaching me.

Her presence aligns my senses in a heartbeat. 'It's nothing,' I assure her, smiling tightly. 'I have a plaster in the kitchen.'

'Maybe put some antiseptic cream on first,' Jack says quietly, and I look at him, finding intense grey eyes nailed to me.

Stephanie laughs and places a dainty hand on Jack's exposed

forearm. His whole body locks, going visibly tense. 'Always so wise,' she says dreamily as my eyes fall to where her hand is resting on his flesh.

Solid arms, braced on either side of my head as he pounded into me.

No!

I shake the flashbacks away and pluck some stability from nowhere. 'What a great start to the night.' I laugh, watching as Jack pulls his arm away from his wife's touch, flicking nervous eyes at her.

Her eyes aren't nervous. They're narrowed. More tension.

'Let's get back to the party.' I gesture towards the door, relieved when Stephanie slaps a smile on her face and leads on, Jack behind her.

I follow them out. Them. Stephanie and Jack. A married couple.

His shoulders are stiff, his profile appearing every few seconds when he looks back at me. Each time, I glance away, dying on the inside, bombarded by so many feelings. I don't know what to do with any of it. The guilt: that's the most potent feeling of all. And then more panic when I see Lizzy coming in from the garden.

Oh Jesus, I've been so caught up in my state of shock I forgot my friends here tonight were also in the bar *that* night. I watch in horror as she pulls to a slow stop, looking straight past Stephanie to Jack, her smile falling away. I fly past Jack, knocking his arm, and reach Lizzy, forcing her to retreat.

'You don't know him,' I whisper in her ear as I whirl around, slapping a smile on my face. 'This is Lizzy!' I declare, making introductions. 'Lizzy, this is Jack, my client's contractor, and his *wife*, Stephanie.' I don't mean to emphasise that word with spite, but just in case Lizzy is slow on the uptake, I need to spell out, loud and clear, my fucked-up situation.

Lizzy presents her hand to each of them in turn, smiling

brightly. She has the casual, blasé mask far more nailed than I do. 'How lovely to meet you,' she gushes, turning to me once she's said her hellos. Her dark eyes are wide. So fucking wide. They should be. 'I'll go and change the music.'

Her head tilts to the side a little in silent signal. I read her mind like I could be reading from a script. She's going to make sure that Nat and Micky don't drop me in the shit. Fuck, I hope they don't recognise Jack; they were all pretty pissed, but I can't risk it. 'I think only Micky will recognise him,' Lizzy whispers as she passes me.

God, I hope so. Colin appears in the doorway. 'Are you okay?'

'It's nothing,' I assure him. 'Did you get a drink?'

'Yes.' He holds up a glass of red. 'I was just seeing to Jack and Stephanie's but I got distracted by your friend Micky. He's a personal trainer, and I need one of those.' Colin flexes his non-existent biceps and makes his way back into the garden. 'Get those drinks and come and join us.'

'What would you like?' I ask Stephanie, pulling the cupboard open and retrieving the small first aid box.

'Wine would be lovely, thank you. White, please.'

'Jack?' I ask, hating how his name sounds on my lips. I definitely hear a deep inhale of breath from behind me.

'Beer, please,' he says, as I make quick work of slapping a plaster over my tiny cut. 'Budweiser, if you have it.'

My fumbling fingers falter. Budweiser. I see him tipping a bottle to his lips and I see me, rapt by his taut throat. And the bottle top. Something to remember him by. 'I have it.' I shove the first aid box back in the cupboard and turn, catching his eye.

'Thank you.' He glances away, kicking me into action.

I make fast work of getting their drinks, but not so fast that Lizzy doesn't have time to suss out the rest of my friends. When she appears in the doorway again, mildly nodding, I very nearly collapse with relief.

'The garden?' I lead the way and introduce Jack and his wife to a few people, feeling him staring at me the whole time.

Nat is oblivious to Jack and who he is, but Micky's stance definitely alters the moment he claps eyes on him. I stare at my oldest friend until he looks at me, then give him begging eyes, hoping he sees and absorbs my silent plea. He shakes his head, looking as disturbed by the situation as I'm feeling, before returning his attention to Colin.

You'd have to be dead not to feel the tension bouncing around my courtyard garden. I'm certain everyone must feel it, yet as I glance around, everyone is chatting normally, unaware. I leave Stephanie and Jack with Nat and rush to the kitchen to find more wine, knowing I'll have company in—

'What the fuck?' Lizzy hisses, joining me by the worktop as I pour with shaking hands.

I nod my agreement and bring the glass to my lips, swigging back half of the wine.

'Tell me you didn't know.'

'I didn't know,' I say calmly, not insulted by Lizzy's demand as I swallow my wine and turn, resting my arse against the counter.

Micky falls into the kitchen with wide, worried eyes. 'Annie, you okay?'

I nod and sip more wine. 'He's married,' I mumble mindlessly, staring into my glass. 'My amazing one-night stand is married, in my house with his fucking wife, and he's my client's contractor.' I look up at my friends. 'I have to work with him.' I laugh. 'You couldn't fucking write it!'

'The wanker,' Micky spits, slamming his glass down on the counter.

'Nat was too busy dancing and throwing back shots to take any notice of him in the bar,' Lizzy says, looking outside, no doubt checking the coast is clear.

'I can't believe this,' I splutter. 'All that time I wasted thinking about him.'

'Here.' Lizzy pours more wine into my glass and Micky comes over, wrapping an arm around my shoulder.

'I'm such an idiot.'

'No,' they snap in unison.

'I am. I fell right into his hands, and now I have to look his wife in the eye knowing I fucked her husband.' The thought sets my panic off again and I begin to tremble, my wine splashing up the side of my glass.

'This isn't your fault.' Lizzy grinds the words out, annoyed. 'Look at me,' she demands, and I do. 'Calm down. Get through tonight and then we'll reconvene in the morning.'

'What am I going to do?' I ask. 'I can't work with him.' I'll have to quit Colin's project. It's my dream design coming to life, and I'll have to abandon it.

'For now, you're not going to let him ruin your night. Tomorrow we'll . . .'

The room falls silent when another presence is noted by all three of us, and we all look towards the door. Jack's standing in the doorway, absorbing the fiery glares pointed at him. 'I need to talk to Annie,' he states confidently.

'What?' Micky pipes up, almost laughing at the cheek of his declaration. 'You turn up here large as life, with your fucking wife?'

'I have one person to explain myself to,' Jack says calmly. 'Five minutes, Annie, please.' He lands me with grey eyes full of desperation. I force myself to disregard his evident despair and tell myself I'm owed an explanation. Because I am.

'Five minutes,' I confirm, glancing at Micky and Lizzy, knowing I must be as mad as they think I am. But I need to hear what he has to say. I need closure. 'I'll be fine.'

They both leave, clearly reluctant, and once we're alone, that energy between Jack and me – the energy that frightens me – surges forward. It's so powerful it makes me move across the room hastily to put as much distance between us as possible and, perhaps, to make the situation look as casual as possible should anyone walk in. Just two people having a chat about business in the kitchen. 'Go ahead, Jack. Explain,' I say, cutting straight to the chase.

His hesitation is obvious. 'Before I explain anything, you need to know that I have never cheated on my wife. Not ever, Annie. Not until you.'

I scoff, unable to force it back. 'And that makes everything okay?'

'I didn't say it makes everything okay. I just want you to know that I don't make a habit of cheating on my wife.' He moves forward a few steps, and I hold my hand up, silently stopping him from coming any closer as I glance over my shoulder into the garden. His wife is chatting with Lizzy. My friend is keeping her occupied while her husband is in here with me. I wince, swallowing down the building guilt. 'Have you thought about me?' he asks.

I snap my eyes to Jack's. 'No.' Admitting it would be stupid.

'Don't lie to me,' he warns, totally serious. 'Don't pretend you didn't feel it.'

'What the hell does it matter now?' I hiss. 'You lied to me. Where was your ring?'

He throws his hand up, showing me his ring finger. It's still bare. 'I don't wear one. I broke a knuckle when I was working as a builder and haven't been able to get it on since.'

'Then you should have told me.' I imagine plenty of women throw themselves at him. He should have a sign on his forehead or something, some kind of visible warning not to go near.

'Told you?' He almost laughs. 'I already said, Annie. I couldn't. I couldn't even *think* the words. I saw nothing except *you*. Thought of nothing except how much I wanted *you*. Everything else paled. All I see are your green eyes staring up into mine. All I can feel is your skin against me. Your breath in my ear.'

'Stop!' I demand, ignoring the fact that I had a similar re-action to him. But I'm single. I'm allowed to feel like that. He shouldn't. Not when he's taken!

'No.' He comes over to me, and I find myself quickly check-ing behind me again, all skittish, before looking at him. He's too close. It's dangerous for more reasons than his wife possibly walking in here. 'I can't stop, Annie.'

I shake my head and move away, opening a cupboard and pulling down a bag of pretzels, anything to look busy and casual. 'You're married. It ends here,' I say firmly and evenly, not allowing his words to pierce my resolve.

'Do you want it to?' he asks, knocking me back a bit.

I don't answer nearly as quickly as I should, distracting my-self with pouring the pretzels into a bowl. 'Are you suggesting an affair?'

'I'm asking you if you're curious about us.'

'There is no "us",' I whisper-hiss, performing another check of our surroundings.

'What if there should be?'

I baulk, astounded. '"Should be"?'

'I've played tug of war with my conscience all week, Annie. I've told myself that this isn't the right way to get out of my marriage. I've tried, I've tried so fucking hard to stop thinking about you, and then shit happens with Stephanie and I'm back to square one, obsessing over you and how you made me feel. The smiles you pulled from me. The feelings you spiked. You are clouding everything.'

Shit happens with Stephanie? I hate myself for wondering too hard what that shit is. I can't ask. *Shouldn't* ask.

'You will stay away from me.' I pivot and leave the kitchen before Jack can come back at me with anything else that may dent my determination, slapping a smile on my face as I enter the garden.

I just need tonight to be over so I can commence with the

meltdown that's undoubtedly going to floor me. He felt it, just like I did – the connection, the overwhelming chemistry. But it was just lust, stirred up and made more potent by alcohol. And spontaneity. I have to keep telling myself that. It's the safest way. I never thought I'd see him again, that he would remain a beautiful, albeit frustrating, fantasy in my head. A benchmark for all men who may come after. I doubt I'll find that crushing attraction with anyone else. I've been teased, experienced something incredible, only to discover I can never have it again. That I should never have had it in the first place. Denying yourself is one thing. Being denied by something out of your control is a whole new ballgame. It just makes you want it more.

I watch as Stephanie chats with Colin, and Jack stands silent at her side, obviously distracted. No matter how hard I try, I can't stop my eyes from straying to him. Every time I catch his gaze, I quickly glance away, pushing down my thumping heart as it works its way up to my throat. I fight to keep myself in conversations, but I'm too unfocused, seeing mouths move but hearing no words being spoken. My head is full of reminders. Of things Jack said to me. Of the way he touched me and made love to me.

I discreetly glance over to him again, but this time his attention is on his wife as she speaks to him. Colin raises his hands, as if in surrender, and backs away from the couple warily, making his way over to me. Stephanie looks angry, and though I try my hardest to lip-read her, I can't make out what she's saying to her husband. Her husband. Jack. Stephanie's husband.

'It's kicked off over there,' Colin laughs, a little tipsy as he reaches me.

'What has?' I ask, playing ignorant, keeping one eye on him and one eye on Jack.

'Jack is a diamond of a bloke, but it seems the rumours are true.'

'What rumours?' I ask, frowning as I watch Stephanie's face get closer to Jack's and he retreats a little, shaking his head and closing his eyes. He's gathering patience.

'Well,' Colin starts. 'I've only met the woman tonight, but I can see what people mean. She's a bit . . . of a handful.'

Handful? I can't rip my eyes away. Jack is clearly trying to keep Stephanie calm, leaning in to speak to her and placing a comforting hand on her arm. My eyes root to that hand, feeling it touching me all over again. What is wrong with her? Is she suspicious? Has she sensed the friction between Jack and me?

My eyes jump between them, trying desperately to figure out what's going on. Jack catches my eye, and he breathes in deeply as Stephanie shrugs him off and throws her wine back on a sneer. She marches off to top up her glass, and I find myself stuck in position, wanting to move away but unable. I start to shake, fearful of the lack of control I have over my body where Jack's concerned. And, worse, my mind.

'Best keep out of the way of domestics,' Colin says, pointing to my empty. 'Another drink?'

I strain a smile. 'I just need the toilet.' I force my shaky legs to take me inside and to my bathroom. I close the door and fall back against the wood, trying to breathe some calm into my lungs.

I feel like I could crack under the pressure of Jack's presence, my mind going into overdrive, wondering if the tension between us is obvious. Wondering what his wife's grievance is. I'm not the paranoid type. I'm not unreasonable. Yet right now I feel like I have a sign stuck to my back detailing my sins.

'Annie?' There's a knock on the door behind me and Lizzy's concerned voice drifts into the bathroom. 'You okay?'

'I'm fine.' I rush towards the sink and brush at my flushed cheeks, then spot the bottle top on the shelf. I'll never be able to look at Budweiser in the same way again. Clenching my jaw, I grab the cap and throw it in the bin. 'Just coming.'

'They've gone,' she says quietly through the door.

I swing around, air gushing from my lungs in relief. 'They have?'

'Yes, just left. His wife seemed a bit drunk.'

I open the door and face my friend's pursed lips, trying to smile. It's an epic fail. 'A bit?'

'Okay. Totally fucked.' Lizzy eyes me carefully. 'To be fair, she was sinking wine like water.'

I wince. 'I think they were arguing. What if she knows?' I start to shake again.

'She doesn't know, Annie. Calm down.'

I try to breathe steadily, and Lizzy takes my arm. 'Come on.' She pulls me out of the bathroom, where I think I'd happily hide for the rest of my life. 'Micky's lined up shots, and I think you need ten of them.'

I spend the rest of the evening pretending to listen to conversations while constantly wondering what Jack's thinking, what he's doing and what he's saying to his wife.

Micky and Lizzy make their excuses to hang back when everyone leaves, though the knowledge of an impending inquisition doesn't fill me with dread like it probably should. I need their support, plus Lizzy spent most of the night talking to Stephanie. What did she find out? Do I need to know? Or, more importantly, do I *want* to know anything about them? Because they are a *they*. A couple. Married.

I shut the door behind the last people to leave, then turn to find Micky and Lizzy standing in the hallway, both sober, both waiting for . . . I don't know what. So I just shrug, the evening sinking into me and weighing me down.

'I can't believe it,' Lizzy says, shaking her head.

'Happy Housewarming to me,' I murmur, wandering towards them. They part and let me through to the lounge, where I pick up a few cushions and chuck them on the couch on my way to the kitchen. I pour myself a nightcap in the form of a large glass of wine, and take a long glug as I stare out of the kitchen window. 'Well that was fun,' I say seriously.

Lizzy clears her throat and comes to stand on one side, Micky on the other, like they're sensing my need for support. I look to each of them in turn and smile a small, hopeless smile.

'You okay, treacle?' Micky's palm slides onto my shoulder and squeezes.

'I'm fine,' I say resolutely. 'Honestly.' I shake my head to my-self and finish off my wine, hoping it'll knock me out and put me out of my misery.

Both eye me doubtfully, and they have every right to. I'm not fine. I don't sound it, and I'm certain I don't look it. My stable, controlled existence has been rocked to the core, and I'm scared. More than I was scared by the crushing connection we had.

Because everyone wants what they can't have.

Chapter 7

Monday morning comes far too quickly, and I feel far from fresh going into my meeting with Colin and his contractor. Jack.

I did a little research on his company last night and found that Joseph Contractors was formed by Jack in 2009, when he was only twenty-eight. I mentally noted that that makes him thirty-five today. He did manual labour for years as a builder, which would explain the stunning physique – a physique that he's clearly set on maintaining – before starting his own building firm that has gone from strength to strength. It was clear from what I learned that any architect should feel lucky to work alongside him. Me? I just feel scared to fucking death.

I've agonised constantly about how to deal with working together. I've given up Colin's project ten times in my head, then reinstated myself quickly after. The prospect of kissing this opportunity goodbye makes me feel empty and weak. But I'm not weak, and I'm not about to let a man make me that way. I owe it to my career to move forward. I owe it to *myself*.

Jack's the contractor. Just the contractor, and I'm not going to let his lies and deceit affect what I've worked my arse off for.

So I put on a pale grey pencil dress, leaving my hair down and wavy, then gather Colin's file and get on my way.

I call Lizzy as I walk to the Tube, hoping for a little pep talk. 'I'm due to start a bikini wax in two minutes,' she says when she answers. 'So let me cut to the chase. How are you going to handle him in this meeting?'

'I'm going to pretend I've never met him before Saturday night,' I tell her, my voice now wavering from the sureness I'd found, just at the thought of doing so. 'He's a liar and a cheat and, frankly, I hate him. It shouldn't be hard to keep it business.'

'Good girl.' There's a buzz of activity from down the line, and Lizzy curses a few times. 'Shit! I just spilled hot wax. I have to go. Good luck!'

I hang up, straighten my shoulders and head for my meeting.

My plan was to arrive early, get a coffee and settle at a table before the men got there, and maybe talk my nerves down, but when I walk into the bistro I find them both already sitting at a table at the far end.

They're talking, looking over some paperwork, and when I'm only a few feet away, Jack slowly turns to face me, like he's sensed I'm close. My lungs shrink at the sight of him, my feet slowing as I fight to breathe. His straight expression doesn't clue me in on what reception I might get from him, and that makes me all the more nervous.

That chest, rippling above me, undulating as he drives into me steadily.

I jolt myself from my untimely flashback, and a dart of my eyes to Jack tells me he hasn't missed it, his expression questioning.

I take a deep breath and will myself forward.

'Annie. Here, take a seat.' Colin motions to the chair next to Jack, but I opt for the one at the other side of the table instead. Not too close.

'Morning,' I greet them, smiling at Colin as I unload my files onto the table. 'Jack,' I say formally without looking at him.

'Annie,' he replies, just as formally, taking his coffee cup and lifting it to his lips. My eyes catch a slight tremble of his hand as I involuntarily follow the cup to his mouth. I think of him drinking that bottle of Budweiser, his neck stretched, begging me to lick the column of his throat. *Bending me over the bar, his big hands on my hips.*

'Great party,' Colin chirps, snapping me back into the bistro. Jack is watching me watching him.

I shake my way back into the meeting, telling myself to concentrate, to not let him distract me. 'It was. Thanks for coming.' I smile, thinking I never want to think about that night ever again.

The waiter approaches and I order a large latte, declining the offer of pastries. I would never be able to hold anything down; my stomach is somersaulting repeatedly, and I'm getting annoyed that I can't control it.

Colin looks down at his watch. 'I have to be at an auction in thirty minutes, so let's get this schedule agreed upon.' He motions to my files. 'Do you have the revised drawings for Jack?'

'I do.' I pull them out and push them across the table to Jack, avoiding making eye contact, which is hard when I can feel him staring at me. This is so strange. I spent a night in a hotel with this man, the most amazing night of my life, and now I'm acting like I've never set eyes on him, let alone his naked body.

All this formality, this distance, isn't coming naturally to me. Being consumed by Jack felt *so* right and easy – looking at him, admiring him, talking to him, listening to him. It all felt so natural. 'The details of the French roof manufacturer are on there too.'

'Thank you,' Jack says, unfolding the first drawing and scanning it over. 'I'll take them back to the office and go over them with Richard. He's my site manager, who'll be overseeing the build, by the way.'

'Good to know.' I make a mental note of Richard's name.

'We have various machinery arriving tomorrow so we can start clearing the site.' Jack folds up the drawing and places it on the table with the others, finding my eyes and locking stares with me. 'We anticipate a few weeks to strip it back to the bare bones.'

Strip. Bare. My skin starts to prickle with heat, and I glance away from him, making notes on my pad. 'Okay. So you'll have the site pegged out as per my drawings by . . .'

'Week three,' Jack finishes for me, pulling my attention up. He smiles, and I have to take a deep breath and force my attention back down to my notepad.

I power on. 'And by week four, you'll have . . .'

'The trenches for the foundations dug out.'

My pen falters across the page. 'Good,' I say quietly. 'And the concrete slab for the floor should be complete by . . .'

'Week five,' Jack murmurs.

I close my eyes briefly and will him to stop being so on the ball. It's a perfect scenario for an architect and contractor to be so aligned when it comes to a project, but now, between Jack and me, it isn't helping me hate him.

'That was what you were thinking, wasn't it?' he asks, almost pensive.

My smile feels strained. 'It was.'

'Good.' Jack gets a diary out of his briefcase and opens it up to a planner, presenting it to me and Colin. Then he takes over, detailing the schedule and phases of the project carefully from week five, running through a timeline for the next few months to completion. I hate that every step, every tiny detail he has written down, is all where I'm at in my head with this project. Every time he hesitates, I'm able to finish his sentence, and we're already talking about slight modifications to make the plans even stronger. We're in perfect sync.

Our sweaty bodies flash through my mind, moving in tune, our hearts beating in time. I jerk in my chair and clamp my teeth on the lid of my pen. In perfect sync. In *every* way. I focus on what Jack's actually saying as opposed to the sound of his voice saying it, fighting not to allow the deep timbre to get under my skin. Fighting to not allow my mind to morph what he says into other words – words he said to me on that night. I'm not doing very well – too many memories, now potent and vivid, running circles in my head. Keeping my eyes off his hands too, as he talks with them, is a killer. A total killer. Those hands have explored every part of my body. So has his mouth.

Stop it! 'Can I get a copy of that?' I ask him, my voice shaky as I point to the schedule in his diary.

'Sure.' Jack looks at me, cocking his head a little to the side. 'I'll send a scan later today. I just need your e-mail.'

Biting down on my lip, I pull a business card from my bag and slide it across the table, trying not to think about the fact that I've just given him every contact detail he could need for me.

'So we're all on the same page?' Colin asks, rising from his chair.

'We're on the same page,' Jack confirms. I look across the table at him, reading between the lines. 'Aren't we?' he asks, swallowing hard. 'I know where I stand.'

He knows where he stands. I read his code message loud and clear. 'Same page,' I confirm on a gulp, feeling relief course through me as I silently thank him for not making this harder than it needs to be.

He nods knowingly, snapping his diary shut.

'Great.' Colin swipes up a huge art folder. 'I just know you two are a match made in heaven.' He breezes out of the bistro as I stare at his back in utter shock, and Jack coughs over his coffee.

He looks at me, his face expressionless. 'A match made in heaven.'

I don't allow myself to fall into the depths of his twinkly eyes. 'Professionally, maybe,' I say, getting my bag from the back of my chair, resisting the urge to point out that we can't possibly be a match made in heaven ... since he's married. My stray thought turns my stomach as I unzip my slouchy leather bag to retrieve my purse.

Jack pulls his wallet from his inside pocket. 'Put your money away. I'll get this.' He reaches over and halts my hand from going into my bag, and I jump so much my chair actually shoots back. Jack retracts his hand in shock. 'Sorry; I didn't mean to make you jump.' He sounds sincere, and I feel utterly stupid. But his touch. Oh God, his touch.

'Thank you for the coffee,' I say, getting to my feet but keeping my eyes on the table.

'No problem. Can I give you a lift anywhere?'

I actually laugh. 'No, but thanks for the offer.'

'What's so funny?' He stands, towering over me, and I get another onslaught of flashbacks as a result. He's naked, looming over me, asking if I'm ready for him.

I squash my thoughts and take a deep breath. 'Nothing.' I hand my drawings to him while keeping my gaze far, *far* away from his. 'Don't forget these.'

Slowly, *too* slowly, his hand lifts and takes them from my grasp. 'I promise to keep this strictly business, Annie,' he tells me candidly.

'Good.' My voice is shaking terribly, adrenalin racing through my bloodstream and making my heart pump crazily. I can feel him staring at me, and as hard as I know it's going to be, I tell myself I mustn't *ever* look at him. At least not in the eye. I brush past him and pace out of the bistro, feeling his stare on my back the entire way. He might have promised to keep it business, but that doesn't stop my entire being from responding to him like it does. And it doesn't erase the memories, either.

When I get back to my studio I fire up my laptop, fetch a coffee and get on with submitting a planning application and e-mailing building control before sifting through piles of e-mails and cleaning up my inbox. I sip my coffee and jot down notes in my diary as I go, confirming a few potential client meetings. The weeks ahead are full-on, and I'm relieved. I need to keep busy.

As it approaches midnight my eyes are beginning to glaze over. I flag my final e-mail and guide the cursor to the top right-hand corner to shut my e-mail down, but the ping of a notification stops me and a new message icon appears in the bottom right-hand corner. My heartbeat dulls to an uncomfortable pulse as the sender's name glows brightly at me:

jack.joseph@josephcontractors.co.uk

I move away from my laptop slowly, placing my mug on the desk and my hands in my lap, trying to psych myself up to open it. *It's just a damn e-mail, just words.* I click the message open.

Annie,
Please find attached the schedule of works detailing the four phases of Colin's project. Any questions, just shout. Richard and I have been over the revised drawings. He has a few questions. Are you available to meet him on site tomorrow to go over them?
Best,
Jack
CEO, Jack Joseph Contractors

I sit back in my chair, reading over his e-mail once more. It's nearly midnight. I question what he's doing working this late until I remind myself that I'm working too. His e-mail is formal. So formal. Just how it should be, so why is my heart thrumming nervously?

My fingers shake when I start composing a reply, making me hit the wrong keys over and over again. 'Damn it,' I curse myself, pulling my hands away and taking some steadying breaths. This is so stupid.

> Jack,
> Many thanks for the schedule. I'm available at 10.00 if that suits?
> Regards,
> Annie
> A. R. Architects Ltd

'Best'? 'Regards'? It's utterly ridiculous considering what Jack and I have done together. We've explored every inch of each other's bodies, shared the most intimate parts of each other, and here we are acting like it never happened. My e-mail dings again.

> Annie,
> I'd ask what you're doing working so late, but that wouldn't be keeping it business, right? Tomorrow at ten is good. I'm currently looking over the landscapers' designs for the garden area. I found these giant glass cases online (link attached) and thought a few hung on the brick wall adjacent to the extension could look amazing, and they'd complement your roof perfectly. Let me know what you think before I put forward the suggestion to Colin.
> Best,
> Jack
> CEO, Jack Joseph Contractors

I raise a sardonic eyebrow at his light joke and click the attachment open, immediately taken aback by the beautiful simplicity of the wall-hung glass cabinets with aluminium trim. 'Wow,' I murmur, scanning the details and dimensions.

Jack,
Right.
Regarding the glass cases, I love them, and I'm certain Colin
would too. A great idea. I'll see Richard on site tomorrow.
Regards,
Annie
A. R. Architects

I close down my laptop and take myself to bed, happy that I
got through my day in one piece and managed to keep it business. But no matter how professional I act on the outside, on
the inside I'm still in fucking chaos over Jack Joseph.

Chapter 8

I'm a bag of nerves when I arrive on site the next day. I've psyched myself up for this meeting all night, telling myself that I can do it. I *can* do it. I'm meeting Richard. Not Jack. I just hope I get to deal with him for the most part on this project.

Colin meets me as I'm walking up the sweeping driveway, a broad smile on his face. 'Here's the lady of the year,' he says, collecting his briefcase from the steps leading up to the building. 'I have a meeting to get to, so I'll leave you with Richard.' He points past me, and I look back to see a tall, fair-haired guy in a high visibility jacket guiding a skip lorry off the road. My heart jumps a few beats when I recognise him.

'Richard,' I parrot back to Colin.

'He's Jack's right-hand man.'

He's also the guy who was with Jack in the bar the night I met him. 'Okay,' I breathe, trying to settle down my building heart rate. 'No Jack?' *Please say no!*

'Not that I know of. Richard's up to speed on things, so you should be able to get on. Oh, watch your back.' Colin takes my arm and leads me to the side, out of the way of the reversing lorry.

Richard slaps the side of the vehicle when it grinds to a stop, then makes his way over to us. I know he's recognised me when he cocks his head. 'Hey. I know you.'

I manage a smile, my mind whizzing. Has Jack told him the sordid details, or am I just a girl he was chatting with in a bar?

I don't know, so I wipe my face of all guilt, or I try, and turn on my professional switch – the one that's getting harder and harder to find. 'Hi, I'm Annie.' I offer my hand and he takes it, giving me a solid, manly shake.

'Nice to meet you. Officially, anyway,' he adds. His friendliness tells me that he has no idea about Jack and me, which would make sense, since Jack's *married*.

Colin smiles and makes off down the driveway. 'I'll leave you guys to it. Call me if you need me.'

'Have a great day,' I call, going to my bag to get my car keys. 'I just need to grab my hat and vest.'

Richard wanders over to a nearby car and pops the boot. 'Here, you can use these.' He pulls out a high visibility jacket and a matching hard hat. 'Probably a bit on the large size, but they'll do you for now.'

'Thanks.' I accept and put them on. 'So you have the drawings?'

'Yes, I've just been going over them.' He motions to the entrance of the derelict building that will soon be transformed into a beautiful art gallery. 'I have a few questions. Shall we?'

'Sure.' I start to make my way up the steps to the front door with Richard, stopping at the top when I hear wheels skidding up the gravel of the driveway. Both Richard and I turn to investigate, but I bet it's only *my* heart that punches its way out of my chest when we see where the noise is coming from: a silver Audi S7 with Jack at the wheel. Oh, fuck. I swallow and immediately start breathing through my rising anxiety. *Be calm*, I tell myself. I'm here for a reason, and it isn't Jack.

He seems to sit at the wheel forever, staring forward at me on the steps.

'Finally,' Richard mutters. 'Is he going to sit there all day and watch us?' Richard's rhetorical question goes right over my head, my files beginning to jump in my hands. Yet when I know I should be moving onward, going inside and getting on with things, I find my legs simply will not cooperate.

Jack eventually lets himself out of the car. He looks anxious. A bit dishevelled. And beyond the stoniness of his expression is something else. Stress. My conclusion is only reinforced when he shoves a frustrated hand through his hair and slams his car door shut violently.

'For fuck's sake, not again,' Richard mutters, marching over to him.

I rip my eyes from Jack's and look at Richard, seeing his tight, pissed-off jaw. *Not again?* What does he mean? Jack takes a few steps towards his right-hand man, yanking on his suit jacket as he does, his head dropped. There's too much distance between us for me to hear Richard's hushed whispers, but it's plain to see that something is wrong with Jack. Is it me?

I back up, beating down my curiosity, and make my way into the building. *Work. Just get on with your work.*

I find the old table where Richard has the drawings laid out and stare down at them, if only for something to do.

'Sorry I'm late.' Jack's voice hits my back and makes every hair on my neck stand.

'You didn't say you were coming.' I keep my eyes cemented on the drawings, dropping my bags to the floor next to the table. His tan brogues appear in my downcast vision, the same shoes he had on that fateful night. I close my eyes and work hard to calm myself down.

'I didn't?' he replies. He knows damn well he didn't.

'Does Richard know?' I need to find out what I'm dealing with.

'No.'

I breathe out my relief, hearing the sound of boots on the concrete behind me. 'Okay, let's—' Richard cuts off when his phone starts ringing. 'Yes? Shit, yeah, I'll be right out.' He curses under his breath. 'The scaffolders are here and the skip lorry is in the way. You guys crack on. I need to go and teach people how to drive.'

My eyes spring open, finding a pair of familiar hands spread on the table before me. Big, capable hands. Hands that handled me with confidence, authority and care. I look up, straight ahead at the brick wall in front of me, rummaging through my mind for anything work-related to say. There's nothing. No words, only mental visions of that night. This is supposed to be getting easier, not harder!

'How are you?' Jack asks quietly.

'Great, thanks,' I chirp, way too over the top. I scold myself for sounding so completely fake. 'You?' Why would I ask that?

'Struggling on.' His arm brushes mine, and I jump from his touching distance, pointing at the drawing nearest to me.

'I'd like you to go over these numbers with me.' I'm not even pointing at numbers. I'm pointing at a damn window spec.

Jack reaches forward with a finger and places it next to mine near the window, and I hear him inhale deeply. There's a long, uncomfortable silence, until Jack finally breaks it. 'These drawings really amaze me, Annie. Richard and I were marvelling over them yesterday.'

'Thank you.' I brush off his compliment and straighten, turning to him and looking past his shoulder. 'Shall we walk the site? I have a few questions too.'

'Why can't you look at me?'

My eyes drop, and I scream at him in my head to keep to his word. He promised. He promised to keep this strictly business! 'It's this way,' I say, passing him and making my way to the rear of the building. 'There's a tree that I'm worried will jeopardise the glass roof.'

'Right.' Jack sighs and his footsteps kick in, following me. When I exit the existing old UPVC patio doors, I point to the colossal horse chestnut tree that canopies one-quarter of the outside space.

Jack wanders around the trunk, looking up. 'Have we checked if this thing has a preservation order on it?'

'It hasn't,' I confirm. 'But, obviously, we should avoid chopping it down if we can. Though to get the full impact of the roof, we need to lose some of these branches.'

'I agree.' Jack smoothes a hand down the bark of the tree, and my gaze follows it, my damn body responding like it's feeling his touch all over again. I look up and catch his eye but quickly look away, knowing he's reading my mind. 'I'll call the tree surgeon in,' he says quietly.

'Thank you.'

'No problem. We should also be mindful of the roots when we dig down for the footings of the extension. She's one beast of a tree.' Jack looks upward, stretching his neck.

I wince and look away, but dart my eyes straight back to his throat in a double-take, squinting. What's that mark on his neck?

'How are we doing?' Richard appears, getting Jack's attention so he lowers his head and I lose sight of the blemish. Or was it a shadow?

'We need to keep an eye on these roots, mate,' Jack says, stubbing the toe of his shoe on the trunk. 'And we need to call in the surgeons to get rid of a few branches.'

'Got it,' Richard confirms. 'Can I borrow Annie for a moment? I have a few questions about the steel supports.'

Yes! Please borrow me! Get me away!

'Sure,' Jack says softly, but I'm walking back into the building before I get his go-ahead. And I can feel his fiery stare on me the whole damn way, raising my temperature higher and higher.

'Is it me, or is it really warm today?' I ask Richard's back, pulling at the sides of my high visibility jacket.

'It's you.' He laughs and points to a wall splitting two rooms. 'This here is a supporting wall.'

'Right,' I confirm. 'And the wall on the next floor is too, so we need a pretty hefty steel in there. The calculations are on the drawing. I suspect we'll need to get it specially made.'

'I'll speak to the fabricators.' Richard reaches into his pocket and pulls out his card. 'You'll be needing this.'

'Perfect.'

'And this.' Another card appears, held between the fingers of Jack's big hand.

'Thank you.' I take it without looking at him and slip them both into my trouser pocket.

'It's gonna look amazing,' Richard remarks. Any other time, I would feel a sense of pride, but right now I'm riddled with too much apprehension to feel anything else.

'Colin's filled you in on the roof situation?' I ask.

Richard laughs. 'Yes. You're one brave woman. If that roof arrives with a chip or crack, this whole project will be knocked off schedule.'

'I have a question.' Jack steps forward, and I can't stop my eyes from meeting his. The grey I remember is clouded and dull, not sparkling and glittery. He's definitely suffering here, and I get no pleasure from it. I'm suffering too.

'What?' I ask tentatively, my head spinning with all of the questions that are probably on his mind, none of them work-related.

He lifts a heavy arm and points at my torso. 'Can I have my jacket back?'

Richard starts laughing, and I tense from top to toe, looking down my front. 'It's yours?' Quickly shrugging the jacket off, I hand it to Jack with an awkward smile.

He takes it slowly, and then his arm starts to lift towards me again. I find myself discreetly pulling back, my stare following his outreached hand as it moves towards my head. What is he doing?

'And this,' he says quietly, taking the hard hat from my head.

I let my tense muscles relax as he pulls back. 'Thanks for letting me borrow them.'

'I didn't.' He swings his jacket on, stilling when he's shoved one arm through the sleeve, his face lowering to the collar a little. He almost scowls, and I know it's because he just got a waft of my girlie perfume lingering on the threads. 'Richard did,' he finishes, looking at Richard like he hates him.

I have a feeling that jacket will be going on a super-hot wash to get rid of my lingering scent the moment Jack gets home. Maybe even in the bin. Arranging the collar, he flexes his neck, and I see it again. Marks, but this time I'm a lot closer, and I can see there are four perfect lines. Scratches?

'What have you done?' I ask before I can stop myself, my hand lifting to his throat to touch gently below one of the raw red marks.

Jack freezes, his wide eyes burning into my concerned ones. It's silent for a few tense seconds; not even Richard says a word. 'It's nothing.' Jack moves away from my touch and back over to the drawings. 'Do we have the bifold door spec on here too?' he asks.

I look at Richard, my arm dropping to my side. His narrowed eyes turn on me, and he shakes his head, his lips in an angry straight line. 'Bottom right corner,' he answers for me.

'They've changed. The drawing I have states five metres wide.'

'Colin wanted more light,' I say quietly, my head spinning. What has happened?

'Get them requoted,' Jack orders shortly, and Richard nods. 'I have somewhere I need to be.'

Without so much as a second glance, Jack storms out, leaving me and Richard standing in awkward silence. I know it's not my place to ask, and I know I really shouldn't, but . . .

'Don't ask,' Richard grunts, marching off after Jack. I remain where I am for a few moments, stunned and quiet, and once I've finally found the will to move, I do so on heavy feet, collecting my bag and files and making my way out to the front.

Jack's car is still in the driveway, him sitting in the driver's seat, the door open with Richard leaning in. Although quiet,

I can see strong words being exchanged, and Richard puts his hand on Jack's shoulder. It's a reassuring gesture, one that gets my curiosity raging more, no matter how hard I try to beat it back.

I stand there, quietly observing while they talk, Jack's head getting lower by the second. Until his eyes shoot up and catch me watching him. His stoic expression and his hard stare make it impossible for me to move. I hold his eyes, as he holds mine, electricity sizzling between our distant bodies like they're touching. I see it all again, every second from that night, in clear, vivid detail. I start to breathe slowly, seeing Jack's chest rising and falling too.

It's only when Richard moves back that we both snap out of our trances, and Jack grabs the door, yanking it shut. He practically wheel-spins off the gravel, leaving me with a racing mind and Richard shaking his head in despair as he marches back towards the building.

'Everything okay?' I ask as he passes me, unable to hold back my misplaced concern.

'Personal problems,' Richard grunts, disappearing through the door.

As I roll into suburban hell on Wednesday evening, I spot my dad on the front lawn trimming his shrubs. The garage door is open and his old Jaguar is in the drive, sparkling like new despite being twenty years old. As I pull up at the bottom of the driveway, he looks up and frowns. 'Don't plonk it there!' he calls, waving his shears over his head. 'Makes the cul-de-sac look untidy!'

I roll my eyes and throw my arms into the air. 'Then where shall I park?'

He huffs and puffs and stomps over to his Jaguar. 'Behind Jerry.'

'Jerry the fucking Jag,' I mutter, ramming my car into first and speeding up the driveway. Dad's face is a picture of horror as I screech to a stop inches away from the bumper of his prized possession. I jump out, just as Mum comes dashing out of the front door, an apron wrapped neatly around her waist, protecting her flouncy skirt. She has a mixing bowl and wooden spoon in her grasp. 'Hi, Mum.'

'Annie, darling!' she sings, delighted to see me.

I shut the car door and pass my father, who's still staring down at the bumper of his Jag, like he's worried my filthy Golf might stick its tongue out and smear the sparkling paintwork. 'How are you?' I ask, kissing her cheek gently as I pass her on the doorstep.

'Wonderful.' She follows me into the kitchen and the smell I thought I'd be glad to see the back of when I lived here invades my nose. I stop and inhale it all. 'Roast chicken,' I breathe.

'You know your father loves his roast dinners, darling.' She places her bowl on the countertop and brushes her hands down her apron. 'It's an all-day affair preparing the bird and mixing the batter for his Yorkshire pudding.' She rolls her eyes like it's an inconvenience. I don't know why. She thrives on faffing around him.

'I'm starving,' I say, flicking the kettle on. This is what I need. One of my mum's home-cooked dinners. Comfort food.

'Good,' she says. I've made her day. Now she has two people to faff over. 'And I did a crumble.'

My mouth waters. Mum's crumble is the nuts. 'I can't wait.'

She looks at me, slight suspicion in her eyes. 'You look stressed.'

I lift my files for her to see. 'Work,' I lie. I don't get stressed out with work. I love work. I get stressed out by handsome married men who neglect to mention that they're married. 'Mind if I load up my laptop at the dining table?'

She smiles, losing her suspicious look in a second. She's so easy to fool, wrapped up in her perfect little world, baking and faffing over Dad. She'd pass out if she knew what her daughter has been up to. Adultery. The ultimate sin.

'I'll clear it for you.' She's off into the dining room quickly. 'Though you'll have to stay at one end so I can set the table for dinner.'

'Thanks, Mum. Want any help?' I ask, pulling down some mugs from the cupboard and finding the teapot before I let my mind spiral into the realms of my sins again.

'You make the tea, darling. And remember your father likes half a teaspoon of sugar.'

'God help me if I put in just one granule too much,' I say to myself, measuring out a perfect half-teaspoon and tossing it into the cup.

'Pardon?'

'Nothing,' I sing, wondering how I lived with them this past year. Then I wonder for the first time if Mum truly enjoys her life waiting on my father hand and foot. That's her sole purpose, especially since he sold his firm and retired. Faffing. She had no aspirations, no career ambitions, except being a stay-at-home mum and housewife. Now that I'm all grown up, she passes the days faffing. Faffing around the house, faffing in the garden, faffing over my father and faffing over me when I'm home. I look like my mother, the dark hair, the pale green eyes, but the similarities end there. She faffs. She's wholesome. I, however, am not. I fuck married men.

'You should be ashamed of yourself!' Dad barks as he wanders into the kitchen armed with his garden shears.

I jerk at his voice. Did he hear my thoughts? Oh God, he knows. He knows what I've done! Beads of sweat – guilty sweat – start to form on my forehead. They'll disown me.

'Your car is an absolute disgrace,' he goes on. My hands hit the side of the worktop, holding me up. Shit, I'm being paranoid.

'You can wash it if you like,' I breathe, gathering myself and finishing off the tea, handing him his mug. He eyes the tea with caution, and I know it's because my mother hasn't made it. 'Half a sugar,' I confirm before he asks.

He places his shears on the side, making Mum shriek in horror. 'Stanley, dear good Lord!' She darts over and swipes them up. 'Now I'll have to clean the worktop again.'

Dad rolls his eyes and turns on his heel. 'Well, it's been at least an hour since you last disinfected it, June. I'll be in the garage.'

'Yes, dear,' Mum chimes, not showing a shred of annoyance at my dad's grumpiness. I don't know how she does it. Since he's retired, he's a real grouch.

'I'll be in the dining room,' I say, leaving Mum scrubbing the worktop. I park myself at the dark wooden circa-1990s table and load my laptop, falling into thought as it fires up. A bad move, but those marks on Jack's neck are a constant in my mind, now accompanying Jack's face *and* his wife's.

'You work too much,' my mother says, wandering over to the sideboard and dusting off a minuscule speck of dust from the shiny surface.

'That's how people become successful, Mum.'

'And what about the other things in life?'

'Like?'

'Like a husband and children. When are you going to make me a grandmother?'

Grandchildren? I laugh to myself. More people for her to faff over. 'Give me a chance, Mother.'

'Well, you're knocking on thirty.' She nods at the drawings splayed out on the table before me, while I look at her incredulously. 'Does that really make you happy, Annie?'

I swallow and return to my laptop. 'Yes. Very happy.'

I hear her sigh, leaving me to get on with my work quietly. 'Maybe when the right man comes along you'll think of something other than work.'

I close my eyes, wilting in the chair. I'm already thinking of something other than work. Except he isn't the *right* man.

After a pleasant dinner with my parents, I pack up my things and kiss them both goodbye, promising I'll pop over this weekend. I'm scrolling through my e-mails as I make my way to my car, checking for any that are going to keep me up late. One jumps out at me from the French company that is manufacturing my super-duper glass roof, and I frown as I open it, hoping the production is still on track as they promised.

'Oh shit,' I breathe, scanning through the e-mail. 'No, no, no!'

I pull my car door open and throw my bags onto the passenger seat, then fall into the driver's.

'How can you miscalculate the weight?' I ask my phone, diving into my work bag for my calculator and drawings.

I urgently punch at the keys, hoping beyond all hope that they've made a mistake in saying they've made a mistake. If the roof is two hundred kilos heavier than they've stipulated, it's going to throw all the engineers' calculations askew.

'Fuck!' I slam my head against the headrest when the figure on my calculator matches the revised calculations in the e-mail. 'You bloody idiots.'

I start my car and reverse down the drive quickly, kissing goodbye to my planned early night.

When I pull up at the project site, it's dusk and the driveway is now jam-packed with skips, scaffolding and materials, the two entrances blocked off with security railings. I park down the road and grab my things, my mind searching for a remedy to the spanner in my works. I can think of none, and the thought that I may have to kiss my glass roof goodbye makes me want to cry.

Of course, I ignore the warning signs all over the metal railings telling me not to enter the site, and pull back one of the panels, squeezing through the gap. I let myself in, hurrying straight to the rear of the building where the extension will be built from the back external wall. Flicking a light on, I get my drawings out and find the calculations I need while pulling up the e-mail with the new, actual weight of my roof. It takes approximately ten seconds for me to conclude that my roof doesn't stand a chance of being held up by the proposed steel frame without another load-bearing wall to support it. And there is no other damn load-bearing wall nearby that I can tap into. My heart sinks, and I reach up to my forehead to rub away the instant headache.

Thud!

I jump and swing around, my hand moving from my head to my chest. What was that? My eyes scan the space, wary. 'Hello?'

Thud!

And my heart kicks up ten gears.

Thud!

I reach for my mobile, moving warily towards the sound coming from outside.

Thud!

The noise continues, consistent and even, and I pull to a stop, wondering what in heaven's name I'm doing moving towards it. I should call the police, but just as I start to back up, ready to leave, I hear a light curse. The voice gets me moving back towards the sound, and I round the corner to find the door to the garden open. I lose my breath when I see what the source of the noise is, and I reach for the frame of the door for support.

Thud!

Jack slams the shovel into the ground and wedges his booted foot on top, working it down before heaving the spade up and tossing the dirt aside. My body goes lax and my phone slips from my hand, hitting the floor at my feet. He swings around quickly and I'm nearly knocked to my arse by the sight of him in dirty old jeans, his chest bare and sweating and his muscled torso glimmering in the dusky light. His hair is damp, his face smeared with mud. *Oh Lord have mercy.*

'Annie?' Jack moves forward, squinting, as if he's not sure he's seeing right.

I gulp and look away from the enthralling sight of his naked torso and perfectly dirtied face. 'I'm sorry, I didn't realise anyone was here.'

'I'm just . . .' His words fade, and I look up at him. 'Digging a trial pit.'

'Don't you have employees to do that?' I ask, thinking I'm sure none of them would look as good as Jack does digging a hole.

He glances down at the pile of dirt he's built up, wedging his shovel in the ground next to him. 'I like getting my hands dirty every now and then,' he tells me quietly.

'At eight o'clock in the evening?'

He looks up at me as I bend to collect my phone. 'What are *you* doing here?'

The scratches on his throat catch my eye again, though they're fainter than they were yesterday morning. 'A problem with the roof.'

His gorgeous face furrows in confusion. 'What problem?'

'Oh, it's nothing.' I dismiss his question and back up, knowing I need to leave. It's tricky enough being in his company as it is, my willpower and conscience constantly being tested to the limit, but here now, when he's half naked, sweaty, and his muscles are pulsating, it's beyond perilous. 'I just needed to check some measurements.'

'At eight o'clock in the evening?' he asks, a small smile on his face. It's only a hint of the full beam I've seen and loved, but it's still wonderful, nevertheless. Inviting. Reassuring. It makes it all too easy to confide in him.

'It's not really nothing.' I relent on a sigh, silently questioning my need to tell him. I should be leaving. Walking out.

Removing myself from this situation. 'The manufacturers have made a monumental cock-up.' I shrug. 'I'm trying to figure out a way around it, and I'm not coming up with much.'

Jack moves forward, and as a consequence I instinctively move back. He stops, regarding me closely. 'Want to show me?'

'Yes.' My answer comes without hesitation, stunning me, and he smiles, this time brighter, getting a little bit closer to the blinding signature Jack Joseph smile. I find myself returning it, unable to stop myself. 'Please,' I add.

He drops his shovel and approaches me, and my damn eyes are glued to his the entire way, my stomach doing cartwheels, until he stops a few paces before me. 'After you,' he murmurs.

I quickly turn and head back inside, feeling him close behind me. My whole being lights up, and I close my eyes and silently pray for strength. Why did I accept his offer? I glance over my shoulder as we enter the huge back room, meeting his stare again. 'You should put a T-shirt on,' I say out of the blue, my thoughts falling out of my mouth.

'I should?' He looks down at his chest. 'Is it distracting you?' His teasing smile as he looks up through his lashes sets off a carnival of beats in my blood.

I shake my head and return my focus forward, adamant that I won't feed his playfulness. 'Very cute.'

'You're quite cute yourself.'

His words, a repeat from that night, have my steps faltering too much for him not to notice. *Ignore it*, I warn myself silently, pulling it together and concentrating on keeping myself that way, arriving at the table where my drawings are laid out and pointing with a shaking finger at the one detailing the roof. 'They've miscalculated the weight of the roof.'

His hand appears and wraps around my wrist, and my whole bloody body bursts into flames. I flick my eyes up to his, tensing every muscle in my body, fighting back the heat. 'Why are you shaking?' he asks, squeezing my wrist.

'Because you make me nervous.' I come right out and say it, and regret it just as fast. 'I mean . . .' My words die on my lips. There's no going back from that. 'Please, Jack,' I beg him. 'Can we just stick to business?'

He slowly peels his hold away and rests his hands on the table. 'Right. Business,' he confirms, looking over the drawing. 'How much have they miscalculated by?'

I silently thank him for being professional, even though he's chosen to ignore my request to cover his gorgeous chest. The smell of him is potent this close, his body nearly touching mine. 'Two hundred kilos.'

He whistles, confirming the shit I'm in. 'I'm no structural engineer, but even *I* know that puts us right up shit street.'

I sag next to him. 'I know.'

'This is seriously going to hinder the progress of the project.'

'I know.' I sag some more.

'And we have a four-month deadline before Colin's launch. It's already tight.'

My hands hit the table and my head drops. 'Are you going to say anything that will make me feel better? I was hoping for a miracle.'

He laughs, light and lovely. 'I'm a contractor, not a miracle worker, Annie.'

I pout to myself, feeling more and more despondent by the second. I could cry. My blow-your-mind project is just an average project without that roof.

'You look gorgeous when you pout,' Jack says softly.

My lips quickly unpout themselves and purse instead. 'You look gorgeous all the time.' I look around me, startled. *Who said that?*

Jack laughs, and the sound seems to dilute my problem. For a second, everything fades and all that matters is listening to his laugh. 'Keep it business, please,' he teases.

'You started it.' I shake my head at myself in dismay, thinking

I need to fix my brain-to-mouth filter pronto. I feel him gazing at my profile, and I peek out of the corner of my eye at him, assessing him, taking him in. 'Why are you really here this late at night?' I ask, stalling on fixing that filter. I don't believe for a moment that he likes getting his hands dirty once in a while. There's something more to it, and though I damn myself for it, I can't help wondering more and more about Jack and his wife.

'I needed to get out of the house.' His answer is very dismissive, and for once he doesn't look me in the eye, choosing to look down at the drawings instead.

His evasiveness just ramps up my curiosity. 'To get some fresh air?' I ask.

'Something like that.'

I stare at his profile, my hand taking on a mind of its own and reaching up to his neck, where the scratches seem to glow at me. Jack catches my hand before it lands on his skin, prompting my gaze to jump to his. His grey eyes have regained a little bit of sparkle as he holds my stare and my hand, gently working his fingers around mine.

I find my eyes taking in our tangle of fingers, the sight morphing into the tangle of our sweaty bodies rolling around in a hotel bed, our mouths kissing wildly, our moans drenching the air. I lose myself in those thoughts, my mind tunnelling, my body feeling it all over again.

'You're in the hotel again, aren't you?' Jack whispers, hunkering down to meet my gaze. 'Reliving that night like I am every single fucking minute of my life.'

I can't talk. Can't move. The rush of feelings has paralysed me, leaving me at the mercy of the man who's consumed my mind, body and soul since he found me in that bar.

'I can see it all in your eyes, Annie.' He moves forward, and the heat from his breath hitting my face spreads through my body like wildfire. He enraptures me, knocks all sense out of me. *His wife. What am I doing?*

I swiftly pull my hand away, turning back towards the table and holding the edge for support. I stare down at the drawings, my head whirling. 'You promised me.'

'Jesus, Annie, how the hell are you doing this? You make it look easy.'

'Because it is,' I spit at the table. 'Because there is nothing there for me, so stop trying to find anything. You're wasting your time.' I wince at my own scathing words, but I have to remain strong. Easy? He thinks this is easy? The notion makes me mad.

'I'm sorry,' he whispers, hurt tingeing his apology.

His sincerity plays havoc with my willpower. It's already painfully difficult to face him on a professional level. It's painful, but it's doable. I already feel consumed by guilt, ashamed of myself. This is impossible. The undercurrent of our connection is still there no matter how hard I fight to disregard it. But it doesn't mean I can act on it.

'I should be going.' I push myself away, all in a fluster, my work predicament forgotten and the urgency to remove myself from the situation now dominating my mind. I grab my bags but forgo the drawings, knowing it'll take me too long to fold them all up. I need to get out of here now before I let my attraction and want get the better of me. Before I cave under the pressure of his struggle, because it would be all too easy to fall into his arms again. So easy. Yet the aftermath and backlash would be unbearable.

I hurry away, keen to get myself home and talk some sense and strength into myself.

'Annie, wait!' Jack calls after me.

I ignore his plea and keep going, knowing I'll be doomed if I let him stop me.

'Annie!'

I hit the fresh air and take the steps fast, but come to an abrupt halt when Jack overtakes me and blocks my path. 'Jack, please don't.' My breath is laboured, not only because of my rushed escape from him.

'I won't, I promise.' He steps back, giving me space, his hands held up in surrender. 'I'm sorry.'

I fix him in place with a sure, curt expression. 'Then. Let. Me. Leave,' I say slowly, watching as he breathes in deeply. After what seems like ages, he finally moves to the side to let me pass.

I hurry away, fighting against the magnetic pull trying to drag me back to him.

The pull that's getting tougher to resist by the second.

Chapter 9

I spot Micky outside the café and hurry over, landing in my chair with a thud. It's been a long bloody day of technical drawings and calculations on my roof . . . and the total head-fuck that is Jack Joseph. I'm drained, my mind bent in more ways than one, and I didn't sleep a wink last night, memories of his words and of his bare, sweaty chest refusing to leave my mind. That vision plagued me all fucking night. Still is.

'All right?' Micky asks, eyeing up my stressed form.

'My brain is frazzled,' I sigh, dumping my bag down on the chair next to me. 'Problem at work that I've been trying to fix.'

'You work too hard. When was the last time you went on holiday?'

I cast my mind back . . . and back . . . and back.

'I rest my case.' He shows the sky his palms with a shrug. 'You look tired. Take some time off and relax. Do nothing. Your business isn't going to fall apart if you take a break.'

He's wrong. It most definitely *would* fall apart. Besides, even if it wouldn't, going on holiday and doing nothing means I'd get to think too much, and I don't want to be thinking right now because there's only one subject my brain annoyingly wants to focus on. 'Maybe next year,' I murmur, looking past Micky into the distance.

'Oh no.'

I snap out of my short daydream immediately and find Micky looking at me, all worried. 'What?'

'That look. What are you thinking?'

'Nothing.' I laugh and start faffing with the spoon at my place setting.

'Annie . . .' My name is said on a long, warning exhale of air, and I laugh again, with a lack of anything else to do. Micky has known me my entire life. I'm not fooling him. 'Tell me.'

'Nothing to tell.' I wave a hand in the air, feigning indifference, and pray he leaves it right there. 'Work's crazy.'

'And have you seen him?'

'Not really,' I reply weakly, hating myself for not being able to sound convincing. I'm too tired to find the energy to be convincing.

Micky moves back in his chair slowly, eyeing me with caution. 'Please tell me you've not been there again.'

I slam my mouth shut and avert my eyes from his. 'No.' Though I haven't physically been there again, I have in my head, a million times, and that's making me feel just as guilty.

'I hope not.' Micky leans across the table, probably to ensure I can see with perfect clarity how stern his face is. 'You know, because he's fucking *married*!'

'Will you be quiet?' I hiss across the table, my frantic eyes checking the vicinity, looking as paranoid as I feel. 'I've not been there again, and I don't plan to either.'

Micky throws himself across the table threateningly, and I withdraw, worried. I've never seen him look so angry. 'I don't like this. Is he pursuing you?'

'No,' I lie, for fear of my lifelong friend taking matters into his own hands. He looks perfectly capable right now.

'Are you pursuing him?'

'No.' That's not a lie. I haven't. 'I'm working with him, Micky. It's hard not to see someone when you're being forced to work with them.'

'No one is forcing you to do anything.'

'Are you suggesting I should throw away my dream job because some arsehole led me on?' At that very moment, my phone starts buzzing on the table, and Jack's name flashes up at us. I reach and reject the call, stabbing at the screen of my phone heavy-handedly. I look up at my friend and his lips purse.

'I know you, Annie. I know when something is on your mind, and I know that it isn't work.' He shakes his head, dismayed. 'Why didn't you take that?' he asks, pointing at my phone. 'If it's purely business, why?'

'Because I'm having coffee with you.'

'He's married,' he says simply, twisting the knife in further. 'You don't go there, Annie. You don't even *think* there!'

'I'm not.' I grit my teeth harshly. 'It's work. Nothing more.'

His face softens as he reaches over and takes my hand. 'You deserve more. Don't get yourself caught up in that shit. It won't end well.'

I drop my head, even more exhausted than when I arrived here. 'I called you for coffee and a catch-up. Not an earache.' I force a smile and shift my hand so I'm holding his, nodding my assurance. 'It caught me off guard. The whole situation. But I'm fine, honestly. You know me.' I look up when the waiter slides a coffee towards me. 'Thank you.'

'Should I have ordered something stronger?' Micky asks seriously.

I snort, thinking that he most definitely should have. 'Probably. How's work?' I ask. 'Specifically, the new client?' I waggle a cheeky eyebrow.

My lifelong friend sniffs in the most blasé way possible, toying with the napkin at his place casually. But just like Micky knows me, I know him, and this new client has clearly got under his skin. 'All right.'

'That's it? All right?'

'I suggested she might need an extra session per week.'

I laugh and take a needed hit of caffeine. 'Of course she does.'

Micky grins around the rim of his cup. 'Hey, I saw Jason yesterday.'

'That's nice. Did you tell him you'd screwed his ex?'

'No.' Micky rolls exasperated eyes. 'Lizzy and I were a drunken mistake.'

'Yeah, yeah. So what did he want?'

'He wants to start training.'

I laugh sarcastically. 'What, to get himself in better shape for the twenty-one-year-old he cheated on Lizzy with?'

Micky shrugs. 'Not my business.'

I'm laughing again, but this time on the inside. I wish he'd adopt the same approach to me and my fuck-up. I look down at my phone and sigh. 'How'd it get to four o'clock?' I ask the screen, bracing myself to get my arse back to my studio so I can agonise over my problem some more. And I mean the roof problem. I'm going to have to admit defeat soon and revise all my plans, and then break the bad news to Colin.

'Four? Shit!' Micky jumps up from his chair and throws a tenner on the table. 'I have a session with Charlie.' He rushes around the table and smacks a kiss on my cheek. 'See ya later.'

'Have fun!' I call, gathering up my things and getting on my way. My phone rings three more times before I make it to the Tube – all Jack – and I reject every single call. After last night, avoiding Jack is top of my priority list.

I look up from the pavement as I near my house, my feet slowing to a stop when I see a silver Audi parked up over the road. What the hell?

The driver's door opens, and Jack gets out of his car, his tall body straightening to full height slowly. I spend a few too many seconds taking him in, as if I need to remind myself of his sheer magnificence. The sleeves of his pale blue shirt are rolled up, his hard forearms on full display, as well as his throat from his open collar.

I ignore him, pretend he isn't there, and focus on putting my front door between us.

'Hey.' Jack's soft voice blazes a trail up my back, igniting panic as I get closer. I start frantically searching for my keys in my bag.

'Annie?'

Where the hell are my keys? Suddenly his hand is on my back, and I whirl around clumsily, pressing my body into the wood of my door. 'What do you want?' I blurt, sounding as scared as I feel.

Jack's head tilts, and he shakes it as if trying to gather some patience. 'Why haven't you answered my calls? Or replied to my voicemail?'

'I think it's best I deal with Richard in future.'

His face takes on an angry edge, his nostrils flaring. 'Why's that?'

'Because . . .' I don't want to say it out loud. I don't want to admit that whatever this is between us is slowly breaking me down, and if I don't remedy it soon, I might go where no woman should go. 'I just think it's for the best.'

'I don't,' he replies shortly.

I look at him in shock. 'What you think doesn't matter.'

His grey eyes narrow to slits. 'I've been trying to get hold of you because I thought of something.'

'What?' I ask warily.

'A solution to your problem.'

'Which problem?' I blurt out without thought, making him recoil a little. *Shit!* I seriously need to fix that filter.

'I was referring to the roof,' he says, looking at me with interest. 'Why, is there another problem?' He's goading me, trying to press my buttons and force a confession out of me – how I can't stop thinking about him, how my body burns with want for him. He can try all he likes.

'No, there's not.' He knows as well as I do that we have more than a construction problem here, and we need to sort it out quickly. If it can be sorted out at all. 'What's your solution?'

'To which problem?' he asks seriously.

I breathe in a patience-building shot of air. And maybe a resistance-strengthening one too. 'My roof problem,' I clarify, keeping my face straight and serious.

'Oh, that problem.' A sick smile ghosts his lips, a *knowing* smile.

'This isn't funny, Jack.'

'I'm not laughing, Annie.' He points to his car. 'I think I have a solution to our roof problem. I'll show you.'

I look to his car, as wary as I should be, and back to Jack. 'Show me what?'

'A project we undertook last year. A museum.' I frown, and he goes on. 'The structure wasn't adequate to take the roof.'

My back straightens. 'And what did you do?'

He sighs tiredly, stepping back to give me space. 'Let me show you?' He's not begging, but he's not far from it. 'I want to see your roof come to life as much as you do, Annie. I want to help you.'

I try to read his body language, try to figure him out, totally torn. I don't know whether he's purposely trying to entice me, or whether he genuinely wants to help me. But there's only one way to find out.

'I'll follow you there,' I say, hoping I'm not making a huge mistake.

The drive takes a good twenty minutes, me tailing his silver Audi in my Golf, and the whole time my mind is batting back and forth between my work problem and my personal problem. Every time I think work, though, Jack overpowers those thoughts and I find my mind reeling with so many questions. Questions about his wife, their relationship, the so-called rumours about her. But as quickly as those questions pop into my head, they go when I remind myself that it's none of my business *or* concern. *Focus, Annie. Focus on work.*

I pull up behind Jack outside an Edwardian-style building and join him on the pavement. 'This?' I ask, looking up at the stone façade.

'It's at the rear.' He wanders ahead, leaving me to follow. 'This way.'

I make my way around the back of the building, keeping my distance, finding myself in a beautifully manicured garden. 'This is a museum?' I ask, taking a few steps towards the face of the building.

'Dedicated to a local artist who died in the fifties.' Jack points upwards, and I follow his indication to look at the roof. 'It's not glass, but it's pretty hefty.'

'And how did you support it adequately?'

Jack moves to a window and points inside. 'Come here.'

I make my way over, curious, and join him at the window, but my height prevents me from seeing through the raised glass. 'I can't . . . oh!' I'm lifted from my feet and presented to the window. 'Jack!'

'See that back wall?' he asks, ignoring my panicked screech.

I try to numb myself to the feel of his big hands on my waist, looking through the window. 'Yes,' I practically squeak.

'That was where the building ended. The original wall was too old and weak to sustain the pitched roof of the extension, so we basically demolished it and rebuilt it with a double skin using reclaimed stone. It meant no support columns had to be used, so the space remained open.'

'And you think we could do the same on Colin's project?' I ask, trying not to let my excitement get the better of me before we know for sure.

'We'll need to have the structural engineer confirm it.' He lowers me to my feet, moving his hands away. I faff with my dress in an attempt to look unaffected by the fact that his big hands had me held at that window with absolutely no effort. 'But I can't see there being a problem at all.'

I lose the ability to contain my excitement, looking up at him. 'Really?'

Jack smiles brightly, and this time it's that full-blown, gorgeous Jack smile. 'You're back on track, Annie.'

Forgetting myself completely, totally overcome with relief and a ton of other emotions I dare not analyse, I launch myself at him, so bloody grateful for his help. 'Thank you,' I breathe, squeezing his shoulders.

His strong arms lock around my whole body and lift me from the ground, his face sinking into my neck. 'Any time,' he replies softly.

It would be appropriate to detach ourselves from each other right about now, yet neither of us shows any signs of releasing the other, both of us content to remain locked together. I can feel his heart beating, his chest pulsing into mine, and his smell, pure and Jack, takes over my senses completely. I begin to succumb to every intoxicating element of Jack Joseph, feeling myself weakening where I'm held in his arms.

'Is this how you do business?' he asks after an age, inhaling into my neck. 'Because if so, we need to work together a lot more in the future.'

I smile despite myself. 'I'm sorry.' I reluctantly break away from him, now avoiding his eyes. 'I got a little overwhelmed.'

'So you should.' He folds his arms over his broad chest, and I fleetingly wonder if it's a move to prevent him from taking me in his arms again. 'You're a very talented woman, Annie. I wish every architect I worked with was as dynamic and creative as you are.'

Every time Jack says my name, something happens inside me. Something electrifying. And when he praises me like he just did, it inspires me, drives me to want to do so much more. I swallow down the lump in my throat and point over my shoulder. 'I should be getting home,' I say, and he nods mildly. 'Thank you, Jack.'

His eyes. Oh, his eyes. They say a million things, even if his mouth doesn't.

I slowly turn and walk away, shaking. But not so much with excitement. More with the restraint to not run back into his arms, where for a welcome moment my rocking world was steady again.

When I make it to my car I drop into my seat and take a few steadying gasps of oxygen, looking back up to the building, waiting for him to appear. But he doesn't, and I start to wonder what he's doing back there. What he's thinking. He's helped me. He found a solution to my problem, and his face when he saw my elation could have knocked me to my arse. He was happy for me. He wants me to succeed.

'Go home, Annie,' I say to myself, turning the key in the ignition. The engine drones for a few seconds before going dead. 'Oh, come on,' I say, trying it again. This time, I get nothing. Not a peep. 'Well, this is great.' I flop back in my seat just as Jack appears from the back of the building, his head dropped and his hands stuffed deeply into his pockets. He looks like he has the weight of the world on his shoulders, and when he looks up and finds me still here, he cocks his head in question. I raise hopeless hands.

Making his way over, he opens my car door. 'What's up?'

'It won't start.' I turn the key again, demonstrating the lack of life.

'Open the bonnet,' he orders.

'How?'

He laughs lightly on a little shake of his head and reaches into the car, down by my legs. I hold my breath and quickly shift my knees when he skims them with his hard forearm. 'Here,' he says, flicking me a knowing look and pulling the hidden lever. I smile awkwardly, my mind blanking on me, as he slowly withdraws his arm. I only start breathing again when he's out of touching distance, making his way around to the front of my car. He lifts the bonnet, taking him out of my view.

I get out of my car and stand far enough away from him so there can be no more touches, accidental or not. 'Are you good with cars?'

'Basics,' he says, licking his finger and touching a metal knob. 'Your battery is dead. I don't have any jump leads.'

'What are jump leads and where can I get them?'

He laughs again, harder this time, and looks at me, thoroughly amused. 'They *may* get your car started, but there's nowhere you'll find them around here at this time of night.'

'Oh. So what do I do?'

'You let me take you home.'

I shoot him a look. 'Jack, I really don't thin—'

He's claimed my hand before I have a chance to argue further, pulling me towards his Audi. 'It's a good idea,' he finishes. 'Why?'

And, fuck, my whole damn body goes up in smoke. I look down at his big hand wrapped around my tiny wrist, knowing I haven't a hope of yanking myself free. He pulls us to a stop and turns to me, catching me off guard. I hit his chest and jump back, zeroing in on his open collar. I mustn't look at his face. I. Must. Not. Look. At. His. Face.

My tongue goes all heavy, but I manage to spit some words out. 'Fine, you can take me home.'

'It wasn't up for debate.' He opens the door and pushes me down into the seat.

Chapter 10

The tension in the small space of Jack's car is palpable. For the entire drive, I find myself fidgeting in my seat, constantly talking myself down from doing something stupid. Like diving across the car and taking what I know he's capable of. What I know he *wants*. Or saying something stupid, like how much he's on my mind. Like how hard I'm fighting my instinct to let him have me.

When he pulls up outside my flat, I literally dive out of the car and run up the steps to my front door, fumbling with the lock to get inside. My skin is tingling terribly. The need to run back to him is strong.

Married!

I slam the door and rush through to the kitchen, shrugging out of my coat and kicking my shoes off on my way, deciding a glass of wine is in order to try and calm myself down. Wine, and maybe a bath. No more work tonight. No more thinking.

'Motherfucker!' I screech, grabbing the kitchen door and virtually climbing up the wood. 'Oh my God!'

I feel all the colour drain from my face as I stare into a pair of beady eyes watching me from the kitchen floor – eyes that belong to the biggest mouse I've ever seen in my life. My heart is clattering in my chest as I grapple at the top of the door, keeping my feet off the ground. It's just staring at me, totally unperturbed, bold as fucking brass.

'Oh my God, oh my God, oh my God!'

We're in a staring deadlock, me hanging off the door, the

elephant-sized mouse holding position in the middle of my kitchen floor. Then it moves suddenly and I scream, watching in horror as it scurries across the kitchen floor and disappears behind a cupboard.

'Mouse!' I shriek, dropping from the door and running at full pelt down the hallway to the front door. I throw it open, the wood hitting the wall behind it and crashing loudly, echoing in the night air. Then I stumble down the path and run across the road, as far away from my flat as I can get. Mice. Oh God, I fucking hate mice! My breathing becomes rushed. I'm hyperventilating.

I shudder from top to toe and glance down the street. What now?

'Annie?' Jack's concerned voice pulls my attention to my right, where he's standing across the road by his Audi. He's still here?

I point to my front door. 'Mouse,' I mumble meekly.

He stares at me. And then he laughs. He fucking laughs. I don't know why. This is about as funny as a nasty rash. I look at him, releasing a scowl of epic proportions, and manage to see through my fear and irritation that he's absolutely in bits, his hands holding his stomach. He looks so fucking handsome. Delightfully so. The fact that he's simply here is enough to cause another meltdown. With his infectious smile and the sound of his laugh, I'm in trouble. Jack . . . and a mouse. Two meltdowns happening all at once will probably kill me.

He looks at my shaking form across the road, smiling brightly, his face alive with happiness, and my world starts spinning wildly out of control at the sight.

I'm screaming on the inside. Positively falling apart, and the mouse is only half the reason why. The mouse, Jack . . . and that familiar sizzle of electricity bouncing between our bodies. He finally finds the will to calm his amusement, and realisation dawns on his face. The scene, him standing on one side of the road, me on the other. Staring at each other. Tension. Want.

The silence lingers painfully. I can't deal with it, but before I can speak to move things along, Jack does. 'Where in the kitchen should I look?'

My relief that he's keeping this to business, so to speak, is obvious. I exhale deeply. 'It ran behind the cupboard by the double doors.'

'Are you okay out here on your own?' he asks. I can see so many things he wants to say in his grey eyes, and I silently beg that he doesn't.

'I think it's safer for me to stay out here,' I say quietly, knowing he understands the hidden meaning in my statement. A mouse in my flat is enough to keep me out. Jack in my flat too makes it the most hazardous zone ever.

I remain where I am as he slowly makes his way up to the open doorway and strides down the hallway with no hesitation or caution.

His back.

Solid and wide.

My fingers scraping into his flesh as he drives into ...

My hands come up and encase my head, my fingers clawing into my scalp like they can squish the thoughts. He's in my flat. I turn away, looking up to the sky as I battle to stop my fortitude from disintegrating. This week has been fucking exhausting. I need it to be over so I can spend all weekend getting trashed and restocking on willpower quickly before I flake. Before I venture into forbidden territory.

It feels like hours of waiting. Hours of holding onto my conscience. Hours of remaining where I am and keeping my thoughts in check. Hours of running through every reason why he's not to be touched. Thought of. Admired.

I wrap my arms around my body and turn back towards my front door, listening carefully for any bangs that will signal the demise of the mouse. I hear nothing. I'm standing in the street, in a skimpy summer dress, not even any damn shoes on my feet.

The temperature has dropped a little, enough to make me start shivering.

Jack eventually appears in the doorway. 'Gone,' he says simply, but this news doesn't relax me like it should, because there's still another hazard looming.

'You killed it?'

He nods, holding me where I am with his hard, hooded stare.

'Thank you,' I say quietly, studying him, definitely detecting that he's deep in thought. *Don't ask, don't ask, don't ask.* I need to get back into my flat without engaging with him, which could prove tricky when he's blocking the doorway and looking like he has no intention of shifting to let me in.

I take long, confident strides across the road, hoping he'll be wise and move before I make it to my door. He doesn't. If anything, he widens his stance, his body now completely filling the entrance. 'Thank you for your help,' I say politely, forcing myself to look at him so he can see the resolve in my eyes. As always, it's a mistake, but I work hard to keep myself in check and disregard his lovely face.

'Annie,' he breathes. 'I'm struggling so badly.'

'I'm not doing this.' I swallow, pushing my way past him. He grabs me by the top of my arm and holds me in place. 'Let me go, Jack.'

'I've already told you I can't do that. Annie, I'm drowning here. I'm going out of my mind, and the more time I spend with you the fucking worse it's getting. Listening to you, talking to you, sharing a passion with you that goes *way* beyond the amazing time we had in bed together.'

'You have to forget!' I yell, knowing anger is the only way forward. Be angry with him. Let it dominate me and rule me, because the alternative scares me to fucking death.

He pushes me into the hall and slams the door behind us, forcing me to back up. 'No,' he says, straight and even. 'No,' he repeats, moving one more step forward, except this time I don't retreat. Because I can't. Because he has me locked in place with those grey eyes, and now they're back to their full glory. Sparkling, even if it's with anger. He reaches for his shirt and starts unbuttoning it before shrugging it off and throwing it to the floor, revealing the chest that's haunting me.

I quickly look down at the pile of material, my mind reeling. His chest. His perfect damn chest. 'What are you doing?'

'I have no fucking idea.' He reaches for me and slides a hand around my neck, pulling me to him. Our chests meet, and my determination to repel him vanishes under our connection. Wrongs turn into rights. Conflict turns into craving.

'I can't get you out of my head, Annie.' His forehead meets mine, his palm massaging away the tightness in my neck muscles, softening me up until I relax in his hold. 'I want you all over again, and I can't even find the will to worry about how much more that'll make me want you.' He breathes down on me. 'I've played that night on repeat. I've dreamed of holding you in my arms again. I've craved the sound of your voice, the feel of your touch, the softness of your lips on mine. I know I shouldn't want you. But I do. Nothing has ever made me feel this insane with need. Nothing has taken up so much space in my head. I can't fucking help it, Annie.' His grey gaze sinks into me, my heart steadying to an even thrum. His head starts to shake mildly, his splayed hand moving up to the back of my head and fisting my hair. 'I don't want to help it,' he growls. 'I want you. I don't care how wrong it is.' His clenched fist tightens, gripping my hair harshly. 'I know I've been on your mind since I fucked you every which way in that hotel room. Stop denying it. Don't insult me and tell me you don't crave that amazing feeling all over again. I can see it in your eyes every damn time I look into them. You. Want. Me.'

It's me who moves in first. All me. I lunge forward and smash my lips to his, the magnetic force winning. His words winning. Jack winning. My heart winning. I coax his mouth open with hard, hungry kisses. I've lost my mind to a craving too powerful to fight off. And, like Jack, I don't care how wrong it is.

Lost.

Yet as he walks me backwards until my back slams into the wall, I feel found again.

I cry out, and Jack moans. We're clumsy and desperate. He's pushing me up the wall with the force of his kiss, then he's rolling away, taking me with him until it's his back slamming into the wall. It's the lift all over again. The atmosphere is sizzling. I'm on fire. He scoops me up, pinning me to him, and carries me into my bedroom. I focus on him. Only him and the return of feelings that I've fantasised about since that unforgettable night. All the guilt is abandoning me, and I let it, unprepared to let anything stop me from taking the forbidden.

He lowers me to my feet, keeping our kiss up, and starts to unfasten his trousers while I pull at the waistband, desperate to get them off.

'Steady,' he mumbles against my lips, considerably calmer than before, probably because he has me now. We're both on the same page. Neither of us are prepared to settle for that one time. It's made us insatiable. It's teased us. It's intensified the desire and anticipation, because now we know what to expect. Now we know that our minds are going to be blown in the best possible way. Now we know that him plus me equals amazing. I can't resist him. I've tried; I've tried so bloody hard. I want him. *Need* him.

Taking my grappling hands gently, he holds them between our bodies and breaks our kiss, making me reach up on my tiptoes to try and maintain the connection. His grey eyes are glimmering brightly, full of want and desperation.

'I want it to be slow,' he murmurs, pulling my dress up over my head and casting it aside. 'I want to take my time and enjoy the fact that I have you again.' Lowering his mouth to my shoulder, he kisses it gently, sending a million bolts of pleasure straight to my groin.

I moan loudly, my eyes closing while he works his mouth across my flesh. He slides his hands up my sides and rests them on my waist.

'I made a promise to myself, Annie. I promised myself that if the Fates brought you back to me, I wouldn't let you go.' Lifting me high to his chest, he carries me to the bed, looking up at me, my hands draped around his neck. 'And now you're here.'

Lowering me, he gets me comfortable on my back, and then rises to his full height, standing over me as he strips his trousers off, taking his sweet time about it, testing my patience. I've put the blockers on any thoughts that try to enter my mind. I'm frightened that the absent guilt and my conscience will return at any moment and stop me from taking him.

'Please hurry,' I breathe, watching as he slowly reveals himself to me. I go lax on the bed, enraptured by the sight of him, my eyes making a slow journey across his skin, soaking up every tiny piece of him. If there was any hope of me repelling Jack Joseph, it's just been squashed. My mind is taking mental pictures of him and locking them away tightly. His melt-worthy naked frame is poised above me, his cock jutting from his groin, visibly throbbing.

His chest expands and he rests a knee on the mattress, followed by a fist near my head to hold himself up. Looking down between my thighs, he starts to shake a little, swallowing hard. For a fleeting moment, I worry that he's had second thoughts, but then his other hand rests on the inside of my thigh and pushes it wide, encouraging me to open up to him. 'Put your arms above your head,' he orders softly, glancing up at me.

I obey without question, despite needing to touch him and feel him. He reaches between his legs and takes hold of his cock, my eyes following with fascination as he works a few slow strokes across his velvet flesh. A glimmer of pre-cum beads at the tip, and I lick my lips. 'Watch,' Jack whispers, circling his wet head across my sex. I cry out, my body arching violently. 'Watch, Annie.'

I start to moan as he rubs against me, spreading the wetness. 'Jack!' I cry, forcing my arms to remain above my head.

'Just watch,' he affirms, and my eyes drop to between my legs, seeing his erection held firmly in his grasp. 'Watch me sinking into you.' He dips a little, pushing into me a fraction. 'Because we both know how fucking amazing it feels when I'm buried deep inside of you.'

Tormented whimpers come thick and fast, my core convulsing wildly, screaming for full penetration. 'Jack, please . . .'

He looks up at me, his eyes wild with want. 'Tell me how badly you want me.'

'Jack!'

'Tell me, Annie.' He withdraws and tactically swipes the slippery head of his cock from side to side across my sensitive flesh. I cry out, beginning to lose the plot. Jack nods, acknowledging my desperation. 'I need to hear how badly you want me. Tell me and you can have me.'

'I want you!' I scream, sweat beads springing onto my brow. 'Jack, I want you. Badly. More than anything I've ever wanted.'

'So I'm not crazy?'

'No!'

'I fucking knew it.' His jaw tightens as he levels up and advances, sliding into me with one long thrust. 'Shit,' he chokes, falling to his forearms, his eyes clenching shut. He's shaking terribly, vibrating all over me.

'Are you okay?' I ask, defying his request to keep my arms above my head, bringing them to his shoulders and holding him. He feels like he needs it.

I hear him swallow, gathering himself. 'I'm fine,' he whispers, turning his lips to my cheek and kissing me tenderly. 'You make me feel so alive.'

I can't help but smile, even if there's a tinge of sadness in it. Because when you feel this alive, there's only one way to go.

The scratches on his neck catch my eye and his wife's face starts poking its way into my mind. I swallow, my thoughts running away with me again. 'Don't think about it,' he says, breaking into my reverie. 'Please. Don't think about anything but here and now.'

He finds my lips and kisses me slowly, swivelling his hips and grinding deeply, withdrawing and driving forward again. I suck in air and store it, holding my breath as Jack finds a meticulous pace that soon carries me away from the dirt tarnishing the moment, proving that it really is possible. In his arms, under his ardent attention, it is possible.

Our bodies work in complete harmony, like they know each other soul deep, our tongues lapping lazily. He rolls us and pushes me up on his lap, mumbling and shaking his head when I grind down hard, feeling him hit my womb. Strong fingers dig into my thighs and hold tight, his cheeks puffing out as his grey eyes watch me riding him slowly. One hand comes up and claims my neck, pulling me down to his mouth. I maintain my rhythm, circling my hips onto him, kissing him like there's no tomorrow. Fighting off the notion that there won't be is harder than I want to admit, because that would be facing my reality. He's not mine. I'm taking something that doesn't belong to me.

'Annie,' he growls, like he's read my thoughts, pushing me over onto my back and slipping back in quickly. His face is stern, his jaw tight. 'Stop.' He executes a perfect drive and holds himself deep and high, watching me unravel beneath him. 'Focus on now. On this. On us.'

I shout my frustration, my back bowing on the bed as I fight the unwanted thoughts away. 'Make me forget!' I yell, throwing my arms over his shoulders and clawing at his back, hiding my face in his neck.

'Damn it, Annie.' His pace speeds up, dousing my tormented conscience with a pleasure like no other. My eyes spring open, my hips flexing to meet his. 'There you are,' Jack murmurs, nudging my face from its hiding place and slamming his mouth to mine, swallowing down my moans. Sinking his teeth into my bottom lip, he pulls away and stares down at me. 'Your face is a fucking picture.'

'Jack,' I breathe, seizing the telltale pressure that's settling in my core and locking it down. 'Faster.'

He picks up his pace and pistons back and forth, our lovemaking turning frantic as we both search for our release. 'Oh shit!' he yells, jacking himself up on his arms, getting more leverage behind his drives. His face is pouring with sweat, his grey eyes wide with wonder.

I can feel him expanding within me, the pressure getting too much. Jack's head drops back, and he shouts to the ceiling, stilling suddenly above me. Then he jerks and the pulse of his cock, followed by a low, rough moan, signals he's gone. One deep breath in, and his face twists as he withdraws and slowly pushes forward, the carefully calculated move taking me into ecstasy with him. My legs lock and I pull him down to my chest, tightening my inner muscles on slow, even pulls. Our moans are collective and full of fulfilment, and they stretch out for an age until both of our bodies go lax and we're heaving against each other, trying to catch our breath.

I feel totally overcome, almost relieved that this time was everything I remembered. Powerful, emotional and mind-blanking. My thoughts sting. I shouldn't be relieved. I should be panicking, because the thought of letting him go is about as painful as any.

I sink my nose into his neck and tighten my arms around his shoulders, clinging onto him. It feels so natural, so right, and when he responds, sighing despondently and holding me strongly, hopeless tears escape and stream down my cheeks.

'Stop,' Jack whispers, sounding as overcome by emotion as I am. 'Please don't cry.'

I shake my head into him, trying to rein it in, but I feel so fraught, unsure and vulnerable. The feelings are new to me, and I have no idea what to do with them. There's no doubt I've just increased the difficulty of my situation. I know I should have resisted him, pushed him away and stood firm, but my integrity and morals drown at the sight of him. My want for him, maybe even my greed, makes it unbearably hard for me to reject him when he's near. Not that he's letting me. I've fallen into a black hole of hopelessness, and though I know I need to drag myself out before I lose myself in it forever, I fear I'll never be able to refuse him. I'm frightened to death that an addiction to Jack is rooting itself deep inside me, and I'm even more scared that I won't let anything stand in my way of taking what I can get. Not my morals, not my conscience . . . and not even his wife.

The silence stretches for too long, leaving nothing but quiet for me to torture myself with. I can walk away. I can end this now. Yet my arms don't release him until he pushes himself up, peeling his body from mine and slowly lifting his hips. His semi-erect cock slips free and he rolls onto his back beside me, leaving me feeling abandoned and hurt. I glance across to him and find him staring at the ceiling, one arm splayed over his head, his other resting on his stomach. I want to know what he's thinking. I also *don't* want to know, so before I let my curiosity get the better of me, I get up from the bed and go to my bathroom, shutting the door behind me.

I look at my naked body in the mirror, reaching up to feel my damp cheeks. My nipples are still flushed pink with desire and the inside of my thigh is glistening with evidence of our combined release. Lifting my gaze to the reflection of my face, I see despondency in my green eyes. I also see words springing into the air around my head. *Adulterer. Weak. Immoral. Heartless bitch*. My hands meet the edge of the sink and my head drops, unable to face myself. I don't know this woman. What have I become?

A light tap on the bathroom door interrupts my self-loathing thoughts and pulls my heavy head up. 'Annie?' Jack's soft voice is evidence that he knows damn well what I'm doing in here. Beating myself up. Ripping myself to shreds. 'Can I come in?'

The lump in my throat won't allow me to talk, so I nod like an idiot, even though he can't see me. It's beyond a stupid idea to invite him in, but stupid seems to be controlling me these days. The door quietly opens and his beautiful head peeks around nervously, searching me out. His brown hair is a mess, his grey eyes still bright. It's been minutes since I last saw him, but it's like seeing him for the first time all over again. The thud of my heart, the rise of my body temperature. I stare at his reflection in the mirror, unwilling to look away. Or unable to. The understanding on his face nearly cripples me. He pushes the door all the way open and walks with purpose towards me, turning me around and yanking me into his chest, hugging me fiercely.

My emotions get too much to hold back. 'This isn't me,' I sob into his chest, finding comfort in the smell of his clean sweat. It's something else that catapults me back to the night that I fear will haunt me forever.

'It's not me either, Annie.'

'Then why are we here?'

He lifts me to his body and encases me in his hold. 'Because I know it's where I *should* be,' he whispers, almost solemn.

My heart clenches in my chest painfully. I think every other person on the planet would disagree with Jack. He should be with his wife. Not here with me, and that notion pains me. I don't know what's happening. This is so crazy. He's still virtually a stranger to me, but the thought of not seeing him again is unbearable. The question *what now?* hangs from my tongue, but something stops me from asking. It's fear.

'Come,' he breathes, steadying me on my feet and taking my hand. 'I need some caffeine.' Leading me through my flat, he finds his way to my kitchen and indicates the cupboards. 'Mugs?'

I smile, trying to disregard how perfect he looks standing naked in my kitchen. 'Yes.'

He matches my smile, pulling two down. 'Ask me how I knew that.'

'You've been breaking in and rummaging through my cupboards and drawers?'

He gives a faint laugh, reaching for the cupboard that houses my coffee. 'I knew because that is exactly the cupboard I would have put them in. And the coffee.' He reaches for the drawer where I keep my cutlery. 'And the spoons are in here, right?'

'Right. And, amazingly, the milk is in the fridge.'

He shoves the drawer shut with a jerk of his arse, tapping the spoon on his palm as he regards me. He takes one step forward. I take one step back. He smirks. I smirk. Then he lunges forward threateningly, and I squeal as he seizes me, wrapping me in one solid arm and tickling me with his spare hand. 'Jack!' I gasp, bucking against him. It's futile; his weight and strength versus mine is always going to win. 'Jack, stop!'

'Are you mocking me for having good cupboard awareness?'

'No, I love your cupboard awareness!' I laugh over my words, relishing his playfulness, his nakedness against mine, and the fact that he would have put the coffee cups in that cupboard too.

I'm finally released from his torturing clutches and slapped on the arse. 'Finish the coffee, gorgeous. I need the toilet.' He strides out. 'Bet I know where you keep your spare loo rolls.'

I chuckle and finish off the coffees, before making tracks to find him. 'Jack?'

'In here,' he calls. I follow the sound of his voice until I'm on the threshold of my studio. I find Jack's naked body standing over my workbench, and I wander over to join him, finding him looking over the drawings for Colin's extension. Glancing up at me, he smiles. 'Architect Annie.'

I laugh softly, remembering him calling me that on the night I met him. 'Jack the joker.'

Jack laughs too, his eyes sparkling. 'You loved my joke.'

I can't deny it, so I don't. 'What are you looking at?'

'I'm just wondering why you chose bare brick for the internal wall of the extension.'

'Colin's art is very modern. Almost industrial. The building is early nineteen hundreds, and I thought . . .'

'The contrast of old and new would be striking,' he finishes for me, as if reading my mind.

'Exactly that.' My heart falls a little as Jack glances up at me, smiling mildly.

'Great minds.'

'Great minds,' I counter softly, handing him his coffee. It's not only our bodies that work in complete harmony, but our thoughts too. It scares me to think how perfect this man is for me. How stimulating, beyond our sexual chemistry.

Jack takes his coffee, seeming to fall into a daydream. I wonder if he's having the same thoughts as me. But I don't ask.

I do, however, ask him something. 'Why?' I pull him from his daydreaming, and I don't have to extend my question.

'Honestly?' he asks, prompting me to nod. Jack frowns and spends the next few seconds sipping his drink. Something tells me he's buying time, trying to figure out whether he *should* be honest. 'I needed to let off some steam. To just get totally fucked,' he tells me. I nearly spit my coffee out, forcing him to go on quickly. 'I don't mean getting fucked like that. I mean getting fucked in the drunken sense. Just so I could forget about . . .' He fades off and glances away from me, sighing as his eyes jump across my workbench.

I step back, studying his sudden despondent expression. 'Are you happy?'

'When I'm with you, I'm deliriously happy. I already told you that.'

'You know I don't mean that.'

He smiles, but it's a sad smile. 'No, I'm not. But does it make the fact that I can't stop thinking about you acceptable?'

His question gives me pause, despite the answer being very easy. Easy but painful. 'No,' I admit, looking away from him. Nothing would make this acceptable.

Within a second, Jack has removed my mug from my hands and has me wrapped in his arms, hugging me tightly. It feels so good, so comforting, like I'm not shouldering all of the guilt alone. I relax into him with a sigh, thinking how I could happily remain here forever.

'My phone,' Jack mumbles quietly, reluctantly releasing me. I hear the sound of his mobile ringing and watch as his naked back disappears through the doorway. I follow him back to the bedroom to find my dressing gown. Jack dips and scoops up his trousers, rummaging through the pocket and pulling out his mobile. I know who it is before he looks down at the screen and his body deflates. The life drains out of me too.

'Stephanie,' he says when he connects the call. He holds his phone to his ear with his shoulder as he drags his boxers and trousers on and walks out to the corridor to get his shirt, his jaw definitely tight. It's then I hear her shouting down the line at him. I stand back, like I'm trying to escape the private conversation. Jack's nostrils flare, and his eyes clench shut briefly. 'I'm sorry. I'll be there as quickly as I can,' he replies calmly and quietly. 'Apologise to your parents for the delay.'

He hangs up, and I stand in the doorway silently while he

fastens the buttons of his shirt, my mind racing. He didn't even react to her rant. There was nothing in him. No emotion whatsoever. My eyes drop to my feet, scanning the carpet, my questions growing. I can't conclude anything except one thing, and it's a conclusion that frightens me because it could fuck with my immoral conscience even more.

I hate his wife.

How she spoke to him just then, I hate her for it. But I have no right to hate her. I've screwed her husband. Twice.

Once Jack's sorted himself out, he stands quietly for a moment, watching me from across the room. My heart is begging him not to go. But my head is throwing him out and telling him to leave me alone. 'See me tomorrow,' he says, not as a question, more as a statement.

I just look at him, unable and unwilling to reply. What I want to do so desperately is ask all about his marriage, but that is a place I know I shouldn't venture. It's laughable. It's not as if I'm not dancing on dangerous ground already. Yet I fear that whatever I learn from Jack will just be another reason that I can use as a weapon to justify my actions. Knowing things were rocky before I came along isn't beneficial. It'll just help blanket my reasoning. It's fucking backwards. I can't win here. So I do the wisest thing and keep my mouth shut. The less I know the better.

'Annie,' he whispers. 'Answer me.'

I drop my gaze to the floor, feeling my eyes flood with infuriating tears. 'It didn't sound like a question,' I retort softly. I need him to leave, because I don't want him to see me break down again. I'm on the edge, my body beginning to tremble with the restraint it's taking to hold it together.

When I hear his steps coming near, I close my eyes and breathe strength into myself. His soft touch meets my cheek and strokes delicately for a few seconds before he dips and kisses my forehead. Then he turns and walks out.

And I crumple to the floor and sob like I've never sobbed before.

Because he said that if the Fates ever led me to him again, he wouldn't let me go.

And he just did.

To go and meet his wife.

Chapter 11

How can you become so attached to something with such limited contact? The answer is easy and unbearable all at once. I feel like Jack was made especially for me, and the fact that I can't have him is cruel. Plain cruel. He is forbidden. I shouldn't have had him the first time. I *definitely* shouldn't have had him the second time. And I'm so mad with myself. I may have been misled in that bar, I may have given in to his potency, but I knew full well what I was getting myself into last night. It's unforgivable.

I lay in my bed mentally beating myself up all over again, the guilt returning tenfold. I tried not to allow myself to wonder if his lack of any fight on the phone with her was because of guilt. I tried not to imagine him being so subservient to her and accepting her rant, even if he deserves it. But Stephanie doesn't know about me. So what is she yelling at him for? Simply being late for dinner?

I didn't sleep a wink, my mind not shutting down, but I did reach one solid conclusion. This has to end now. Whether their marriage is struggling is of no consequence. I have no place in their lives. Their problems are not my problems, and I shouldn't make them mine.

I'm better than this.

By 6 a.m., I've given up on sleep, so I put myself in the shower and ready myself for a long day at work. After getting my car sorted out with a local garage, I stop off for a large cappuccino and drink it while I make a few calls and e-mail the structural engineer to arrange a meeting to discuss the roof issue.

He comes back to me quickly saying he's free at two for half an hour. I have no choice but to take the slot and rearrange my diary. This can't wait until next week.

I'm chewing on the end of my pen an hour later, working out some numbers, when my mobile dings the arrival of an e-mail. I snatch it up while jotting something down and glance at the screen. His name glares up at me, getting the usual expected re-action from my heart. Then the relentless flashbacks commence too, except now there are more scenes, more feelings, more images. More words to hang onto. I read the first line of his e-mail and quickly establish that it's in no way work-related. 'Damn you, Jack.' I stop reading and delete it. We've crossed the line twice. It can't happen again.

'Totally doable,' the engineer says, simple as that. 'I'll have the recalculations done and get them to you before close of play tomorrow.'

'You are a saint.' I give him praying hands. 'Thank you.'

He smiles and gets his pad out, starting to make notes. As I pass the existing double doors that lead into the garden, I spot Richard pointing up at some branches of the horse chestnut tree. He spots me and waves me out.

'Annie, this is Wes. He's gonna get rid of these branches.'

'Hi.' I shake Wes's hand when he offers it.

'Which ones am I lopping off?' he asks, looking up.

'Lopping off?' I laugh.

'I'm all about technical language.'

'Right.' I catch Richard's laughing eyes too, as I point the branches out. 'That one and that one.'

'And that one,' Jack says, appearing across the garden. I cringe on the inside, quickly looking away before I have the chance to admire how good he looks in his suit.

'I don't think that's necessary,' I reply formally. 'Just the two will suffice.'

Wes and Richard look between the two of us. 'I disagree.' Jack reaches us and points to the lowest branch. 'If you remove that one, it'll dislodge the one behind and the problem will still exist.'

I press my lips together, breathing some patience into myself. He's pissed off. I can tell by the bulge in his neck and his clipped tone. And I know why. I only peeked at each of the five e-mails he sent me, and deleted them swiftly the moment I gathered they weren't work-related. Therefore I haven't responded to any, and when he rang, I rejected every single call. 'And if we remove *that* branch, you'll be exposing the garden to the buildings beyond,' I point out.

'Well.' His lips twist in annoyance. 'I did e-mail you numerous times today regarding this, but you haven't bothered to reply.'

I shoot him a shocked glare and open my mouth to fire a few choice words at him, but quickly force my gob shut when I remember we have company. He did not e-mail me about trees or anything work-related, and he knows it. 'I've been busy,' I reply shortly. 'But we're clear now.' I walk away, leaving Wes and Richard with wary eyes, and Jack with a fuming face. 'The branch stays,' I call.

Jack's caught up with me before I make it inside. 'Why have you ignored my e-mails?' he hisses in my ear, following close behind. 'And my calls.'

'Because they were about us.' I swing around, infuriated. 'And that back there was your way of punishing me for not answering you. By making me look incompetent in front of colleagues, just because I didn't reply? Just because your ego is bruised?'

'You think this has *anything* to do with my ego?'

'Yes,' I hiss.

'You're bloody deluded. The branch needs to go!' he barks childishly.

'It's staying!'

He growls, advancing towards me, forcing my steps backwards until I'm pushed into a corner. *No. Oh, no, no, no!*

'It's easy to ignore me when I'm on the end of a message, isn't it?' he says, his voice low and dangerous. 'What now, Annie?' He grabs my hand and slams it over the crotch of his trousers. 'What am I supposed to do with this?'

He's solid. He's angry and he's fucking solid. I gulp, anxiety gripping me. He's wrong. It's not easy when he's on the end of an e-mail. It's not as hard as this, but it's still a battle that I'm losing. Or have I already lost?

'And this?' He moves my hand to his chest. His heartbeat is crazily fast. Just like mine. 'What do I do with this?'

'Why don't you ask your wife?' I inwardly wince at my quiet retort, but Jack *physically* winces, dropping my hand and standing back, a look of pure disgust on his face.

He breathes in, slowly raising a finger and pointing it at me. 'You don't get to say that. Not after last night.'

'You forget.' My jaw could crack under the pressure of the bite on my back teeth. 'I can say what I fucking like, because no one owns me. And definitely not *you*.'

His features twist, his disgust doubling, and he slowly places his hand on my hip. I jolt under his touch, and he smiles victoriously. 'Really, Annie? Keep telling yourself that.'

'Um . . . Jack?' Richard interrupts us, definite awkwardness in his tone, and I quickly dip away from Jack, moving on shaky legs to the drawings.

'What?' Jack yells, pulling my shocked stare up.

Richard doesn't even flinch. 'I think you need to come out front, mate.' Richard's face is full of apologies, and Jack's is suddenly full of dread. Then I hear it: a woman yelling.

I look towards the front of the house, wondering what on earth is going on. 'Jack!' a woman screams. 'Jack!'

Jack's hands go to his head and yank viciously, and he shouts, a carnal sound full of frustration. He glares at me, his eyes raging with fire. I turn to dust on the spot, cowering away. Then he strides off.

I look at Richard. Richard looks at me. 'I'd avoid the front for a while if I were you.'

Of course, that means I just go right ahead and make my way out there, curious. Too curious. Dangerously curious. I find Jack halfway down the driveway and his wife waving her arms, looking deranged, while plenty of workmen look on. What on earth?

'Why haven't you answered my calls?' she screeches.

Jack's hands come up in a pacifying way, his body language now entirely different compared to when he left me a few moments ago. 'I've been busy, Stephanie. I'm running a business.' He sounds calm too.

'Yeah, it's all about fucking work with you. What about me? What about your marriage?'

I watch, rapt, as he seems to talk her down before taking her arm. She yanks herself free and shoves him away viciously, though Jack's big body hardly moves at all.

'Daddy says *I* should be your priority! He says you're selfish, and I'm inclined to agree!' Her final vomit of insults is delivered on a slight slur. Is she drunk? *Daddy?*

'That's enough, Stephanie. You're showing yourself up.' Jack grabs her arms and leads her to his car, but she pushes him away again, stumbling a little in her heels on the gravel. She's definitely drunk.

'I'll get myself in the car,' she spits, falling into the seat.

Jack looks back at me, his face a picture of stress. Then he shakes his head mildly at me and mouths, *This isn't over.*

I take a backward step and find the nearest thing to cling to in order to hold me up.

I spend all weekend lost in work in an attempt to distract myself. It doesn't work, and it's not going to when Jack's been persistently trying to get hold of me. I've ignored him. It's been hard, but I've managed. Just. I stop off at the supermarket on my way home on Monday to pick up dinner for this evening. As I'm traipsing up aisle after aisle trying to decide what I fancy, my phone chimes the arrival of a text. I reach for a paella as I open the message.

We need to talk. Meet me. Jack

My stomach drops. It doesn't take a genius to conclude that this won't be about business. And it isn't even a question. Once again I start imagining what he wants to say, my mind going into overdrive, no matter how hard I try to stop it. Why can't he drop it? *This isn't over.*

My lips dry and my stomach flips. I delete the message quickly before I do something stupid . . . like reply. Why is he doing this? I need to give up Colin's project. It kills me, but I have to. I can't work with Jack. I *shouldn't* work with him. I'll just take on more projects, anything to swallow up all my time and take my mind away from my dangerous thoughts. That's the plan. I just hope to God it works, because every time I see Jack, the deep ache inside me intensifies. My want deepens, my heart splits with pain when he leaves, and when he holds me, I dream about him holding me every day, encouraging me every day, inspiring me every day. For the first time in my life, I'm imagining my world with a man in it. I'm imagining giving up some of my independence to make room for Jack. Because with him, it doesn't feel like I'm giving anything up at all – only gaining. I'm imagining him poring over designs with me, offering advice, telling me constantly how proud he is of me. Ignoring all of these dreams is draining me. I'm all out of resistance.

Dropping my half-full basket to the floor, I abandon my plan to eat and rush home so I can dive into my office and lose myself in work. I finish drawings, e-mail them, call the structural engineer for his opinion on a few things . . . and draft an e-mail to Colin advising him of my intention to pull out of his project, but recommending some colleagues who will be happy to assist and see it through to completion.

I take a call from a potential client and schedule a meeting. It's nowhere near the scale of Colin's project, but it's something else for me to get stuck into. I check in with Mum and Dad, reply to a text from Micky telling him I'm fine, so *so* fine, and even clean my bathroom. It's been a productive day. The only thing that'll finish it off nicely is clicking *Send* on the e-mail I drafted to Colin.

But as my cursor hovers over the icon, nothing I say to myself convinces me to click it. I close my eyes and will my finger to push down. Just press it. *Just press that little icon and your problems will go away.* I sit back in my chair, staring at the screen for a good ten minutes, searching for the will and the sense to do the right thing.

Ding!

I look down at my phone and see Jack's name, and though everything tells me not to open his message, my stupid finger doesn't hesitate to click down on *that* icon.

You don't get to ignore me now, Annie.

A second later, my phone starts ringing, and I push myself away from my desk in my chair to put some space between me and it. 'Go away, Jack,' I whisper.

As soon as it stops ringing, I quickly dial Lizzy, breathing my way through my panic. I'm going to cave into his persistence soon. 'Hey, what's up?'

'Fancy a coffee?' I ask.

'Sure. I just finished. Usual place, twenty minutes?'

'See you soon.'

I spot Lizzy weaving her way through the tables up ahead, my eyes following her until she lands in the chair opposite me.

'How's work? Everything okay?'

'Yes, it's all fine. I hardly see him actually,' I lie. This wasn't the plan. I need distraction. I could never tell Lizzy I slept with Jack again, especially given everything she's been through with Jason. I can never tell *anyone*. I'm a disgrace. A weak, pathetic woman. I also can't tell her that I'm giving up Colin's project. She'll know why.

I plaster a smile on my face, feigning normality. 'Besides, there's nothing like a wife to realign things, is there?'

Lizzy laughs loudly, and for the first time I see the funny side. Because it's actually quite fucking hilarious. I'm never overwhelmed by a man, and when it eventually happens, the bastard is married.

'Doesn't the sanctity of marriage mean a thing any more?' I ask, truly exasperated.

'More marriages end than survive.' Lizzy picks up her tea-spoon and points it at me. 'And mostly because of infidelity. I had a lucky escape. I'm never getting married.'

'Me neither,' I agree, feeling like I'm subconsciously kissing goodbye to my happy-ever-after, as well as my dream project.

'Fuck coffee,' Lizzy says. 'Let's get pissed. Call the others.' She grabs a menu and proceeds to order alcohol en masse.

'Now?'

'Yes, now. And hopefully you'll get laid as well.'

She's right. I need to get back in the saddle. 'You need a good screw too.'

Her eyebrows jump up.

'By someone other than Micky,' I clarify as I grab my phone to call the guys, my mouth now watering in anticipation for the mojito that will soon be landing on the table in front of me.

Unplanned drinking sessions are the best. The fact that it's on a week night makes it all the more thrilling. We've ended up in a beer garden in Camden; it's 8 p.m. and we're both tipsy. Not pissed, just a nice gradual state of drunkenness. We've talked about everything and nothing, my mind being perfectly occupied by alcohol and a dedicated friend.

'I've missed this,' Lizzy says, looking past me to a group of men at the back of the beer garden.

I follow her eyes and smile. 'You've missed ogling men?'

'No.' She waves her wine between us. 'This. You've been working so hard on your business, and I get that, but I've missed our girlie time.'

'Me too,' I confess, watching Lizzy plaster a knockout smile on her pretty face, obviously having attracted the attention of the group of men. 'Hey, come on. We're having a nice time without men,' I point out, smacking her arm to win her attention back.

I look past Lizzy and see Micky stroll into the beer garden. I can virtually hear all the female hormones in the vicinity go potty. He laps it up and struts over. 'Shit, how many behind am I?' he asks, taking in our tipsy state.

Lizzy burps in reply, and I start giggling. 'I'll get more drinks.' I snatch my bag up and head for the bar. 'And keep your hands to yourself while I'm gone.' I level a warning look at Micky, and he holds his hands up in surrender.

'Reading you loud and clear.'

I make my way to the ladies' to freshen up before heading to the bar to get our drinks in. By the time I've made it back to the garden, Nat's found us too. Everyone cheers my return and dives on the tray when I place it on the table. 'Wow,' Nat chimes, toasting me. 'It's a school night and Annie's not in her studio. What's happened?'

I ignore her sarcasm and throw my arm around her shoulder. 'Drink,' I order. 'We're three ahead of you.'

'To being single!' Nat sings, and we all chink our glasses before getting our drinking session under way.

*

It was so needed – the alcohol, the friends, the limited space to allow my mind to venture further than the laughs being had in the pub garden. I feel normal again. Sane. Even if I'm smashed.

Micky drops me home in a cab at around eleven, the amount of alcohol I've indulged in evident as I zigzag my way up the path to my front door. 'Hey, Annie!' he calls from the cab. 'Run in the morning?'

I snort unattractively and give him the finger, making him laugh as he slams the door and the cab pulls away. Getting my key in the lock proves tricky. I close one eye and zero in on my target, but each time I hit the wood to the side, chipping at the paintwork. 'In you go,' I slur, getting up close and personal with my door, my tongue hanging out a little in concentration.

'You're not doing very well there, are you?'

I jump and whirl around, just barely managing to keep my balance, and find Jack standing behind me.

I smile brightly and point at him. 'Well, if it isn't the married man himself!' I sing, and then slap a clumsy hand over my mouth to silence myself, giggling like an idiot. 'Oopsie,' I say into my palm. I might be drunk, but he definitely scowls at me, and I even manage to find the sense to be offended by it. 'Did you just scowl at me, Jack Joseph?'

'You're drunk,' he mutters, coming towards me. My challenged vision runs a sluggish check over him, finding him looking delightful in some battered old jeans and an old grey T-shirt, his biceps bulging.

'Yes.' I stagger a little, my back meeting the door. 'I am drunk. And it's not your concern.'

He takes the top of my arm and moves me to the side, prising my key from me and opening the door. A deep warmth penetrates my skin, making me look down on a frown to where he's got hold of me. 'Why does that happen?' I ask my arm.

'What?' he mutters, irritated. He's in a mood. I laugh hysterically on the inside. What, has he had a row with his wife again?

Good! I hope she's figured out that he's a cheating arsehole.

'I go all funny whenever you touch me.' I shudder on the spot, and he looks at me as he pushes my door open.

'"Funny" isn't the word I'd use.'

'What word would you use, then?' I challenge, pulling my arm free, but it's soon claimed again when my hasty withdrawal has me staggering backwards.

'I'm not having this conversation with you when you're drunk.' He guides me into the hallway, following.

'No, you'd better get back to your wife.' I laugh, snatching my arm back and slumping against the wall.

'Stop it, Annie,' he warns, placing a palm on the wall next to my head and leaning in close. Too close. 'Why haven't you answered any of my e-mails or calls?'

'Because I want nothing to do with you,' I spit, making him recoil, shocked. He has a nerve.

'Stop fucking lying to me.'

I drink in air, searching for some poise before I slap him. Too late. My arm flies out clumsily, but I miss his cheek by a mile, my arm ricocheting off his shoulder. He doesn't even jolt, whereas I lose my footing and stumble forward awkwardly. 'I hate you,' I snipe as he catches me in his arms, cursing under his breath. 'I hate you, I hate you, I hate you!'

'Shut up, Annie,' he seethes, lifting me off my feet. 'Don't ever fucking try to hit me again.'

'Why?' I snap, wriggling to break free.

'Because it doesn't suit you.'

As we pass through my bedroom door, the sight of my bed makes me start squirming more, but Jack just holds on tighter. 'Get off me!' I begin to flail my arms, but they have no effect on him as he strides across my room with me locked tightly to his body.

'Cut it out,' he warns, a threatening edge to his tone.

'No!'

He lowers me to my arse on the bed, but I'm scrambling back up a second later, getting up in his face. It's a bad move. This close, his gorgeous features make me even dizzier. I slam my eyes closed and lose my footing again, plummeting to the bed. I'm a mess. Useless. Pathetic.

'Just go,' I plead, burying my face in my palms to hide from him. 'Leave me alone.'

My stomach lunges, and my mouth becomes watery. Oh no. I jump up from the bed and make a mad dash for the bathroom, banging into everything on my way, whether it's blocking my path or not. I hang my head over the toilet and throw up on long, loud retches.

'Oh God,' I groan, going limp around the bowl, clinging to it with weak arms.

I feel fingers weave through my hair and pull it away, and a warm palm smoothes across my back. Slumped over the toilet, I rest my head on my arms and close my eyes. 'Please don't hate me,' he murmurs.

I black out.

Chapter 12

You know it's going to be a bad one when your head is throbbing and you've not even lifted it off the pillow. And your body hurts when you try to move and get comfy in your bed. And your mouth is drier than the driest desert, but you can't figure out if you'd prefer to remain unmoving and put up with the dehydration, or attempt to get to the kitchen in search of water and risk throwing up on the way. This is a bad one. Maybe the worst I've ever had, and that's an achievement since I've not even got up yet.

I groan and attempt a stretch, hissing as I lengthen my body, spreading myself out in search of a cool patch. I peel my eyes open, my bedside table coming into view, a glass of water sitting waiting for me. And propped up against it, a note saying, 'Hydration'. I frown and sit up, spotting two pills on a note that says, 'Pain relief'.

What on earth? I still and try to think back to last night. Oh God. I slowly cast my eyes over my shoulder, cringing as I do, bracing myself for what I might find.

What's spread across my bed gives me a fucking heart attack, and I bolt upright, immediately grabbing my head for fear that it might fall off. I hiss and wince as I fall back to the mattress, unable to give the seriousness of my situation the attention it deserves in my feeble state. 'Jack,' I moan, throwing my leg out to kick him. What have I done?

He groans but remains on his back, and my eyes take a greedy roam down his naked body, arriving at his cock. There's a note there too: 'Breakfast'.

'Jack!'

His lashes flutter and his lids open, revealing deep grey pools of adorable sleepiness. 'Morning,' he rasps, not in the least bit perturbed by seeing me.

'What are you doing here?' I ask, starting to panic for both of us.

His hand comes across and rests on my hip. Which is naked. 'How's your head?'

'Confused,' I admit, pulling away from him before his touch has a chance to scramble my mind further. He looks down to my hip, now free of his hand, and back up to me. 'We didn't . . .' I wave a finger between us, trying my hardest to pull some memories out of my beaten brain. 'You and I, we didn't . . .'

'No,' he says quietly, almost apprehensively.

I'm relieved, but I still don't know why the hell he's in my flat. 'What are you doing here?'

'You didn't answer my messages or calls.'

'So you thought you'd break in?'

'I didn't break in. I found you plastered trying to unlock your door when I came to talk.'

I swallow down my anger and push myself to the edge of the bed. 'I have nothing to say to you.' Taking a deep breath to push away the dizziness, I rise to my feet. I spend a few precious seconds ensuring I'm not going to face-plant, then make my way to the kitchen in search of water, abandoning the glass Jack kindly laid out for me in my need to abandon *him*.

'Please leave, Jack,' I call.

I make it to the kitchen and turn the tap on, running it while I collect a glass. I glug back two pints of water on the bounce, parched, before slamming my glass on the drainer and pivoting to leave the kitchen. Brushing past him as I exit is unavoidable when I find he's blocking the doorway, and as soon as our skin connects, I gasp, my pace faltering. But I fight myself to keep moving.

I don't get very far. Jack's hand shoots out and claims my wrist. 'Don't do this,' he practically growls, squeezing his hold. 'Don't you dare, Annie.'

I wrench my arm free, my teeth gritting hard. But I don't say anything. My seething expression must say it all. I glare at him as I walk away, my jaw aching from the pressure of clenching my teeth.

'Annie!' Jack shouts, his bare feet thumping the wooden floor as he comes after me.

'Get out.'

I push my way into my bathroom, shutting the door behind me and locking it. In an instant, his fists are banging on the wood. But I ignore them, flipping the shower on. After scouring my teeth to within an inch of their life, I get in the shower and scrub the stench of stale alcohol away. He has no right to be here. He may not have taken advantage of me, but he took advantage nevertheless.

I start shampooing my hair roughly, blocking any thoughts and questions from muscling their way into my achy mind. After rinsing and washing down, I step out, grabbing a towel from the towel rail, listening for movement beyond my bathroom door. There's nothing.

As I dry off and throw a T-shirt on, I mentally plan my day. I need to revise some drawings. Maybe I could take Micky up on his offer and squeeze a run in. It could be a good stress alleviator. I should call the girls too, to see if they're in any better shape than I am. And I mean hangover-wise. Not fucked-up-married-man-wise.

After towel-drying my hair I flip my head up, just as the door flies open, the lock jumping off the wood. I swing around, finding Jack in the doorway. 'Get out!' I shout incredulously.

'No.'

I spin away from him, doing everything I can to avoid meeting his eyes in the mirror, knowing I mustn't risk being hauled into their burning depths. It's not a battle I can win. An invisible force pulls my stare to his in the reflection. My spine lengthens. He's just there, no expression and no movement, but it makes no difference to my uncontrollable reaction to him. A reaction I shouldn't have. A reaction I can't help.

'Your wife,' I say. 'She doesn't deserve this.' No woman deserves this, no matter what. I've encountered her only a few times, seen her behaviour and heard the rumours, but it still doesn't make this right.

His nostrils flare as he scans my face for a few thoughtful moments, maybe considering what a selfish arsehole he's being. What an awful situation he's putting me in. 'Don't think you're destroying a perfect marriage, Annie. You're not.'

'It's still a marriage,' I mumble meekly. 'Perfect or not, I have no place in it.'

'That's not true. You *do* have a place in it, because you are the only thing that can save me from it.'

I feel my brow furrow. 'Save you from it?'

A small smile crosses his handsome face. 'Stephanie is . . .' His words die as he evidently struggles to piece together what he wants to say. 'Volatile.' He sighs. 'Our marriage is over. I know it, she's knows it, but she refuses to accept it.' Jack shakes his head and squeezes his eyes closed, the frustration clear. 'I can't live like this any more, Annie. There's no going back for me.' Opening his eyes, he levels a determined stare on me. 'I don't *want* to find a way back again. Especially now. Especially since I met you.' He shakes his head a little in frustration. 'See me again,' he orders quietly.

'Are you crazy?' I ask, dumbfounded. I've already spent limited time with Jack, and it feels like I've known him for years. Adding any more hours to our time together would be monumentally stupid. I've been stupid enough already.

He moves across the bathroom towards me, coming to a stop behind me. He doesn't touch me, but ensures our eye contact remains intact. 'Quite possibly,' he answers simply.

I swallow and shake my head, but he counters by nodding his own, confident with his declaration. I can feel myself slipping from the safety of my conscience again. 'No,' I murmur.

'Yes,' he counters, watching me as he lowers his mouth to my shoulder and rests his lips on my flesh. I jerk and grab the sink for support, but I don't pull away. Stupidly, I let him at me, consumed in a second by his power over me.

He kisses my shoulder lightly and takes my hand, extending it out to the side and kissing his way down my arm to the very tips of my fingers. My skin bursts into flames, my head drops back and my mind blanks out once again. Only Jack exists. I slide my hand up his arm and curl my palm around his neck, applying a light pressure, telling him to come to me. He expresses no victory. He circles me until he's before me and slides his hand onto my cheek, lowering his mouth leisurely to mine.

I'm gone, lost in that special place he takes me to, where passion and longing cloud everything.

Then Stephanie's face is suddenly all I see, and I shout, pushing him away from me. 'No,' I snap, turning and walking away from him, my hands coming up to my temples and physically trying to force the image of her from my head. It's stuck there, tormenting me, torturing me. I can't cave again. I *mustn't* cave again. 'Get out.'

'Annie, don't walk away—'

'Get out!' I scream, swinging around in a blind rage. His pursuit halts as soon as he catches sight of my incensed face. 'I don't want you!' I seethe, snatching up his jeans and T-shirt and throwing them at him viciously.

He lets his clothes hit him and fall to the floor. 'Stop fucking lying to me!' he roars, stalking forward and claiming me. 'Stop saying what your head is demanding and start listening to your fucking heart, Annie!'

'My heart is saying nothing!' I fight with him, scared to death of remaining in his hold, feeling him breaking me down with every second he's touching me.

'Then why can I fucking hear it?' he yells. 'Loud and fucking clear, woman. It's saying the exact same thing mine is.'

I wrench myself free and move away, breathing heavily. 'Leave me the hell alone and go home to your wife. It's that simple.'

'Simple?' Jack asks seriously, gesturing an accusing hand up and down my front before smashing a fist into his chest. 'Then why the *fuck* does it hurt like hell every time I think about not seeing you again?' he yells. 'Explain it to me, Annie, because I really am going fucking crazy!'

I shrink on the spot, shocked, yet I fully comprehend what he's saying. I feel like I'm going out of my mind too, and I'm definitely hurting. I start to shake. It's anger, but it's also fear.

'Get out.' I need to put aside the crazy chemistry and bat down the butterflies. I mustn't be blinkered by lust again. 'Just go, Jack.' I drop my eyes to the floor before I can take in any more of him. And those memories. His face, my face, our bodies. I squeeze my eyes shut and push the heel of my palm into my forehead.

'It doesn't work,' he says quietly. 'I've tried it.'

I start to shake my head, my cheeks becoming wet with tears of frustration.

'Nothing works, Annie. Not shaking my head, not distracting myself, nothing.'

'Stop it,' I whimper pathetically.

'I can't stop,' he hisses, taking a step towards me. 'It was bad enough having you constantly up here.' He taps his temple aggressively, his face twisting. 'Now you're *actually* fucking here. I can't eat, I can't sleep.'

He takes another step towards me and I retreat again, trying my hardest to keep the distance between us. Being this close to him is dangerous. It's screwing with my resolve, eating through my conscience.

'You're married,' I grate, furious with him. So furious! 'I made a horrible mistake. Get out of my flat.'

He just stares at me for a few moments, and I can tell he's assessing my mental state. He's trying to find that one little chink in my armour, any way in. I won't give it to him. Not again.

'I said, get out,' I repeat, certain and strong. 'I never want to see you again.'

'Colin's—'

'I'm giving up the project.'

Jack backs away, his face a picture of hurt, maybe even devastation, but I refuse to let it dent my resolve. I make sure my expression remains determined, watching as his jaw goes so tight it could possibly crack.

'You want that?' he asks.

'I don't see any other way.'

'I do.' Jack's face is suddenly determined. 'You're right. I can't look at you every day and know you're lying to yourself. And to me.' He tugs his jeans up his legs and shoves his feet into his boots, all angrily. 'But you're not giving up. This project means too much to you, and I'm not going to be the reason you walk away from it.'

I withdraw, moving back. 'I don't understand.'

'I'll be off the job by tomorrow evening.' He turns and walks out, pulling his T-shirt on as he goes, and a few seconds later I hear the front door slam with brutal force.

My breathing becomes shallow and strained, my throat clogging up. What just happened? He's resigned. Jack's solved my problem for me. I'll never see him again. I'll carry on with my life as if I never met him. It's for the best. I know it's for the best. I can't go on like this. I'm caught in limbo, desolate without him, desolate with him. I feel like I'm yo-yoing between strength and shakiness, never knowing which way to turn. I'm never going to see him again. Hear him. Feel him.

Those thoughts make my knees give, and I crumple to the floor into a heap of grief. I'll never see him again. My eyes well up, blurring my surroundings. My whole world blurs too. I'll never see him again. Never feel him, hear him, smell him. My shallow breathing virtually diminishes to nothing, my sobs now racking my folded body.

I know this is for the best. So why does it feel like I'm slowly dying?

He's walked away so I don't have to. Because he knows what this project means to me. I drag myself up from the floor, sobbing uncontrollably.

I don't know what I'm doing, but everything is telling me to do it. I stagger to the door, my vision distorted through my teary eyes, and throw myself out onto the street. I frantically search for his car and spot him down the road getting into his Audi. 'Jack!' I scream, and he looks up, holding the top of his door. I stand where I am in a T-shirt and nothing else, my feet bare, my face undoubtedly a tear-stained wreck. 'I don't want you to,' I sob, breaking down completely. 'I don't want you to go.'

He slams his car door and runs towards me, worry written all over his face. He just catches me before my body gives, scooping me up into his arms and squeezing me to his chest. My arms hold him so tightly, my heart telling me this is right. Me and him. It's so right.

'It doesn't have to be this hard,' he whispers, walking up the steps and into my hallway, shutting the door behind him. Detaching me from his body, he brings his hand to my face, and when the heat of his touch meets my cheek, the warmth spreads throughout me. Those powerful, consuming feelings take hold. Just one touch. He brings his face close to mine, his other hand settling on my hip as we stare into each other's eyes. I see so much pain behind his mesmerising grey gaze. And so much life.

'Don't make me give you up, Annie,' he murmurs quietly, his voice broken with emotion.

My throat clogs, my eyes refilling with hopeless tears. 'I have no fight left in me.'

'Good, because I'm fucking exhausted battling with you.' He dips his head and claims my mouth gently, sensing my fragile state, his hand sliding into my hair and fisting, holding me in place.

Falling.

I return his kiss, no questions, no fighting and no hesitation. It's slow, it's accepting and it's loving. And everything is better once again.

Then things begin to get desperate. Things start to get frantic. Jack moans, over and over, and I swallow them all. The pace of our swirling tongues begins to increase until we're going at each other with a desperate urgency, ripping each other's clothes from our bodies, stumbling down the hallway, banging into the walls and groaning loudly. Our desperation is spiralling. A trail of clothes is left in our wake as we cause a hurricane with our urgency to get to the bedroom.

Jack doesn't push me to the bed as I expect. He slams me into the wall, our hands feeling everywhere they can reach. I'm lost in him, and I have no wish to find myself. I have to have him, and while he's ravishing me with such conviction and confidence, I have no hope of stopping this. And no desire to.

The forbidden is too irresistible. It has a dangerous allure and a compelling magnetism. And it's certainly going to inflict pain and anguish. It defies reason for me to willingly allow myself to be possessed like this. To surrender to a man who belongs to someone else. But I can't fight my heart. I want him. My sanity will be compromised no matter which road I take. I'm doomed.

Jack takes us to the floor, our naked bodies rubbing in all the right places, as he holds me beneath him, pinning my arms above my head. I shout, I writhe, I arch my back violently. His mouth is all over me, every kiss filled with fire, every lick sending surges of energy through me. His lips latch onto my nipple and suck hard, licking and nibbling at the tip.

'Jack!' I scream, bucking desperately under him. I'm being tortured in the best and worst ways possible.

He doesn't let up. Keeping my arms securely over my head, he crawls all over me, kissing me everywhere, his lips eventually finding their way to my mouth and devouring me. Deep plunges, wide swirls, harsh bites of my lips. I'm going out of my mind. Pulling the flesh of my bottom lip through his teeth, he opens his eyes and watches me coming undone as he releases my lip and kisses his way down the centre of my stomach. Our eyes lock and he brings my arms down to my tummy, holding both wrists in one hand on my abdomen so his mouth can reach . . .

'Oh God!' I fling my head back and snap my spine into a harsh arch, trying to yank my hands free. They're going nowhere. I try to relax, try to savour the indescribable pleasure. I look down at him, panting my way through it, the slick warmth of his tongue swirling far and wide sending me dizzy. I flop back and hold my breath, feeling the rush of pressure dropping fast into my sex.

'Jack!' I cry as my climax seizes me, tossing me into an oblivion of stars and white noise, my body violently vibrating under him. The pleasure goes on and on, ripping through me like the most powerful of tornadoes, knocking everything out of me. Everything – the guilt, the tormenting conscience, the ability to care about what I'm doing. It's all lost in a haze of Jack.

My body liquefies and I go lax on the floor while he laps lazily around my clitoris, sucking gently, easing me down. I feel utterly useless beneath him, my arms flopping above my head. I exhale on a moan, feeling him crawling up my body, until his lips are level with mine and he's exploring my mouth again, this time gently. I swallow his hums and breathe him into me, relishing his weight spread over me and his cock pulsing against my leg.

'How was it for you?' he asks as he nibbles his way across my mouth. I can't help but smile. It's probably misplaced, but, good Lord, I feel like I've had the pleasure of a million orgasms all at once, and during the process, my shaking world has aligned completely.

'Good,' I admit, nuzzling into the scruff at his neck. I've never felt so sated. Finding some strength, I drag my arms up and curl them around his shoulders, humming happily.

'Sounds like someone is satisfied,' he muses, pecking my lips one last time and pulling away.

'Is that a hint?' I ask, cocking an eyebrow at him.

'Speaking of hints . . .'

'Oh, your cute little note?'

He grins, the God-glorious grin that I haven't seen for too long. A grin that I've never seen on his face when he's been with his wife. I make him happy. 'You didn't take much notice, though, did you?'

'I was in shock.' My eyes fall to his neck, and my hand automatically lifts to ghost my finger across the faded marks.

Jack's smile is now sad, and he takes my hand from his neck, pulling it to his mouth and kissing my knuckles. 'She lashes out.' He looks so unaffected by it, and that's the worst thing of all. It's normal to him. This big, strapping man. I get a sudden vivid recollection of me swinging at him last night in my drunken state, and how angry he was. Ashamed of myself, I vow here and now to never let that happen again, no matter how frustrated I am. 'Why didn't you say anything?' I ask.

'Because when I'm with you, I'm free, Annie. I'm not tearing myself up inside wondering what the fuck went wrong with my marriage and why Stephanie is the way she is. I'm not obsessing about blame and where it falls. And I'm not trapped and miserable. I'm me again.'

My welling eyes fall from his handsome face. 'Why do you allow it?'

'What am I going to do? Hit her back? I'd kill her with one punch.'

'Leave her,' I whisper, my throat ragged and broken. The thought of her physically hurting him tears me up inside, no matter how capable he is. No matter how big and strong. He just has to accept it? 'Just leave her.' Tears build in my eyes, and Jack rolls into my side, propping himself up on an elbow.

He tenderly wipes them away, bringing his face down to mine. 'Don't cry for me.'

His gentle order has the reverse effect, and I start to sob, my face turning and hiding in his neck. How can he be so accepting of this? The thought of someone physically hurting him destroys me inside.

Jack forces me out, putting his body on top of mine, getting nose to nose with me. 'She doesn't hurt me, Annie. The only person in this world who can hurt me is *you*. Do you hear what I'm saying to you? I'm untouchable if I have you.' He starts to dot light kisses all over my wet face, wiping away the tears with his mouth.

'You have to leave her.' I reach over his shoulders and hold him to me, like I can protect him from her. Take him away from his nightmare.

'Trust me. When I can, I will.' He lifts his head and gazes down at me, brushing my hair from my wet face. 'You've given me a purpose. A real reason to get out. My own happiness wasn't enough to leave. It just wasn't worth the pain and backlash. Your happiness *is* enough, and I know I can make you happy. Just like I know how happy I can be with you.'

His spew of words hits me hard. Every single one of them. He doesn't just need to leave her, he wants to. For me. When he can, he will. 'When will the time be right?' I ask on a mere whisper, starting to grow concerned by what this *really* means.

It means people will know. It means *she'll* know.

'I don't know.' He gives me sorry eyes. 'A few weeks ago, before I met you, I'd have said never. Now, I will make sure I find the right time. But I have to tread carefully. And you have to trust me to do this the best way. Please, just give me time.'

What I should do now is walk away. Let him sort out that part of his life before I even *think* to continue this. That's what I *should* do. It doesn't mean that I can. 'Are you telling me you're going to leave your wife?' I ask again, if only for clarification. If only to hear him say it again.

'Yes,' he answers without a second's hesitation. 'I need to get out for my own sanity and health. I'm leaving her because I need there to be life left in me, life that I want to give to you. There's something still alive inside of me, Annie, and you've found it.'

I pull him down and cuddle him. I wanted him before I knew I couldn't have him. My want has only multiplied by a million since then, no matter how much guilt tries to mask it. I've never wanted something so badly that I'll willingly sacrifice my integrity to have it. I would never demand he leave his wife. That's his move to make when he thinks it's best to make it. In the meantime, I get some of him. I *need* some of him. Even if it's just for my own sanity. Nothing with Jack isn't an option.

'I'll take whatever you can give me for now.' It pains me to say it, but it's the truth. I have to finally face the fact that I'm falling for a married man. I've tried to run away and got nowhere. Not only because Jack won't let me, but because my heart won't either. He's asked me for time, and though I know most people will think I'm certifiably mad, I'm willing to give it to him, because he's worth the wait. I trust him. I don't want to make his life any more difficult than it already is.

I kiss his neck, tracing circles across his back, and stamp out the thoughts threatening to ruin the moment. Right now, he's mine. In this moment, he's mine.

'I trust you,' I whisper.

Moving back, he kisses me with the most incredible amount of meaning injected into it. 'Thank you,' he breathes.

He trails his lips across my face and I smile sadly. Because no matter how much I try to fool myself, a piece of Jack isn't what I want at all, and I know deep down that there will come a point when I can't make do with part of him. I just hope Jack finds whatever strength he needs to leave his wife before that time comes.

Chapter 13

We made love all day. Slow, soft and meaningful love. He looked down at me, our breath mingling, our hands exploring, as he drove into me firm and exact, over and over. It was blissful. It was beyond incredible. It left me dazed and struggling to keep my eyes open. Which is a good thing, because I didn't have the energy to disintegrate when he kissed me gently on the forehead before he left last night.

I fell into a deep slumber and dreamed of Jack. It was the most satisfying night's sleep I've ever had. The only thing that would have made it better would have been to have Jack wrapped around me the whole night through. But entering into this, I have to accept that *that* can never happen. It feels like a small price to pay after the time we've just spent together, full of acceptance and total devotion. Just a small price to pay. For now.

I feel full of life and energy as I shower. Strangely, there's an overwhelming sense of relief, like a weight has been lifted from my tired shoulders. Like I have someone else to help carry the burden of my choices with me.

I'm standing in the mirror looking at myself, kitted from top to toe in sportswear. My cheeks have a healthy glow, my dark hair is glossy and my light green eyes are sparkling brightly. And I have a delicious heaviness between my thighs. I feel good, and ignorant as it may seem, I don't question it.

I grab my iPod, load a playlist and hit the street. A run. I have no idea where the urge has come from, but I'm going to make the most of it while I have the drive. The sun is warm on my back as I make tracks towards Hyde Park, feeling fresh and rejuvenated. That may not be the case in a few miles, but for now my legs are working with little effort and my breathing is consistent and easy. It defies the fact that I haven't worked out in over a year. And I'm smiling. Above & Beyond's 'Sun & Moon' is pumping in my ear, spurring me on, as I race through the park, my focus set firmly forward. Fellow runners nod and return my smile as I continue to breathe steadily.

Jack is a constant vision in my mind, except now I'm not fighting to get him out. He's embedded in my brain, and I like him there. His grin, his sparkling eyes. His voice, his laugh, his cheeky banter. His passion for my work and his encouragement. Everything about him. Our moments have been just stolen pieces of time, but no matter how brief, they're still so incredibly powerful, the feelings lingering on, and I'm hoping that makes the time in between without him more manageable.

I smile and take a sharp right, running towards the Serpentine, the fresh morning air breezing across my skin. Something catches my attention out of the corner of my eye and I look across the grass to see Micky waving frantically at me. I pull the buds out of my ears and wave back.

'What the fuck's got into you?' he shouts, showing the sky his palms.

'Felt like a run!' I call, keeping up my pace.

He laughs loudly and then turns to the woman who's on her hands and knees in front of him, her long blonde hair skimming the grass. I smile like crazy when I see him drop to one knee and take her hips, looking over to me and fist-pumping the air. 'Tart,' I say to myself, following the path and heading up alongside him, watching as he manipulates the woman into various positions.

'Morning.'

'Shit!' I yelp, jumping mid-stride, looking up to see Jack running next to me. I blink rapidly when his shimmering beauty hits me like a right hook to the eye. Fucking hell; he looks otherworldly. My breathing that was perfectly controlled goes to shit. I'm breathless. 'What are you doing here?'

'I run every morning.' He performs a quick, expert turn and starts jogging backwards a few paces in front of me. 'But I've never had this amazing view before.' He puckers his lips and kisses the air.

I laugh through my laboured breathing, dropping my eyes to that lovely, huge, *solid* chest. 'Do you always run bare-chested?' I ask, ripping my stare away from the thrilling sight.

'Only when I'm trying to impress.' He turns back the right way, and I feel him look down at me. I peek out of the corner of my eye. He winks cheekily.

I grin. 'I'm impressed.'

'Me too,' he counters, taking a lazy trip down my body with equally lazy eyes. 'Really impressed.'

I suddenly feel more eyes on me and look across the grass to find Micky standing again, watching us warily. Shit. 'Micky's here,' I say, returning my focus forward and trying my hardest not to look guilty. Just a pleasant morning run with a colleague. The colleague who fucked me stupid. The colleague who is married. The colleague who I'm now having an affair with. 'Don't look.' I snap when I see Jack start to glance around. 'He will seriously lose the plot if he finds out about us.'

'Take a left up here,' he orders.

I look up to see the path forking up ahead and follow his instruction, peering over my shoulder to find Micky no longer in view. 'Jack, we can't be seen together,' I pant, now struggling like hell with my breathing, maybe assisted by a little panic.

He turns to me mid-stride and grabs me, swiping me from my feet and carrying me behind a tree, his hand slapped over my mouth. Once he has me pushed up against the bark, he removes his palm and replaces it with his mouth. I'm instantly consumed, matching his hungry kiss. My hands are on a mission, feeling every part of his bare chest. 'Hmmm, you taste fucking good, girl.'

I smile into his mouth and reach up to fist his hair. 'I'm sweating.'

'And I want to lick it all off.' Jack's tongue runs from my cheek to my ear and traces the shell, making me pant, shudder and push myself onto his mouth. He growls, circling his hips into my lower tummy. 'So fucking good.'

'You have a thing for licking me, don't you?'

He pulls back, a spectacular smile on his face. 'Are you objecting?'

'No.' He can lick me until I disappear for all I care.

He reaches forward and traces the bridge of my nose, looking at me fondly. 'What are you doing today?'

'Finalising some drawings, submitting an application, chasing decisions on another one.'

He stifles a yawn, glancing away, losing interest completely. 'Sounds riveting.'

'Hey!' I smack his arm, spiking the cutest chuckle.

He grabs my cheeks and squeezes them until my lips are pouting. Jack mirrors my protruding pout around a grin. 'I'm not sure how I feel about being with a woman who's potentially more talented than me.'

'Potentially?' I mumble through my squished mouth.

'Well.' He shrugs. 'The jury's still out over your bedroom skills.'

I gasp, disgusted, and Jack mimics it, totally taking the piss. I scowl at him, and he scowls right back. My nose wrinkles, and his wrinkles in return. I force my tongue through my lips, childishly sticking it out at him in a demonstration of how affronted I am. He grins and releases my cheeks, hauling me into his chest and cuddling me. 'I love your work ethic, for the record. Not many people can say they love their job. You're one of the lucky people in this world who get something more than money out of it.'

I return Jack's hug. 'And what about your job? Are you one of the lucky people?'

'I guess so,' he says into my hair. 'Though my work is more of a good distraction these days.' He releases me and fusses over my face for a few moments, ridding my sticky skin of hair. I'm not sure how to read that statement. So I don't.

'Ready?'

'Yes,' I assert, joining him when he starts to jog back to the main path. 'Act normal,' I say, knowing Micky is about to come into view again at any moment.

'Right,' Jack says sharply. 'How was your day yesterday?'

I throw him an incredulous look. 'What?'

'I'm making conversation.'

'Seriously?'

'Yes, I want to know how your day was.' He's hiding a smirk as he focuses forward, not indulging my narrowed eyes.

'Amazing,' I confess, deciding to go along with his playful banter. 'But I didn't get much work done. Yours?'

'I got *lots* of "work" done.' He grins. 'And it was the best day ever.'

I smile up at him and he looks down at me, his grey eyes the brightest I've ever seen them. The notion that I am the cause of such a beautiful sight does things to my heart that are beyond comprehension.

Puckering his lips, he kisses the air. 'I better go. Call you later, gorgeous.' He sprints off and I get the pleasure of his wet, naked back for too short a time before he disappears from view as I gradually slow my pace and come to a stop.

'What the hell did *he* want?' Micky asks, strolling across the grass towards me.

'Nothing.' I raise my arms in the air and stretch, dead set on nailing coolness.

'Is he bothering you?'

'No.'

'Then what did he want?'

'I bumped into him, that's all,' I say tiredly, dropping my palms and pushing them into the ground, looking up at him. 'It's done with, Micky. I already told you that.'

He's bristling like a threatened bear, but it doesn't stop him from pushing his palm into my back. 'Straighten your back,' he grumbles. 'If you're going to stretch, do it properly.'

'Your man-bun is wonky,' I quip, hissing when my hamstrings burn. 'That hurts!'

'Quit complaining.'

I unbend and stand up straight, tossing him a dirty look. 'Go and stretch your client.'

He frowns and looks towards the woman currently spread-eagled on the grass. 'I'm working on it.'

I laugh. 'Is that Charlie?'

'Yes.'

'You're losing your magic, Micky.'

He scoffs and loops his arm around my neck, hauling me in. 'I am not losing my magic.' He leads me back towards his client, roughing up my ponytail. 'And if I ever do, you must kill me.'

'That would be an injustice to female eyes everywhere.'

'True,' he agrees, releasing me when we reach his workout area. 'Charlie, this is Annie.'

She smiles coyly, her pretty face flushing. 'I've heard a lot about you.'

'I bet,' I laugh, backing away. 'I'll leave you guys to it. I have to get to work. Nice to meet you, Charlie.'

'And you!'

I flip Micky an approving look before turning and jogging home.

*

I glug back a pint of water and toss my iPod into the fruit basket before throwing the double doors open and breathing in some more air. I push my way through the leaves of the willow tree and land in the deckchair, stretching my legs while checking my phone. I have a text message from Jack. I open it quickly.

Running with a hard-on is fucking painful.

I laugh loudly and relax back in my chair, daydreaming for a few minutes as I think back over yesterday and this morning. Jack runs every morning, which means I might have to too. Will half an hour every day be part of our ongoing routine? I want to be grumpy about it, but I can't, not when it means that 1) I'll get to see Jack, and 2) I'll tone up in the process. We just might have to think about where we run to avoid being seen together. I start to punch out a reply to him, but I'm interrupted halfway through my message when my phone rings.

I don't recognise the number. 'Annie Ryan,' I announce when I answer.

'Miss Ryan, my name's Terrence Pink, CEO of Brawler's.'

'Oh, hello.' I sit up straight in my chair, wondering why a world-renowned tech company would be calling little old me. 'How can I help you?' I'm raging with curiosity.

'We're expanding, building new premises, and we've heard your name on the grapevine. I'm hoping we could meet to discuss.'

They've heard of my name? 'Of course.' I rush into the kitchen and grab my diary. 'When is convenient for you?'

'The sooner the better. Today?'

I wince. My day is packed, especially after yesterday when I achieved a great big fat zero in the studio. 'Could we do tomorrow?'

'I'm sorry; I know it's short notice, but we've already seen other people and hope to make a decision very soon so the project can move forward.'

I bite my lip and bite the bullet. This is too good an opportunity. 'Two o'clock?'

'Two o'clock it is. We're floor ten, 25 Churchill Place, Canary Wharf.'

I scribble it down. 'See you then.' I hang up and the message I'd half typed out in reply to Jack appears on my screen.

Morning sex would remedy . . .

But I delete it instead of finishing it and sending it. Because that would just be reminding him that there will be no morning sex in this relationship, and I don't want him to feel as grumpy as me at that notion. I pout, bringing my phone to my mouth and chewing the corner. No morning sex yet, but when? No snuggling in bed and simply being together, either. I stamp those thoughts away and run into my office ready to hit Google and research Brawler's in preparation for the meeting.

Chapter 14

I walk into the building that houses Brawler's, gazing around at the impressive space, not quite believing that I'm here. Everyone knows that Brawler's is the giant in the tech world. That they dazzle with their innovative approach to marketing and development. What I didn't know is that this project, the new offices, is a move being made after Brawler's announced they're launching a partnership with one of the world's largest social media platforms. To say I'm intimidated by this meeting would be a slight understatement. But, as I've reminded myself countless times, while their area of expertise is tech, mine is designing buildings. And that's what I'm here to potentially do.

I step inside the lift with a guy and scan the list of companies on the wall sign to the side.

'What floor?' he asks.

'Ten, please,' I answer, my scanning eyes freezing when I make a note of the companies that operate from floor ten. 'What?' I say out loud, my mouth going dry. I look up to see we're at floor eight already. 'Oh no,' I squeak, turning back to face the doors just as they slide open and reveal the biggest silver engraved sign saying JACK JOSEPH CONTRACTORS, above a sign that says BRAWLER'S. They share a floor?

'You okay, love?' the man asks, waiting for me to exit. No. No, I'm not okay.

I force myself out of the lift, looking cautiously around, not quite believing that I've found myself in Jack's office. It's modern, smart and impressive. Just like Jack.

I announce myself at Brawler's reception, then take a seat in the waiting area, unable to stop my eyes from flitting everywhere nervously. He might not be here. He might be out for a meeting. I'm scanning the space again, reaching up and loosening the floral tasselled scarf that I have wrapped around my neck. I feel like I'm suffocating. I can't deny I would love to see him, but I can't promise I'll be able to keep my hands to myself. Is he here?

And like he's heard me ask, a door across the waiting area opens and Jack walks out, fastening his suit jacket. Good Lord, he looks too delicious for his own good, his grey suit pristine, his tie perfectly knotted and his hair a sexy mess. Fucking hell. He looks straight at me, like he knew I'd be here, and then it occurs to me: he *did* know I'd be here.

Jack strides forward with purpose until he comes to a stop before my seated form. His hand comes up and cups his chin, stroking down his scruff as he stares at me. 'Annie,' he rasps, making my heart gallop and my tummy flutter. He presents his hand. 'Good to see you.'

I briefly close my eyes to gather myself. He needs to stop saying my name, and I really shouldn't entertain his prompt to make physical contact with him. I'm already struggling to cool down my rising temperature before I burst into flames at his feet. 'You too.' I push myself to my feet and place my hand in his, for no other reason than the receptionist will think it odd if I don't. I go stiff from head to toe when he locks me in his grasp, squeezing gently, his grey eyes dancing. 'Gotcha,' he whispers.

My mouth drops open a little, and I quickly and discreetly reclaim my hand and look away from him before I give myself away. 'Don't say that,' I warn seriously, at risk of self-combusting. I look up through my lashes and catch his mild grin. 'You knew I'd be here.'

'I recommended you.' He shrugs like it's nothing.

'Why would you do that?'

He leans forward, bringing his face close to mine. 'Because I wanted to lure you here under false pretences so I can fuck you over my desk.'

My mouth falls open in shock and my panicked eyes quickly scope the surroundings. 'I should slap you,' I retort indignantly when I've ensured no one's in earshot.

He laughs softly. 'I recommended you because you are an amazing architect and I just *know* you can pull this off. Plus, my company will be doing the build so it means I'll get to see you more.'

I narrow suspicious eyes on him. 'So it's not a *completely* selfless move?'

'We're all winners.' He signals me down the corridor on a cheeky grin that I can't help but match. I can't believe he's done this. 'We're in Brawler's boardroom. Last door on the right.' I take the lead, following Jack's extended arm. 'And after the meeting, I want you on my desk,' he whispers into my ear, making my shoulders roll and a shudder travel down my backbone.

'You're coming into the meeting?' I ask, my alarm growing. I have to be all professional in front of him? Jesus, I've been trying to do that since I found out he's Colin's contractor, and I've not been very successful.

'I'm coming into the meeting.'

Oh God. 'Please don't look at me.'

'You're asking the impossible, Annie,' he says seriously, slowing to a stop when the lady from reception appears, looking apologetic.

'Mr Joseph, your wife is on the line.'

I nearly dislodge a back tooth with the force of my bite, discreetly looking at Jack. His face definitely takes on an edge of unease. 'Tell her I'm in a meeting.' He clears his throat and overtakes me, opening the door to the boardroom and gesturing me in.

I wander past Jack, glancing up at him. He smiles, but it's

small and strained. I hate that just the mention of his wife wipes away the sparkle in his eyes that I love so much. It makes me want to take him and run away, to get him away from the source of his misery. And now my misery too.

The boardroom is big, a huge table taking up nearly all the space, with at least thirty executive chairs positioned around it. There's a projector screen on the far wall and a sideboard loaded with glass bottles of water and platters of cakes. Richard is sitting at the table, along with three other suited men and a woman.

'Annie, you know Richard,' Jack says. 'And this is Terrence, who I believe you spoke with.'

Terrence nods, his eyes glimmering at me as he stands and offers his hand. 'Pleasure to meet you, Annie,' he says around a big, toothy grin. 'Jack's told us wonderful things about you.'

I laugh, slightly uncomfortable, feeling my cheeks flush. I bet he has. 'Nice to meet you, Terrence,' I reply, accepting his hand. His delighted eyes take in my form, and I look at Jack when I hear a low, throaty growl emanate from his direction. His eyes, narrowed to slits, are trained on Terrence.

'These are my partners Dick and Seth, and their PA Lydia.' Terrence motions to the two men seated next to him, and then to the woman.

I shake hands with them all and take a seat as Lydia pours everyone a glass of water and sets some plates and the cakes between us on the table. Her smile is friendly and her fifties-style glasses suit her heart-shaped face perfectly.

Jack slips his jacket off and hangs it on the back of his chair – the chair directly opposite me. He lowers to the seat and begins to tap his pen on the leatherbound writing pad before him.

He smiles, the smile that's so dazzling and genuine it makes me smile too. 'You've got this,' he mouths across the table.

My nerves vanish just like that, and the fact that he's here suddenly fills me with comfort and ease. I've just fallen for him a little bit more.

'Guys.' Jack looks to the men from Brawler's. 'We're working with Annie for the first time on a new art gallery in Clapham.' He pushes the drawings across the table to them, and they all look down with hums of praise.

Like he's read my thoughts, he glances towards me, a secret smile hiding behind his professional front. 'She's diverse, hugely talented and passionate about what she does.'

I melt all over the chair, and Jack breathes in, holding my eyes for perhaps a moment longer than should be acceptable for business associates. 'She won't disappoint.' He clears his throat and realigns his focus. 'I assure you.'

I just stare across the table in silent awe, watching his mouth move as he speaks. He looks so fucking sexy, relaxed back in his chair, reeling off words that are making me fall harder and harder for him. He recommended me. He set this up, gave me this amazing opportunity.

He takes his phone from his pocket and spins it in his hand. 'So, guys.' Jack waves his mobile between me and the people from Brawler's. 'Over to you. This is a long-term project. We need to get off to the best start.'

His grey eyes meet mine fleetingly, and I frown across the table at him, my head tilting. *Long-term. Best start.* My brain threatens to go off at a tangent, but I quickly rein it in. I can't allow myself to think beyond today.

I cough and realign my focus, set on nailing my meeting. 'So, tell me about the project,' I say, giving the other people in the room my undivided attention. 'Your partnership with a giant social media company means expansion.'

'Yes. We've acquired a plot of land in Blackfriars,' Terrence says, pushing over a portfolio. 'It has planning permission for a ten-storey building, our new home.'

I open the folder and scan the details – square footage,

surrounding buildings, etc., happy to see other modern buildings in close proximity to the space. 'You want to stand out.' I state it as a fact, because I know it is. Brawler's has an ego as big as its share prices. Fucking huge.

Terrence smiles. 'Can you make us stand out?'

'You mean make you the envy of every company operating within the area?' I ask, closing the file.

I hear Jack laugh softly and Richard smiles, as well as Terrence. 'If that's how you'd like to put it.' Terrence links his fingers and lays them across his broad tummy, his smile widening.

I return it. 'No point beating around the bush, is there, Terrence?'

Jack coughs and my eyes shoot across the table, finding him clenching his big hand around his tumbler of water, and as he lifts his glass to his mouth, he glances at me, his lips straight with displeasure.

'Your top priorities for the new home of Brawler's?' I ask, pulling my attention back to the team of people that I'm trying to sell myself to. He's feeling threatened, and while it's quite an amusing sight, I can't let it distract me.

'Light and space,' Dick answers. 'Clinical, clean and modern. When it comes to the interior people getting involved, we plan on having open working spaces to connect the entire company, but with clear distinction between departments. That gives you a good indication of the theme we're going for. We're excited to see what you come up with.'

I smile and start making notes, my mind going into overdrive and building Brawler's in my head as I sit here. 'Outside space?'

'Definitely. Take indoors outdoors.'

I visualise a courtyard in the centre of the building connecting all four sides, every floor visible from every part of the structure. 'Do you have any leaning towards a sustainable energy-efficient ethos?'

'Of course.'

I nod, happy with his answer. 'I'd need to research the surroundings in regard to landscaping and orientation, et cetera.'

'We can arrange a site meeting, no problem,' Terrence says. 'Now, let me ask you a few questions, Annie.'

'Fire away.' I smile and get ready to sell myself hard.

I'm positively buzzing once the Brawler's people have shown us out of their boardroom. 'Great job, Annie,' Richard says as he wanders off. 'They'd be stupid not to give you the opportunity.'

'Thanks, Richard.' I turn, ready to say a professional goodbye to Jack, but just as I draw breath, my arm is seized and I'm pushed down the corridor urgently. 'What are you doing?' I gasp, my cautious eyes darting warily.

'We need to debrief.'

'We do?'

'Oh, we do.'

My body is instantly singing with need. And my mind is racked with worry. 'Jack, what if someone sees us?'

He opens a door, pushes me inside and locks it behind us. I swing around and find Jack yanking the buckle of his belt undone as he stalks towards me. He looks coiled with desperation and ready to explode, and my body is responding – my heart thumping, my tummy twisting and a pulse kicking between my thighs. I gasp when he grabs me around the waist and carries me to a desk. He sits me on the wood and pushes me back, lifts my dress and spreads my thighs. Oh fuck! He moves in and cups my cheeks, sealing our lips and kissing me hungrily. My body temperature rockets, and I'm instantly in the game, feeling my way to the top of his trousers and unfastening them.

'That was the most painful hour of my fucking life,' he mumbles, licking and biting his way up my cheek.

'More painful than running with a hard-on?' I ask, pushing

his trousers down his thighs before slipping my hand into the top of his boxers. I grab his cock and squeeze, revelling in the heat and hardness of his smooth flesh.

He jerks on a groan, releasing my lips and resting his forehead against mine, blinking slowly. 'I'm in pain whenever we're not touching,' he says softly, dragging his thumb across my swollen bottom lip. His eyes close as I draw my palm down his erection, his forehead becoming wet on mine. 'Have you any idea how you make me feel?'

I smile on the inside, wondering if he feels as alive as he makes *me* feel. 'I think I do,' I reply, rolling my thumb around the pulsing head of his cock, spreading the moisture.

His hand comes down and grips mine for a second before he pulls it away and hauls me to the edge of the wood. 'Are you going to let me fuck you on my desk?' He pushes my knickers to the side and nudges at my opening teasingly. The heat is almost unbearable.

'Do I have a choice?' My head drops back, my hands weaving through the hair at his nape as he pushes his way inside me.

'No,' he admits on a long exhale, edging in that little bit more.

'God, that feels good,' I breathe.

Jack does this to me. He makes me forget everything, consumes me to a point where I forget my name. He brings his hands to my arse and tugs me forward until we're locked together, deepening our connection. My head falls forward, my forehead finding his for support. Slowly he widens his stance, pulling out before plunging forward again, repeating his move in a steady, meticulous flow. The relentless pleasure of him stroking my inner walls leaves no space for anything but that. Indescribable, mind-numbing pleasure. I lock my ankles around his lower back.

'Feel good, baby?' His soft words are a caress, and I nod against him, unable to catch a breath to voice my answer. Jack mirrors my nod, swaying into me while his palms cup my bottom and pull me gently forward, meeting his advances perfectly every time. We're so close, the clothes between us not taking even a tiny bit away from our intimacy.

I let my hands roam across his damp neck, slipping across his skin, moulding and squeezing softly. 'You're pulsing,' he whispers, obviously feeling me clenching him. 'You'll have to be quiet when you come, Annie.'

My breathing becomes erratic as the signs of my orgasm steam forward. 'Kiss me,' I demand, pushing my lips to his and forcing my tongue into his mouth, urgency overtaking me.

'Slowly,' he orders, sweeping through my mouth delicately, matching his drives. My legs begin to tense around his waist, my back straightening and pushing my front harder into his. He nips at the tip of my tongue, and then buries his face in my neck. I take his lead and do the same, sinking my face into his shirt where his shoulder meets his neck, panting vigorously. We're locked in a cuddle, his arms now wrapped around my waist, mine around his shoulders, as he thrusts us both over the edge. 'Fuck,' he mumbles into me, freezing and holding himself deep.

My moan of release is muffled and long, my body convulsing in his hold, the pressure draining right out of me on delicious, satisfying pulses. I'm clinging to him tightly, hiding in his neck, loving the feel of us locked so tightly together. 'Oh wow,' I breathe, my face sticky with sweat. I feel him jerking a little on a silent laugh, squeezing me to the point I can't breathe.

'That was a very welcome mid-afternoon pick-me-up,' he says, making me smile. I pat his back and ease out of his hold, wincing when he slips free. He places a light kiss on the corner of my mouth as he breathes in, and I gaze around the impressive space, taking in his office.

'So this is where you work?'

'This is where I work,' he confirms, smiling at me as he

releases me and sorts his trousers out before handing me a tissue.

'Thanks.' I slide off his desk, grimace as I wipe between my thighs and pull my knickers and dress back into place. I look at the tissue with a frown and Jack laughs, taking it from my hand and throwing it into the bin next to his desk. I grab my slouchy bag and sling it over my shoulder. 'This is all a bit risky.'

He almost scowls, his lovely grey eyes narrowing a touch. 'It was either here or on the boardroom table in front of everyone.' He buckles his belt and steps towards me, smiling at my blushing cheeks as he runs the pad of his thumb over one. 'Though Terrence might have enjoyed that.'

I press my lips together. 'Did you growl, Jack Joseph?'

'He fancies you. I'll be keeping a close eye on him.' He plants a chaste kiss on my lips and starts to walk me to the door, but we both come to an alarmed stop when the handle starts jiggling. I look up at him, hoping he might clue me in on who it might be so I can assess how panicked I need to be. He looks blank.

'Jack?' Stephanie's yell hits me like a bullet to my temple. His mouth drops open. I begin to shake. 'Jack, you in there?'

'Oh fuck,' he breathes, staring at the door as the handle continues to rattle.

I clench my eyes shut and try to breathe through my panic.

'This way,' he grates, taking my arm and pulling me across his office towards another door. 'I'll get rid of her. Give me two minutes.'

'We work together, Jack,' I whisper-hiss. 'We could just be having a meeting.'

'With the door locked?' he asks, tugging me along. He's right: that would look so dodgy, and actually, I don't want to face Stephanie. I'll probably shake before her with nerves, guilt and a million other things.

He pulls the door open and ushers me inside. To complete darkness. I swing around and glare at him. 'A fucking cupboard?' I hiss, outraged, but unable to refuse what he's suggesting.

He gives me a pained face – a sorry face – before he shuts the door and I'm alone in the dark. Fucking brilliant.

'Jack?' I hear Stephanie shout again, and then his phone starts ringing. 'I know you're in there.'

I suck in a breath in an attempt to keep silent. I hear his office door swing open. 'Hey,' Jack greets her, super-chirpy. And guilty.

'What's going on?' Stephanie sounds affronted, and I wilt on the spot, expecting her to come charging through the door that's keeping me out of sight at any moment.

'It's chaos around here today,' he reels off with ease. 'I was trying to get some peace so I can work through some figures.'

I sag against the wall.

'I see,' I hear Stephanie say, and in my mind's eye she's gazing around his office suspiciously. My anxiety nearly chokes me as I remain deathly still, dying on the inside.

'What brings you here?' Jack asks, his footsteps getting louder. He's walking to his desk? *Good Lord, don't lead her this way!*

'It's been such a stressful morning!' she wails.

'What's happened?' he practically sighs. There's no concern in his tone at all.

'I was supposed to have lunch with Tessa.' Stephanie's voice gets louder too, telling me she's following Jack towards his desk. I close my eyes even though I'm in darkness. A chair creaks. She's sat herself down. 'And she cancelled!'

'And that's awful?' Jack breathes.

'Well, yes,' Stephanie snipes harshly. 'She said she had an appointment that she forgot about, but I know she's having lunch with her new friend from yoga.'

'Stephanie, she's probably cancelled because she really does have an appointment.'

'I'm not stupid, Jack. Her new friend doesn't like me. She wants Tessa all to herself.'

I frown, opening my eyes and scanning the blackness of my confined space. Stephanie sounds completely unreasonable.

There's a brief silence lingering, and in that time I build a mental image of her staring at Jack across his desk. 'So what do you want me to do?' Jack asks simply.

'Well, I don't know.' Stephanie huffs. 'Tessa's *my* friend, and I'm not going to let some interloper push me out.'

My mind twists as my wide eyes stare into the darkness. Whoever Tessa is, I feel sorry for her.

I hear Jack breathe in, clearly trying to gather some patience. 'She's allowed more than one friend.'

'No she's not, Jack. It's always been me and her.'

'Stephanie, I haven't got time to babysit your friendships.'

'No, you don't have time for anything other than work, do you?'

'How else am I going to pay for the life to which you've become accustomed, Stephanie? Get yourself a job. Something to do other than worry about who your friends are friends with.'

She gasps, truly horrified. 'Me? Work? I don't think so. What would people think?' I stare at the door, flummoxed. 'Anyway,' she goes on, that obviously the end of that, 'I was thinking you can finish work early. We'll have dinner. Somewhere nice.'

She sounds hopeful. I close my eyes, and as much as I don't want to, I let the flood of guilt wash over me and scrub at my skin relentlessly. Because no matter which way you look at this, what I'm doing is wrong. What Jack is doing is wrong. How we're feeling is wrong. A harsh dose of reality has just been rammed down my throat. I hope it chokes me. I deserve it. I look around my prison, feeling hopeless and deplorable and immoral.

'Sure,' Jack answers. 'That would be nice.'

'Great!' She sounds so happy despite the lack of enthusiasm in Jack's voice.

A knife wedges itself in my chest and twists repeatedly. And I accept the agony. Because I deserve it. But I'm not delusional. Knowing you're doing something so terribly wrong doesn't make it easy to stop.

Chapter 15

I snuggle down on the couch under my blanket and stare at the wall. I'm in hell and I'm in heaven. I'm flying and I'm drowning. I can't walk away from him. It's that simple, if fucking horrendously complicated. Maybe the guilt is something I'll just have to get used to. At least the guilt tells me I still have a conscience. It's a small consolation, and maybe a little irrelevant, since I don't plan on clearing it. Clearing my conscience means no Jack, and no Jack isn't an option. I've tumbled hard, fast and furiously for him. Unstoppably. I've finally fallen for a man – a forbidden man. A man I shouldn't have.

In an attempt to stop my mind from dwelling on my fuck-up of a situation, I grab my laptop and try to focus on work. I get into my stride, researching the area of Blackfriars where Brawler's have bought their land and making endless notes, my vision for their new building getting clearer as I work.

When I hear a light rapping at the door, I check the time, surprised to see I've had my head down for nearly three hours. Pulling the door open, I find Jack looking anxious, and he visibly deflates before my eyes as he takes me in.

'Aren't you supposed to be somewhere?' I ask as I hold the door open.

'Are you okay?' There's no umbrage lacing his tone after my reminder that he has a romantic dinner planned with his wife.

I shake my head, my bottom lip trembling. This is something else I promised myself. I told myself that I wouldn't cry on him from now on, but I feel too fraught, hopeless and exhausted to fight it off. I was on cloud nine, being worshipped by Jack on his desk, and then I was in the deepest depths of hell, locked in a cupboard in his office wrestling with my conscience. The conflict is wearing me down already. A lone tear tumbles down my cheek and splashes my arm. 'I'm sorry,' I whimper feebly, looking away from him. He looks beaten, as exhausted and hopeless as I do.

'God, Annie.' He comes to me, closing the door behind him, and wraps his arms around my shoulders, pulling me into his chest. I know it shouldn't, but his warmth and closeness eases me, makes me feel safe and untouchable. As though any trauma I endure is worth it if I get to have him holding me after. He kisses the top of my hair, breathing into it. 'It's me who should be sorry. I never should have risked putting you in that situation.'

Maybe he's right, but I didn't refuse when he dragged me to his office. I didn't say no or fight him off. Snatching moments with him here and there whenever I can is how it needs to be, and that was a moment. An amazing moment . . . until his wife turned up. 'Where's Stephanie?' I ask quietly.

'At her parents'.' He pulls away from me and takes my hand, leading me into the kitchen. At her parents'? What happened to dinner with her husband?

'Sit down,' Jack orders gently, guiding me to a chair. I watch as he fills the kettle and boils it, finding his way around my kitchen with ease. As if he belongs here. With me.

He takes a seat and slides a cup of tea towards me. I smile my thanks, wrapping both palms around the mug.

'Talk to me,' he says gently.

'What do you want me to say?'

'Tell me what you're thinking.'

I look away from him, trying to escape his probing, but he reaches across the table and takes my chin, forcing me back. When he gives me high, expectant eyebrows, I lamely shrug.

'Annie, I understand that this is hard for you.'

'Do you?' I ask.

'Of course I do. You're a gorgeous, young, single woman. You could go out tonight and have your pick of the thousands of men out there.'

'I don't want any of the thousands of men out there,' I admit quietly, spelling it out loud and clear.

'You want me?'

I look at him carefully, wondering where he's taking this. Is he asking me to demand he leave his wife right this minute? I can't do that. Call me stupid, but he has to make that move himself. 'I don't understand where you're going with this.'

'Do you want me?'

'Yes.' I don't hesitate.

Jack nods, relieved, and squeezes my hand. 'I just needed to hear you say it again.' He swallows, and I don't like the deep breath he draws, like he's psyching himself up to tell me something. 'I didn't want to burden you with every crappy detail of my shit, Annie, but I'm scared to death that you're going to talk yourself into leaving me.'

Every crappy detail? I don't like the sound of this. Besides, I know enough. 'I think the less I know the better,' I protest, desperate to keep my connection with his wife, his life beyond me, as limited as possible.

His face is pleading with me. 'I need you to understand, Annie.'

This time I don't protest, seeing his need plain and clear.

He sighs, slumping back in his chair. 'I was doing so well building up my business. Stephanie's father was one of my first clients, and I met her during the project.' He shrugs. 'She was nice enough. Her father was relentless in his attempts to get us together. He was a valuable client with a huge ego. Stephanie and I dated, and it wasn't long before she started pushing for marriage. My business was the perfect excuse to put that off. I told her I wanted a more solid foundation, to get at break-even point. I was hoping to buy myself some time, because I didn't know what I wanted. I wasn't sure she was the right woman for me. Then her father offered up cash for investment and . . .' He shakes his head. 'Well, problem solved. I realise now how spineless I was. I'd be where I am now even without Stephanie's father's money. It all ran away with me.' He smiles, but there's a sad edge to it. It breaks my heart, for no other reason than he's clearly full of regrets. I can't help feeling like his saviour in a weird, fucked-up kind of way.

'So you married her.'

He swallows and looks down into his mug. 'I married her. I got caught up in the arrangements, convincing myself I was doing what was right. I knew I'd made a mistake only a few months later. I paid her father back the money he lent me, but it was too late to give his daughter back. Her temper, her controlling nature, her spending habits. My business became my escape. Escape from the suppression, control and . . .' He drifts off and takes a deep breath. 'And my wife. There's no happy medium with her. There's no bearable middle ground. She's done . . .'

'She's done what?' I press, not liking the internal battle he's clearly having trying to tell me. 'Tell me, Jack. She's done what?'

He looks away, obviously gathering strength from somewhere. He looks beaten. 'I didn't want to give you the dirty details.' He gives me his eyes again, and I see a million problems in them. A million woes. I know I'm going to hate what I hear.

He must read the questions in my eyes, because he continues without my prompt. 'I've left her before.'

My mouth falls open. 'And you went back?'

'Yes, after I'd picked her up from the hospital.'

I frown, not understanding.

'She took a knife to her wrist.'

'Oh my God!' I gasp, recoiling in my chair. 'That's emotional blackmail, Jack!'

'Maybe. I might not love the woman, but I don't wish her harm.' He slumps back in his chair, scrubbing his palms down his suddenly tired face. 'I didn't want to tell you because I know it'll play havoc with your conscience. It would just be another reason for you to leave me.'

Play havoc with my conscience? Is he serious? Because there's not enough playing havoc with it already? My heart sinks. 'You're trapped,' I whisper. *We're* trapped. There's no way out. Stephanie has a hold on him and he can't leave her because of what she might do to herself. And I wouldn't want him to. That would make me inhuman, and despite everything I've done, all of my wrongs, I'm not a wicked person. I don't wish her harm, either. I couldn't live with myself.

Jack looks at me, and I see the torment in his eyes. And the guilt. It's still there. Guilt for feeling like this. Guilt for not loving his wife. He grabs my hands with force, gritting his teeth. '*You* make me happy,' he grates. 'So fucking happy.' He's getting worked up, and it's so upsetting to see how frustrated he is. How hopeless he feels. His wife knows just what to do to keep him. Because it's worked before.

I hold on to my emotions as best I can. My situation hasn't changed. It's the same, but the stakes have been raised. I can't imagine what Stephanie will do if she finds out about us . . . which means I have to ensure that she doesn't.

I feel the tears of despair getting the better of me and use every scrap of strength I have to keep them at bay. I won't be walking away. Not before, and most definitely not now.

He promised me he wouldn't let me go again if the Fates ever brought me back to him. Well, they did bring me back, and they brought me back for a reason. I can't control my feelings for him. I can't stop them. He's supposed to be mine. I need to free him from his nightmare, not for my own selfish reasons, but because he doesn't deserve this. He should have what he wants, and if I am everything that he wants, then I have to help him have me.

'We will be together, Annie,' he vows. 'No matter what.'

I get up from my chair and walk around to him, putting myself on his lap and showing him where I'm at. With him. Always with him. And I believe him. We *will* be together. But at what cost?

Chapter 16

Four months later . . .

I never thought I'd be the kind of person to settle for second best, and only having a piece of Jack is second best. But it's a sacrifice I've had to make for now. A sacrifice that I've learned to cope with until we're both ready to face the shit storm that'll break when he leaves her.

In the meantime, we snatch moments here and there, meeting in hotel rooms on the odd afternoon and running together in the morning. The runs mean no touching, which is hard, but mostly I just love to be with him. To talk and laugh and forget reality, even for just half an hour.

It's a constant challenge to keep our relationship secret at work – the looks that pass between us, the desperation to barge everyone out of our paths and throw ourselves at each other, damn anyone who's watching. The sneaky touches, the private jokes. I loved my job before. Now, with Jack by my side on the projects we're working on together, it's truly amazing. I've found I seek his counsel. I ask him for his opinions and whether ideas I have can work. Knowing it's Jack who is bringing so many of my ideas to life makes them more than *just* a project. They're now all part of our story. We're building more than just feelings and love.

I won the contract with Brawler's. Jack made sure of it, singing my praises at every opportunity. I wasn't about to let him down. The drawings were passed with only a few minor amendments, and he made a point of delivering the news before Brawler's did. He called me while I was on my way to a meeting, and hearing how excited he was for me made me cry. Tears trickled down my cheeks as I stood at the entrance of Warren Street station. It's my biggest project to date, and a huge addition to my portfolio. I always seem to be buzzing these days . . . until I think about *her* and the dirt tarnishing my happiness.

There's been no mention of what happens next, and when. When Jack and I are together, we tend not to focus on depressing subjects . . . like his wife. Like how his day has been. I don't need to ask. I see it on his face for a fleeting second every time I see him, before he breathes in deeply and throws his arms around me. And in that moment, everything is better again. I'm following Jack's lead, trusting him . . .

Because I'm so hopelessly in love with him. I can't make this any harder for him than it already is.

As much as I try not to, I've become more and more dependent on Jack, how he makes me feel, the encouragement and support he gives me. The devotion he lavishes me with too. But he's not wholly mine. I've promised myself never to give him that ultimatum. I won't make demands and throw my weight around. He deals with that enough already. Besides, my fucked-up inner self never wants him to have the opportunity in our future to throw the words *I left my wife for you!* in my face. Call me stubborn. Call me nonsensical. I don't care what. Maybe I'm a glutton for punishment. Or maybe I'm protecting whatever shreds of integrity I have left.

I've managed to keep the fact that I've fallen in love with a married man from my friends. They wouldn't understand. I've seen the reactions of people who have found out about affairs. They tarnish each and every adulterer with the same brush. I accept that many affairs are based on nothing more than sex – something exciting and daring in a life of boredom and discontent. But what about the people who meet that little bit too late and share something special like Jack and I do? Are we supposed to let that person pass on by, turn away from someone who finds your soul and kisses it?

I know in my heart of hearts that Jack is my soul mate. He's the missing piece of me. Without him now, I'd be lost. It's as simple as that. Call it wrong. Call it sinful. I can't turn my back on the man I love. I can't do it to him, and I can't do it to myself. That's my reality. A reality I now accept.

I've been busy keeping up with all my projects. Today I'm on Colin's site overseeing the installation of my spectacular glass roof. Each individual pane of glass has been cut in France and shipped across the Channel. I'm praying they've made it here without any damage, and as I stand on the street watching the lorry rumble up the road towards us, I frown. 'I thought we specified a HIAB lorry,' I say, looking at one of Jack's men, Bill, standing next to me. He's a crabby old sod, but as Jack reminds me daily when I gripe about him, he's a good worker and he knows what he's doing.

'The HIAB broke down at Dover.' He makes his way towards the lorry, guiding it down the narrow street.

'Great,' I mutter, following him. 'Then we need to leave the panes on the lorry until the crane gets here.'

'No can do, love.'

'Yes can do,' I argue indignantly. 'Those glass panes cost a fortune!'

He ignores me and whistles, getting the attention of the driver of a small forklift. 'Around the back, mate!'

'You are not moving my roof with that thing.' I gawk at Bill, between panic and anger. 'And where's my fucking crane?' I shout, losing my shit.

'Caught in traffic in Westminster,' Bill says, unperturbed by my hissy fit.

'Bill. I don't think you're hearing me.' I calm my tone and try to reason with him. 'This roof is special.'

'And I don't think you're hearing *me*, Annie,' he argues

back, calmer than me, as the delivery vehicle comes to a stop. 'This lorry is blocking the road and causing anarchy. The crane could be hours. We need to get those panes off and clear the road.'

I look up at the packaged glass, praying to every transportation God there is that it's all still in one piece. If the roof has to be reordered, it'll blow the schedule *and* budget to pieces. 'If this goes wrong, the haulage firm will seriously wish they'd never met me.' I'm speaking hypothetically, obviously, since the haulage company hasn't *actually* met me.

Bill laughs a big belly laugh. 'Have faith.' He pulls on his safety gloves. 'Up!' he yells to his forklift driver.

I watch with bated breath as the first pane gets negotiated from the back of the lorry, a dozen men spread around the sheet to control it as it's shifted to the side of the pavement. 'You're just going to dump them there?' I ask incredulously. 'On the side of the road like a pile of trash?' Oh shitting hell, this isn't good.

'Where else do you suggest we put them?'

'On the fucking roof!'

'I don't think the crane is gonna reach from Westminster, love.'

I yell, frustrated, and grab my phone, dialling the plant hire firm. 'Annie Ryan,' I announce, stomping over to the first pane as it's lowered to the ground. 'I should've had a crane in Clapham two hours ago and it isn't here.'

'It's stuck in West—'

'I know it's stuck in Westminster,' I say quietly, my jaw tense. 'But that doesn't help me, does it?'

'I can't control traffic in the city, sweetheart.'

'Don't "sweetheart" me. What time did it leave the depot?' There's silence, and I scowl down the line. 'And don't fob me off with traffic jams when you failed to dispatch with enough time to make it to the site.' I know how these hire companies operate. 'I have a bespoke glass roof blocking the road. I need to get this roof on by the end of the day, and if that doesn't happen, I'll be heading your way.' I hang up before he gives me any attitude, wincing as I watch Bill pull back some of the protective packaging that's keeping my roof safe. 'Tell me it's in one piece,' I beg.

'One down, three to go.' He turns a smile onto me, and I bring my hands together in front of my face and look to the sky. Then jump when I feel someone at my ear. 'Site safety first, Annie. Where's your hard hat?' Jack's voice wipes away ninety per cent of my stress, even if it's slightly scolding.

'I'm having a disaster with the roof.' I turn around to face him, scanning the surrounding area for peeking eyes, so I know how *friendly* I can be. Just when I think the coast is clear, I spot Richard wandering down the street, a definite look of interest on his face. I step back and swallow, returning my eyes to Jack. He's spotted Richard too, and has also moved back a step.

'Where's the crane?' Jack asks, clearing his throat.

'Stuck in Westminster.'

Out of the corner of my eye, I see Richard chuck something in the skip and make his way back to the building.

Jack sags a little when he's out of sight. 'I've fucking missed you this week,' he declares, sounding a little despondent. As always when he seems so worn down, I stop and wonder what he's had to contend with to make him sound so disheartened. But only for a second, because I try not to think about his wife and focus on the fact that I can make Jack feel better. It's been a long, busy week for both of us, except we haven't been busy with each other, either at work or privately. It's positively sucked. It's not really that long, but millions of years too. That's a problem I'm coming to fear now. I want him every day. Every hour. Every minute. 'Can you make it to the St James's Hotel for four thirty?' he asks hopefully.

'Yes,' I confirm, as if there would be any other answer. 'I'll climb up on top of this extension and get the roof on myself if I have to.'

He laughs lightly, the low, sexy sound, as always, bringing a huge smile to my face. Jack's laughs are like melted chocolate – smooth and addictive. I can't get enough of them. 'No need.' He claps his hands loudly and whistles to Bill, pointing down the road.

I look over my shoulder and gasp. 'My crane!' I screech, watching it round the corner up ahead. 'My crane is here!'

'Let's get this roof on, baby,' Jack says quietly, striding off towards the crane.

I grin to myself, watching him fly into authoritative action, shouting orders as he goes. God, what I would do to have him alone right this minute. I look down at the screen of my phone and start to count down the minutes to four thirty.

I run up the steps of the hotel, nodding to the bellboy as I pass, checking my phone for the room number Jack sent me. When I reach the door, I knock as desperately as I'm feeling, and then start patting down my hair and brushing down my black shift dress. I don't get nearly enough time to sort myself out after rushing here. The door swings open, Jack seizes my wrist and yanks me inside, slamming the door behind him. I yelp, startled, as I'm hauled into him. I'm yet to see him properly because everything is a blur from the speed of my movements.

'You're two minutes late.' He snatches my bag and tosses it aside, then dips and grabs me under my thighs, pulling me up to his body. I yelp again, but it quickly transforms into a giggle when he runs through the sitting area and launches us into the air.

'Jack!' I scream, delirious, sinking my nails into his shoulders, which I now note are naked. We land on the softest bed I've ever been in, and his mouth is immediately on mine. I haven't had the chance to indulge in his face yet, nor appreciate the fact that he's naked, but when I find his lips on mine, I let the losses slide. I coil every limb around him and kiss him with everything I have, filling my sense of smell with his scent. I sink into the mattress on a happy sigh, shifting my palms to his bristly cheeks and holding his face firmly.

'Damn, I've missed this,' he says into my mouth, moving his lips to my cheek and pecking his way up to my ear.

I flex my hips, feeling his erection push into my thigh. 'I can tell.' He bites my earlobe and gets himself to his knees, collecting my arms from around his neck and shoving them above my head, holding them there, his torso suspended over me. And now I have his face. His grey eyes could have fireworks exploding in them, and his smile breaks records in the brightest category.

'Hello,' he says simply, though low and husky and drenched with longing. Just one simple word.

We stare at each other for the longest time, Jack suspended above me, his thighs straddling my tummy, his hands holding my wrists down. And we just grin at each other, both happy to admire each other for a while. When he raises his eyebrows, I raise mine. When he teasingly pushes his groin into my tummy, I reciprocate by flexing my hips up. And when he seductively licks his lips, I lick mine. Both of our smiles stretch wider.

'Well done with the roof, baby,' he says, keeping me restrained.

I smile. 'Doesn't it look fab?'

'Amazing.'

'But I didn't come to talk about roofs.' I make it clear. 'How long have I got you?'

'How long do you want me?'

My eyes narrow, and the word *forever* tickles the end of my tongue, waiting to drop out. But I hold it back, unwilling to spoil our precious time together with the ache of the unknown. Besides, I'm certain he knows already. 'Long enough to ravish you.'

He nods a little. I think it's in understanding, not only to my voiced answer, but to the answer I'm holding back too. 'Before we get to ravishing, I have something for you.' He plants a chaste kiss on my lips and frees my arms, getting off the bed and strolling through to the lounge area. I prop myself up on my elbows and follow his path with my eyes, held rapt by his wide naked back and perfect arse. 'Come on,' he calls.

'But I'm comfortable here,' I complain, pouting.

Jack looks back to me sprawled on the bed and smiles, flicking his head in silent demand that I go to him. I do, now curious of what he has for me. Padding my way into the separate lounge area, I find him sitting on the couch. He pats the seat next to him, and I sit beside him, all the while keeping my questioning eyes on him. He produces a Selfridges bag and holds it out to me.

'What's this?' I ask, gingerly accepting it.

'It's for you.' He sits back and gets comfy. 'Open it.'

I grin down at the bag and start to pull the bow loose, flicking my eyes between Jack and the yellow bag as I find my way in. Once it's open, I peek inside, discovering something wrapped neatly in tissue paper. I pull it out, set the bag aside and place the package on my lap, then start to peel at the stickers securing it all together. I pull the tissue paper open and find a small pile of black lace.

'You bought me underwear?' I ask, lifting the bra and holding it up.

'Do you like it?' He sounds apprehensive.

I look at the beautiful piece, the delicate black lace of the balcony bra hanging from the fingertips of both of my hands by the straps. 'It's gorgeous.'

'And the knickers?' He reaches for them and holds them up,

showing me. They're low-rise lace Brazilian briefs with a pretty gold charm in the centre of the waistband.

'Love them,' I confirm.

I can sense his relief, and I conclude that Jack has never bought underwear for a woman before. The notion fills me with satisfaction. I don't care if it doesn't fit, or the style doesn't suit me. Jack bought it for me. 'And now this.' He pulls a small box from behind his back and holds it out to me.

I bite my lip as I look down at it. 'Is it a special occasion?' I ask, keeping my eyes on the box.

'It's been four months since I found you drunk in a bar and licked you.'

I quickly look up at him. 'It is?' I'm not sure why I sound so shocked. It's flown by, yes, but I feel like it's so much longer than that. I feel like I've known him forever. 'And I wasn't drunk.'

He chuckles, his grey eyes twinkling. 'Of course you weren't. Open.' He thrusts the box towards me and I take it, just as gingerly as I accepted the bag containing the underwear.

'I didn't get you a gift,' I say, feeling a little guilty.

'*You* are my gift, Annie.' He reaches over and slides his hand onto my cheek.

My heart melts and I throw myself into his arms, unable to resist the urge to cuddle him tightly. 'Thank you.'

He laughs lightly, holding me as he pushes his lips to the back of my head. 'You don't know what it is yet. You might hate it.'

'I won't hate it,' I argue, letting him detach me and push me back to my side of the couch. I pull the ribbon tie and slowly open the box, blinking when shards of sparkling light shoot out from within. A small hitch of air catches in my throat as I take in the bracelet glistening against the black velvet cushion. In the centre there are two small diamond-encrusted words. One says 'Me' and the other says 'You'. The two words are separated by a tiny heart. I press my lips together as I stare at it, not wanting to cry all over him. I feel a little overwhelmed.

'It's platinum and diamonds,' he says quietly.

'It's beautiful,' I breathe, running the pad of my finger the length of the precious metal.

'I've had the fastener reinforced with a safety catch.' He points to the small clip that secures it. 'So you never lose it.' Slowly and carefully, he drapes the bracelet over my right wrist and fastens it. It's a perfect fit, not too loose and not too tight, with just enough room to slip two fingers between my skin and the platinum. Something comes to me, and I look up at him. 'You were measuring my wrist,' I say, not meaning to sound accusing. 'Last week when we lay in bed, you kept circling my wrist with your fingers.'

He holds his hand up, the tip of his middle finger meeting the tip of his thumb, forming a circle. 'About two inches smaller than this.'

'Sneaky,' I exclaim, going in for another cuddle. 'I love it.'

'Me and you, Annie,' he whispers, constricting me in his arms. 'Me and you.'

The happy tears I was holding back win and a few stream down my cheeks, splashing his shoulder. I hope he doesn't feel them, but when he starts pushing me out of his embrace, I fear that he has. I have no time to brush them away, especially when he's holding my wrists. I drop my eyes in a vain attempt to hide my face.

'Why are you upset?' he asks, genuinely concerned.

'I'm just so happy,' I confess, shaking my head, cross with myself. Because now my mind is going into overdrive, venturing into places that I always promise myself I won't go. If I'm this happy settling for just a piece of him, then imagine how happy I would be if I had *all* of him. Yet I still can't bring myself to ask him when that will be possible. I don't want to put pressure on him. I'm dancing between two very fine lines, both of them blurred. Everything is so distorted and my mind confused. I'm not sure what is best for who and when.

This is exactly why I try not to think about it. It dampens my mood and has my mind going around in circles. I never ask about Stephanie or his home life. I don't want to know, and I know Jack doesn't want me to, either. All I know is that Jack works ridiculous hours and he never stops smiling when we're together. What happens when we're not together isn't something I can bring myself to think about.

He takes my chin and lifts, forcing me to look at him. Then he leans over and rests his lips on mine. 'Go put your new underwear on,' he orders. I smile on the inside, grateful for his intervention. I don't get him for nearly enough time. The last thing I want to do when I *do* have him is talk about the crappiness of our situation. It's easy like this. Our own private happiness that no one can destroy with judgements and devastation. Or suicide attempts.

Gathering up my new underwear, I give him a peck on the cheek and make my way back through the bedroom to the bathroom. The space is overrun with black marble, and the huge tub, which is filled with steaming bubbly water, has a television embedded into the wall at the end. We're having a bath. Jack's naked wet skin all over mine. I shiver with anticipation as I strip down and slip my new bra and knickers on, finding they fit like a glove. Music suddenly begins in the bathroom, and I smile, listening to the intro of Klangkarussell's 'Sonnentanz'.

'Fuck me,' Jack breathes, appearing in the mirror behind me. His eyes are like saucers. 'Your arse looks fucking amazing.'

I thrust my bum out cheekily and yelp when he slaps me clean across my left cheek. 'Ouch!' I'm grabbed, whirled around and thrust up against the mirror. My hair is yanked, my lips attacked. I meld into his body pushed up against mine, spreading my legs when his knee comes up and nudges between my thighs. I'm lifted up by my waist, my back sliding across the mirror with ease, the slight condensation coating the glass creating a slippery friction.

Jack's kiss is relentless and hungry, his moans and growls desperate. My fancy knickers are yanked to the side, he levels up and pounds into me unforgivingly, pushing me up the mirror on a grunt. My hands go straight to his hair and grip, knowing I'm going to need the support. The feel of him buried to the hilt inside me sends my world spinning wildly. He's too desperate to take it slowly. I am too. I kiss him hard and he lets loose, smashing into me on constant shouts. I bite at his lips, pull at his hair and scream on every hard pound. We're loud and frenzied, fervent and messy. The depths he's achieving are both pleasurable and painful. I throw my head back and shout at the ceiling, feeling his fingers claw into the backs of my thighs harshly. My back is repeatedly hitting the mirror, my skin squeaking across the glass when he withdraws, before crashing forward violently again and again. I close my eyes and focus on seizing my orgasm, feeling the pressure collecting fast.

'God!' I shout on a particularly brutal drive.

'You want me to stop?' he asks, not slowing in his pace, continuing to smash into me like a depraved madman.

'No!' I scream, dropping my head and dragging my lids open. I find his eyes are just as wild as his pace. I almost snarl, yanking at his hair viciously.

He grins and ups his stride, digging his fingers into my thighs further. 'Are you close?'

'Yes!' My orgasm takes me by surprise, exploding between my thighs and robbing me of breath. My whole body starts to convulse uncontrollably, and my hearing becomes muffled from the pounding of my pulse in my ears. The muscles in my neck fail and my head collapses forward onto his shoulder, the intense waves ripping through my body ruthlessly. It's almost too much to take. I'm limp against Jack, still being pushed up the mirror as the warmth of his seed fills me until he's rocking gently into me, gulping for oxygen.

'Jesus, that was intense,' he pants, folding to the floor and taking me with him. I spread myself over him, my cheek against the centre of his chest, my palm resting on his pec. We stay on the hard floor of the bathroom for an age, a tangle of arms and legs, both of us heaving loudly. I feel dazed and sucked dry of energy.

'Bath?' he asks on a laboured breath, starting to fiddle with a lock of my dark hair. I hum my half-hearted agreement. I can't move. 'Come.' He wrestles me up from the floor and holds me up with one arm, removing my underwear with the other. Lifting me, he places me in the tub and I immediately sink down into the water, sighing my appreciation. The heat is an instant relief for my muscles. 'Move up,' Jack says, stepping in.

Shuffling forward, I wait for him to settle behind me before reclining and coming to rest on his chest. His legs open and his arms come around and hold me, his nose falling into my neck. 'That was good.'

I nod my agreement, still working to catch my breath. He laughs lightly and rests back, placing a palm on my forehead to encourage me with him. His fingertips glide up my wet thighs, onto my stomach and up towards my breasts. My nipples harden simply by the closeness of his touch.

'Happy to see me?' he teases, reaching them and circling the dark edges slowly.

'I'm always happy to see you.' I shudder atop him, resting my hands on his thighs and smoothing across his dark hairs. 'This is nice,' I muse quietly, closing my eyes. It's relaxed and peaceful. Totally blissful. 'Thank you for my gifts.'

'And thank you for mine,' he counters, making me smile into my darkness. 'I've been thinking.'

'What about?'

'About snatching a whole weekend with you.'

My eyes spring open. 'How?' I ask, trying not to let my excitement run away with me. A whole weekend with Jack? I'm giddy at the mere suggestion.

'There's a construction convention the weekend after next. I'm signed up, but I don't actually need to be there.'

I turn myself over so I'm lying front down on his chest. He must see the exhilaration in my eyes. 'Where?'

'Liverpool. Friday night through to Monday morning. Do you think you could come?' His hand meets my cheek and pushes some wet strands of my hair away from my face. I mentally race through my diary: nothing too important springs to mind. I can tell the girls and Micky that there's some architects' exhibition or something. They won't check, and they definitely won't volunteer to come.

'What will we do?' I ask, already planning it all in my head. We'll be like a normal couple. No sneaking around or looking over our shoulders. I'm getting more excited by the minute.

'We'll eat out, go shopping.' He mirrors my smile. 'We'll just be together.'

I feel like a kid on Christmas Eve. I'd happily hide in a hotel for two full days as long as Jack is with me. 'Lots of affection?'

His smile cracks and he laughs, sliding his palms under my arms and pulling me up his chest. Our noses meet, our eyes hold. 'Lots and lots of affection.'

'Then I'm in.' I seal our mouths and seal the deal, unable to wipe the huge grin from my face. 'I can't wait.'

'Me neither, gorgeous.' Jack sucks on my bottom lip until it pops from his mouth. 'Richard knows about us.' His declaration comes from left field, even though I wondered when I caught him watching Jack and me.

My heart jumps a little, suddenly worried. 'Did you tell him?'

'I didn't need to.'

My eyes drop. 'We haven't been careless.'

Jack pulls my chin up and smiles. 'I work closely with him,

Annie. I can't hide my happiness when you're around.'

I mirror his beam, only mildly. I'm worried. 'He wouldn't say anything, would he?'

'God, no.' He laughs at the suggestion. 'He's a good guy, and he knows . . .' Jack trails off, but he doesn't need to finish. Richard knows what Stephanie is like. That's what he was going to say. I remember a few occasions when Richard passed comment, or muttered something under his breath when Jack's wife turned up on site in a deranged fit.

Jack takes a breath and kisses my nose. 'Our secret is safe. Now, tell me about your week.'

Our secret. I so wish we weren't a secret. I let Jack turn me back over, and he curls his forearms around my shoulders, keeping his face close to mine. We lie there for over an hour while I give him a rerun of my projects. He drains the tub a little every now and then and tops it back up with hot water to keep us warm. He listens and asks questions, and never once does he sound bored. I love how he can just let me ramble on about structures and technical stuff, speaking up when he has a suggestion or opinion. It works in reverse. I could listen to Jack reel off any old gobbledegook, just to hear his voice. Just to know he's close enough to hear.

Once we've got out and dried ourselves off, we dress and the atmosphere noticeably changes. We're not chatting easily any more. I watch him while I blast my hair dry. He's sitting on the couch checking his phone, but he's not totally focused and there's an air of despondency around him. I wonder what he's thinking, seeing him look up blankly to the wall every now and then, lost in thought.

When I'm done and have gathered all of my things, I wander through to him. 'Ready?'

He slowly stands. I can see it takes some effort, his body appearing weighted down by something. 'Ready,' he confirms, slipping his phone into his pocket. He closes the gap between us and pulls me in for a hug, probably one of the tightest he's ever given me. 'I hate this part,' he whispers.

I smile sadly. Is he reaching the crossroads? Is he on the verge of making the move that will toss our secret blissful bubble into heartache and hurt? Aside from the limited time we have together, what we have is easy. Too easy, which makes it harder to take the steps that will undoubtedly change that. I don't know if I'm ready for the backlash.

What sane woman gets herself caught up in an affair? What woman with any self-respect and integrity would venture there? A woman who's in love. That's who. They say you can't help who you fall for. I wholeheartedly believe that now.

I remember how much it hurt to fight the feelings, pushing Jack away and shutting down. I'm so frightened by the prospect of him telling Stephanie that he's leaving her. I'm frightened that she will convince him to stay and work on their marriage. That her emotional blackmail will get the better of him again. That terrifies me the most.

I see her in my mind's eye, hysterical and devastated, begging him not to go. There's a knife in her hand, held on her wrist. I feel guilty. Jack will feel guilty. Guilt has a way of influencing your decisions. It's easier to succumb to guilt and disregard what your heart is telling you.

'I'll see you next Friday at Colin's launch,' he says on a hushed whisper. 'We'll do something after, yes?'

I nod into his shoulder, unable to feel excited about it. Next Friday feels like aeons away.

Jack holds me in his arms, seeming unprepared to release me, so I gently break away from him and reach up, giving him a little kiss on his cheek. 'See you then,' I say, and then walk away, feeling him watching every step I take until I close the door behind me.

Keep it together, I tell myself. *Breathe through it*. I make my way out onto the street and quickly find a wall to perch on to gather myself. I don't know how much longer I can see him like that. How much longer I can keep walking away.

'Annie?'

I glance to my right and find Lizzy approaching. 'Hey!' I shoot up, way too quickly, and I sound way too pleased to see her too. I glance around, panicked. 'What are you doing here?'

She frowns at me, and I strain a fake smile through my guilty face. 'I have a dinner date.'

'Here?' I ask. Of all the fucking hotels in London, she's having a date here? At this particular time?

'Yes, here.' She smiles through an even deeper frown. 'What are you doing here?'

'Had a meeting with a client,' I blurt, shrugging. I'm behaving strangely, and it isn't escaping her notice.

'Are you okay?'

'Yes, I'm fine.' Oh fuck, she has to go into the hotel. What are the chances of her and Jack crossing paths? I don't know, but I can't risk it. Yet I have no clue what to fucking do about it, either.

At that very second, I see Jack coming down the steps of the hotel, and I scream in my head for him to turn around and go back. He looks up, smiling when he sees me a few feet away. My eyes go around, trying to silently tell him to pay attention to who's with me.

His steps falter, and his smile falls. But my attempt to warn him doesn't register in time, and Lizzy starts to turn around. 'Jack?' she asks.

Jack's face is a picture. It's so bloody obvious, and Lizzy must see it. How the fucking hell am I going to get out of this one? It's too much of a coincidence that I'm here and Jack's here, even if we're working together. Why would we be meeting here?

Jack seems to gather himself quickly. 'Hi, Lizzy. And Annie's here too! You girls having dinner?'

I'm utterly stunned by his coolness. How? 'No,' Lizzy says

slowly, looking at me. I strain another smile. 'We just bumped into each other.' Her eyes are accusing, and I die on the inside. 'What are the chances of you two being at the same hotel?' She cocks her head in question.

I shrug and cough, forcing myself to locate some energy to play it as cool. 'Like I said, just finished up with a client.'

Jack starts buttoning up his suit jacket. 'Excuse me a moment.' He turns to the bellboy and slips a note into his hand. 'My wife, Mrs Joseph, is on her way out. Please hail her a cab when she's ready.'

'Yes, sir.' The bellboy nods sharply.

'Thanks.' Jack turns back towards us, smiling brightly. It's so fake. His wife's on her way out? It's quick thinking, granted. But she isn't on her way out. He pulls his phone out of his pocket and glances at the screen. 'It was nice to see you two.' Putting his phone to his ear, he smiles brightly, backing away. 'Oh, and we're still on track with the gallery schedule, Annie. Colin said you were asking.'

I nod sharply as Jack turns and leaves. I waste no time swooping in for a subject change. 'So who's your date with?' I chime, injecting tons of excitement into my tone.

'Oh, I'd better go. I'm late.' Lizzy, suddenly awkward, hot-foots it up the steps into the hotel.

'But who's your date with?' I call after her.

She totally ignores my repeated question, not that I'm bothered. I need to be out of here pronto. 'Call you later!' she sings.

I sag all over the pavement, but quickly pull it together when she turns and faces me. 'We're going out next Friday,' she declares.

I wilt, despite not being disappointed that I can't make it, but Lizzy needs to think I am. 'I have a cocktail party at Colin's new gallery. I'll call you if I can get away early.' I could get away early, no problem, but meeting up with the gang means not seeing Jack. I can go out with my friends any time I like, whereas my opportunities to spend time with Jack are rare. Nothing will make me pass them up.

'Okay, call me.' She breezes into the hotel, and I stagger towards the main road, exhausted by it all.

I really don't know how much longer I can keep this up.

Chapter 17

The days running up to Colin's launch pass by surprisingly quickly, thank God; most of my days are spent at Colin's gallery, checking over the installation of the roof and having building control pass it. It's been chaos there, the decorators and landscapers working through most of the nights to get everything done on time so the launch can go ahead. It is a push, all hands on deck, but we scrape in just on time.

I stop off at the Tesco Express to pick up a bottle of wine, planning my night ahead while the cashier rings it through. A soak in the bath. A glass of wine while I get ready. I have a taxi booked for eight, so I have two hours to slowly preen before I head back to the gallery to celebrate its opening. Stuffing my bottle of wine in my huge slouchy bag, along with a bottle of fizz for Colin, I pay and get on my way, rootling through my bag for my keys when I make it to my front door.

'Hey, Annie!'

I frown at the wood before me, my grip on the key becoming hard. I recognise that voice. I don't want to recognise it, and for a fleeting moment I hope I'm hearing things, but as I slowly turn and look over my shoulder, my hopes die. My muscles tense, and the bracelet that Jack gave me starts to burn around my wrist. I glance down, worried, checking that the sleeve of my trench coat is concealing it.

'Hi, Stephanie,' I say, tugging my key from the lock, but not before I've got the door open so I can escape quickly once we've had our pleasantries. What the hell is she doing around here?

In particular, outside my flat? Panic begins to consume me as I slowly turn to face her, trying to clear my face of all guilt. She's pristine as always, her lips blood red to match her long nails. Those fucking nails. I want to cut them off with a hacksaw.

'I'm parked just down the street,' she sings, pointing down the road. 'Jack's dry cleaner's is out on the main road, and it's a total bitch to park there.' She holds up a suit bag. 'I knew it must be you.'

I give her a strained smile. 'How are you?' I ask, my mind in chaos.

'Oh, fine. Just running a few errands. Jack needed this for some work thing he's going to tonight.' She rolls her eyes, and I just smile, a rabbit caught in the headlights. 'Got any plans?'

'Just drinks with some friends,' I blurt, breaking out in a sweat. Fuck, does she know it's Colin's launch night? I should have mentioned that I'm going. Why didn't I mention that I'm going?

'Don't get too drunk.' She laughs hysterically. 'I'll have to wait until tomorrow to let my hair down. Jack and I are out for a nice dinner and a few cocktails.'

'Sounds great. I hope you have a lovely evening.' I'm lying through my teeth, of course. I actually hope they have a blazing row and Stephanie realises there's a serious lack of love coming from Jack's direction. And *she* leaves *him*. Problem solved.

'Oh, we will.' She rearranges her bag on her shoulder. 'Hey, we must do lunch sometime. How about next week?'

I smile tightly, alarmed. What the hell? 'Sure,' I murmur, edging into my front hall. 'That would be nice.'

'Great.' She makes off down the road, waving as she goes. 'Lovely to see you, Annie.'

'You too,' I call, then shut the door and fall back against it, utterly exhausted. Shit, I need a drink. She was so bloody happy, and the unreasonable part of my brain is asking if she and Jack are getting on all of a sudden. I can't think that. I rush to the kitchen in search of the wine and pour as I dial Lizzy, needing to talk to a friend to take my mind off . . . things, even if that friend doesn't have a clue what's going on in my life. Distraction. 'Hey.'

'*Bonjour!*' she answers. '*Comment allez-vous?*'

'Why are you talking French?'

'Because I had a French client in today, and *oh là là*, is he something pleasant to look at.'

'Ooh, French, ah?' I sip wine as I make my way to the bathroom to run the bath.

'Hot as fuck.'

'Did you make your attraction known?'

'He's married. Restricted zone.'

I swallow down my wine on a hard gulp, thanking the Lord I'm not having this conversation with Lizzy face to face. I must be bright red and radiating guilt from every pore. I place my wine on the side of the bath and flip the taps on. 'Damn shame.'

'Not for his wife.' She laughs, and I force myself to laugh too. I swear, my phone is heating up with me. It's burning my ear.

'Hey, have you seen your new man again?' I ask. Apparently their first date went well, and there have been two further dates since, though she's being sketchy with the details.

'I'll tell you about it tonight.'

'I might not make it tonight. I have the gallery opening, remember. Tell me now. You've not even shared his name.'

'Can't you slip off early?'

'I don't want to be rude, Lizzy.' I tip some bubbles into the tub, pushing the guilt away for lying to her. Lying. I'm getting way too good at it, and it's not a quality that I'm proud of. 'If I can, I'll call you.'

'Okay,' she relents on a drawn-out sigh. 'Have a good evening at your fancy gallery opening.'

'Will do,' I confirm, my guilt now being pushed aside by excitement. I get to spend some time with Jack after the gallery opening. I just have to keep myself together while we're actually at the gallery. But as soon as we're out of there, the gloves are off. As well as his clothes.

I hang up, toss my phone to the side and start to strip down, frowning when I realise Lizzy avoided my question of a name again. I make a mental note to call her tomorrow and get one.

I lower myself into the water but I can't get comfy. The hardness of the tub on my back when I recline annoys me. I shift and move, trying to find a comfortable position, wondering what gives. When one of the diamonds in my bracelet catches one of the spotlights above and sparkles brightly, I realise what's wrong. I sigh, fondling the charms thoughtfully, shifting and wriggling in the tub. It's no good. I have no Jack to lie on. Baths will never be the same again. I give up on my relaxing soak and take a shower instead.

I stand at the end of the driveway that leads to Colin's gallery staring up at my new creation, feeling an immense sense of pride. It's just about perfect, and though it looks shiny new after the renovations, it doesn't stick out like a sore thumb as was argued by the local authorities on numerous occasions.

I make my way up the drive armed with a bottle of bubbly and wander through the open door. The impressive entrance has spectacular art displayed at every turn.

'Annie!' Colin appears and seizes me as I laugh.

'Hi!' I let him squeeze me before handing him his champagne.

'You shouldn't have.' He hauls me through to the huge extension at the rear. 'Just look at it,' he marvels, gazing up towards the roof. 'Isn't it the most spectacular thing you've ever seen?'

'Wonderful,' I admit, absorbing it for a few moments before

taking in the people dotted around in small crowds; some admiring the art, some the building, and some just chatting and sipping fizz. I don't see Jack, but I spot Richard. He notices me and raises his glass.

'Here.' Colin swoops a flute off the tray of a passing waiter and places it in my hand. 'Have a drink, mingle, and listen to everyone sing your praises.' He motions to the outside space through the bifold doors. 'There's a wealth of people waiting to meet the woman who designed the new home for my masterpieces.'

I actually blush a little, walking out into the minimal garden, where crowds of people are gathered drinking and chatting. But still no Jack. I see the glass cases that Jack suggested, three of them hanging proudly on the brick wall, housing three pieces of Colin's extraordinary art. 'Are you hungry?' Colin asks, indicating a huge table with a buffet laid out. 'Help yourself if you're peckish.'

'Thanks, Colin.' I forgo the food in favour of my champagne. 'I'll grab something soon.'

'As you wish.' Colin leads me over to a group of people standing around a tall table.

'Hi,' I say, shaking every hand that's offered to me.

'Annie, this is Rick.' Colin introduces me to a stocky man with grey hair and an impressive moustache. 'I know you're technically off duty tonight, but he'd love to talk to you about a property he's thinking of buying.'

Rick smiles brightly at me. 'Annie, pleasure to meet you.' His shake is solid; his huge sausage fingers completely wrap around my hand.

'Pleasure, Rick. Tell me about this property.'

'It's a historical building. Protected.' He almost grumbles, clearly not impressed by that. 'Off Grosvenor Square. What can I do with it?'

I laugh. 'Not a lot. Is it derelict?'

'Completely.'

'Renovations will be welcome, but English Heritage will be watching like a hawk. Materials will be specified, demolition a total no-go, and specialist tradesmen will need to be drafted in.'

'What are you saying?' Rick asks, looking rather displeased.

'I'm saying it'll cost you an arm and a leg. But you might be eligible for a grant from English Heritage to help with the financial burden. It's worth looking into.'

He laughs loudly, taking a swig of Scotch. 'Maybe I'll rethink that idea. It sounds stressful. So, tell me, where did you get your inspiration for this place?' He motions around the garden, up to the roof. I have to say, it looks bloody amazing, everything I hoped it would be.

I smile and let myself get pulled into conversation about work. It's a welcome reprieve from my racing mind. Where is Jack?

Richard finds me when I'm inside getting a refill, and I motion down his front. 'This is a nice change,' I say, smiling at his suit.

He laughs and gets a new glass for himself. 'It's been a job and a half, but well worth it, I'm sure you'll agree.' He looks up to the roof, and so do I.

'It was the best and worst design move I've ever made.' This roof has caused me more stress than most projects in their entirety.

'Jack had every faith in you,' he muses, dropping his eyes back to me.

I sip my champagne, not knowing what I'm supposed to say to that. So I smile awkwardly, looking around the room. 'He's not here?' I try to sound casual, but I know I've failed when Richard shakes his head a little.

'He's been held up,' he replies quietly.

I glance at him, fighting to keep cool. He's been held up? I don't like Richard's knowing expression. It's as if he's trying to tell me something without actually saying it out loud. Why is Jack held up? What's happened? I contemplate rushing to the toilets to text him or e-mail him, but I know that would be stupid. Stephanie seemed upbeat earlier during that awful encounter with her. But that's what the outside world sees. I know it's not all rosy behind closed doors.

Suddenly fretful, I empty my glass in one gulp and grab another. 'I hope he makes it,' I murmur weakly, backing up. 'Excuse me, I need the ladies'.' I turn on my heel but get no further than that. My hands immediately begin to shake. My eyes are fixed on the entrance into the gallery, where Jack is standing.

With his wife.

'Annie!' Stephanie cries, delighted to see me, like I'm her best friend. She grabs a glass of wine from the waiter and literally throws it down her neck before claiming another. 'I thought you said you were out with your girlfriends.' She struts over and plants a peck on my cheek, and my skin literally crawls.

I risk a quick glance at Jack. His face is grave, the twinkle in his eyes dead.

'I'm not staying for long,' I murmur. 'Heading into town to meet them soon.' The night I've been looking forward to for days and days vanishes before my eyes. I'm totally devastated.

'How lovely.' Stephanie frees me and moves on to Richard, who is eyeing Jack with all the concern he deserves. 'Hello, Richard.'

'Stephanie,' he says, smiling tightly through a nod. 'You look stunning as always.'

Her palm hits her chest, her red lips pouting. 'You're too kind.'

Yes, he is. She looks like a dog's dinner, dressed to the nines, her body draped in a long satin dress that's fit for the opera house, not a gallery. Jack moves in, swallowing hard. 'Annie.' He nods formally at me and smiles mildly at Richard, taking what looks like a much needed drink. I'm desperate to ask him what's happened. Why she's here. What the hell is going on?

'Isn't it wonderful?' Stephanie gushes, stopping another waiter as he passes and exchanging her empty for a full glass. 'I mean, really wonderful.' She raises her glass and toasts the air. 'To my husband.'

This is fucking awful. 'To Jack.' Richard chinks her glass, and I follow suit, mentally planning my escape.

'And Annie,' Jack pipes up, making my eyes go all wide. 'We only built what she told us to.'

I feel my spine stiffen. 'Thank you.' I swallow and dive back into my champagne. It's the only thing keeping me going right now.

'Of course.' Stephanie places her well-manicured hand on Jack's arm, and my eyes involuntarily fall to it, silently screaming at her not to touch him. 'Annie, Jack's been so impressed with you.'

I shoot Jack a look, shocked. He's been talking about me? Is he stupid? 'It's just a job.' I brush it off as best I can.

'Annie and I are going to make plans for lunch.' Stephanie sings, clearly thrilled. I, however, am the furthest from thrilled that a person could be, and Jack looks plain horrified.

I've got to get out of here. I look past Stephanie's beaming face, feigning surprise. 'Oh, there's Gerard.' I pluck a name from nowhere and point to the garden. 'Please excuse me; I must say hello.'

I'm out of there like a shot, walking outside and finding a group of people to muscle in on. The voices in the conversation are a blur of nothing. I try to engage, to listen, just to stop my mind from racing and my eyes from wandering, but no matter how hard I try to focus, my head has other ideas. I glance back casually and see a few more people have joined Jack, Richard and Stephanie, all engrossed in conversation. Jack's there, but he isn't, as Stephanie drapes herself all over him, stroking his arm, smiling up at him every so often and throwing glass after glass of wine down her throat. I can't bear it.

Breaking away from the group, I find my phone and text Lizzy, asking her where they are.

'I couldn't get out of it.' Jack's voice hits the base of my spine and licks its way to the top, making me shiver. But not in the way it usually does, when I get tingles and have to take a breath and contain my need to devour him. He rounds me and puts himself before me, searching my eyes. 'I'm sorry.'

'What happened?' I ask.

'She insisted on coming. What could I do?'

I shake my head and move away from him, watchful and wary of our surroundings. 'I don't know,' I admit. 'Jack, you have to talk her out of arranging lunch with me.'

He laughs, low and sarcastic. 'How the hell am I going to do that?'

I wilt when I realise he can't, and it's mighty unreasonable for me to expect him to. 'I was so looking forward to tonight.' I instantly regret letting my thoughts speak. This isn't his fault. I shouldn't be making him feel guilty.

'I know, Annie. I know. She mentioned you ran into each other.'

'Outside my flat,' I confirm. 'She was picking your suit up from the dry cleaner's.' I motion down his grey three-piece with my glass. 'Looks nice, by the way.'

He smiles mildly. 'You look beautiful, and I can't even fucking touch you.' His eyes burn into mine, so much hunger clouding them. 'I need to see you later. Tell me I can see you later.'

'How?' I ask. 'You're with your wife.' I don't mean to sound resentful, but the truth of it is, I am.

'I'll find a way,' he promises.

'Now's not the time to become careless, Jack,' I warn. 'Richard knows, and if we're not careful, your wife will soon figure it out too.'

'I need to see you,' he grates, daring me to deny him with his hard stare. 'Just answer your phone when I call.' He breaks away, slapping a smile on his face.

'There you are.' Stephanie croons, slipping her arm through Jack's when she joins us. 'Talking boring work?'

'As always,' Jack confirms, looking down at her glass. It's empty again.

'Well, enough of that.' She turns her full body to him and places her lips on his cheek. I vomit in my own mouth, my stomach churning terribly. 'You need to show your wife a good time.'

My phone chimes in my hand, and I rip my eyes away from the unbearable sight of another woman all over the man I love. 'Excuse me,' I murmur, heading back into the gallery as I read Lizzy's text. I'm going to get *so* drunk.

I find Colin, thank him and make my excuses, not prepared to allow his evident disappointment make me feel too guilty. He holds on to me, temping me with more fizz, but I stand firm, not letting him succeed in persuading me to stay a bit longer. Nothing would convince me to.

I head to the toilet to freshen up my lipstick, and as I enter the ladies', the first thing I see is myself in the mirror. I look as terrible as I feel. Pale and traumatised. Bracing my hands on the edge of the stone vanity unit, I breathe in, trying to give myself a pep talk.

Bang!

My eyes shoot past my reflection to the row of cubicles, scanning from side to side, listening carefully. What was that?

Bang!

Sounds of shuffles and whispers come from beyond the door of the far cubicle, and I force myself into stillness, or I try to. My heart isn't listening to my silent demand to pipe down.

Then the hushed whispers turn into low moans. My blood freezes, the sounds working their way into my brain and cementing themselves there, making sure I'll never forget them.

Stephanie's moans.

Moans of ecstasy and pleasure. 'Take my dress off,' she pants. 'Take it off now, Jack.'

My stomach convulses and I double over, physically retching over the sink. Then the shouts start. 'Oh, Jack! Yes. Take me here. Take me now.'

'Stephanie,' Jack growls.

I run out of the ladies', the combination of heaves from my nausea and body jerks from the instant tears making me stumble and trip as I go. I feel like I could vomit. Panicked and knowing there's no way I can go back in the ladies', I fly into the disabled toilet and slam it shut, bracing my hands on the toilet as I try to regulate my breathing. I feel lightheaded and dizzy. I feel sick and betrayed.

A hopeless sob pours free, and I clench my head to try and crush the tormenting sound that's looping on repeat in my head. 'No,' I sob, falling apart, my body racked with ragged emotions. I have to leave. Now.

I wrench the door open and run out of the gallery, and I don't stop until I reach the end of the road. I flag down the first taxi and dive in. I'm going to find the girls and I'm going to drink myself into oblivion. I hope it's enough to take me away from this nightmare. I've never ventured there. I've not allowed my mind to, but when it's screwing behind a door in front of you, it's hard to ignore. I feel hurt. Totally devastated. And fury is burning a hole in my senses. I can't stop it.

Chapter 18

'Here she is!' Lizzy shouts as I wander into the champagne bar, spotting them all perched on tall stools around a bar table. Micky waves me over, pointing to a stool with a glass of wine on the table in front of it. 'Good boy, Micky,' I praise him, landing on my seat with a thud.

'You okay?' he asks, giving me a once-over. I don't know how good a job I did of fixing my face in the cab, but I'm guessing even with perfect make-up right now, my distress would still be detectable.

'I'm fine,' I say, holding up a hand to halt Lizzy when she goes to speak. She snaps her mouth shut on a pout and watches as I neck my wine. 'Just fine,' I repeat, slamming my glass down.

Nat, Micky and Lizzy all regard me carefully for a moment. 'Fine.' I breathe in and out, in and out.

'She's fine,' Lizzy says slowly, nodding her head at me. 'You sure?'

I nod back. 'Just an arsehole taxi driver.'

Lizzy rolls her eyes. 'So let's get my news out of the way.' She sits up straight, and everyone else at the table looks at her. She begins to fidget. 'Well,' she begins, focusing on her wine glass. 'I have something to tell you all, but before I do, I want to make it clear that I've thought long and hard about it and I'd appreciate your support.'

We all noticeably sit back on our stools, and I look to each of my friends, trying to figure out their thought processes. They look intrigued, like me.

'I'm back with Jason,' she blurts out before scooping up her drink and downing the lot, shrinking on her stool.

Realisation dawns on me. 'That's who you were meeting for dinner!' I say. 'Jason.' No wonder she's been so cagey.

She shrugs. 'I agreed to meet him, yes. I didn't see the point in mentioning it because I thought I'd tell him to be on his way and that would be that. But seeing him again, seeing how guilty he feels . . . I love him.' She shrugs. 'You can't turn that off.'

When the atmosphere becomes unbearably awkward, I dive right in and reach across the table, taking her hand. 'Do what makes you happy,' I say, wholeheartedly meaning it.

Tears of relief flood her eyes and her lips press together to the point they're white. She can't speak, bless her, so she nods in return. I feel terrible for her. I saw how cut up she was when she found out about Jason's affair, and I damned the woman who'd walked uninvited into her life. A woman like me.

Giving Nat a discreet kick under the table, I sit back and let her do her bit, though it's plain to see that she's significantly less enthusiastic about it than me. Poor Micky, however, just watches as us girls do our girlie shit. 'I might go meet the lads,' he mumbles, rolling his eyes.

'In other news.' Nat raises her glass, grinning wickedly, and I wonder for a fleeting moment if she's perhaps decided to give John a break. Then I remember the chewing gum incident with his kid and dismiss the thought immediately. Her hair has a way to go before it's back to its former long, luscious glory. 'I've joined a dating agency.' There are a few funny looks tossed around the table before we all burst into fits of laughter. 'What?' Nat asks, disgruntled. 'At least I can make it clear what's acceptable and what's not.'

'Like kids?' Lizzy asks, dismayed.

'Just like kids,' Nat confirms. 'Fathers need not apply.'

'Holy shit,' Micky breathes, exasperated. 'Can we talk about football before my balls shrivel to nothing?'

I laugh and reach over to pinch his cheek. 'You'll fall in love one day.'

He scoffs, disgusted by the suggestion. 'There's a reason you and I are still friends, and it ain't because you have photo evidence of me dressed up as He-Man brandishing a rolling pin as a sword.'

Right. Apparently we're friends because we're both allergic to relationships. He's talking nonsense, obviously. We're actually friends because we've known each other since day one, but that knowledge doesn't stop me from wilting. I swallow hard and divert my attention away from him, suddenly remembering why I'm clinging to my wine glass like it's a life jacket. Then I notice it's empty. I grab the bottle from the middle of the table. *Get plastered. Drown the memories in alcohol.*

'He-Man?' Nat chimes in. 'You dressed up as He-Man?' She jumps down from her stool and throws an imaginary sword in the air. 'I have the power!' she roars, before folding in half in fits of laughter with Lizzy.

It's a while before they look at me in question, like why am I not laughing? I shrug. I have nothing to give in the humour department, despite my life being a fucking joke.

'Twats. All of you.' Micky jumps down from his stool, looking to the door. 'The lads are here. I'm off to find my She-Ra.' He lopes off with a grin, leaving the girls to be girls, which currently involves Nat and Lizzy laughing their tits off.

It could be an hour later, or it might be two. I'm not sure. All I know is that I'm tipsy and my mind is numbing more with each sip of wine I have. It's respite. I turn on my stool and find Nat on her own on the dance floor, her wine glass in the air, her head dropped, swaying out of time to Hot Chip's 'Boy from School'. I keep my eyes on her as I blindly reach for Lizzy to get her attention, the sight too amusing not to share. 'Look at that.'

'Jesus, no man will entertain that, kid or no kid,' Lizzy quips, sliding off her stool. She strolls over to Nat and gently coaxes her from the dance floor, helping her walk as she staggers and trips her way back to us. Steadying her on the seat, Lizzy takes a stool beside her and moves in close enough to catch her if she slips in her drunken stupor. 'I have to ask,' Nat slurs, looking up at Lizzy with one eye closed. 'Why would you even dream of taking Jason back?'

I sag on an audible sigh. 'Nat, it's Lizzy's decision. We should respect that.'

'I know, but we're all thinking it.' She slaps a hand down but totally misses the table, forcing Lizzy to catch her before she topples from the stool. 'What about the other woman?'

'That's none of our business,' I pipe up, eager to halt the direction of the conversation dead in its tracks.

'It's fine,' Lizzy appeases me. 'We need to get this part out of the way.'

'Yeah,' Nat slurs, feeling around the table for her wine glass. Lizzy moves it away and pushes a glass of water towards her, and Nat grabs it, waving the highball at Lizzy. 'What kind of woman sniffs around a taken man? Not even *I* would stoop to that level.'

My throat closes up on me, leaving me silent at the table while the topic I've dreaded for months steamrolls forward, threatening to make my night even worse.

'Men think with their dicks!' Nat rocks back on her stool. 'Their brains are in their balls!'

I die on the inside. Part of me knows it's wise to keep my trap shut, and part of me wants to give another angle for Nat to consider. Yet I don't. I can't. I have no other option but to sit back and listen while they slam into said *other* woman, calling her every name under the sun, surmising what a nasty piece of work she is and generally ripping her to shreds. Brutally. Harshly.

Justifiably.

I shrink further and further, my head starting to hurt, my heart starting to ache. I'm a fool if I think for a minute that anyone will understand me. The tiny scrap of hope I had of support from my friends just died. I can't take this any more. I grab my bag, jump down from my stool and rush to the ladies', forgetting to declare my need for the loo in my desperation to escape the bitching session. I can feel tears stinging the backs of my eyes and I can't let my friends see them.

I lock myself in a cubicle until my churning stomach eases off, my mind slowly settling. I wasn't prepared for that. It's easy for me to bully my conscience into a certain way of thinking, but I can't control how other people think. For the first time since I embarked on this affair, I feel so alone. Where's Jack? Where is he to hold me and tell me everything is going to be okay? Anger simmers in my gut, kick-starting the churning again. He's with his wife, fucking in the toilet at the gallery. My phone chimes, and though I know it'll send my anger into frightening realms, I still open his message.

Where did you go?

My lip curls in disdain as I delete his worthless words from my screen. I leave the toilet and head straight for the bar, ordering more alcohol. My phone rings this time, and I psych myself up to answer it. 'Hello.'

'Where are you?' he asks in a whisper that I'm struggling to hear over the music. He's found a quiet corner to call me, away from her. 'Annie?'

'I'm busy.' I hang up, but before I collect our drinks, it rings again. 'What?' I snap when I answer.

'What's the matter with you?'

'Nothing. Get back to your wife, Jack,' I spit, cutting the call and ignoring his next three attempts to ring back as I get the wine and take it to the table. I wave for Nat and Lizzy's attention on the dance floor, and both give me a thumbs-up when they spot the bottle in my grasp.

'Is that Annie Ryan?' a male voice asks from behind me, pulling my attention around. I find a strapping bloke with a cute smile on his face, leaning against a nearby table. And I see thighs. Thick, rugby player thighs.

'Tom,' I say, trying not to make it sound like a question. This is the last man I slept with before Jack. Jason's friend of a friend.

'Well done,' he teases. 'How have you been?'

'Good, thanks. You?'

'Can't complain.' He indicates my empty glass. 'Drink?'

My blazing fury gets tackled from the side by the unexpected potential opportunity that's fallen at my feet. I thought alcohol was my only escape. Maybe I was wrong. I disregard the full bottle I've just placed on the table. 'Why not?' I say, smiling. 'Sauvignon, please.'

'Small? Large?'

'Large.'

Tom heads for the bar and orders while I fight back the stupid part of my fucked-up mind that's telling me not to do something that I'll regret. It's not really that hard to disregard it. My only regret right now is putting myself in an affair. I remind myself that I'm technically still single. I'm technically free as a bird to do what I want, when I want. I'm not the married one. If Jack can have his cake and eat it, then so can I. I look across to the dance floor where Lizzy and Nat are throwing themselves around like the drunken fools that they are, and catch both their eyes. When Lizzy grins, and Nat gives me double thumbs-up, I know they've clocked Tom. They think I've been celibate these past four months. They'll physically put Tom in bed with me if they have to.

I accept my drink with a smile of thanks as I reacquaint my eyes with Tom. He's handsome but rugged. His nose has clearly been broken a few times, and he has a tidy scar across his brow bone. His hair is short but styled, and his neck thick. 'How have *you* been?' I ask, getting the conversation started as he perches on Lizzy's stool.

'Great, actually. I've been in Scotland for the last year at a training academy for kids.'

'Sounds good. But you're back?'

'It was a year-long programme at one of the league clubs. We're starting one here at Twickenham next month.'

I nod. 'So you play rugby, then?'

He laughs. 'How'd you guess?'

I shrug and place my glass on the table. 'Must be the cauliflower ears.'

'Hey!' He reaches over and lightly punches my jaw. 'I wear a head guard.'

I smile coyly. 'I'm teasing. Sounds like a great job.'

'It is. What do you do, Annie?' He takes a swig of his pint, grinning. 'We didn't exactly talk much last time I saw you.'

I return his grin, remembering the night well. It involved lots of alcohol and laughs, and ended with very drunken sex. 'No, but we did a lot of something else.'

'I tried calling you after.' He watches me closely. 'Why did you give me your number if you didn't plan on taking my calls?'

'Work kind of took over my life.'

'I thought maybe you were involved with someone.'

'No.'

'And are you now?'

I swallow and breathe in deeply. 'No,' I say clearly, evenly and with one hundred per cent conviction.

Chapter 19

Don't ask me what I'm doing because I couldn't tell you. It's the story of my life these days. All I know is that I'm in agony inside and I'm hurting all the more because deep down I know I have no right to feel betrayed. My mind is a wild mess of questions. I feel deceived. It's a crazy claim. Maybe this is karma. Maybe the Fates have decided that Annie Ryan doesn't get to be happy. She doesn't get to have what she desperately wants because she lied and cheated to try and get it.

I get out of the cab outside my flat, Tom following closely behind. He slams the door and it echoes in the night air around us. We had a little moment outside the bar, nothing too much, just a look, but it was enough for him to ask if I wanted some company, and enough for me to say yes. As I walk up the path, I question what I'm doing and what good will come from it. I have no answer. I'm retaliating because I'm hurt beyond comprehension and it's making me self-destructive. I slip my key into the lock, push the door open and let Tom follow me in.

'Nice place,' he says, shutting the door behind him. 'You been here long?'

'Just a few months,' I reply over my shoulder, making my way to the kitchen. 'Tea, coffee, alcohol?'

'Whatever you're having.'

His answer gives me a moment's pause as I flick my eyes between the kettle and the wine glasses. Seems stupid that something as simple as a choice of drink could pave the way for the rest of the night. 'White okay?' I ask, taking down two glasses.

'Sounds good to me.' He strides over to the double doors that lead onto the courtyard. 'I love this,' he says, unlocking the door as I pour us drinks. 'I'm on the fifth floor of a high-rise. No outside space.'

I gather up the glasses and follow him into my small garden. 'Here.' I hand him a glass and he raises it before taking a sip. 'Cheers,' I say in response.

He wanders over to the willow tree and pulls back some of the branches, peeking into the hidden space behind. 'This is really cool.'

'It's my peaceful space,' I say, getting an unexpected replay of Stephanie's tormenting sounds of pleasure in my head. And then Jack's growl. They're playing on loop. Over and over, getting louder each time. I wince, closing my eyes, but I'm interrupted from my inner turmoil when Tom speaks. 'You never did tell me what you do.'

'I'm an architect.'

'Nice. Designed anything I might know?'

'Like the Shard or something equally iconic?' I ask on a teasing smile.

Tom laughs. 'Now I know the bloke who designed the Shard was some Italian dude. You're not Italian, and you are definitely not a dude.' He winks cheekily, prompting me to laugh.

'His name is Renzo Piano. Sadly, I'm nowhere near his league, but maybe one day.' I shrug.

Tom smiles and takes one step forward, closing the distance between us to only a foot or so. I look up at him, finding soft, searching eyes. 'I'm hoping I haven't read this wrong.'

He moves in and I hold my breath, waiting for his lips to meet mine, and when they do, I exhale and relax, accepting his kiss. His lips are soft and tender, his mouth working slowly over mine. My mind empties. It's a relief. It's a reprieve. I can't pass up the opportunity to free myself from the mental chains I've locked myself in. Even if it's only temporarily.

With my wine glass in one hand, I use my free arm to reach up and rest over his broad shoulders, responding to his kiss. My willingness forces the pace up a few notches. I expect this to take me further away from my pain, but I'm proven wrong when my darkness is suddenly hijacked with images of Jack. I try to push his beautiful face to the side, feeling Tom slip my dress from my shoulders, exposing my bra straps. The bra Jack bought for me. I persevere, taking our kiss up another level in the hope of getting past my momentary lapse in fortitude, but a loud crash brings the moment to a screeching halt and Tom pulls away fast, looking towards the doors.

'What was that?' he asks, a little dazed.

'I don't know.' I start towards the flat to investigate, and just make it into the kitchen when Jack comes crashing through from the lounge. I skid to a stop, shocked by the sight of him. He looks manic, his eyes wild. He stares at me, his chest puffing under his jacket, his shirt hanging from his trousers, his waistcoat undone and the knot of his tie halfway down his torso. He looks a wreck, and when his focus moves and centres on something behind me, his jaw tensing to snapping point, I know he's seen I have company.

I fear Jack might explode at any second and lash out at my *guest*. I can't allow that.

I turn to Tom. 'I'm sorry; I think it's best you leave.' I take his wine glass from his hand and set it to the side, not liking the scowl he has pointed at Jack.

'Who's this?' Tom asks, keeping his eyes on the deranged-looking man in the doorway of my kitchen. I hear Jack draw breath and wait for him to say something, but nothing comes. What can he say? That he's the married man who's fucking me?

'A friend,' I say, taking Tom's arm. 'I'll see you out.' Leading him towards the kitchen door, I look at Jack, my jaw as tight as his. He moves from our path, his nostrils flaring aggressively as we pass. I can see it's taking everything in him not to lunge at Tom and beat the shit out of him.

'I'm not sure I'm cool with leaving you alone with him,' Tom says as we reach the front door. It's open, with splinters of wood hanging off around the lock.

I shake my head to myself. 'He's not that type,' I mumble meekly, trying to smile.

'I don't think your front door would agree.' Tom points at the mangled wood with a frown.

I'm feeling so remorseful for putting him in this position. 'I'm so sorry about this.'

'An ex?' Tom asks, eyebrows high, and I just nod, because what the hell else can I say? 'I don't think he's over you,' he laughs. 'I hope you sort it out.' His sincerity triples my remorse. Leaning down, he gives me a peck on the cheek. 'Bear me in mind if you don't, though, yeah?'

I reach up and give his arm a squeeze. 'Thanks for the drinks and the chat.'

'No problem. See ya, Annie.'

I push the door closed repeatedly, but the latch won't click into place. The damage is extensive: chunks of wood missing, some on the floor. He kicked the door in? He actually kicked the door in and steamrolled through my house like he had some right to stake a claim on me?

I march back to the kitchen and find him leaning against the wall, his head back, his breathing still heavy, his fists clenching. When he hears me enter, he pushes himself away and looks at me, a definite twist to his lip.

'Where's Stephanie?' I ask, matching his threatening stance.

'I don't give a fucking shit,' he bellows, knocking me back a few paces as he straightens and points at me. 'I don't care how unreasonable it sounds, you will not see other men. How the fuck could you do this to me?'

How could I do this to him? How could *I* do this to *him*? 'You selfish arsehole!' I swipe the wine glass off the worktop, sending it sailing across the kitchen and crashing into the wall. The shattering of glass rings through the air, echoing forever. 'Do you think I enjoyed listening to you and her earlier?'

Jack's neck retracts on his shoulders, his eyes wide and wary. 'You listened to us?'

'In the toilets at the gallery!' I scream. 'You couldn't even wait until you got home to fuck her.' I have to cover my ears to try to ease the recurring sounds in my head. I feel Jack's hands wrap around my wrists, trying to pull my hands away. 'Don't touch me!' I fight him, disturbed and hysterical, crying uncontrollably.

'Annie, for fuck's sake.' His attempts to calm me become more forceful as he flings me around and locks my hands behind my back, thrusting my front into the wall. He presses his body into me to hold me in place, his breathing shot like mine. 'Calm down.'

His tall frame pressing me into the wall might be stopping me from escaping, but it doesn't stop me from shaking uncontrollably, rivers of tears streaming down my cheeks. 'Go,' I sob. 'Just go.'

'I'm going nowhere,' he vows, moving his hold of my wrists and locking them in one of his hands. I close my eyes, looking for the darkness to match my world, but I can't prevent the bawls of despair from ripping through me. Jack waits for my sobs to subside before he speaks, keeping me restrained. 'I took her in there to calm down, Annie. She was falling all over the place, getting louder and louder, more offensive and rude.'

'I heard her moaning and you fucking growling. She was telling you to take her dress off. Did you? Did you take her fucking dress off, Jack?'

He spins me around, keeping my hands behind my back

with his, pressed into the wall. The scruff on his jaw is rolling in waves of anger. 'She was trying to get my clothes off. She was drunk, Annie. All I did was fight her the fuck off me. I wasn't growling, I was whispering because I could hear someone had come in the fucking ladies'.'

I push the back of my head into the wall, trying to escape the bullets of fury shooting from his angry eyes.

'Are you hearing me?' he roars in my face. 'Are you fucking listening to what I'm telling you?'

I nod, my chin trembling, my face stinging.

'If you had been in that bathroom any longer, you would have heard the row. You would have seen me storm out of there. You would have seen Stephanie slap a waitress for apparently staring at my arse.'

I gulp down my horror, unable to be relieved or grateful. 'What?'

He laughs sardonically. 'Oh yes, she put on an epic performance tonight.'

'You should have told me,' I whisper.

'You didn't give me the chance.' Jack closes his eyes, his body going lax against me, and then he moves away, pulling his shirt up, turning away from me. My hand covers my mouth when I see the state of his back: red, raw and throbbing. I'm horrified.

'Every time I look at her, Annie,' he says quietly, 'I see the threat in her eyes. She knows I've already left her in my head.' His teeth audibly grind as he drops his shirt and turns to face me, his grey eyes opening and boring into my wide ones. 'She's not going to make this easy for me, even without knowing about you.'

I sniffle, feeling crippling guilt. He's going through this alone – being faced with Stephanie and her manipulation every day – and I've buried my head in the sand.

'You're the only thing that's keeping me going while I try to figure this shit out. Don't give up now, baby. Please.' Jack's gaze drops to my shoulder, and I watch as the hollows in his relaxed jaw start to pulse again. His hand comes up and lightly traces over the strap of my bra. He's not being affectionate.

I realise what's forcing him to keep hold of his temper the moment he turns disgusted grey eyes onto me. 'You're wearing my underwear,' he breathes. He's trying to swallow down some calm. He's failing terribly. Taking the tops of my arms, he holds me in place. 'You have my underwear on and you were going to let another man have you?'

I shake my head meekly.

He recoils. 'Did you kiss him? Tell me you didn't kiss him.'

I fly into defence mode. 'I've been here for months accepting that you get into bed with *her* every night. Not me. *Her.*' A fresh batch of tears tumble free. 'It should be me.' I cough on a sob, looking away.

Jack hisses and releases me, backing away. 'This is poisonous,' he mumbles, raking a frustrated hand through his hair.

Without him holding me up, my knees give and I slide down the wall to my arse. He takes his knuckles to his eye sockets and rubs harshly, letting his head fall back once he's done.

'I know you're scared of the repercussions, Annie,' he says, this time calmly. 'Trust me, so am I, but I'm done with it.'

My heart pounds in my chest as he drops heavily to his knees in front of me, taking my hands and shuffling forward to get close. 'Annie, listen to me.' He squeezes my hands, his face deadly serious. 'If I stay in that hell any longer, there will be nothing left of me.' He drops my hands and grabs my cheeks, holding my face as my tears continue to pour. 'I'm madly in love with you, woman, and I'm hating my screwed-up situation for keeping me from you. I don't care about the consequences. I can't let her manipulate me any more. And I don't care what people will think of me when I leave her.' He kisses my forehead, holding his mouth there, and my hands go to his shoulders and hold onto him. 'We've been walking with our heads in the clouds for too long, baby. I'm not settling for part-time love any more. I just want to be with you. Every day I stall is a day wasted without you. It's another piece of me chipped away.'

I break down in his arms, feeling like everything is coming to a head. The pain and devastation on the horizon is at the forefront of my mind, but I know it's going to be worse than I ever imagined it could be. 'I don't want to lose you,' I murmur weakly, aware that Stephanie has the ability to manipulate Jack, make him feel guilty and influence his decision. How can she be happy knowing how unhappy he is?

'You won't lose me, I swear to God.' He breathes in as he pulls his lips away from my forehead and brings his face to mine, making sure he has my eyes. 'It's not going to be easy, but as long as I have you at the end of it, I can get through it.' Jack's voice quavers, his bottom lip trembling. 'I'm terrified that you're going to decide I'm not worth the heartache and walk away from me.'

'No!' I cry, grabbing his hands on my face. 'I could never walk away from you. I love you too much.' I hate how relieved he looks, as if he doubted it. I might not have told him with words, but I've told him in every other way. I would never have put myself in this situation for anything less than powerful love. The kind that keeps you going. The kind that gives you breath and life. Jack is my life. He's my pulse. He's everything.

He nods and strokes over my hair, his hand falling to my neck and massaging. 'Then we do this together. We'll figure it out.'

He collapses to his arse and hauls me into his body, holding onto me like he's never held me before. His heart is pounding hard, his emotion clear in his constant swallows. 'I love you. I'll never regret not walking away from you that night,' he tells me quietly.

I smile through my wretchedness, squeezing him harder,

reinforcing how I feel without words. 'Crossing that road to you was the best move I've ever made.'

He kisses my head constantly, feeling me everywhere as I snuggle in his embrace, letting myself calm under his touch. 'We'll be all right.' Gently breaking away from me, he smiles mildly, a smile full of the worry and apprehension that I'm feeling myself. 'I should go,' he says regretfully, just as his phone rings. On a weary exhale, he looks down at the screen, as do I. Her name stares up at us and brings on another level of despondency.

'Where is she?'

'At home. I walked out when she came at me with her claws.'

I wince, but a flash of anger creeps up on me. The sooner he's out of there, the better. He stands and pulls me to my feet, brushing my hair from my sticky face. 'I need to fix your door before I go.' Taking my hand, he walks us through to the hall where my door is literally hanging off its hinges. There's no way Jack's fixing that. He'll be here all night.

'I'll call a locksmith.'

'I'm not leaving you with your door like this.'

'Then you shouldn't have smashed it down,' I mutter.

'Then you shouldn't have brought a man—' My hand zooms up and covers his lips, and his eyes widen. Then his mouth opens and shifts a little, and he bites down on my hand.

'Ouch!' I yell, retracting quickly, but my split second of a chance to retaliate is stolen from me when he seizes me around the waist and pins me to his body. Taking my arms and draping them over his shoulders, he gets nose to nose with me. I scowl. He chuckles lightly. I have no idea why. Tonight has been about as funny as a horror film. 'Why the hell are you laughing?' I ask indignantly.

'Because if I don't laugh I'll embarrass myself and cry like a fucking baby.'

I sigh. 'You'd better go.'

His shining eyes dull immediately. 'I don't want to leave you.'

'You don't have any choice,' I point out, detaching him from my body and moving towards the door before I beg him to stay.

'Can I see you tomorrow?' Jack asks. 'I'm in the office all day but can get away for an hour for lunch.'

I fight my hands to my sides when he stops in front of me, giving me hopeful eyes. After everything, I just want to charge at his waist, tackle him to the floor and hide in his chest. And hide him from *her*. 'You're in the office? But it's Saturday.'

'I have stuff to catch up on.'

And it keeps him out of the house. 'Where?' I ask.

'There's a little place at the back of the docks.'

'That's a bit close to your office, isn't it?'

'It's Saturday. No one from the office will be around.'

'Okay,' I agree, without hesitation. If Jack's comfortable with it, then there's no reason for me not to be. 'Noon? I'm seeing Micky for coffee at ten. Shouldn't be more than an hour.'

'Noon,' Jack confirms, stopping at the door and giving the splintered wood another inspection. 'Call the locksmith straight away and text me when they've been.' He turns and gives me stern eyes.

I sigh. 'I can't text you.'

'Yes, you can and you will. I won't sleep until I know it's done.'

Is he becoming a bit complacent? All the signs suggest it. Bashing down my door, meeting for lunch, telling me to text him when he's going to be in bed. I know he's made a decision, but he still needs to tread carefully, as well as think about how and when he's going to do what needs to be done. Cold waves ripple through my bloodstream at the thought.

After kissing my cheek, he wanders down the path. 'I'll text you the address of the restaurant.'

'Okay. See you tomorrow.' I push my door closed as best I can, then go in search of my phone to call a locksmith. They can't specify a time, so once I've let Jack know, I'm given little choice but to sit on the couch and wait for them to turn up, when I'm so desperate to fall into bed and shut my mind down. But there's no hope of that happening. He's leaving her. You'd think it would be what any woman who's in love with a married man would want to hear, but given everything I know, I'm full of dread rather than elation.

Dread for Jack.

My Jack.

Chapter 20

I come awake to banging – relentless, panicked banging. Diving up in a daze, I stumble down the hallway to my front door, trying to straighten my sleepy mind while shaking my dead arm awake. It's full of pins and needles, which results in my hand refusing to grip the handle of the door in order to turn and open it. I mentally encourage my muscles to wake up as the banging continues, my head rattling more with every impatient thump of the door. 'Hold on!' I yell, swapping hands and wrenching the door open.

I growl before my sleepy eyes tell me who the culprit is. I soon wake up when a blurry silhouette of a person becomes Jack. He looks a little flustered. 'What are you doing?'

'It's one o'clock,' he grumbles, pushing me inside and following, shutting the door behind him. 'You didn't acknowledge the address of where we were meeting for lunch, and you didn't fucking turn up.' He points a finger in my face. 'I've been worried sick!'

I blink a few times, letting everything he's just shouted at me drip into my brain. 'It's one o'clock?' I blurt in panic, turning and running into my lounge to find my phone. 'I was supposed to meet Micky at ten,' I cry, pulling cushions from the couch and throwing them over my shoulder. No phone. I shove my hand down the sides in turn, feeling around.

'Looking for this?' Jack picks up my phone from the TV cabinet and holds it up.

'Yes!' I rush over and snatch it from his hand, finding its

battery is dead. 'Shit.' I quickly plug it in and wait impatiently for it to switch on. Sounds start ringing, dinging and singing chaotically when it comes to life. I wince with every separate sound, seeing missed calls and text messages springing onto my screen; not just from Micky, but from Nat and Lizzy too. I can see Micky in my mind now, calling them to try and find out where I am. Going through the texts, I see each and every one of my mates has left a message asking where the hell I am and if my lay was up to scratch. I quickly call Micky, worried that he might be on his way over to track me down. 'Damn,' I mutter when it goes to voicemail. 'It's me. I slept in.' I laugh like an idiot. 'Call me!' Hanging up, I proceed to call Nat, telling her the same excuse, moving away from Jack when she asks, a bit too loudly, if I'm able to walk this morning. I peek at him, and his nostrils flare dangerously. 'I'll call you later,' I say, hanging up. Then I dial Lizzy. She might not be so easy to fob off.

'Where the hell are you?' she answers in greeting.

'Slept in.' I screw my face up, waiting for her scoff of disbelief. In the ten years I've known Lizzy, I've never slept in. Not this late, anyway. I look at Jack and see him roll his eyes, a sign of his annoyance.

'I'm on my way over to check you're not dead.'

'No need.' I shoot Jack a pained look, watching as he flops down on the couch. 'I'm on my way to my mum and dad's.'

'Oh. Okay. So how was it? You seeing him again? I like Rugby Player Tom!'

I turn away from Jack and cringe. 'I can't talk right now.'

'Oh my God! Is he still there?' she squeals excitedly. 'Call me later. I want every dirty little detail.'

'I will.' I hang up and drop my phone on the couch, exhausted after my mammoth session of bullshit. 'I cannot believe I slept in till this time.' It shouldn't be a surprise. The locksmith didn't turn up until 4 a.m. and I didn't get to bed until five.

'Don't sweat it,' Jack grumbles. 'It's not like you've given me a heart attack or anything.'

'What did you think had happened to me?' I ask, passing him to go to the kitchen. 'There was no risk of the madman who beat my door down returning.'

'He's here now,' he replies, low and husky and . . . very close behind me.

I whirl around and collide with his chest. 'Oh!' I'm grabbed and hauled up to his lips, and then indulged with a long, passionate hello kiss. 'Hmmm,' I sigh, relaxing into the smooth, slow rotations of his tongue. 'Hello to you too.'

'Fuck, I've missed you.' He keeps our lips sealed as he lowers me back down to my feet.

'It's been twelve hours.'

'Every minute felt like a century,' he mumbles into my mouth moodily. 'I didn't sleep a wink, I daydreamed my way through my morning and tapped the table in the restaurant a million times with my fork while I waited for you.' He pulls back and scowls at me.

It's then I see it. A nasty red mark on his cheekbone. My eyes root on the blemish, fury burning a hole through my gut.

'It's nothing.' He covers the mark and steps away, avoiding my furious eyes.

'Nothing?' I ask, astounded. *Nothing?* I can feel myself beginning to quiver with the rage building. Last night she shredded him with her fucking nails, and now this? 'You might not be able to retaliate, Jack, but there's nothing to stop me.' I storm past him, enraged, set on finding Stephanie and giving her payback for all the marks I've seen on Jack, *and* the ones I haven't too.

'Annie, stop.' He snakes his arm around my waist from behind and lifts me from my feet, stopping me.

'She can't do this to you.' I shout, wriggling to break free from his hold. 'I swear, Jack, I'll rip her fucking arms off so she can't touch you again!'

'Annie, calm the hell down.' His voice is so level, so composed, as he takes me back to the kitchen. '*You* will be doing nothing.' Placing me on my feet, he tilts me a warning look.

This just isn't fair. 'How would you feel if you found me with one of these?' I ask, pointing at the mark, flinching as I imagine her hand connecting with his face. His beautiful face.

Jack's low, threatening growl gives me my answer. 'Don't ask silly questions, Annie.'

'It's not silly, it's genuine. I want to know.'

His face looks murderous. 'Kill.'

'I rest my case.' My lips form a straight thin line.

Jack visibly gathers patience. 'I didn't come here to argue with you. Please, just let me deal with it.'

I open my mouth to argue once again, but he covers it with his palm. My eyes become angry slits.

'Please.' His plea pierces my fury like a needle, and my swallow is lumpy. I'm stressing him out more, giving him something else to worry about. And though I'd love nothing more than to rip his wife limb from limb, I relent, pulling his hand down from my face so I can speak. 'I'm sorry.'

'Never be sorry for loving me *that* much.' His fingers thread through my hair and grip at the base of my neck. 'Do you hear me?' I nod, and Jack nods in return. 'Good. Now, make us some coffee.' He plants a kiss on the tip of my nose, turns me in his arms, and sends me on my way with a tap on my arse.

I set about preparing us a strong, steaming cup of the good stuff, but I pause as I spoon some granules into my gigantic mug. 'Where is she?' I ask, swinging around.

'On her way over for coffee,' he replies flippantly.

I'm not in the least bit amused by his attempt to lighten our mood. 'You're not funny.'

'She's gone to her parents'.' He rolls his eyes, like I should know that. 'We ...' His forehead wrinkles a little. 'Well, it didn't go too well when I got home.' He points to the mark on his face, and for the first time I ask myself *why* she hit him.

Oh fuck, has she figured it out? Yesterday gave a chain of clues. Did she rewind through it all and piece things together? Or did Jack tell her he's leaving? I start to sweat, and then steel myself to ask the operative question. 'What happened?'

'The usual.' He shrugs his big shoulders dismissively. 'I didn't say what she wanted to hear, so the fingernails and screams come out to play. She's gone to her parents'. It's her father's birthday. They picked her up and took her home for the evening to join in on the jamboree with all the family, friends and business associates. The thought of sitting there pretending my life is perfect, pretending to be the perfect couple, doesn't appeal. Funny that.'

I spoon two sugars in his coffee – just the way I know he likes it – and stir, watching him, thinking how casually he reeled all that off. Because he's used to it – the drama, the fights, the lashing fingernails – and that isn't good. I hand him his coffee and rest back on the worktop, cupping mine with my palms.

'Anyway.' He takes a quick sip and rids his hands of his mug, then proceeds to try to take mine. I put some resistance up, taking a big gulp of caffeine before he can take it away. He laughs under his breath as he slides it onto the counter, and then takes my hips, hunkering down, getting his face close to mine. 'Enough of all that. You're supposed to be my happy place.'

'Happy place?' I ask, slowly pulling back when his palm slides over my waist before drifting down a little and stroking over my inside thigh, just a fraction away from my crotch. I go rigid.

'My happy place,' he declares, restraining his grin.

I gasp, shocked, totally forced. 'Cheeky!'

Jack laughs, a true happy laugh that sinks straight beneath my skin and impales my heart. He dips and hauls me up over his shoulder. I yelp, laughing, as he strides out of the kitchen, holding me in place by the backs of my thighs. 'My coffee!' I protest, not really giving a fuck about my caffeine, but feeling the need to put up a fight.

'Fuck the coffee,' he scoffs. 'I have something far tastier to wake you up.'

I grin like an idiot and hold his hips, eyeing his arse as he hauls me down the hallway to my bedroom. I land on the bed, laughing. Jack pulls off his suit jacket and tosses it to the side carelessly, yanks his tie free, and then his fingers are quickly working the buttons of his shirt. I remain still and happy while I watch him strip down, licking my lips provocatively when he pushes his trousers down his sturdy thighs. He kicks his shoes and socks off, and finally his trousers, leaving him graced with only his boxers. My eyes drop to his groin. He's hard, the shape of his cock prominent and calling for me. Slipping his finger into the waist of his boxers, he pushes them down and it springs free. I lose my breath, my anticipation building.

I reach for him with my hand, asking him to come to me, but he shakes his head, taking a loose hold at the base. 'Take your T-shirt off,' he orders, his voice edgy and firm. My hands go straight to the hem of my T-shirt and I pull it up over my head, revealing my breasts, tipped with hard pink buds. He smiles, his eyes sparkling. 'Now come here.' I'm on my knees and crawling towards the end of the bed, my eyes remaining on his arousal the whole way until the tip of my nose is touching the tip of his cock. He has something tastier than coffee. He wasn't wrong. My tongue leaves my mouth, keen and hungry, but he pulls away before I make contact, devastating me.

'Want a taste?'

I try to play it all cool and nonchalant. I try. But next thing I know, I'm knocking his hand away and wrapping my lips around his flesh. Jack's stomach concaves, his body bending over to try and escape my wicked mouth. I don't let him.

'Holy shit, Annie.' His hand comes to my head and presses

me to him. 'Fuck!' His bark of shocked pleasure soon changes into a deep moan of ecstasy.

I look up as I move forward, getting comfy, loving the feel of the taut velvet skin of his manhood gliding in and out of my mouth. His head is dropped back, his throat stretched, showing every hard swallow he makes. And there are many.

He tastes divine. Better than coffee. I'll take this over caffeine any day of the week. His hands in my hair start to meld against my scalp, and his hips start to rotate to meet the advances of my mouth. I work my hand too, doubling his pleasure. Then he adds to *my* pleasure, his hands leaving my hair and feeling down until he has a breast cupped in each palm. It's me moaning now, my pace faltering for a fleeting moment while I accustom myself to the feel of him caressing my aching boobs and pump my mouth up and down, the tip of his cock hitting the back of my throat each time. I hear mumbles, I hear moans, I hear barks of pleasure-filled despair. It all fuels me. Sliding my hand down his stomach, I reach between his thighs and stroke his heavy balls tenderly. His body convulses. 'Ohhhh . . . fuckkkkkk.'

I smile and draw back slowly until his cock pops free, then I circle my tongue teasingly around the tip, watching him as his head goes limp, dropping. His eyes are closed, but a cheeky bite of the tip of his cock remedies that. They spring open, low and hooded and clouded with want.

'Better than coffee?' he asks. His chest heaves, his eyes falling to his hands moulding my breasts. I should be asking *him* that question, but instead of doing that, and instead of answering him, I start a punishing pump with my fist, ensuring my hold is tight.

'Motherf—' he chokes, jolting forward on unsteady legs, his hold of my boobs becoming brutal. I wince but battle through the slight discomfort, shooting back and forth at an epic rate. 'Shit . . . Annie . . .'

My tongue circles his tip as my fist continues to work him, and then when I sense he's close, I swathe the top third of his cock and suck. It's his undoing. A flow of curses come thick and fast, and plenty of verbal warnings too. I take him all, feeling him come in long, surging pulses, his essence pouring into my mouth.

'Oh, Jesus Christ,' he puffs, grinding his groin against my mouth, trying to catch a breath. Pulling free and falling towards me, he flattens me on the bed with his heavy sweaty body. I smile, satisfied, and swallow. 'You are fucking amazing,' he pants, a dead weight spread all over me.

'And now I really need that coffee.'

He laughs and struggles to push himself up onto his elbows until he has my face in his sights. I blank out the blemish on his cheekbone and give him a dazzling smile, feeling rather pleased with myself. 'I'm booking in one of those for every day of the rest of our lives together.'

'It'll cost ya,' I warn.

'Name your price, baby.'

His serious demand gives me pause. I was being playful. I had nothing in mind specifically. 'Can I think about it?'

'Yes, but you only have until tomorrow.' He dips and kisses my forehead, and then rolls onto his back.

I'm straight up on my elbows, looking at him lying beside me. 'What's happening tomorrow?' Has he decided tomorrow is the day he'll tell Stephanie it's over? Once again I'm breaking out in a sweat, and it has nothing to do with the effort I just put into giving Jack head.

His head falls to the side. 'You're giving me another one of those.' He points at his semi-erect cock, then to my mouth.

I calm a little, falling onto my back next to him. It's only a little, because one thing we haven't talked about is *when* he plans on telling her. I need to know. I need to be prepared . . . and possibly out of the country. I didn't want to ask, and I planned never to, but all of these mild heart attacks I keep having aren't good for me. 'Jack, I'm not asking to put pressure on you, but can you give me some kind of indication as to when you plan on ...' My question rolls to a stop. I don't know why I can't finish.

'I tried this morning before her parents picked her up.' He shakes his head as he glances away. 'But every time I went to say the words ... it's like she knows what's coming and gives me crazy eyes to remind me of what I can expect.'

'You sure she knows?' I ask. Maybe he's wrong. I can't figure out if it's better for her to be expecting it or not.

'Oh, she knows. In bed last night she—'

'Whoa!' I half-laugh, half-gape at him, not quite believing those words just came out of his mouth.

He drops his head to the side and gazes at my disbelieving face, taking my hand and squeezing. 'Just listen,' he orders softly, so I brace myself, breathing in deeply and wincing in advance. 'I got in the spare bed last night, for obvious reasons.' He clenches his eyes shut, and his body definitely shudders. 'She climbed in with me in the middle of the night. I pushed her away, Annie.' Jack points to the blemish on his cheekbone. 'She knows.' I see all kinds of emotions in his eyes, and definitely a bit of guilt. And he must see the fear in mine, because he rushes on. 'She won't make me stay. I promise you.'

I fall quiet for a moment, thinking. He needs to get out. He needs to get out now, and he would need to even if I wasn't in his life. This is fucked up on so many levels. 'Will you tell her about me?' I ask, biting my lip nervously.

'God, no.' He shakes his head vehemently. 'No. I want to keep you as far away from it as possible, which will be fucking hard when I know I'll need you close.'

He wants me out of the firing line. He wants to protect me from the repercussions. But really, things will be no different. We'll still need to sneak around because no one can know about us, which leads me to another question. Yet I don't voice it. How long will it be before we can just . . . be? What's an acceptable period of time for someone to move on? What's an acceptable period of time for a woman to start seeing a man who's recently left his wife? Months? Years?

I fold on the inside a little, wondering how long I have to wait until I can say Jack is mine. Just mine. Some of him was better than nothing of him. I couldn't walk away. Still can't. My only out isn't really an out at all. It feels more like a punishment. When Jack leaves her, people will see the state of Stephanie, because there's no doubt she'll be spiralling downwards. They will judge Jack, and if they find out about me, they will judge me too.

'Annie?' Jack's anxious call of my name pulls my eyes from the ceiling to him. His face is worried as he squeezes my hand. Threading his fingers through mine, he holds on tight, as if he senses my despondent thoughts and he's worried I might up and leave.

'If anyone finds out about us, they'll blame me,' I murmur, looking back up to the ceiling. 'To them, I'll be the cause of a woman's devastation and heartache, and I kind of am, Jack. No matter how you look at this situation. I feel like karma is going to plague me for the rest of my life.'

'Hey.' Jack rolls into me, lying on his side beside me while I remain flat on my back, looking at my bedroom ceiling. 'You are not the cause, Annie. You are a symptom, that's all.'

I laugh lightly. 'Come on, Jack. How many people do you honestly think will accept that? It's a crock of shit. If you hadn't found me at the bar that night, you would have remained in your marriage, happy or not. Right now, I *am* part of the reason. That's the crux of it. I'm not going to kid myself that others won't see it the same way if they find out about us.'

'I love you.' He grinds the three words through a frustrated jaw. 'I left her before, remember? This isn't about thinking the grass is greener, or being blindsided by great sex and excitement.' He reaches for my face and pulls it towards him so he has my eyes. 'I'm not delusional, Annie. I'm head over heels. I don't care what people think if they find out, but I'll do my best to make sure they don't. I need to keep you away from it.' He drops a light kiss on the edge of my mouth. 'I have one shot on this earth. One life. I can't see my days through to the end with someone who I'm *not* supposed to be with. I wish I'd met you fifteen years ago. But I didn't. I can't dwell on that.' His eyes cloud over as his thumb swipes slowly across my bottom lip, his gaze following its journey. 'I just have to be thankful that you did eventually show up.' He slowly returns his eyes to mine, and I feel my bottom lip tremble under his thumb. 'It's you and me against the world, baby. Don't give up, do you hear me?'

My face twists with sadness, my throat closing up on me, and I roll over, putting myself on his chest and burying my face in his neck, needing closeness and comfort . . . needing Jack. 'I love you.' My voice shakes with so many emotions, and my body presses into his as far as I can get it. 'I'll hold your hand through this if you hold mine.'

'I'll never let go, Annie. Not for anything.'

Chapter 21

I look over my shoulder when I hear Jack's footsteps padding into the kitchen, finding him with his phone in his hand, spinning it slowly, thoughtfully. I dip a spoon in my fresh cup of coffee. He's pulled his boxers on, but the sight I'd usually be rapt by is being overshadowed by the blankness of his expression. 'Are you okay?' I ask, slowing my stirring.

'Stephanie's father,' he says, holding up his phone. 'I should be at his birthday celebrations beside my wife.' He smiles, but it's strained. 'Because God forbid anyone notices my absence and surmises what that might mean.'

Placing my spoon on the drainer, I take my coffee and turn towards him. 'If you have to go ...' I start, swallowing down the strength I need to say the words that I really don't want to say, 'then ...' It's no good. I can't tell him to go.

'I don't want to go,' he says softly.

My smile is relieved but sad. 'Okay,' I reply, not sure of what else to say. I don't feel any sense of triumph that he's choosing not to go. This isn't a trivial *he picked me over her* situation.

'I don't want to make assumptions, but I was hoping we could do something.' Jack gives me hopeful eyes.

'Like what?' I ask. We hardly have the luxury of freedom to go where we please and do what we like.

'Like just be together.' He shrugs, almost embarrassed. 'Watch trashy television, eat junk, be lazy.'

I smile. I don't need to venture into public. Not when I can hide in here with Jack and smother him all day long. 'I like that idea.'

'You do?' He smiles too, bright and beautiful, and the knowledge that such a simple thing can make him so elated warms me soul-deep.

'I need to pop to the shop,' I tell him, swilling my mug in the sink. 'I need milk.'

'And junk food,' he pipes up, his excitement growing. 'Get some of those strawberry sweets. The big ones. Giant Strawbs. Lots of them. And how about I cook something?'

'You're going to cook for me?' I ask, loving the sound of that. No man's ever cooked for me before. Not ever, and I love that Jack will be the first.

'Yes.' Jack heads for the drawers and starts pulling them open one by one. 'I'll write you a list. Where do you keep your pens and paper?'

'Here.' I reach to the shelf and pull down a pad, then go through my bag to find a pen. I hand them to him and he takes a seat, starting to write. I look over his shoulder, peeking down at his list. His *long* list. Beef stock? Cornflour? Crème fraiche? He's cooking for me, and he's cooking from scratch?

'Sherbet dip?' I ask, frowning.

'Yes.' He looks up at me. 'You know, the little pouches of sherbet that come with a strawberry lollipop inside? You lick and dip, and when the lolly has gone, you lick your finger and shove it in to scoop out the sherbet.'

Oh God, he's adorable. 'Lick your finger and shove it in? Will that be dessert?'

His eyes try to narrow, but they're glimmering too much. 'I have something else in mind for dessert.'

He rips his list off the pad and hands it to me.

I take the paper and lean down, offering him my lips. 'And what do I get in return for delivering all this sweet stuff?'

Placing his lips on mine, he grins. 'I'm cooking you dinner, woman. What more could you want?'

'I'm sure I can think of something.'

His grin widens. 'A sleepover?'

I recoil, a little surprised. 'A sleepover?'

'She's staying at her parents'.'

To fall asleep with him and to wake up with him? I push my lips to his hard, intending for it to be a forceful peck, but Jack soon turns it into more, pulling me down onto his lap and coaxing my mouth open with a few nudges of his tongue against my lips. I open up to him and lose myself in a few minutes of his mouth's attention.

His groin flexes upwards into my bum, making his hard-on known. 'You'd better go before I take you back to the bedroom for some more affection.' He says it like that's a problem. I hold on tighter to him, my way of telling him that I'm totally cool with that. 'Come on.' He taps my bum and tries to usher me from his lap, ignoring my grumbles of protest.

'How about dessert now, dinner later?' I try, pushing my chest into his and nibbling at his ear, making a point of breathing heavily into it. I'm all worked up as a result of that smouldering kiss. He needs to take responsibility for the condition he has me in.

He laughs, forcing me to my feet. 'Can I use your shower while you're gone?'

'Sure,' I mutter moodily, making my way to my bedroom to throw on some clothes.

'You're walking funny,' he calls, amused.

I ignore him and try to shrink the need that's wedged itself between my thighs . . . making me walk like my knickers are up my arse.

After collecting everything on Jack's shopping list, I make my way to the checkout. I quickly snatch some magazines from the nearby stand and toss them on the conveyor belt, as well as a chocolate bar, then head to the other end and start packing as the cashier rings it all through. After paying, I pull out a magazine, hang the bag from the crook of my arm and start wandering home. I flick through the pages as I chew my chocolate, not looking where I'm going. The weekly gossip mag holds my attention, leaving everyone else to sidestep around me.

'Annie!'

I look up and see Lizzy jogging across the road, looking all sweaty in her running gear, her short hair tugged back in a haphazard ponytail and a Frappuccino in her hand. I shove the magazine in my bag and chew rapidly as she makes it to me. 'What's with the sports get-up?' I ask.

'Wine. That's what. I either need to stop drinking it or try to counteract it. I must have gained eight pounds while me and Jason were split up.' She reaches forward and pulls the side of my bag open a little. 'Been shopping?'

'Just some milk.'

'Milk and sweets?'

'I'm having a bumming day.'

'I thought you were at your mum and dad's today.'

'Work took over.' I hope I look better than I feel when I lie, because I feel like a million bags of shite. 'I have an exhibition next weekend in Liverpool.' Let's get that in while I can. 'Lots of prep.'

'Oh well.' She sounds as interested as I hoped she would: not interested at all. 'Hey, come on, give me all the juicy details.' She starts jogging on the spot, grinning. 'Are his thighs still as impressive?'

I straighten my lips and shake my head. 'He's nice, but . . .'

'Urghhhh,' she groans, dropping her head back in despair. 'You're a hard woman to please, Annie Ryan.'

My mouth forms a tight smile. That's not true at all. I just want Jack. 'How's Jason?'

Her eyes sparkle, and I relish the sight. I just hope the twat doesn't fuck up his chances. 'He's being so attentive and romantic. I know you guys are unsure, but he's trying really hard.'

'Then I'm happy for you.'

'I know you are.' She kisses my cheek and starts towards the road. 'Lunch tomorrow? Nat's up for it.'

'Sure.'

'Call you in the morning!' Lizzy disappears around the corner, and I carry on my way home, ignoring the guilt rising after lying to my best mate. Again.

Jack's waiting for me in the hallway when I walk through the front door, freshly showered and looking edible. His hair is wet and floppy, his scruff bordering ... well, scruffy, and he's back in his boxers. His eyes light up when he sees me, but instead of seizing me and saying hello, he swipes the bag from my hand and virtually shoves his head in, his big body on the verge of shaking with excitement. 'What do I have to do to get a hello like that?' I ask, watching as he rifles through the bag.

He halts mid-rummage and looks up at me with a cute smile. If he wasn't so adorable, I'd still have an indignant look on my face, but instead I'm smiling too. 'Is it sad that I can't think of anything I'd rather do than veg out and eat crap with you?'

'That sounded poetic,' I laugh, kicking off my flip-flops.

He switches the bag to one hand before circling me and picking me up from behind with an arm curled around my waist. He carries me into the lounge. Or what *was* my lounge. Now it looks like it's been set up for a glorified slumber party.

'I got everything ready,' Jack says, heading for the kitchen. 'I'll cook later. After we've watched a film.'

'Okay,' I agree, looking around. He's dragged in all the pillows from my bedroom, along with the duvet, and pulled the throw and cushions down from the couch. My king-size bedcover is spread across the floor, the pillows propped up against the sofa and the cushions haphazardly spread around the sides. He's drawn the curtains, making the room dusky and cosy, and turned the TV on, although the screen is paused. '*Top Gun?*' I ask, bemused.

'Shit, yeah.' Jack comes back in from the kitchen with his Giant Strawbs, takes my hand and pulls me onto the covers. 'Best film ever made.' He starts to strip me until he has me down to my knickers. He wants jet planes and sweets.

I can do no more than let him do his thing and arrange me where he wants me, smiling the whole time. 'Who did you want to be?'

'Iceman,' he answers immediately, not needing an elaboration on the question and not sensing the mockery in my tone. 'You good?' He sits back on his haunches and looks at me propped up cosily on the cushions in my knickers.

'I'm good.'

'Good.' He grabs the remote, settles beside me and starts shoving jelly strawberries into his mouth.

I shake my head with a smile as I lift his arm and crawl into his side, getting snuggly. I'm not going to deny it. This is some seriously enjoyable stuff.

I watch *Top Gun* for the first time in twenty years, but my head's not totally in it. I'm listening to Jack munch, feeling his chest compress and decompress and just generally relishing our closeness. It's a novelty to just . . . be. Every so often, half a jelly strawberry blocks my view of the screen, and I open up and let Jack slip it into my mouth until I'm stuffed and have to push his hand away. 'I won't eat whatever you're going to cook me.' My eyes become heavy, my body naturally moulds into his side, until the last thing I remember is Maverick and Goose rocking out to 'Great Balls of Fire'.

I've never felt so serene and comfortable. I'm somewhere between sleep and consciousness, Jack's chest warm under my cheek, my leg sprawled across his thighs, my palm on his pec. His arm is curled around my waist, holding me to him, his chin resting on top of my head. In my sleepy wonderland, I note the film must have finished, because there's silence except for Jack's light breathing. Burrowing into his body some more, I sigh happily into the darkness, feeling him respond to my move, kissing the top of my head in his sleep. Then I'm drifting back off again.

The sharp jerk of his body beneath mine wakes me, then the soft sound of my name has my lids flickering and slowly peeling open. 'Annie,' Jack says again. I turn my face up to his, but he's not looking at me. He's looking across the room, and when I slowly crane my neck to find out what has his attention, all the warmth I'm feeling turns to ice. I push myself away from his body abruptly, ignoring my waking muscles that are screaming their protest, pulling painfully. There's no time for me to consider giving them the slow moves they need, because though they're not fully awake, my mind is. And so are my eyes, which are open wide and staring at Lizzy and Micky, who are standing at the entrance to my lounge.

Chapter 22

I clam up, looking away, ashamed. The disappointment on their faces is more than I can bear and only a smidgen of what I expect is to come. Their silence is excruciating.

Jack shifts next to me and I look at him. His face is serious, but I can see he's desperately trying to feed me some reassurance. It's in vain. 'Do you want me to go?' he asks quietly, instantly giving me something else to make my mind spin about.

I don't know. Do I? Will Jack serve as a support, or will he fuel the situation? My face must tell him that I'm in a muddle over how best to approach this, because he reaches for my hand and squeezes.

'I'll stay.' He makes the decision for me, and, with my own head not helping me out, I go with his instinct and nod a little.

'You can leave,' Micky butts in. I look across and find my oldest friend looking the most serious I've ever seen.

'I'll be staying,' Jack counters smoothly and firmly, getting to his feet, showing no shyness at being virtually naked. I follow his lead, gathering the covers and pulling them in before standing and facing my friends.

The look of disdain on Micky's face is fierce. 'How about I don't give you the option?'

'How about you do and this doesn't get nasty?' Jack retorts, the muscles of his back tensing dangerously.

'All right!' Lizzy interjects, holding her hands up, looking as equally pissed off as the two men in the room. She closes her eyes and gathers strength. 'What the hell is going on, Annie?'

'She's fucking a married man, that's what's going on.' Micky spits nastily. 'Why don't you run along back to your wife? Tell her what you've been up to? Or maybe I should go tell her.'

Jack lunges forward threateningly, leaving me no choice but to jump in his path before they start scrapping in my lounge. 'Stop!' I shout, placing a hand on Jack's chest firmly. 'I think it's best you go.' I look up at him, and he immediately starts shaking his head.

'No.' He looks adamant. 'Not so these two can make you start questioning what you're doing.'

'That's exactly what we're going to do,' Micky yells. 'Make her see some fucking sense.'

'Just stop!' I yell, turning to face my oldest friend. 'I *know* what I'm doing!'

'You do?' Lizzy pipes up. 'Are you sure, because I'm pretty sure you must have lost your fucking mind, Annie. What has he promised you? He's going to leave her?' She laughs coldly. 'Yes, they all say that, but when it comes to the crunch, they're all ball-less. You're a bit of fun. Something exciting and different. Don't you see that?'

'It's nothing like that,' I yell, starting to lose my shit. Her experience, albeit at the complete opposite end of the spectrum, cannot be used as a comparison. 'And if all you're going to do is stand there and make judgements, you can leave now. You know nothing about this, and you don't look like you're in the mood to listen, so get out.'

Both of my friends recoil, shocked, and Jack's hand rests on my shoulder to calm me. It won't work. I'm infuriated that they think they have our situation nailed. They don't. I'm not just fucking him. I back up into Jack's front, showing where my alliance lies, my face fixed and determined.

'Calm down, Annie,' Jack says quietly from behind, turning me to face him. He looks down at me with a soft smile, reaching up to my eyes and wiping under each tenderly. 'This is just part of the process. One of the challenges we need to face.'

He's talking to me like there's no one else in the room, and it's having the effect he's wanting. Under his soft order, I swallow down my frustration and pull myself together.

'Don't drive your friends away. You need them.' He dips and pushes his lips to my forehead, and though I now can't see his face, I know he'll have a trained eye on my friends. 'I'm going to get dressed.'

He heads for my bedroom, slowing when he reaches the door, needing Micky to move so he can pass through. It takes my friend a few seconds to find the courtesy, but he eventually shifts to the side, allowing Jack to pass, even if it's on a curled lip. I see Lizzy blow out a breath as Jack disappears and Micky uncoils a little.

Then they both look at me again, but before I let their condemnation beat me down, I turn and scoop up my T-shirt from the floor. 'You can put the kettle on if you want to stay. I need to get dressed.'

'I'll put the kettle on,' Lizzy sighs, taking Micky's arm and pushing him through to the kitchen, leaving me alone. I spend the few minutes it takes me to dress trying to dampen down my simmering resentment. I fail. But I need to face this head on. No more hiding.

When I join them in the kitchen, I find Lizzy is drinking wine and Micky has a beer in his hand. I've pushed them to drink.

'I didn't give you a key so you can infiltrate my privacy,' I say as I get my own glass down from the cupboard and pour myself some wine. I've pushed myself to drink too.

Neither of them have anything to say to that, but I'm not kidding myself that the conversation ends here.

'I had a training session with Jason this afternoon,' Micky explains. 'He was telling me he bumped into Tom.' His head cocks, his eyebrows rise. 'And Tom mentioned some bloke breaking down your front door.'

'What the hell are you thinking?' Lizzy jumps in, pointing her wine glass towards the door, as if there could be any confusion about what she's talking about. 'I knew you were hiding something.'

'Is it any wonder?' I ask. 'Why would I confide in you when I knew you would be like this? I don't expect you to understand.'

'What's to understand?' Micky pipes up, dropping to a chair. 'All this time you've been lying to us. You're going where no one should go.'

'Do you think I don't know that? Do you think I walked into this with my eyes closed?'

'You must have.' Micky laughs bitterly.

'This isn't a game,' I shout. 'He's not a trophy to be won. I fucking love him!' I shock myself with the decibel level of my voice, and Lizzy and Micky's eyes bug. But I don't give either of them an opportunity to come back at me with their thoughts. Not until they know the deal. 'I've torn myself to shreds repeatedly!' I yell. 'I've beaten myself up and constantly dreaded the consequences, but none of it has made me lose sight of how I feel. I can't pretend I don't feel this way. I can't turn my back on it because I'm scared.' My voice is starting to quiver, but I soldier on, determined to try and make them see things from my perspective. 'He's worth the shit I know I'm going to go through, because I love him. So much it fucking hurts right here.' I thump my chest. 'It frightens me, but the thought of not having him, of coming out of this mess without him, fucking terrifies me.' I finish off my speech with a long glug of wine, shaking as I bring the glass down to the worktop. 'I'm not asking you to give me your blessing. I'm just asking you not to assume you know the deal, because you don't.'

'He's not yours to take, Annie,' Lizzy says quietly. 'Don't go there, please.'

'It's too late.' I drop my eyes to the floor. 'And I'm not taking him. He's coming to me willingly.'

'Do you think his wife will see it like that?' Micky asks. 'And anyone else?'

'No,' I admit. 'But one thing I'm having to come to terms with is that I can't control how people will see me. I've been through all the labels that I'll have slapped on me. Home-wrecker, slut, whore, selfish bitch. But none of them hurt as much as the thought of being without Jack. He's miserable in his marriage. That mark on his face is because of her. She did that to him!'

There's a brief silence and both of them look at me, stunned. 'Oh shit,' Lizzy sighs, discarding her wine glass, shaking her head. She might not understand, but she comprehends how I feel about Jack. Coming over to me, she wraps an arm around my shoulders, giving me a half cuddle. 'What have you got yourself into, Annie?'

'Love,' I reply simply, because that little four-letter word is the only explanation for me venturing down this painful road.

The moment Jack's eyes met mine in that bar, our hearts began to slowly entwine, and now they're tangled so tightly I have no choice but to battle forward and hope we can't be ripped apart, because if Jack leaves me, he will take part of my heart with him. I'll be destroyed. The growing lump in my throat expands and I break down in Lizzy's arms. I hear Micky curse, and I hear a soft sob come from Lizzy too. I cry into her shoulder quietly, grateful for the comfort she's been forced into giving me, until she pulls away and holds me by my shoulders. Her eyes are glassy with tears as she wipes mine, her face sad.

'You stupid girl,' she says tenderly, her voice broken with emotion. 'Part of me is so happy that you've found a man you're so in love with, and the other part of me is full of dread for you.'

I swallow on a nod of understanding, feeling exactly the same. Micky audibly sighs and comes over, wrapping his big arms around both of us. 'My brain is officially pink,' he mutters, kissing each of our heads in turn. 'For fuck's sake.'

A mild cough interrupts us, and our little crowd breaks up. 'I didn't want to interrupt,' Jack says.

'You'd better be there for her,' Micky warns harshly.

Jack doesn't retaliate, and he doesn't look insulted that Micky's more or less threatening him. I hold back from telling my friends that I need to be there for him too. 'I will be,' Jack answers, not wavering at all.

'And if you break her heart, I swear I'll kill you.'

'There'll be no need,' Jack counters coolly, turning his calm grey eyes onto me. 'If I hurt her, I'll kill myself before you can get to me.'

I hear Micky's small hitch of surprised breath, and I bite my lip as silence falls. There's nothing left to be said. Lizzy nudges Micky from his staring deadlock with Jack, pulling him out of the kitchen. 'I'll call you in the morning,' she says, so obviously torn by today's revelations.

Jack moves from their path and nods respectfully as they pass, and once the front door closes, he turns to me, his hands deep in his trouser pockets, his face grave. It's all becoming so real now. 'You okay?'

I nod, but my emotions don't agree and I crumple once again, unable to process what just happened. Jack crosses the room in a few easy strides and pulls me in for a needed cuddle, holding me tightly, hushing me and kissing my hair. 'We'll be okay,' he says, trying to appease me. 'I promise.'

I hang on to his words like they are all I have, praying that he is right, while physically hanging onto him too. I feel drained of energy already. My lack of fight doesn't sit well. My strength is going to be tested to the limit. I can only hope it doesn't break me.

Breathing in deeply, Jack gives me one last squeeze before cradling me in his arms and carrying me to my bedroom. He lays me on the bed, then disappears momentarily to collect all of the pillows and the duvet from the lounge. Once he's put a pillow under my head and stripped both of us down, he crawls in, forcing me onto my side, and covers us up. The length of his body curls around mine perfectly. 'Every time I leave you, it hurts, Annie. I'm climbing the walls, getting myself all worked up because I don't know how long it will be before I can be with you again. I can't go on like this.' He kisses the back of my head, pulling me closer.

We're locked together.

Sheltered from the outside world. Protected from what is to come.

'No matter what happens, what she does to me or to herself,' he whispers in my ear, 'I'm leaving her tomorrow.'

Chapter 23

The wretchedness that engulfs me when I open my eyes could knock me unconscious again if I allow it. Jack's gone. I roll over and stare at the pillow where his head lay last night, the warmth of his body locked against mine still lingering. My hand slides up the sheets onto the pillow, feeling the warmth there too, telling me it's not been long since he left. The needy side of me hates him for slipping out without waking me. But the sensible side of me knows he did what was best. I don't think I could have let him go. He's telling her today.

It would be easy to hide under my bedcovers all day, but I whip them off and get out of bed. I see a note propped up against the lamp on the bedside table. I take it between two fingers and read.

Don't go anywhere x

He doesn't mean literally, like not to leave my flat. He means from his life. I bring the paper to my nose and inhale, silently promising him that I won't. Then I slide it back onto the bedside cabinet and wander through my flat, intent on getting some coffee before I shower and get on with my day. My plan is simple: lock myself in my studio all day and lose myself in work.

After I've thrown on some ripped jeans, my U2 T-shirt and flip-flops, I make my way into my office and sit at my desk. And I stare at the blank screen. Forever. I twiddle my pen for ten minutes and then doodle on some paper. I start at least ten e-mails and try to answer another twenty. I doodle some more and finally throw my pen down, wedging my elbows against my desk and letting my face fall into my hands. This isn't going to work. I grab my laptop and case, throw a scarf around my neck and dial Lizzy on my way out the door. She answers within two rings. 'Hey,' she greets me, subdued.

'Hey,' I parrot, hitting the pavement. 'How are you?' I ask, for lack of anything else to say. It's obviously strained between us, and I hate it.

'I didn't sleep much,' she openly admits. 'Nat popped around for an hour. She was asking after you.'

'Did you tell her?'

'No. That's not my place, Annie. And I might not like this, but I fully appreciate the sensitivity of it. Your secret is safe with me.'

I reach the main road, my eyes closing briefly, ashamed. She makes what's between Jack and me sound sordid, and I can't argue with that. 'Thank you.'

'Where are you?'

'Heading for Starbucks.'

'Already? It's eight on a Sunday morning.'

'I needed to get out,' I admit, not holding back. 'Jack's telling Stephanie it's over today. I don't know when, but I can't sit around at home all day thinking about it.'

'I see,' she says flatly. 'Is he telling her about you?'

'No.'

'So what does he plan on saying then? She'll want a reason.'

I look down at my feet, hating her coldness, but knowing I can't expect anything more. She may have hugged me when I broke down last night, but that wasn't a sign that she would go full-force into happiness for me. 'There were cracks in their marriage before me, Lizzy,' I say, my voice quivering.

'Of course there were, Annie. There would have to be for Jack to look elsewhere.'

'He wasn't looking,' I argue, not with any malice but as firmly as I can muster.

'Whatever. My point is, many marriages have cracks, but when you take your vows, you promise for better or for worse. You forsake all others.'

I come to a stop on the street. 'Is there a vow that states it's acceptable to physically hurt each other? Do they make you promise to never scratch your husband or cuff his face?'

She doesn't answer, and I sigh.

'Lizzy, I didn't call you to hear this.'

'And I didn't take your call to pump you full of reassurance,' she retorts, making me wince. It also brings more tears to my eyes. I brush at them harshly, trying not to sniff and snivel so she can hear my sadness. I'm not looking for sympathy; I'm just looking for my friend. And I don't think she's here any more.

'I understand,' I whisper, cutting the call. My phone slips away from my ear into the centre of my hand, my arm falling heavily to my side. The tears are falling steadily down my cheeks as I pick up my stride again, and I can sense a few people looking at me as I pass them by.

And I accept that my world with a piece of Jack needs to slowly fall apart in order for it to be rebuilt again. With him. *All* of him.

With a coffee in my grasp, I wander over to Hyde Park. I walk the entire circumference before breaking through an opening in a barrier on Park Lane and strolling down to the Serpentine. I see Micky in the distance, just on the crest of a hill, squatting while shouting encouragement to a guy doing press-ups with a rucksack on his back. I sit on a bench and watch their entire training session, then remain where I am for another hour and watch him putting another client through her paces – this one

Charlie. When they're done, she gives him a hug, and he reciprocates. It seems so affectionate, something that doesn't go hand in hand with Micky. Not with his conquests, anyway. He couldn't have got her in the sack yet. He's slacking; he's been training her for months.

I had no intention of waving to attract his attention, but when he turns and starts towards me, I realise he's probably known I was here the whole time. He's all sweaty, the muscles of his arms glistening in the mid-morning sun as he approaches me. Offering a small smile, he sits next to me, but he doesn't say a word. Neither do I. I'm scared to death of a repeat of Lizzy. Will I lose *all* of my friends in my mission to have all of Jack?

I feel his hand take mine and gently squeeze, and I glance to the side, finding him looking straight ahead. My eyes fall to our held hands resting in his lap. We don't speak for an age, both of us staring out across the grassy planes of Hyde Park as the world goes by.

After a quiet eternity with unspoken words hanging between us, he pushes himself to his feet and bends to kiss my forehead. 'I'm here,' he says, and I look up at him, unable to smile or say thank you, but I make sure he sees the gratitude in my eyes. They're full of water again, and he sighs as he wipes away a stray tear. Then he strolls off, leaving me on the bench.

I count three people who take a seat next to me over the next hour. One old boy for a rest, another man to eat a sandwich, and finally a runner to stretch. They all come, and they all go to get on with their lives. Probably simple lives. Lives not tainted with deceit and hurt and guilt.

A lady on the opposite bench looks across to me when she's settling her baby in its pram, smiling. I return her smile before getting to my feet and going on my way. I don't know where I'm heading next, but my pace is steady. Then it slows, my mind slowing with it, until I come to a stop in the middle of the pathway. I turn back, watching the woman pushing her baby towards me.

The possibility hits me like lightning, the bolts tearing through me and making my stomach churn in dread. I fumble for my bag, feeling around with shaky hands for my phone. When I finally find it, I press the wrong icons again and again in my panic, trying to load my calendar. It takes a few seconds to count back the weeks. Then only a few more for the sick feeling to come over me. I'm suddenly very hot and dizzy. I start to hyperventilate – my breathing diminishing to virtually nothing, sending my surroundings into a whirl.

'Are you okay?'

I look to the side blankly, finding the woman with the pram has stopped beside me. She looks genuinely concerned for me. My eyes fall to the baby, now sleeping peacefully. My stomach clenches and I double over, throwing up at my feet.

'Oh my goodness!' she cries, her hand rubbing my back.

I manage to hold my hand up while I retch, the strain on my stomach bringing water to my eyes. Or are they more tears? 'I'm fine,' I croak, accepting the baby wipe she is holding out to me and wiping my mouth. 'Thank you.' I straighten and rush away, too worried to be mortified by my public spewing episode.

I eventually find myself in a public toilet. Not that I ever imagined I'd be in this situation, but if I had, I would never have anticipated I would resort to the impersonal location of a lavatory that maybe a million people had used. Yet here I am, sitting on the seat of the loo, staring down at a pregnancy test.

Positive.

The two lines are glowing, taunting me, yelling in my face that I'm a careless, stupid bitch. *Careless* isn't a word that will be used by many others. *Deceitful* will be one, as well as *manipulative*, *scheming* and *calculating*. Nothing I can say or do will change that. It's something I will have to live with, along with the judgements for stealing another woman's husband.

The crushing pain is only amplified by the fact that the one person who will trust I didn't do this on purpose isn't available for me to call today. I can't phone him and I can't see him. I have no one to turn to, no one who I can be sure won't annihilate me and will instead give me the cuddle that I need.

My world isn't slowly falling apart. It's crashing down around me, and I feel like it's all out of my control. I feel no sense of achievement while I look down at the positive test. I don't feel even a glimmer of excitement through the turmoil I'm in. This is without doubt the worst thing that could have happened. This changes everything.

I drop the test into my bag, exit the cubicle, wash my hands and avoid the mirror as I walk out. I don't need a reflection to tell me I look like a ghost. I'm cold, my blood feels like it has drained from my body and my breathing is shallow. I feel like a shadow of a woman, and I know I must look like one too.

I think I must have walked around every park in London by the time the sun starts to set. My feet ache, but it's nothing in comparison to my head, my stomach and my heart. There's been no word from Jack. I wonder if he's had to take her to hospital because she's done something reckless. I wonder if he's even told her. I wonder if he's covered in scratches. I can't go home and sit there alone. I can't face my parents or my friends. I have nowhere to go. I've never felt so lonely.

As I drag myself into a coffee house, my phone rings and my heart leaps. I retrieve my mobile from my bag quickly and glance down at the screen. I don't even have the room to feel guilty when I sag with disappointment, seeing the caller's not Jack. I contemplate ignoring Lizzy's call for a few moments, worried that any more negativity might have me folding to the ground here and now, but a glimmer of hope shines through my fear, and I answer.

'I'm so sorry,' she chokes out, her voice trembling. 'I'm just so worried about you, Annie. I'm trying so hard to hope for happiness for you, and it's truly killing me that I can't. You deserve so much more than this shit. You deserve the fairy tale. Why did you have to go and fall in love with a married man?'

'I didn't plan it.' I drop to a chair at a nearby table. 'I so didn't want this to happen. I tried to walk away; you have to believe me.'

'It really doesn't matter now, does it? You're in up to your neck.'

I stare at thin air. She has no idea. 'I love him,' I say simply. We could go around the houses for years, argue about the whys and wherefores. We'll only ever come back to those three simple words. 'I can't turn that off, Lizzy,' I say quietly, shamelessly stealing her words.

'I know,' she sighs. 'Have you heard from him?'

'No,' I admit, wondering once again where he is. What he's doing. What's happening.

'What have you been doing all day?'

'Wandering.'

'On your own? All day? Why didn't you come to me?' she asks, disturbed.

'You weren't exactly warm on the phone this morning,' I point out gently. 'I didn't want to push you.'

'Annie, I don't love you any less. You've done something I don't agree with, but I would never turn my back on you.'

'That's good to know,' I say robotically. 'Because I'm pregnant.' It just falls right out, and I'm not even shocked. I have nothing left in me.

'What did you say?' she asks, her voice high and worried.

'I'm pregnant,' I repeat, though I know she heard me just fine the first time.

'Oh Jesus,' she whispers, truly horrified. 'Oh my God.'

'I know.' It's all I have the energy to say. No explanations. No pleading for compassion or understanding. I'm done for the day. Maybe even forever.

'Where are you?'

'In a coffee house near Regent's Park.'

'Why?'

'Because I don't want to go home. Because I don't know whether Jack's told Stephanie he's leaving her yet. Because I haven't heard from him and it's driving me crazy. Because I can't call him. Because—'

'Come here,' she orders without hesitation. 'Please.'

I smile down the line, strangely reaching the conclusion that I just want to be alone. No talking and no one surmising the crappiness of my situation. I'm doing a stellar job of that all by myself. 'I'm fine,' I assure her.

'Annie, please.'

'Lizzy, trust me, I'm okay. I just need to process it all.' Or more like torture myself some more. 'I'll head home soon, I promise.'

She's silent for a few moments, but she finally relents. 'Call me if you want me to come and get you, okay?'

'Okay.' I hang up, but before I can put my phone away, it rings again. This time it *is* Jack, and my heart commences a strong, consistent beat. I rush to answer. 'Jack?'

'Hey, baby.' He sounds absolutely broken, and I don't know whether that's a good thing or a bad thing. Did he bottle it? Did she beg him not to go? Did he cave under the pressure to stay? 'Where are you?' he asks.

I don't tell him where I am. I don't want him worrying about me. 'At Lizzy's,' I lie. 'Are you okay?'

'No,' he answers quickly and honestly. 'No man should be okay with seeing a woman falling apart at his feet.'

'I'm so sorry.'

'I told her there was someone else.'

'What?'

'She wasn't listening to me, Annie. I got desperate.'

'Did you tell her it's me?'

'Jesus, no,' he breathes.

I'm only mildly relieved. He's given her something. She'll be obsessing on that and going to the ends of the earth to find out who. 'Where are you?'

'At Richard's. I'm having a few beers and trying to wind down. It's been . . .' His words die. He doesn't need to tell me that it's been a long day.

'Okay,' I agree, unable to protest and strangely not feeling hurt that he needs a few bottles and man time. I still need my own space to process something Jack is yet to be hit with. I need to think about how I'm going to tell him, and when.

'I love you,' I blurt out, if only to remind him in his mayhem why we're going through this.

'I never once doubted that, Annie.' He sighs heavily, sounding tired. 'Get a good night's sleep, baby, and I'll call you in the morning.'

'I will.'

'Love you, gorgeous. More than anything.'

His declaration brings a small smile to my face. 'Even more than Giant Strawbs?'

'Even more than them. And I love them a lot.'

'I know you do. I love you too.'

I hang up and start to make my way home. I'd like to think the hardest part is done with, but I'm not stupid.

It's only just begun.

Chapter 24

It's dark by the time I get home. I go to my room and throw my bag on the bed, rummaging to the bottom until I lay my hands on the little plastic stick. Pulling it out, I gaze down at its window, hoping a miracle has occurred. There are still two lines looking up at me loud and proud. I throw it back into my bag and make my way to my bathroom, looking at myself in the mirror for the first time today. I don't think I've ever seen myself look so terrible. My skin is sallow, my green eyes clouded, my dark hair limp and my clothes crumpled. I lower my head to avoid seeing the wretchedness of my face, and my gaze falls to my stomach. My flat stomach. For the first time, I consider the most important question I should be asking myself right now. Not what people will think or how they will react – I should be asking myself if I can do this. Be a mum. Not once has the thought of ridding myself of the problem crossed my jumbled mind. I haven't asked myself whether I'm keeping the baby or not.

I *am* keeping it.

After showering, I make myself a bedtime cup of tea. I don't question the smile I have on my face as I clear up sweet wrappers from around the sofa. And I don't second-guess my reasoning for loading *Top Gun* and snuggling down on the couch to watch it. My eyes wander from the television from time to time, falling to the floor and seeing me and Jack, a tangle of arms and legs, sweets and pillows. And I see a third person: a baby. Me, Jack and a little person – half of him and half of me. My hand falls to my stomach and circles absentmindedly. I'm going to have a little human to take care of within a year. Someone to rely and depend on me. Being a mum has never featured in my plans, maybe because I've never had any plans beyond my career. My life has been turned upside down and I asked for it all. Now I need to take charge. I know what I'm faced with, but with this baby growing inside me, I'm caring less about the reactions of the world and Stephanie, and more about being a good mum. I can do it. With Jack, I can do anything.

For the first time today, I see hope amid the ruins and I cling to it with all my might, lying back on the couch and sipping my tea. I get a text before I doze off.

From Jack.

I was always yours. Even when I didn't know you. And you were always mine. It just took us a while to find each other. I love you

x

I fall asleep with those words on loop in my mind.

I wake up feeling chilly, and the credits for *Top Gun* are rolling on the television. I groan, not wanting to move and take myself to bed, but too cold to stay where I am. I shiver and get up from the couch, flicking the TV off, grabbing my phone and pulling the blanket over my shoulders. Then I trudge to my bedroom sleepily.

I nearly make it to the God-glorious warmth of my bed, where the covers are calling to me, but a knock on the door stops me on the threshold to my room. I look down the hallway to my front door, wondering who it could be at this hour. I glance down at my phone. 10 p.m. Not so late at all.

I shrug the blanket off my shoulders, toss it on the bed and grab my grey hoodie from a chair, putting it on as I make my way to the front door. I decide and hope on my way that it must be Jack. The possibility injects some urgency into my legs and I pull the front door open, ready to throw myself at him and never let go.

But my face falls the moment I register my visitor.

'Stephanie,' I breathe shakily, desperately trying to stop my eyes from bugging in shock. Oh my God, what is she doing here? Shit, what do I do? She looks a wreck, her hair unwashed and pulled into a tatty ponytail, her face red and blotchy and her body huddled up, wrapped in a khaki fluffy-hooded coat. I release my hold on the door when it starts to tremble mildly from my movements.

I must appear as anxious as I'm feeling. She's staring blankly at me, in a bit of a trance. This would be the point that any normal person would ask if she's okay. But I know she's not okay, and I'm not any normal person. I'm the woman her husband has left her for, and I need to get rid of her before my nerves begin to fray again and she figures it all out.

'Stephanie?' I prompt gently, forcing anything close to a friendly face.

'I didn't know who else to turn to,' she croaks, her arms wrapped around her midriff protectively.

'What?' I startle myself with my abrupt tone, fighting to pull myself together. So she came here? *To me?*

She bursts into tears.

Oh fuck.

'He's left me,' she sobs. 'He's gone!'

My insides tangle up. No part of me seems willing to give me a heads-up on what I should do. 'Stephanie, I—'

She falls into my hallway, leaving me no choice but to move back, and thumps the wall. I definitely get a waft of liquor as she passes me. She's been drinking. 'He's gone, Annie! He's gone and left me all alone!' She pulls away and faces my shocked form, her expression suddenly straight, her eyes round and wild. 'But he needs me,' she says evenly.

'I'm so sorry, Stephanie.' My mouth kicks into action, reminding me that I should be acting the sympathetic outsider. 'I'm sure he'll come back to you.'

'Yes, he will,' she sniffs, wiping at her nose. 'He's confused, that's all.'

I nod, giving my enthusiastic agreement, just needing her to pull it together and leave so I can commence with my own meltdown. It won't be as spectacular as Stephanie's, but I can guarantee it'll involve tears and a panicked call to Jack.

Her face cracks and she starts sobbing again, more controlled this time, her body jerking with the constant sniffles and gasps for air. 'What am I going to do?' She hiccups over her words, her head dropping limply.

I have nothing to say to that. I don't know what she's going to do, and that truly scares me. 'Do you want me to call a friend?' I ask. 'Someone you can talk to?' I need to make it clear that I'm not that someone. I wouldn't be even if I wasn't in love with her husband.

'There's no one,' she sobs. 'I have no friends.' She looks at me hopefully. I fear the worst. 'Except you. I'll stay with you for a while. You can make me a cup of tea. I'm not good on my own, Annie.'

'How about your mum?' I press, trying to sound concerned rather than desperate.

She shakes her head. 'She and Daddy are out for dinner. I don't want to bother them.'

I try to swallow down the growing lump of apprehension in my throat. It's not budging. She wants me to be her friend. Or she clearly thinks I already am. She wants to spill her problems to the woman who is carrying her husband's baby.

I can't imagine a worse situation. Jesus, I can't make her leave and spend all night wondering if she's trying to hack at her wrists.

'I'll put the kettle on,' I say, shutting the front door. I'm totally and utterly fucked.

Leading Stephanie through to the kitchen, I let her take a seat and start making tea, my mind racing, dreading how this conversation will go.

'He says there's someone else,' she says out of the blue, with definite amusement in her tone.

'Probably just a flash in the pan,' I reply robotically, deciding as I stir our tea that I have no option but to shut down and act like the friend she thinks I am.

'That's what I said. Some hussy who's opened her legs.'

I grit my teeth and slide her tea onto the table, taking a seat opposite her.

'He'll come back. I mean, he did before when he realised he'd made a mistake. That he couldn't live without me.' She laughs, and my smile is strained. I'm falling apart on the inside. I don't want to hear this. She leans forward, her hands wrapped around her mug, and smiles at me. 'You can help me show him. You work with him, see him all the time. You can tell him that he's making a mistake. What do you say?'

What do I say? I say this must be hell. I smile, physically hurting, my stomach performing constant flips as if to remind me that I have a part of me and a part of Jack growing inside me. 'Okay,' I reply on a swallow.

'Thank you, Annie,' she says, bringing her mug to her lips thoughtfully. She seems significantly more together now. And just as I think that, she slams the mug down and starts howling again. I can't figure out if this is the normal behaviour of any woman whose husband has walked out on them, or just the normal behaviour of Stephanie. 'I'm sorry,' she cries, wiping at her face. 'Do you have any tissues?' she asks.

'In the bathroom.' I'm praying she goes to get some herself and doesn't expect me to. My phone is across the room by the kettle and it's going to look odd if I grab it and take it with me. If she goes, I can text Jack for emergency help. 'You know where it is.'

The chair slides across the floor as she pushes herself up, and I wait for her to disappear around the corner before I make a mad dash for my phone, hammering out a message to Jack.

Stephanie is here!

I take a seat again and hold on to my phone, hearing her blowing her nose in the distance. Jack's reply is almost instant.

What? At your place?

I only have time to reply with a simple *Yes!* before Stephanie appears again. I slip my phone into my pocket and stand. 'Okay?' I ask.

She nods, stuffing the tissue in her pocket. Then she approaches me and wraps her arms around my tense body, which refuses to loosen up no matter how much I yell at it not to give my anxiety away. 'You're a good friend,' she says, pulling away from me and kissing my cheek.

I can't bear this. My alarm bells are suddenly going wild.

A phone starts ringing, and Stephanie gasps, pulling a mobile from the pocket of her coat. The happiness on her face as she looks down at the screen is enough to floor me. 'It's Jack!' she squeals, connecting the call. 'Jack?' She turns and hurries out of the kitchen. 'Yes, I'm on my way home. Are you coming? We'll talk. Properly. I'll listen, I swear.' She disappears in a whirl of excitement, slamming the front door behind her.

I fall to my arse on the chair, the adrenalin that's kept me going draining from my body and shock setting in. My head falls into my hands, but I have no time to rest my weary mind. My phone starts buzzing in my pocket. I pull it out and answer.

'Annie, are you okay?' Jack sounds out of his mind with worry.

'Great,' I quip. 'I've just watched your wife spiral into melt-down and listened to her tell me how she's going to win you back from the hussy you're sleeping with. Apparently I'm a great friend and I'm going to convince you that you're making a mistake. Perfect, eh?'

'What?' He sounds as flabbergasted as I am.

'Jack, I'm worried.'

'I'm so sorry,' he breathes. 'I didn't know she'd turn up on your doorstep like that.'

'Are you okay?' I ask softly, not liking the weariness in everything he's saying.

'I just wish I could be there with you,' he admits, making me smile sadly. 'It's been a shitty day.'

'It has,' I say quietly. He doesn't need to know what my shitty day has entailed.

'I need to see you, Annie. Can you come to my office in the morning?'

'Won't that raise a few eyebrows with staff?'

'We're having a business meeting. That's all.'

'I'll bring my files,' I tell him, getting up and going to my bedroom to find my long-awaited bed. I pull my bag off the end and drop it to the floor before I fall in and drag my covers up to my chin.

'My offices at eleven?'

'Okay.'

'I can't wait to hold you, Annie.' He sounds so exhausted. I close my eyes and imagine myself cuddled into his chest, warm and safe. Together. 'Night, baby.'

'Good night.' I hang up and stare up at my ceiling, trying to piece together how I'm going to break the news to Jack that I'm pregnant. I'm not sure the poor man can take much more.

Chapter 25

The next morning, I'm all kinds of nervous as I sit in the waiting room of Jack's offices after being told he's expecting me. I can't figure out if I'm jittery because Stephanie could turn up again, or whether I'm worried about telling him that I'm pregnant. I don't have time to ponder for long. Jack strides out of his office towards me, fastening the button of his suit jacket. He looks washed out, absolutely knackered, but his face lights up when his eyes meet mine. He has no tie on today – just a white shirt open at the collar, and his jacket and trousers. His hair isn't as neatly styled as the last time I encountered him in his office. It's no wonder, really. I think yesterday took a lot out of both of us.

In contrast, my ripped skinny jeans are worn, my T-shirt oversized and creased, and my flip-flops are highly inappropriate for a supposed business meeting.

Jack nods to the lady on reception. She gives him a half-smile, almost sympathetic. Has he made it public knowledge? Has he told people that he's left Stephanie? I start to fidget in my chair, my nerves accelerating.

'Miss Ryan,' Jack says quietly, holding his hand out to me.

I accept his offering. 'Mr Joseph,' I reply, feeling him pull discreetly to help me to my feet, as though he senses I need the support. He'd be right. I feel drained. I lay awake last night and agonised over telling Jack my news. I feel like I should be the one easing his stress, not adding to it. 'Thank you.' I feel him squeeze my hand gently before releasing it and gesturing ahead.

'My office is this way,' he tells me.

This is utterly stupid. Mr Joseph? Miss Ryan? Telling me his office is this way? Yes, I know, because he screwed me on the desk. Besides, doesn't his receptionist remember me from when I was here for the meeting with Brawler's? I feel her looking at me as I pass. She looks suspicious, peeking over her glasses with interest as we pass by. I'm not helping matters when I blush bright red and cough, quickly avoiding her eyes.

'She's looking at us funny,' I whisper as we walk side by side towards Jack's office. Our arms are brushing with every pace, the brief touches making my breathing even more shallow. Physical contact between us has rendered me breathless from our very first encounter. Now is no exception, despite the horrible circumstances.

'You're being paranoid,' he whispers back, taking the doorknob and opening the door for me. 'After you.' He gives me a little wink, trying to relax me. I hide my secret smile and enter his office, turning as soon as the door shuts behind me. He swoops me from my feet and carries me to one of the couches, sitting with me draped across his lap, holding me as close to him as he possibly can. 'Jesus, it feels like I've been waiting forever for this.' He devotes some quiet time to lavishing me with sweet kisses and tender touches to my face, fussing over me like I need to be fussed over. 'How did you sleep?' he asks, cupping my face and following up his question with a rub of our noses.

'Terribly,' I admit. 'I couldn't get Stephanie out of my head.' Jack nods his understanding. 'She was in such a state.'

'I know, baby. It's awful to see, but I have to stay strong even if it makes me seem heartless. This is for the best, not just for us, but for her too. She can't be happy in this loveless marriage.'

I go limp in his lap, wishing I could rip every thought tormenting me from my mind and be numb to it all. 'I feel so guilty,' I whisper. I decide here and now that tomorrow I'm going to church. I'm not religious, but God's there for everyone, right? He doesn't turn his back on a soul. I'll confess my sins and pray for forgiveness. I hope he forgives me. I might hate Stephanie for what she's done to Jack, but I still feel guilty. I'm both annoyed and comforted by it.

'Hey.' Jack nudges me from my hiding place, his face falling when he finds I'm tearing up. His lips press together as he runs a soft pad of a fingertip beneath my eye, catching the tear before it falls. 'Baby, did you plan this?' he asks seriously. 'And when I say plan, I mean did you wake up one morning and decide you were going to go out to a bar and fall in love with a married man?'

When he puts it like that . . . 'No.'

'Have you killed anyone?'

'Jack,' I sigh quietly. 'It doesn't make it right.'

'I'm not saying it does, Annie. What I'm saying is that you are not a bad person. You're not evil or calculating or manipulative. You fell in love. If that's a crime, then we'll be in love together in hell.'

'You make it sound acceptable.'

'I'm trying to get my head straight. That's all.' He laughs lightly under his breath, the sound full of misery that he's trying so hard to keep from me. 'I've left Stephanie because she made it impossible to love her. I left her because if I stay, there will be nothing left of me. I left her because I want to be happy.' He pinches my chin a little. 'I want *you* to be happy. With me.'

'I know,' I admit, smiling a little, but it's sad and it's strained. 'What happens now?'

'I have a place near Maida Vale. There are tenants serving a few weeks' notice. It'll be empty by the end of the month. Until then I'll shack up in a hotel.'

'I'll be able to see you?'

'Fancy moving in with me?' he kids, smiling when I grin. He could be shacked up in a tent on a crummy campsite for all I care. There would be *nothing* to stop me being with him. But I also get the feeling there's more meaning laced between the words of his question, and it has me gathering my inner strength to tell him what I need to tell him.

'Jack—'

'I've agreed to see Stephanie this evening,' he blurts out, and my announcement gets caught on my lips. 'I wanted you to know so you don't think there's anything in it other than . . .'

'Other than what?' I push my body away from his a little, damning myself for being so obviously slighted and worried.

'Other than talking like grown-ups about the arrangements.'

'Didn't you talk last night? When you called her?'

'Last night all I cared about was getting her out of your flat.'

'So you agreed to see her.'

'It was the only way. I can't go back on my word, Annie. Anyway, she said she's thinking more clearly and thinks some time apart could do us good.'

'Time apart?' I question, not liking the sound of that.

He shrugs. 'It's breathing space. Time for her to get used to the idea. I'm not going to rock the boat and refuse her half an hour of my time if I get a lot more in return. Like my whole life. Trust me. I know what I'm doing.'

This is a ploy. It has to be. I listened to Stephanie last night and I watched her. She's a desperate woman. She'll do anything to keep him. Which brings me to something else . . .

I suddenly feel desperate myself, but I suck back my news and try to reason with myself. I can't tell him that I'm pregnant now. He's right. I have to trust him to do what he thinks is right, even if it kills me to let him. He's undeniably in a mind-fuck, and I can't add to that. I can't make this any harder for him. I have to be patient, and I have to reasonable. After all, it is me who gets him when all this is over. It's me who gets to have my happily-ever-after with the only man I have ever loved. The only man I've ever shared such a deep connection with, on every level. 'Okay.' I push the word out. 'I'll go to Lizzy's.' I can't be alone at home thinking. I'll go mad.

He nods. 'How is she, by the way? And Micky?'

'They think I've lost my mind.' I tell it as it is. 'But they're here for me.'

'I'm glad.' Jack pulls me back down to his chest. 'I love you, Annie.' He breathes in deeply, squeezing me so tightly. 'I love your passion, I love your mind, I love how you pout across the rim of your cup when you're thinking. I love it when you fidget when you're anxious.' His lips push into the back of my head, and I smile a little, loving him telling me all of this. 'And I love your U2 T-shirt, especially when you wear nothing else with it.' Breaking out of his hold, I find his face, suddenly desperate to see him. He smiles, and I find my thumb tracing the edges of his jaw as he goes on. 'I love how you pile your hair up into something resembling a pineapple too. And I love how at the end of the day your mascara is a little smudged just here.' He touches the corner of my lid, a grin tugging the sides of his mouth. 'I love everything there is to love about you.'

'I love your chest,' I say stupidly, falling back into his warmth, wishing I could hide in it forever.

Jack laughs lightly. 'Let's get this week out of the way and go to Liverpool. Three days, just you and me, yeah?'

I nod and settle into him, enjoying this snatched moment of time. I'll tell him about the baby at the weekend, when we're away from London, on our own and relaxed.

I called Lizzy as soon as I left Jack's office. She listened to me while I told her about last night and the fact that Jack has arranged to see Stephanie this evening. I didn't need to ask for company. She told me to get to her place for six when she'd be home from work and we'd eat curry and watch *Titanic* – a movie neither of us tire of, even after watching it a million times.

She greets me at the door with the biggest hug she's ever given me. I needed it before I went to Jack's office. Now, if she didn't release me for the entire night, that would be fine by me.

I take my phone from my bag and hand it to her. I don't need to be checking every minute for a text from Jack. It'll defeat the whole point of me being here. Lizzy takes it and slips it into the back pocket of her jeans. She doesn't say a word, doesn't ask questions or press me: she just silently walks me into the kitchen.

I smile, genuinely happy, when I find Nat and Micky huddled around the table, chatting and laughing. Micky gives me a wink and Nat cheers my arrival. I look to Lizzy, wondering if she's told them of my turmoil, but she just shakes her head mildly, grabbing a bottle of wine from the fridge.

Lizzy hands me a glass, but when I go to take it, I suddenly remember I should be avoiding this stuff. 'Non-alcoholic,' she whispers, going on to refresh the others' glasses with what I expect is the real stuff.

Nat toasts the air and pulls me down onto the chair next to her. 'You look like shit.'

'Thanks,' I laugh, joining her in a sip of wine.

'You do.' Micky winks at me across the table. I pick up a peanut from the bowl and chuck it at his head, and he shifts, catching it in his mouth around a grin. 'Tough day at work?'

'Draining,' I answer tiredly. 'But it'll be worth it in the end.'

'I hope so,' Lizzy chimes in, giving me a look as she joins us.

'I have exciting news,' Micky announces, looking blasé and very *un*excited.

'You sure?' I ask.

'Yes.' He straightens and clears his throat. 'I'm going on a date.'

Silence falls and we all look at each other like the weirdest thing could have just happened. I'd think I didn't hear him right but everyone else is looking as blank as I am.

'Come again?' Nat pipes up, her chin dropping to her chest.

'A date,' he repeats, starting to swivel his bottle of beer on the table while he watches it, pouting to himself.

Nat bursts into laughter, followed by me and Lizzy. This is priceless! 'Give me a fucking break, Micky,' Nat chuckles.

'What?' he asks, offended.

'You?' I laugh.

'A date?' Lizzy is holding on to the table for support.

'The girl you're training!' I jump up from the table. 'Charlie! She isn't *putting* out so you've resorted to *asking* her out.'

'Fuck off,' Micky snipes seriously. 'I could have her like that.' He snaps his fingers.

'Oh my God.' Nat puts her drink on the table to avoid spilling it because she's laughing so hard. 'I can't . . . It's the . . . You won't . . . Shit, this is the funniest thing I've ever heard.'

The kitchen is alive with laughter, all of us in stitches at Micky's 'date'. Does he think we don't know him? For Christ's sake. 'Micky, you're killing me.' I howl, grappling for my fake wine and laughing into my glass as I take a sip. 'Where are you taking her?'

'Ah, now.' He leans forward. 'This is what I need to talk to you guys about.' His motives for having to share news of his date are suddenly all too clear, and it also spikes another bout of laughter. 'Come on, girls,' he whinges. 'Help me out.'

'We don't know her,' I point out. 'Does she like art, culture, food?'

'She loves it when I play with my hair.' He looks at me hopefully. God, I could cuddle him.

'She likes it when you play with your hair?' Nat asks seriously. 'Great. Take her with you for your next haircut.'

I stifle my laugh this time, feeling for my lifelong friend. He can't help being an idiot when it comes to dating women. 'Hakkasan is always a winner,' I offer.

'Really?' Micky asks. 'It's quite pricey, though, right?' He backs up, hands raised in defence, when we all gape at him.

'Burger King,' Nat sighs. 'Take her to Burger King. But I know for a *fact* that they don't do a good fuck for dessert. You'll get a fuck for dessert if you take her to Hakkasan.' She raises her glass in cheers.

I chuckle, as does Lizzy, but Micky rolls his eyes. I love this. I forgot how much. It doesn't matter that my glass is full of pretend wine. I have my friends around me, and it's exactly what I need right now. I look at them all in turn, spending some time thinking about how lucky I am to have them.

Lizzy orders Indian, and we all pile into the lounge to watch *Titanic*. There are no objections, even from Micky. 'Watch carefully.' Nat kicks him in the back when he sits on the floor in front of her. 'Might get some tips on how to woo.'

He turns and gives her tired eyes. 'Put a sock in it, ice queen.'

Nat sniggers. 'Ouch.'

'Shhhh!' Lizzy hushes, pointing the remote control at the TV and cranking up the volume. 'Watch it or piss off.'

Nat throws her an indignant look but pipes down with the assistance of my calming palm placed on her thigh. We barely move, and only the odd sigh or hum permeates the air as we all settle down and watch Kate and Leonardo fall in love. I make it to the point when he paints her. After that, the movie is just a fuzz of words, and Jack's words are clear as day, filling my head.

We'll be okay. I promise.

'Annie?' Lizzy shakes me gently, stirring me. 'Annie, Jack's called.'

She may as well have thrown a firebomb at me. I'm up from the chair like lightning. 'Where's everyone gone?' The living room is empty.

'The film finished an hour ago. I didn't want to wake you. Thought you could do with the rest.'

What she means is, she thought I could do without the opportunity to think. I can't thank her enough, but now I'm awake and my mind is careering into panic. 'Where's my phone?' I shoot past her in search of it.

'On the table,' she calls after me as I land in the kitchen.

I spot it and swipe it up, dialling Jack, but it's taken from my hand before I can connect the call. 'What are you doing?' I ask, trying to win it back.

'He's on his way,' she soothes me, holding it out of my reach. 'I gave him my address. He should be here any minute.'

What she's telling me doesn't even sink in before there's a gentle knock on the door. I gasp and rush from the kitchen like a speed demon, throwing the door open, out of breath. The vision of him, no matter how wiped out he looks – totally shattered, weary and drained of life – still centres my off-kilter world. He steps forward and I dive into his arms, pushing my face into his neck. I'm holding him so tightly; I may squeeze what life he has left in him right out.

'Annie,' he breathes. My feet leave the ground and he walks in, holding me to him with one arm while shutting the door with the other. I refuse to let go of him. Ever.

'I'll leave you to it,' I hear Lizzy say. 'I'll be in my room if you need anything. Help yourself to the kitchen.'

'Thank you,' Jack says quietly, continuing on his way with me wrapped around him like ivy. I know when we're in the kitchen because the sound of his footsteps changes when hitting the floor, but I still cling onto him. 'Baby, sit down.' I shake my head into him, hearing him sigh as he squeezes me before he forces me away gently, pulling a chair out and pushing me down into it. He leaves me looking blankly at him as he rounds the table, obviously struggling to keep himself upright.

'Jack, what's the matter?' I don't like his despondency. It's overshadowing my relief that he's here.

He pulls his own chair out, and I watch in silence as he lowers his arse to the seat, his elbow going straight to the table, his head resting on his palm. 'I need to tell you something.'

My entire body locks up in response. I don't want to ask, because I'm sure as hell going to hate whatever he's going to tell me. I don't like the space he's purposely put between us either. My head is screaming the question that I refuse to ask out loud. What could possibly have him so flattened? Has she hurt herself again? Has she got into his conscience, churned up guilt?

'She's pregnant, Annie.'

I jolt in my chair, as if something has come from nowhere and physically taken me out. My heart starts to pump painfully.

'She's been throwing up,' Jack says quietly. 'She did a test.' His eyes close. 'It was positive.' He doesn't want to believe it either.

'No,' I whisper, pushing myself back in the chair, the room starting to spin. The beats of my heart slow with each painful second that passes, and my limbs are beginning to lose all sensation. She's pregnant. He's tied to her forever. She'll be in the background of our lives forever. Our lives? I look across the table at Jack's beaten form. Our lives. 'You're not going to leave her, are you?'

Jack's heavy head gradually lifts until his grey eyes meet with mine. The life in them has completely gone. They're empty. 'I can't leave my *child*, Annie.'

My throat closes up on me. I feel like I'm slowly dying. Desperation is telling me to scream my confession, to tell him that I'm pregnant too. But Jack goes on before I can straighten out my head and release the words. 'I can't believe this is happening. She knows I don't want a baby.'

My announcement falls to the pit of my stomach and rots. He doesn't want a baby. I'm becoming more numb by the second.

'This is fucked up.' He slams his fist on the table. Fucked up. He's right; it is. All of it. I don't want him to be with me out of pity like he will be with Stephanie. I don't want to stoop to her level. She's manipulating him. This is just another form of her fucked-up manipulation. Another symptom of her screwed-up way of thinking. I refuse to force him to be with me. I can't do it to Jack and I can't do it to myself. I'm not begging. I'm not falling to my knees. I've lost enough integrity already. I can't ask him to abandon his child – the child Stephanie is carrying – any more than I could ask him to leave his wife for me.

That's it.

Done.

I'm on my own.

And I'm suddenly furious. I'm furious with him for being so fucking careless, for giving her the opportunity to trap him like this. 'You were sleeping with her.' I look up at him.

His face falls. 'Not for months, Annie. And she was on the pill.'

'Then how?'

His head drops, ashamed, confused, sorry. 'She forgot to take a pill here and there. That's all it takes. She must be over four months now, because that's how long it's been since we were—'

'I don't need to hear it, Jack.' It doesn't matter how far gone she is or how it happened. It's happened. Nothing can change that. 'Go.'

I'm fighting to keep my world together. I feel let down, and I have no fucking right to. And I'm now damning myself to hell for being so careless too. 'Just go, Jack.' I speak levelly. It's a far cry from how I'm feeling on the inside, yet my objective now is to bat the devastation down. I feel like all the life has been sucked out of me. I feel empty.

Jack's head shakes mildly. 'Annie . . .' He reaches across the table for my hand but I pull it back, placing it with the other in my lap, keeping my gaze low.

'Don't make this any harder than it needs to be.' Keeping my breath steady is taking everything I have. 'Please,' I add, closing my eyes on a swallow. This is going to be the challenge of my life. But at least I don't have to spend the rest of my days with someone I don't love. At least guilt isn't dictating my future. It is for Jack.

I push myself up from my chair, being sure not to look at him. *Detachment. Close down, shut off. It's done.* 'You should go.'

'Annie, please, lis—'

'Is it going to change anything?' I ask, and despite myself, I look at him. I find a face invaded with pure misery and hopelessness. I flinch and glance away. 'If I listen, will it change anything?'

'I have to be there for my child.' He grates the words on broken air. 'I can't abandon my baby.'

The irony of the situation doesn't escape me. This is what I deserve. This is karma. There's another baby, one he doesn't know about. And one that he won't know about. I hate him right now. But I hate myself more. 'Go,' I demand.

'Annie . . .'

'Just go!' I scream, losing it. 'Get out!'

There's a brief silence before I hear his chair scrape the floor. 'I'll always love you, Annie.'

'Don't say that,' I whisper, unable to be near him any longer. 'I don't need to hear that.' I get up and walk away from him in a blur of ruin and pain, my eyes furiously welling with tears. He watches me go. I feel his eyes trained on my back every step of the way. But I don't look back. Not now. Not ever again.

Chapter 26

I've dragged myself through my working week, staggering blindly from meeting to meeting, fighting to keep it together. It's been the fight of my life, constantly batting away the quiver in my voice and the tears that threaten to break free. When I've been home, my flat has been drenched in darkness while I've hidden from the world and fought to find the determination I need to take the next steps in my life.

Aside from my meetings and work commitments, I've only ventured outside twice this past week. To go to the doctor, and then to the private clinic. Lizzy came with me, supportive of my decision.

I'd hoped another test would spring up negative. I hoped in vain. A scan told me I'm six weeks pregnant. A discussion with a nice lady who works at the surgery helped me make my decision. It's the right decision. I can't do this alone, but more significantly, I can't be reminded of Jack every day for the rest of my life. No child deserves a single mother riddled with bitterness and regrets.

Lizzy has been a constant support. She hasn't thrown any *I-told-you-so*'s in my face. She's just been here for me, cuddled me when she's seen my mind drift and made sure I've eaten. She has been here all morning helping me prepare for today. By tomorrow, I will no longer be pregnant. If I give too much time to processing the magnitude of that, I'll undoubtedly fall into the deepest depths of the black pit I'm balancing on the edge of and never claw my way out. Numbing myself to it all is easier.

It's the only way I can be sure to get through this horrific stage in my life. And I asked for it all. I deserve it all.

Karma isn't just a bitch. She's a barbaric psychopath.

Lizzy hands me my bag packed with everything I need for the clinic, along with my leather slouchy bag. 'How about we decorate your bedroom?' she says, steering me away from thinking about where we're heading. 'When you're on your feet again after . . .' Her words fade to a wisp of air.

'After I've had an abortion,' I finish for her. 'You can say it, Lizzy.'

She glances away, thinking, but she doesn't say what she's thinking. I know exactly what that is. *Am I sure?* She's asked me the question without judgement or any sense of disapproval a dozen times. My answer has been consistent and automatic. Yes. Every time, yes.

'Ready?' she asks.

I nod and we head for her car. Our drive is quiet but not uncomfortably so. The private clinic in north London looks welcoming as we roll up. It's been over-decorated on the outside with shrubs, pots of flowers and plants, making it seem like a happy place. I smile at the irony of it. The receptionist is over-friendly and the interior over-cosy. Everything is over-done. Lizzy checks me in while I take a seat, glancing around the waiting room at the other women I'm sharing a room with – all younger than me, some obviously with their mothers. Young girls who have got themselves into trouble. Young girls who have come here to have their problem sucked out of them. I flinch at my agonising thoughts, looking up at Lizzy when she hands me a clipboard.

'You need to fill this out,' she says, taking a seat next to me and handing me a pen.

Resting the form on my lap, I begin the task of completing my details – name, address, date of birth. It's all straightforward, but every time the point of the pen meets the paper, I start to shake terribly, unable to write down the simple answers.

'Here,' Lizzy prompts gently, relieving me of the task. 'I'll do it.'

'Thanks.' I go back to studying the women surrounding me, finding a few of them also watching me. I bet they're wondering what my story is, just as I'm wondering what theirs are. But we're all here for the same reason, to fix the shit situation we've got ourselves into, no matter how it happened for each of us. I wonder if any of them imagined themselves here. I wonder if their sins are as deep as mine. We all have one thing in common, but are their reasons for being here valid? Are mine? I look down at my stomach, reminding myself that this is the best decision for me.

'Annie,' Lizzy says quietly, pointing the pen at the form and looking at me apologetically. 'What do you want me to put here?'

I lean in and read the question. My reason for undergoing the procedure? I don't know what comes over me. I start laughing, drawing the curiosity of everyone in the room, yet the attention doesn't embarrass me, nor does it make me stop. I take the clipboard from Lizzy, ignoring her alarmed face as I continue chuckling.

Then I write the most inappropriate response I guess has ever been written on one of these forms. I fill the box with a shortened version of my life these past few months. I note the wife, her pregnancy, and I finish it off with, 'I bet she won't be here to have her baby sucked from her womb.' I sign where indicated, slam the pen down and shove the form back into Lizzy's lap. Then my laughter abruptly transforms into body-jerking sobs. I cover my face with my hands and let my tears pour into them.

'Oh shit, Annie.' Lizzy sighs, placing the clipboard at her feet and throwing her arms around me, hushing me gently. 'It's not too late,' she soothes, rubbing at my back. 'You can't do this unless you're one hundred per cent sure. I won't let you.'

It's way past too late. 'I'm sure,' I weep, lying, breaking away from Lizzy and wiping at my eyes.

All the thoughts I've safely pushed to the deepest parts of my mind have come thundering forward as I sit here in the waiting room, waiting to be called so they can rid my body of my final reminder of Jack. Unexpected anger starts to bubble in my tummy. I focus on the perfection of my surroundings, the relaxed atmosphere, the friendliness of the staff and the luxurious environment. They're trying to make everyone who walks through that door as comfortable as possible about what they're going to do. Make them forget. Because something as hideous as an abortion couldn't possibly happen in such a lovely place.

'Miss Ryan?' I look up to find another smiling member of the staff standing over me. 'We're ready for you. If you'd like to come with me.' She gestures the way.

Like? Would I *like* to? I get to my feet with Lizzy's help and slowly start to follow, my legs heavy, my heart heavier.

We're shown into a room. More luxury. I'm directed to a chair. More comfort. I'm spoken to by a nurse. More friendliness. I blindly sign more forms with the nurse's lovely silver pen. I feel like I've stepped out of my body. I'm standing to the side, watching people talk at me as I sit in the chair like a zombie, someone holding my hand comfortingly. Lizzy is next to me, answering questions, helping things along.

It's a blur. Everything is a blur. I'm surrounded by activity in slow motion and a fuzz of white noise. I nod when I think I should be nodding and I stand to let Lizzy help me into a gown. Then I'm being guided through another door, Lizzy holding my hand until she's forced to drop it when I'm out of reach. I hear her suppressed sob as I enter a room that's clinical and white. There's a bed and medical equipment at every turn – medical equipment that's going to kill my baby. My breaths start to come shallow and fast, my body chilling to the bone but sweating. I don't want to do this. I can't talk as my hand is taken, can't speak to tell them that I've changed my mind. I'm helped onto the hard bed. A friendly face appears, floating over me, his mouth moving but I'm not hearing his words. My stomach swirls, my head spins.

All I can hear is *Stop!*

Stop them!

I feel tapping on the back of my hand. I see a needle coming closer. 'No,' I mumble. 'I ca . . .' My words fade to a slur.

Then everything goes black.

I feel groggy, exhausted and sick. The heat that my body is giving off is unbearable, yet I'm shivering uncontrollably. I move a little, feeling a thin sheet shift across my body. Then I open my eyes. And I remember where I am. And intense pain steams forward and makes my stomach convulse. I roll onto my side and throw up in long, painful heaves. But nothing comes up. Just bile.

A flurry of activity breaks out, nurses appearing from every direction. 'Annie!' Lizzy's stricken voice hurts my ears and I moan, dropping onto my back. 'Annie, can you hear me?' I blink, waiting for my vision to clear, and when it does, I see her suspended over the bed with pure dread distorting her pretty face. But she only holds my bleary attention for a few seconds, because someone standing behind her steals it.

Jack.

He looks like he's in shock, standing still and silent in the background while people fuss around me, asking how I feel. Numb. I'm numb.

Approaching slowly, his haunted eyes fixed on mine, he comes to a stop at the side of the bed. 'Why didn't you tell me?'

I look away, tearful and ashamed. It's too late now.

His hand rests on mine and he sits on the edge of the bed. 'Annie, look at me,' he demands with a harsh edge. I refuse, so remorseful.

'Sir, I'm going to have to ask you to move,' a nurse says, gesturing curtly for Jack to move to the side.

'One minute.' Jack snaps, standing firm. 'Just give me one minute.' He takes my face and turns me to him, forcing me to look at him. To face what I've done. His eyes are watery. 'What were you thinking?'

'Sir, please. I need to check Annie's blood pressure.'

Jack's jaw begins to pulse, the pressure of his fingertips firmer on my cheeks. He flinches and looks up when Lizzy takes his arm, encouraging him to move and give the nurse the space she needs. Jack shifts to the side under duress and watches the nurse move in.

'How are you feeling, Annie?' she asks as she presses a button on a machine to the side of me and slips a small gadget on the end of my finger.

'Okay,' I mumble, feeling the band around my arm begin to inflate.

'That's good.' She makes a note of my blood pressure on a mobile device in her hand before removing the band from my arm. 'Let's get you sitting up, shall we?' She helps me up a little, and I manage with surprising ease. 'What a pickle you've got into,' she chuckles. 'Patients usually pass out on their way *to* the operating theatre, not on the table.'

I look at her in a daze. 'Sorry?'

'You fainted, dear,' she says matter-of-factly. 'We didn't even get a chance to knock you out. You went white as a sheet! But don't worry. There's still time for the procedure if the doctor thinks you're well enough.'

My mouth goes a little lax, and I look to Jack. 'She won't be having the procedure,' he practically snarls.

'I'm still pregnant?' I mumble mindlessly.

'Yes, dear. Do you think you can stand?' She gives me raised eyebrows. I don't know. My legs still feel useless, but there are definitely some tingles of life now. I'm still pregnant? I look to

Jack, confused and shocked. What's he doing here?

His shoulders drop a little and he makes his way over to me, insisting on taking over from the nurse. 'I've got her.' He sounds pissed off.

The nurse gives me up to him willingly and leaves the room. 'I'll give you some privacy,' she calls, sensing the thick atmosphere.

'And me.' Lizzy heads for the door too. 'I'll wait in reception.' The door closes and we're alone; just Jack and me and a whole load of unanswered questions.

I hear Jack's light sigh as he holds me. 'Sit down,' he orders quietly, moving me over to the chair in the corner.

'I'm fine.' I gently shrug him off and head back to the bed, finding my bag, needing to get out of this gown and out of *here*. I pull my jeans and T-shirt on and slip my feet into my flip-flops. 'Why are you here?'

'Why d'you think, Annie?'

'I don't know, Jack. That's why I'm asking you.' I pull my hair into a ponytail and reach for my slouchy bag.

Jack snatches it away and throws it to the ground. 'Will you fucking stop?' he snaps impatiently, taking the tops of my arms and shaking me. 'Why didn't you tell me?'

'You said that you didn't want a baby.' I sound like a machine.

He looks at me in utter disgust. 'With Stephanie!' he yells, but winces at the volume of his voice, breathing in to find some calm. 'I don't want a baby with Stephanie, Annie.' He lets go of my arms and drops his head back, clenching his eyes shut.

'You never said that,' I murmur, letting my gaze plummet to my feet.

'I didn't think I needed to.'

'I didn't want you to feel trapped.' I grit my teeth, forcing myself to make eye contact with him. His grey eyes have not one spark of life in them. 'I didn't want you to pick me because you felt you had to.'

'Fuck the pity party, Annie.' He releases me and stalks away. 'I've just walked out on my wife. Again! Except this time I've walked out on my pregnant wife.' He falls back against a wall, looking up at the ceiling. 'I didn't know you were pregnant when I made that decision. Lizzy called me as I was walking out of my house with Stephanie hanging off my fucking back.'

I scan Jack's body over his clothes, seeing a few rips in his white T-shirt. 'Lizzy called you?' I mumble mindlessly.

'Yes, she called me. Angry. Tearful. I can't fucking blame her. An abortion, Annie?'

My jaw quivers – I'm mad, sad, relieved. 'I wanted you out of my life completely.'

He flinches, swallowing down the hurt my statement has spiked. Then he starts to gently knock the back of his head against the wall, the hollows of his cheeks pulsing. 'I've spent the past week trying to make sense of this fucked-up situation. Stephanie's flounced around with such a satisfied grin on her fucking face, ordering baby equipment like it's going out of fucking fashion.' He stops with the head bumps and clenches his fists. 'And not once did it feel right. Not once did I feel happy, and she hasn't even questioned it. She's quite content with my misery. Because a baby is going to solve everything. It'll make me love her.'

He laughs sardonically, thumping his forehead with the flat of his fist. 'I found her contraceptive pills,' he breathes. 'Unopened. Not one of them gone. She hasn't missed a few. She hasn't been taking them at all. Not for months. I confronted her, and she denied it. She lied to my fucking face. I realised in that moment that I hated her. I couldn't stay in that madness. Not even for a baby, and now I'm wondering what kind of fucking arsehole I really am.'

He rubs his eyes, and I can tell it's to hold back the tears. He's reached his breaking point. The big, strong man I love has finally cracked.

My heart breaks for him. He's a mess, but rather than rushing over there to comfort him, my legs give and I have to lower myself into the chair. 'She did that to you,' I say, looking at his shredded T-shirt, knowing there'll be angry claw marks beneath.

'She didn't want me to leave.' He pushes away from the wall and comes to me, kneeling between my legs. 'My head has been everywhere, Annie. When Stephanie told me she was pregnant I felt like someone had snatched away the rest of my life. And then the guilt that came because of that ate me alive.' He takes my hands, his grey eyes begging me to understand. 'I didn't know what I was doing. I was lost.'

He pulls me forward until our foreheads meet.

'All I could think of was you,' he says. 'How I would carry on without you. How I'd survive without ever touching you or holding you in my arms again.' His hands move to my face and smooth down my wet cheek. 'Every day became darker until my world was black. I can't live like that.' His voice breaks, and one stray tear rolls down his face. 'I can't live without you.'

Despite my own tears, a small piece of my heart clicks back together as I listen to him pouring his soul out, trying to make me understand. 'I'm pregnant,' I whimper pitifully, like that news might have escaped him. My body starts to tremble as I crumple in the chair, feeling fraught and weak. But I'm relieved too. So relieved. My mind might have failed me in that room, but my body didn't, choosing to shut down into protective mode and bring everything to a stop when my mouth failed to voice my demand to halt the doctors.

Jack smiles. It's a huge smile, full of genuine elation, and it's truly a sight to behold. It makes his eyes sparkle crazily as they fall to my tummy. I see life in him again. He dips and kisses my T-shirt, then rests his head in my lap, slipping his hands around my back.

We're sitting in an abortion clinic. I suddenly feel like a

monster, dirty and immoral. My senses have been clouded by grief, my thought processes purposely stemmed in an attempt to curb my hurt.

'I need to get out of here,' I murmur. 'Please, get me out of here.' Jack helps me to my feet and collects my bag from the floor before holding a firm arm around my waist as he walks me out of the room, constantly looking down at me as if checking that I'm okay. I'm so okay. I have my Jack.

We meet Lizzy in the waiting area and walk out to the car park together, saying our goodbyes with hugs and promises to speak later. Jack thanks her, which she accepts with an affectionate rub of his arm. Her gesture is small, but it means the world to me.

Jack helps me into his car, gets me comfy, fussing and faffing around me until I resort to batting him away. 'Jack, I'm fine,' I assure him, and he scowls at me in response. 'I'm fine,' I breathe, leaning my head back, my hand involuntarily resting on my stomach.

The whole drive home, he holds my hand while I let my mind run away with me, wondering exactly what happens now. I have Jack back. My happiness should be complete. Yet I can't ignore my apprehension, and I don't think I should. We're going to have to think carefully about how we approach this, decide together and be strong. This isn't going to be easy. But my reward is Jack. Whether I deserve him or not is something I'm past agonising over.

Once we've reached my flat, Jack gets out of the car, rounding to meet me on the pavement. 'Okay?'

'Okay,' I assure him as he relieves me of my bag. I head straight for the kitchen and flick the kettle on while Jack throws my bags on the floor next to the sofa.

'I'll do that.' He muscles in, confiscating the teaspoon from me. 'You go get on the couch.'

'Jack, I'm fine.'

'You look a little pale.' He scans my face, pouting. 'How d'you feel?' His palm meets my forehead, feeling for my temperature.

Oh my God! 'Perfect.' I laugh, reclaiming my spoon and loading my mug with sugar. 'You're not going to be irritating and smother me, are you? Because, just so you know, that's going to drive me mad.'

'I can't make any promises.' Jack seizes me from behind and whirls me around, pushing me up onto the worktop.

I drop my spoon on a tiny gasp of surprise. Given the circumstances, is it wrong that I'm reduced to a pool of lust? I'm not sure. I can't think. He nuzzles into my cheek and breathes me into him.

'I've got you back,' he says quietly. 'Thank God I've got you back.' Pulling away, he holds my hips and gazes at me like he can't quite believe it's me. 'I'm going to make it up to you,' he vows. 'For everything I've put you through.'

'Jack . . .'

'No.' His finger meets my lips, silencing me. 'It's not up for discussion. Now' – he drops a light peck on my cheek – 'go and get into some comfy clothes so we can slob out. I'll finish the tea.' He leads me by the backs of my shoulders to the door. 'Go.'

I submit, looking over my shoulder as I leave. 'Jack,' I say as he goes to turn, hindering his return to the kitchen.

He looks at me questioningly. 'What?'

'What are you going to do about Stephanie?' I don't actually mean *her*; I mean more about her condition, and he knows it.

'I haven't figured it all out yet,' he admits. 'I honestly don't know where to start.'

'And what about me?'

'I'll have to tell her about you eventually.' He nods to my stomach with a small smile. 'Not yet, but soon. Once the dust settles.'

'Okay.' But I wonder if the dust will *ever* settle.

'But maybe first I'll move you to another country.'

I smile, despite it not being a laughing matter. He's worried. *I'm* worried. 'I think I'll like you fussing over me,' I tell him, loving the elation that springs onto his face. I have to let him do his thing. And I want to. I want to let him fuss over me. Who would have thought?

'And I'm going to love doing it.' He winks and continues on his way. 'Brace yourself, baby.'

I chuckle and go to the bathroom to freshen up and find some cosy clothes. Once I've brushed my teeth, washed my face and dragged on some sweatpants and a vest, I find my slouchy bag by the couch where Jack dumped it and grab my phone before making my way to join him in the kitchen, colliding with him as I enter. 'Oh!' I drop my mobile and it hits my bare foot. 'Fuck!' I yell, bringing it up and hopping around with a screwed-up face.

'Ouch!' Jack says on my behalf. 'Come here, clumsy.' He picks me up and carries me into the lounge, putting me on the couch. 'Let's see.' He claims my foot, crouching by the sofa.

'It hurts,' I complain, feeling a throb begin to set in, peeking down to my foot as Jack rubs the sharp pain away.

'Let me get some ice.' Setting my foot on the cushion, he hands me the remote and disappears, returning seconds later with my phone and the ice. After he's fussed over my foot, he hovers over me, bracing his arm on the chair and lowering his face close to mine. 'Don't move until I'm back.'

'Where are you going?' I ask, sounding affronted. We just got here.

'Shop. My sweet tooth is raging. I want to curl up on this couch with you and stuff myself stupid with Giant Strawbs. Then I'll cook that meal I owe you.'

He's going to cook for me. In my kitchen. 'Get extra Strawbs,' I order, giggling when he dips, crowding me and smothering my face with wet kisses. 'Stop!'

'I love you.'

'I love you too!' I laugh, pushing him away. 'Hurry up.' The sooner he goes, the sooner he'll be back. I need to stick myself to him and I don't plan on unsticking myself for a while.

Jack laughs as he leaves, and I flick through the channels . . . and flick . . . and flick, searching for anything decent to watch. 'Rubbish,' I grunt, tossing the remote control aside and scooping up my phone when it rings. It's Lizzy.

'Everything okay?' she asks in greeting.

At this particular moment in time, yes. Everything is perfect. I just have to have faith that this all works itself out. 'For now, yes. Thank you for being there today.'

'I'd say I wouldn't have had it any other way, but that would be a lie.' I smile, fully aware of the trauma I've put my friend through.

'I'm sorry. For lying to you, for putting you through today.'

'And I'm sorry for judging you,' she replies, bringing fresh tears to my eyes. 'Now, don't make a fuss, but Jason's taking me to some posh place in Oxford. I need to borrow a cocktail dress.'

I smile at my phone. 'Come over when you're ready.'

'On my way.' She hangs up, and I go back to pointlessly flicking, snuggling down and flexing my foot back to life.

I'm still flicking when there's a knock on the door twenty minutes later. Scrambling up from the couch, I go to let Lizzy in, pulling the door open with a huge smile on my face.

But it's not Lizzy.

My smile falls and every drop of blood drains from my face.

Chapter 27

'Stephanie,' I all but breathe, stepping back a few feet in shock.

'Hey, Annie.' She beams at me, bright and ... normal? She *looks* normal too. Composed and ... normal. 'I felt I should apologise for the other night.' Pulling her bag onto her shoulder, she walks straight in without me even inviting her.

She doesn't know about me, I tell myself. *Act normal!* I look back onto the street, mindful that Jack could come back at any moment and change that.

'How are you?' I ask, just for the sake of it, because I haven't the foggiest idea what else to say.

'Great.'

Great? She looks normal. She claims to be great. What the fuck am I missing? 'That's ... great.' I smile awkwardly. I need to get her out. 'I was just popping out,' I say as non-offensively as I can.

She smiles and I'm sure her eyes drop to my stomach for a split second. No. I'm being paranoid. My stress is playing mind games with me. 'I won't keep you. Jack will be home from work soon.'

He will? I'm speechless. 'You've sorted things out?' I try not to pose it as a question, but my voice is high and squeaky, betraying me.

'Yes, didn't he tell you?'

I pull back. Why would she say that? Why would she think that Jack would tell me? 'I haven't seen him.'

She smiles again, except this time there's an evil edge and I'm definitely not imagining it. I'm not being paranoid. 'Do you think I'm stupid?' she asks, stepping forward.

My lungs drain on a shaky exhale. Deny it. Just deny it. 'What are you talking about?' I laugh. It's nervous and she doesn't miss it.

'All that time you were pretending to be my friend.'

I back away, aware of just how precarious this situation is. She might appear calm, but her words are telling me otherwise. Pretending to be her friend?

She looks volatile. Her eyes are on my stomach again, and her palm flattens across her own belly. She smiles fondly as she slowly circles her midriff, something disturbing in her deep-set eyes.

'It was you all along. You are a pathetic whore, Annie,' she muses quietly, looking up at me. 'He'll never leave me.'

My flesh goes cold. I mustn't confirm what she suspects. I need to play dumb. Keep my cool. 'Stephanie, I don't know what you're talking about.'

She sniffs, looking down at her wrist, inspecting it. She's planning where she's going to make the cut.

'It won't work,' I blurt, losing control of my mouth, fighting down the anger her subtle hint has spiked. 'Not again.'

Her eyebrows jump up, surprised. 'I beg your pardon?'

'He's told me,' I confirm. It's too late now. 'He's told me everything.'

Her lip curls. 'You'll be a distant memory by tomorrow, you vindictive bitch. You and that bastard child of yours. A minor indiscretion. That's all.'

I want to scream in her face, tell her he loves me, but something stops me. It's not the sudden comprehension that I'm dealing with a woman who doesn't think twice about lashing out at her husband, therefore won't hold back from going at me with those talons of hers. It's the sudden comprehension that she knows I'm pregnant. I snap my mouth shut. She *was* looking at my stomach. No one else knows I'm expecting. Only Jack and Lizzy.

'How do you know I'm pregnant?'

She scowls. 'Jack told me.'

'No he didn't.' Jack wouldn't do that, not with her being so volatile. He hasn't even told her about *me*. Yet she knows. And she knows I'm carrying her husband's child.

I rack my brain, and quickly step back when something crazy and very disturbing starts to itch at the corners of my mind. I rewind to the night Stephanie turned up unexpectedly at my flat, looking for a friend after Jack left her. She used my bathroom. She had to go through my bedroom to get to my bathroom. My leather slouchy bag was on my bed. My pregnancy test was in my bag.

My thoughts seem ridiculously crazy. But then this is Stephanie, and I know how crazy *she* can be. I rush over and grab my bag from the floor where Jack dropped it in the lounge, rummaging through it to find the test. I've been using this same bag for over a week since that night. I don't recall seeing it in here. Where is it?

I turn the bag upside down, emptying the contents onto the floor and scanning it all. No test. Then I rifle through the inside pockets, just to check it hasn't slipped into one of those. Nothing.

I gasp, my eyes shooting upwards, finding Stephanie in the doorway to my lounge, watching me frantically search. She knows what I'm looking for. I'm not losing my mind.

'You stole the test from my bag,' I accuse on a burst of stunned breath. 'You took it and claimed it was yours.'

'You will stay away from him!' she screams, slamming her fist into the doorframe. Her knuckles split on impact, the force of her strike echoing around my flat. 'Do you hear me?' she roars, her fists clenching. 'I'll fucking kill you and that bastard baby of yours. Don't think I won't!'

I see the scratches on Jack's neck. The mark on his cheek-bone. The state of his back. And then I see pure red fury but just hold my composure before I return the favour and rip her to shreds. 'You can't hurt me, and you can't hurt Jack any more either.'

Her eyes go wild and she lunges at me, catching me off guard. I'm dragged into the hallway and slammed into the wall. My breath is knocked out of me, and I don't get a chance to get it back before her palm connects with my cheek. Pain slices me in half, and she just keeps coming and coming at me, attacking me. 'You asked for this!'

As each blow connects, I struggle through the chaos to try to defend myself. My arms are wrapped around my stomach, protecting it, willing to accept her rage on any part of my body but there. But then her fingers are clawing around my wrists, trying to pull them away.

I see a baby. A defenceless baby relying on me for protection.

With sudden strength, I violently shove her away. She hits the wall opposite me with a bang, but I give her no opportunity to gather herself. I yank the front door open and grab her by her hair. My only purpose is to put a barrier between us. I feel murderous, and adrenalin is thundering through my veins.

'I'll kill you!' she shrieks. 'I'll make you pay for trying to take him from me!'

I don't shout back at her. I don't scream and wail, and I don't try to hurt her. My only focus is just to get her away from me. Get her away before she does either of us any damage.

I use all my strength to shove her out. Slamming the door, I fall against it, gasping for breath. I expect her to start banging on the wood, but there's nothing. I run into the lounge and grab my phone before I rush to the window. She comes into view, standing still on the pavement outside.

'Oh my God,' I whisper, my eyes falling to her wrists, where she's holding a knife. 'Stephanie, no!' My instinct has me dashing for the door and running out to stop her. 'Stephanie, stop!' My stare zeroes in on hers, and I manage to appreciate the intent in her deep-set blue eyes as I near. She'll do it. I have no doubt. I pelt forward, ready to knock the knife away or snatch it; I'm not sure which. All I know is that I have to stop her.

She doesn't move, doesn't try to escape me. No. Instead, she smiles and turns the knife towards me. It takes a few too many seconds for my brain to engage and register what she's doing, the reckless glint in her eyes confusing me. I tell my legs to stop running, to bring me to a stop before it's too late.

Stop!

'No!' I cry, skidding to a halt and bending my body, bringing my stomach in as much as I can to avoid the blade as she charges forward.

'Bitch!' she screams. 'You won't have him!' Her body collides with mine, knocking me to the side on a grunt. I gasp and feel my stomach, searching for blood. I can't see anything. Nothing obvious, but I don't look for long. I haven't got the luxury of time. I run back to my flat, too aware of the damage she could do to me if I don't get away. I bolt the door and run to my window, gasping for breath.

There's no sign of her anywhere. I have another quick check over my abdomen and freeze, waiting for pain to kick in. Nothing. Tears of relief burst from my eyes as I grab my phone and call Jack, returning to the window to look for her.

'Hey, baby,' he answers, sounding happy. Content.

'Stephanie was here,' I shout urgently, exhausted, my breath loud and strained. 'Jack, she has a knife. She attacked me with a knife.'

'Jesus!' he chokes, and the background noise of his engine gets louder, evidence of him hitting the floor with his foot on the accelerator. 'Where are you?'

'Inside. I got her out and locked myself inside.'

'Are you hurt?'

'Nothing major.'

'Nothing *major*?'

'A few scratches, that's all.' I look down at my arm and see evidence of her nails, just like I've seen on Jack's body. 'She's not pregnant, Jack. She stole my pregnancy test from my handbag.' I return my attention to the window, my eyes darting left to right, searching for her outside. She's gone.

'What?'

'The pregnancy test. It was mine.'

'But she did it while I was there.'

'Did you watch her? On the toilet?' It sounds like a stupid question, but she could have switched them.

He's silent for a second before he whispers, 'No. She was in the bathroom. I waited outside.'

I close my eyes, reaching up to my cheek and pressing into the burn. 'It was mine,' I repeat quietly. 'She knows it's me. And she knows I'm pregnant.'

I hear his sharp inhale. 'Call the police. I'm around the corner. Don't open the door until I'm there.' He hangs up before waiting for my agreement, and I watch the street from the window as I dial 999 and bring the phone to my ear. When I see his Audi round the corner, I nearly fold with relief.

'Emergency. Which service do you require?'

'Police.'

Jack zooms into a parking space across the street and jumps out, heading quickly around the car to the road. But he pulls to a stop abruptly, looking over his shoulder, something snatching his attention. My heart stops in my chest as he backs up, turning towards something. Or some*one*. I can't see who; there's a van blocking my view, but I don't need to see. She'll be waiting for him.

'Jack!' I shout, banging at the window. 'She has a knife!'

He doesn't look my way. He can't hear me. I start to tear up as

I drop the phone, then rush for the door and unbolt it, running out onto the street.

'Jack!' I yell, frantic. He looks to me, frowning, as I leap into the road just as someone walks out from behind the van. But it's not Stephanie.

My brain vaguely registers Lizzy and her widening eyes at the sight of me running across the road towards them, and my mind pulls up, as do my legs, slowing me down until I come to a confused stop. I look to Lizzy, then to Jack. He's frozen in place, his mouth slightly open as he looks down the street. It's then I hear the screeching of tyres.

I turn slowly, seeing a car speeding towards me.

'Annie!' Jack roars. I hear his shoes hitting concrete as the car comes closer and closer.

'Annie!'

I'm a statue.

'Annie, move!'

Jack's hysterical plea is the last thing I hear.

My bones, my flesh, my head . . . they all scream on impact.

But I don't feel a thing.

Chapter 28

Beep. It's all I can hear. The damn sound has embedded itself into my brain – the short, sharp, repetitive shots of noise assaulting my ears. I'm sure that's all I'm going to hear for eternity.

My world is black and I can't move. My body feels heavy – so, *so* heavy – and my head is pounding terribly. My brain feels as if it's been bouncing off my skull. Everything *hurts* – my head, my bones . . . even my skin.

Why am I in so much pain? Where am I? The blackness engulfing me shows no sign of fading. There's no light anywhere to be found, and no matter how hard I try to convince myself to move, I can't. My eyes won't open and I can't talk. Everything is failing me.

My mind descends into panic, and then quickly my panic turns to pure, raw fear. In my head I'm falling to pieces, hysterical and frightened. I'm crying but I'm not crying. I'm flailing but I'm not moving. It's my own personal hell, and I begin to wonder if that's where I actually am. Am I dead?

Beep!

That sound. It's unbearable.

Beep!

A spasm in my eyelid surprises me, and I wait, wondering if I imagined it. I push my fear away and wait some more. Another twitch, this time in both eyelids. I focus, concentrate hard on the muscles in my eyes, willing them to open.

I'm filled with hope when I detect another spasm – small but definitely there. I get a glimpse of light, spurring me on. I need more. I can't bear this blackness any longer. I shove the pain away and gather my determination and strength.

Beep!

My eyes open, seeming to wake my lungs as they do. Air gushes into me and my body inflates. My eyes quickly close again on a flinch. The combination of harsh light and searing pain bolting through my body makes it too difficult to keep them open.

I can't scream. I can't move to curl into a ball and curb the agony. My eyes fill with tears behind my lids, and the tears force their way to the corners of my eyes and trickle down the sides of my face into my ears. I work to regulate my breathing into smooth, even inhales and exhales, and the pain subsides a little.

Then I begin to open my eyes again, bit by little bit, squinting back the glare. My surroundings come into view. I don't recognise anything. It looks like a hospital room.

Beep!

If I could make anything work, I'd sit up. Or get out of bed and find someone to tell me what on earth is going on. I try to turn my head and the movement triggers a wave of pain that rips through me again. I scream in my head. Oh God, I've never felt pain like this. More tears come, blurring my vision.

Beep!

And then I see him.

He's slumped in the chair next to me, asleep, his head propped on his hand, his elbow on the arm of the chair. He looks haunted, even in his sleep. His skin is almost as grey as I know his eyes to be, and his scruff is the scruffiest I've ever seen. He's wearing old jeans and a white T-shirt, and a blanket is spread across his lap.

My Jack.

Suddenly, the pain doesn't feel so brutal.

His hand is wrapped loosely around mine, resting by my side. I see a bracelet. It has two charms. *You* and *Me*.

The sight of Jack along with the bracelet opens the flood-gates to my mind. I close my eyes, willingly walking towards the memories. I'm at a bar with Jack drinking tequila. He's licking me. And I'm staring at him in a complete, awed daze. I'm standing on the opposite side of the road from him. I'm pushed up against a rough wall, and then soon after a smooth window in a hotel room. I wake up in a bed with his beauty spread out beside me. I run. I relive every moment of the week that followed, remember obsessing over the intensity of our en-counter and regretting not leaving him any way to contact me. I see his face when I open my front door on the night of my housewarming party. I hear glass smashing at my feet. I feel his touches and hear all his words, experience every kiss again and every painful thought. I feel his arms around my body when I threw myself at him after he gave me a solution to my roof pre-dicament. I see him sitting across the boardroom table looking at me as if he were the proudest man alive. I see a pregnancy test. I see his wife and the crazy light in her eyes. And finally I see a car speeding towards me.

Beep!

My eyes snap open and I gasp for breath, my chest pumping. More pain, except this time it's worse. This time I know why I'm hurting.

'Annie.' I hear Jack in the distance and turn my eyes, find-ing him suspended over me, his face grave. 'Annie?' He reaches above my head and slams his fist into something before return-ing his attention to me, watching me convulse on the bed.

His hands are stroking my face as I look up at him with wide, frightened eyes. 'Jesus, baby.' He chokes, reaching for the but-ton again and smashing it hard. 'Come on!' He looks over his shoulder when a hive of activity breaks out, the door swinging open. 'She's awake but I think she's having a seizure.'

A nurse appears above me, pushing Jack out of the way. 'Annie?' she calls loudly. Too loudly. She pulls the skin under my eyes down, looking closely into them. 'Annie, can you hear me?'

I nod, fighting to rein myself in to stop the pain. A mask lands over my face and I suck in air ravenously. The hit of oxygen gives me instant relief, widening my airways and dislodging the panic.

'Is she okay?' Jack asks, appearing by the nurse's side. He looks just awful – drained, tired and anxious.

'Are you in pain, darling?' the nurse asks, ignoring Jack.

I nod again, and she immediately looks across the bed. 'Check her chart and tell me the last time she was given morphine. Intravenous.'

'Eight this morning,' a female voice replies. 'Straight after the first transfusion.'

'Hook her up again.'

'Straight away.'

'Annie, we're getting you some more pain relief, darling. Won't be long, okay?' The nurse makes fast work of hooking up a fresh bag of drugs, and I close my eyes, welcoming the cool liquid into my veins, hoping it numbs not only my broken body but my mind too. The door closes quietly and I try to relax, focusing on Jack's closeness. He's here. Everything will be okay because he's here.

'Annie, can you hear me?'

I feel his touch on the tips of my fingers and force my eyes to open, my head resting comfortably to the side. Jack pulls the chair closer to the bed and perches on the edge, leaning forward to take my hand in both of his, squeezing gently.

'Hello, gorgeous,' he whispers, his expression harbouring all kinds of trepidation. It doesn't matter how terrible he looks. I'd put money on the fact that I look worse. I flex my hand a little in his, my way of replying, and he smiles, his lips trembling as he exhales deeply and drops his forehead to our cluster of hands on the bed.

I stare at the back of his head for an age, building up my strength to speak, soothed by the relief from pain that the morphine delivers. 'J . . . ack.' His name comes out of my mouth jagged and broken, and I find myself able to lift my head a little, now that the pain isn't hindering my movement.

His own head whips up considerably faster than mine. 'Don't move, baby,' he rushes to say, gently pushing my head back down to the pillow. 'Don't move.'

'I'm stiff,' I complain, feeling like I need to crack every bone in my body into place, especially in my hips.

'You mustn't move.' Jack faffs with my pillow, not really making much difference, but I let him tend to me nevertheless.

My arm feels like lead, and I look down to find it concealed in a cast, from the tips of my fingers to the very top of my arm. It's ramrod straight. I look at Jack, who's watching me assess my injury. Or one of them. His bristly face is close and straight, his grey eyes cloudy. He drops the most delicate kiss on the corner of my mouth, and I manage a small smile.

'Better?' he asks, scanning my face for any sign of discomfort.

I nod. 'How are you?' I ask, watching as he more or less plummets back to the chair, leaning in and resting his forearms on the bed, his hand holding mine.

He huffs a short, quiet puff of amusement. 'Don't ask me how I am when you're lying here looking like you've been run over by a bus.'

'It was a car, wasn't it?' I reply simply and emotionlessly, making Jack pull up in his chair.

'You remember?'

'Who was driving?'

He starts patting at the bedding around my thighs, avoiding my eyes. 'Let's not do this now.' He's trying to avoid the conversation that we're going to have to have at some point, but I'd rather just get it done with. 'For now we focus on getting you well.'

'It was her, wasn't it?' I don't mean to allow emotion into my voice, and I wholeheartedly hate myself for letting it, because Jack's face is a picture of pure misery as a result.

'She was arrested at the scene,' he whispers. I look away, my lips pressing together to stop the cries of devastation from escaping and crippling him even more. 'She said she didn't see you in the road.'

'She saw me,' I say quietly, looking down at my tummy, not wanting to ask the question that's most important to me. Jack's hand appears in my downcast vision, coming to rest lightly over the bedcovers on my stomach. I look at him, my eyes brimming with tears that are ready to tumble. 'Our baby?' I murmur, my hand coming to lie atop his, hoping and praying that my battered body protected our unborn child. 'Please tell me our baby is okay.'

Tears begin to stream down Jack's cheeks as he shakes his head. And my heart breaks clean in two. 'I can't.' He swallows, his handsome face distorting with grief. 'I can't, Annie. I'm sorry,' he whispers. 'I'm so, so sorry.'

A ragged sob rips through me, my broken body jerking as a result. I'm in agony. 'No,' I whimper, my eyes bursting with tears, encouraging more from Jack. 'No.' My body begins to spasm uncontrollably, my world exploding into a haze of devastation. 'No, no, no!'

Jack shoots up from his chair and bends his body over the bed, getting as close to me as he can to comfort me. 'I'm sorry,' he sobs, trying desperately to console me as we cry in each other's arms. 'I'm so sorry.'

I shake my head, not prepared to accept it, hiding my face in his neck. 'She killed our baby.'

Jack doesn't say anything more – no apologies, no attempts to calm me. All he has the energy left to do is hug me and cry his heart out along with me.

The darkness returns, and so does the pain. But now it's

agony. She tried to kill me and she succeeded in killing our baby. This is my penance. For all of the wrong decisions I have made, for touching the forbidden, this is the ultimate punishment.

I will never forgive myself.

Chapter 29

I've had so much blood pumped into me, I don't even think I'm me any more. I had internal bleeding caused by a splintered rib that nicked a blood vessel. The mass of blood behind my ribs was excruciatingly painful, but once it started to disperse, the pain lessened over the weeks until regular paracetamol sufficed and I could lose my drip. My left arm is broken in three places and three tendons were severed above my wrist. I have a tidy gouge in my thigh, and I'm all kinds of black and blue from scrapes, cuts and grazes. Quite honestly, I look a royal mess, even six weeks later.

Yet I'd endure this pain forever and happily look like this for the rest of my life if I could change just one thing.

But I can't. My only comfort is that our baby didn't suffer like we have.

Stephanie was charged with attempted murder. I didn't know, but a few neighbours up the street have CCTV cameras installed at the front of their properties, and after careful analysis, apparently her intent became clear. The footage of her coming at me with a knife only moments before cemented it for the police.

I chose not to see that footage, but Jack did. I don't know why he needed to, and I didn't ask. They also did tests on the car; the speed on impact was estimated to be around 50 mph. I shouldn't even be alive. Stephanie's been put on suicide watch while on remand, and her lawyer has appealed for mental assessments. I've heard she's claiming diminished responsibility.

I'm hoping that means she'll be certified mad and shipped off to a mental institute. I don't care where they take her, just as long as it's far, far away from me and Jack.

After my parents got over the shock of the accident, my father ripped into Jack with an anger I've never seen before. Jack bowed to his fury, putting up no fight and not retaliating with any kind of excuses. The guilt that consumes him worries me more each day. He's here, but he's not here. He smiles, but behind the smiles there's a perpetual sadness. It wasn't supposed to be this way. No one was supposed to suffer *this* much.

My friends and parents have been in and out of my flat checking up on me, but their help hasn't been needed. Jack's taken compassionate leave from work to be with me, to wait on me hand and foot and fuss over my healing body. I can't say I don't like having him around so much after all the time we've spent snatching hours here and there to be with each other. But I just wish the circumstances weren't so tragic. We lost our baby. It's something neither of us knows how to deal with. All we have is each other; I pray that's enough.

We've watched *Top Gun* a hundred times and eaten a million Giant Strawbs between us. Jack has taken me to physiotherapy every other day since my cast was removed. In between sessions, I perform the exercises that were given to me, on various hard-backed cards, at least six times a day. Six times! So basically all I've been doing are arm exercises, and Jack has made sure of it, sitting with me for twenty minutes each time and doing the movements with me, as well as pulling me up if he thinks I'm not doing it effectively. I'm bored of arm exercises.

Now I'm reclined on my couch, flicking through the channels, when Jack wanders in with those damn cards. 'Not again,' I sigh, the remote control falling to the cushion with my limp arm. 'We just did some.'

'Be quiet,' he scolds me gently, shifting my legs and sitting next to me.

'But it's much better. Look.' I reclaim the remote control and aim it at the television, ignoring how heavy it feels. 'I can do this.'

'Yes, but I want you to be able to do this.' He fists his hand and starts thrusting it in the air, mimicking some hand action on an invisible cock. I gape at him, not because it might be inappropriate for him to do that, given where we're at, but because I see a slight glimmer in his grey eyes that's been missing for weeks. The corners of his mouth twitch, and I find mine following suit. And then he laughs lightly, the sound acting like the best kind of medicine there could be. I giggle, my head falling back to the cushion. It feels good, another piece of my broken heart slipping back into place.

My grief will never diminish completely, but I have to hope the pain will eventually become bearable enough for me to move forward. I hope Jack is moving in the same direction too. I drop my head and find he's smiling. It's such a stunning sight, and it fills me with hope that with my fading pain comes his fading guilt. 'You're very good at that,' I say, reaching for his hand and squeezing it. 'Been getting a lot of practice?'

He flicks through the cards, looking up at me with a raised brow. 'Wanking pales by comparison after you've had the hand of the woman you love wrapped around your cock,' he replies huskily, winking, expanding my grin.

'Did you just say that?'

'Yep.' He holds the card up and I look, seeing the familiar pictures. 'Now focus on this.'

'After you've just said something so romantic?'

The full-blown Jack Joseph smile makes an appearance. 'Concentrate,' he orders.

Grudgingly I look at the card. 'Easy,' I claim, starting to clench and unclench my fist, over and over. 'Next.'

'This one.' He holds up another card.

'There.' I bend my arm at the elbow with a stifled yawn. 'Next.'

'Annie, you need to extend your arm fully.' He reaches over and pulls my arm straight. I hiss, feeling my stiff tendons stretch too much. 'Yes, much better,' he quips sarcastically. I scowl. He gives me a warning look. 'Are you going to carry on arguing with me?'

I grumble my annoyance and start to bend my arm, slowly this time, stretching it back out as far as I can. 'Happy?'

'I'm just trying to help.'

'Help me by taking me out,' I plead, with no hope that he'll listen. I feel like a prisoner, and aside from my mundane visits to the physiotherapist, Jack's kept me safe inside wrapped in cotton wool. I'm slowly losing my mind. 'Or at least let me in my studio so I can do some work.'

'I was thinking of taking you somewhere, actually.' He reaches up to my face and traces the line of a cut on my cheek. 'But I don't want you pushing yourself.'

'I feel so much better.' I need to get out and try to pick up something close to normal life instead of lying here with nothing to do other than relive that awful day. This isn't healthy for Jack, either, being my nursemaid twenty-four-seven. He needs to get out too.

'I'll make you a deal,' he says, bending over my reclined body and coming in close to my face.

'What?' I'll do anything.

'I'll take you out somewhere if you . . .' His words fade, his eyes flicking past me fleetingly.

'If I what?'

'If you agree to move in with me.'

I recoil. I don't mean to. We haven't spoken about this. Or anything, for that matter. Since I was discharged from hospital, all of our efforts have gone into my recovery, and we've both seemed content doing that. I didn't want to go over and over the dreadful events that put me in hospital and snatched away our unborn child. Jack's been here at my flat the whole time, and I didn't question it. Move in with him? Where? His home has been empty, since he's here and his wife has been locked up. And I know he never wants to set foot in the place again. My flat is small.

'Maybe we could buy somewhere,' he goes on, sensing that I'm spinning off endless silent questions, and maybe knowing what they are. 'I can't sell my place just yet, until we know what's happening with . . .' He trails off again. There's been no mention of her name and I doubt there ever will be. Jack's filed for divorce and has left the complicated logistics of it in the hands of his solicitor. 'I want somewhere with you. Away from here. Somewhere to call ours.'

'Ours?' I ask, liking the sound of that.

'Just ours.'

'Just ours,' I parrot, struggling for what else to say. Somewhere that is just ours.

'A fresh start. Me and you.' He takes my wrist and fingers my bracelet, prompting me to look down at it. 'If you want me.'

Another small piece of my shattered heart drops into place. I add my fingers to his and join him in playing with the precious charms. The dynamics of our relationship have been forced to change. Before, when we were only able to see each other in stolen moments of time, our clothes were usually ripped off within seconds, both of us ravenous with hunger for each other, our time together spent losing ourselves in our private bubble of happiness. Now, when we're spending every second of the day with each other and I'm laid up, our time is spent . . . just being. Loving. Supporting. Healing each other as best we know how while being physically unable to take each other into the mind-numbing haze of pleasure that's got us through so many months. But it's still pleasurable. Through the grief I've been dealing with, being with Jack is still beyond fulfilling. And if anything, it's only strengthened our love. He's seen me at my weakest. I've seen him at his. Yet together we're probably stronger than ever. I look up at him, letting my lips tip a little at the corners. 'You were always mine, even before I knew it.'

He nods, combing his fingers through my hair. 'I'm just so sorry that—'

I take his nape and pull him closer, our lips nearly touching. 'I'll be okay,' I say, cutting him off. 'I have you, so I know I'll be okay.' I'm mindful that my hurt could eat him alive if I let it. I mustn't let it.

'I've put you through so much,' he whispers.

'I put *myself* through it,' I point out. This isn't just his doing. I accepted the repercussions the moment I knowingly got caught up in a web of lies and deceit with a married man. I just didn't anticipate the extent of the pain and heartache we would go through. I didn't anticipate Stephanie.

His lip curves a little. 'I didn't exactly give you much choice, did I?'

'You mean when you relentlessly tempted me with your gorgeousness?'

He closes the space between our mouths and kisses me carefully. 'I knew I was supposed to find you drunk in that bar that night.'

'I wasn't drunk.'

'Of course you weren't.' He smiles against my mouth. 'Want some help in the shower?'

I nod against him and let him help me up from the couch, making myself keep the slight discomfort quiet so he can't withdraw from his end of the deal.

'You're in pain, aren't you?' he muses as he holds my waist, walking behind me and matching my sluggish pace.

'I'm fine,' I retort, my face screwing up a little when an un-expected shot of pain bolts through my thigh. I'm still limping slightly, but I'm pretty sure that's simply because of my lack of regular movement. My muscles and bones are just objecting any time I move because they're used to feeling redundant.

Jack guides me into the bathroom and flicks on the shower. I hate myself for it, but I have to sit on the toilet seat while he starts collecting towels. I'm exhausted from that short, leisurely stroll from one end of my flat to the other. He doesn't miss my movement, raising knowing eyebrows at me that I choose to ignore as I start to remove my T-shirt. I lose sight of him when I pull it over my head, and when I win the sight of him back, he's removed his own T-shirt. I smile at his abs, his chest, his downright stunning torso. And I sigh.

I drop my T-shirt to the floor as Jack unfastens his jeans. Slowly. Then pushes them down his thick thighs. Slowly. He's purposeful and means to be. Things happen between my legs that haven't happened for a long while.

'I'll wash you down.' His jeans hit the floor. 'Up for it?'

I fly up from the toilet seat. And yelp. 'Fuck!' I drop back down and grab the sink, breathing through the pain.

'Annie!' Jack's kneeling before me in the blink of an eye, assessing my condition. 'Take it easy.'

My cheeks puff out as I exhale, looking up at him. 'Ouch,' I murmur pitifully.

'Okay. No outing. It's too soon. And no joint shower.'

I growl and grab his hair, yanking him forward threateningly. 'You're coming in!' I hiss. 'And then you're taking me out.'

'Fuck, Annie!' He chuckles as he reaches up to prise my clawed fingers away. 'Okay, okay.'

'Good.' I go back to breathing, cool and controlled. 'Sorry for being so insistent.'

Jack laughs, a proper belly laugh. It's like music to my ears. 'I look forward to a lifetime of insistence, gorgeous.' He rises before me, offering his hand. 'Ready?'

I take his hand and let him gently ease me up and strip me of my shorts, knickers and bra before directing me patiently to the shower. 'What do you expect when you brandish that body, anyway?' I ask, hearing him chuckle. 'And look at me like that.

And speak to me in that tone. And say those things.'

'I'll keep my mouth shut.' He gently turns me at the shower bench and helps me down. 'And keep my clothes on,' he adds.

'You don't have to do that,' I object. That would be a travesty.

My bum meets the wood of the shower bench and I grimace, hating needing it. I was hoping today would be the day I'd be able to stand while I have a shower. 'I feel like an invalid,' I grumble, watching Jack drop to his knees before me.

'You are,' he points out, making my face screw up more. He takes the sponge and wets it under the spray, adding some shower gel. He clasps my ankle and gently lifts, keeping a cautious eye on my face for any hint of pain. 'You good?' he asks, just to be sure, and I nod. 'Good.' He starts soaping me down. 'Want me to shave your legs?'

I look down at my legs, reaching to smooth up my skin. I've been trying to shave, but with limited movement comes limited reach. 'Please.' I can't believe we're at this place in our relationship already, but Jack's completely unperturbed by the task and happily fetches the razor and starts running it up my leg in precise, gentle strokes. 'Our love has reached a whole new level,' I muse to myself, seeing his mouth stretch into a smile as he carries on with his self-appointed job.

'Our love is the greatest kind, Annie.' He finishes up and washes the remnants of soap away, running his palms down my legs to check his handiwork. 'Perfect,' he says, looking up at me. I suspect he's not talking about how good a job he's done of shaving my legs. He's talking about our love.

I reach forward and feel his bristly jaw. 'Perfect,' I counter.

He turns his mouth into my hand and kisses it gently, breathing in and closing his eyes. 'I love you.'

I inch forward on the bench, wanting to get closer to him. He's having none of it, holding me back. 'I want to hold you.'

'Then I'll come to you.' He walks forward on his knees and places his hands on my thighs, looking at me for an okay. I open my legs in reply and reach for his shoulders, pulling him in and constricting my thighs as much as my body will allow before it hurts. 'Careful,' he warns, his wet chest meeting mine, my face sinking into his neck, his face into mine. We both hum. 'God, that feels good,' he sighs.

It so does. Warm. Comforting. Right. We stay there for ages, locked together, enjoying the first proper cuddle we've had in too long. Nothing hurts me. I have no space for anything other than appreciation. I could stay here forever, so content in his arms, so when he starts to break away, I grumble and cling to him even more tightly.

'I thought you wanted to brave the big wide world,' he says, nudging my face from his neck with determined effort.

'I've changed my mind. Let's just stay here.'

'Forever?'

'Yes.'

He laughs. 'Someone's decisive today. How about I promise to hold you all night long?'

'As opposed to lying on the edge of the bed as far away as possible from me?'

'I was afraid I'd knock you in my sleep.' He pushes himself up and retrieves the shampoo.

'I feel better after five minutes of you holding me than I have after six weeks of being static.'

He pauses with the bottle upside down, looking at me. I shrug. It's the truth. He has a healing touch. 'Then I'll hold you all night,' he declares.

'What about tomorrow night?'

'And then too.'

'And the next night?'

'Annie, I'm going to hold you every night for the rest of our lives together.' His hands come to my dark hair and massage, working it up into suds. 'And I'll be thankful every minute that I can.'

I fall into total bliss, feeling Jack's hands working tenderly through my hair, like he could be handling the most fragile of things. I guess right now he is. 'You must be sick of seeing me looking such a wreck,' I sigh. I've forgotten what make-up is, and I've been in slobby clothes for weeks.

'You look beautiful every day,' he says, simple as that. 'Be quiet.'

I obey and let him take care of me, having to keep my eyes closed. His naked lower stomach is at perfect eye level, and if I drop my eyes a little, something else. I know I'm not ready for *that*, so taunting myself would only add to my fading pain.

'Up you come.' Jack slips his arm around my waist and lifts. 'Easy.'

I wince and hiss and ooh my way up, after just a few minutes on my arse. I grudgingly admit that I have a way to go yet until I'm fighting fit. 'Thank you.'

He doesn't acknowledge my graciousness, being quick to wrap me in a towel and help me to the sink. I look at myself in the mirror. I look pasty. Beautiful every day? I scoff and reach for my packet of contraceptive pills, popping one out and bringing it to my mouth.

But the tablet doesn't make it past my lips.

Because Jack's palm is wrapped around my wrist, hindering me from putting it there. I look at his reflection in the mirror, my eyebrows pinching in the middle. What's he doing?

'How about you don't take that,' he says quietly, observing me carefully for my reaction.

I'm thunderstruck. Does he mean …? 'Then I'll likely fall pregnant when you finally give in to my need to have you asap.'

His lips twist a little in amusement, still holding my wrist firm. 'Like I said, how about you don't take that.' He tips my hand to the side, and the pill tumbles from my palm and falls into the sink. I look down, watching as it rolls around the plughole a few times before disappearing. The pill is gone, but

I still stare at the porcelain of the sink, trying to wrap my mind around what he's suggesting.

'Jack, I don't need you to—' His finger meets my lips and hushes me, his body moving in close to mine.

'I'm not trying to make things right, Annie. Not with a baby, anyway. And I'm not trying to replace the one we've lost.' The mention of my miscarriage stings terribly, and he must notice because he encases my cheeks with his big palms and brings my face close to his. 'I want to build a life with you,' he says softly. 'I feel like I've waited forever to feel like this.' His thumbs caress my cheeks, and I close my damn eyes when tears pinch the backs of them. Jack kisses each of my lids in turn, so tenderly. 'I want to make babies with you, Annie. Hundreds of them.' I sniff back my emotion. 'I want to look at you every day and smile because I picked *you* to be the mother of my children. Because I know if I'm to have it all, then I should have it all with you.' I open my eyes and sink into the grey depths of Jack's. The sadness that was lingering there: it's nearly gone. 'You are my all, Annie Ryan.' He kisses my forehead sweetly. 'No more pills.' His kiss tells me so much. It tells me he'll protect me. It tells me he'll always be there for me. And it tells me that however wrong people think my choices have been, they were the right choices for me. And for Jack.

'Just give me time,' I whisper.

'As much as you need.' He pulls back, a small grin on his face, one that I can't help but mirror. 'I can do condoms. I just need you to know I'm ready when you are.'

'Okay,' I agree easily, as simple as that. Because I also know that if I am to have a child at all, then it should be with Jack. I stare into the grey eyes of a man who was forbidden. A man who should never have been touched. A man who wasn't mine. 'I draw the line at four babies,' I murmur. His smile. God, his smile. It's bright, almost dazzling, and it's pouring with hope and love. The biggest piece of my broken heart slides back into place. Jack's smile symbolises our life. And the lives of our children. It symbolises happiness. And freedom.

'I want six.'

I ignore the searing pain that bombards me when I throw myself at him. 'I love you,' I sob like a fool into him. 'I love you so much.'

'Thank you.' He holds me like I would collapse if he releases me. I would, but not with pain or exhaustion. I'd collapse with a happiness that's almost too intense to comprehend. Like most things I have with Jack. 'Come on, then. I'm taking you out.'

'Where are we going?'

'It's a surprise.' He drops a kiss on my nose and releases me gingerly. 'Want some help getting dressed?'

'What am I wearing?'

He takes my hand and leads me to my wardrobe, then proceeds to flick through my rails of clothes. 'This.' He pulls out an oversized Ralph Lauren shirt. 'With these.' And some skinny jeans. So nowhere fancy, then.

Slowly and carefully, he helps me get dressed and oversees me applying the first bit of make-up I've worn in weeks. 'My hair?' I ask, frowning at my mane. It could do with a cut and colour.

He pulls the hair-tie off my wrist and gathers up my long dark hair, securing it in a messy ponytail.

'Perfect.'

I wouldn't say that, but it's an improvement on the ragged mess I've been sporting since finding myself in hospital. 'And my feet?'

'Something comfortable.' He rests his big, strong palms on my shoulders and massages lightly for a few pleasurable moments.

I close my eyes and soften under his touch. 'That feels nice,' I sigh.

'Come on, before you fall asleep.' Leaving me at the mirror, he pulls some jeans on and a T-shirt over his head. 'Ready?'

I nod, slip my feet into my Converses and frown down at my untied laces. Jack's kneeling in front of me, taking care of it, before I can even try to bend down. I smile down at the back of his head, feeling grateful instead of useless. His care. His attention. It's easy to accept, because it's Jack.

Chapter 30

I suspect I know where we're heading when Jack gets us out of the city, but I keep quiet, happy to let him take charge of where we're going and what we're doing. It's something I never dreamed I would be content with: letting someone else look after me. It just feels right, not because I'm an invalid at the moment and can't carry out the simplest of tasks, but because it's how we are supposed to be. His hand remains tightly held around mine in my lap for the entire journey, my head relaxed back as I stare at him, take him in, try to come to terms with the fact that he is mine. All of him. He wants it all, and he wants it all with me. Despite my lingering pain, physically and emotionally I don't think I've ever been happier in my life. And it's all because of this man. This beautiful, wonderful man.

The final turn Jack takes confirms I was right about where we're going. 'My parents'?' I ask as Dad's Jaguar comes into view, shiny as ever on the driveway. 'What are we doing here?'

'Visiting,' Jack says, simple as that, as he pulls up outside my mum and dad's house.

Visiting? When I asked to be let out into the big wide world, I was thinking a bit further than my parents' house. Unclipping my seat belt, I wait for Jack to open my door and help me out, forcing back my hiss of pain as I rise from my seat. He curls an arm around my waist and walks me up the path to the front door. Mum, as always, answers before we can knock. She has a tea towel in her hand, a smile on her face.

'Annie, darling.'

'Hi, Mum.' I let her claim me from Jack and hug me, and boy does she hug me. 'Not so tight.'

'Oh, I'm sorry! It's just so good to see a bit of life in you.' She helps me into the hallway, and the usual homely scent of her cooking fills my nostrils. And the sound of voices fills my ears.

'Who's here?' I ask as we shuffle towards the kitchen, Jack following. Mum doesn't answer, and instead diverts us into the dining room.

'Everyone, darling.'

I stop at the doorway and take in the small space, and everyone quietens down and looks in my direction. Lizzy with Jason, Micky with Charlie, my dad and Nat. The first thing that comes to mind is, *Mum will be in her element with all these people to faff over.* The second thing I think is, *What are they all doing here?* I raise a wary hand in a lame hello, and then turn to Jack and give him questioning eyes.

He just smiles, takes my hand and leads me to the table, where a chair is waiting for me. Easing me down, he bends and kisses my cheek. 'They've promised not to fuss over you.'

I laugh, a little nervous, and watch as Mum hands Jack an apron. He doesn't question it, accepting it and slipping it on. 'You're helping Mum?'

'Apparently.' He shrugs and heads off to the kitchen, leaving me pretty astounded. Mum's letting Jack help?

I look across to my dad. 'Is she okay?' I ask seriously. She has a way with everything. Especially in the kitchen. *Her* way.

'She wants to bond with that new fella of yours.' Dad shrugs.

Micky laughs, and I look across to find his arm draped casually around Charlie's shoulders. 'Poor Jack.'

Bond. She wants to bond. The notion is deeply warming, given the circumstances of them discovering everything about Jack. The fact that she's invited him into her kitchen is a huge deal, and her way of accepting him. But visions of Mum's panicked face when Jack fails to do things to her liking fill my mind. 'He'll be kicked out within ten minutes,' I conclude.

'Five,' Dad counters with a grunt. 'He'll run out screaming in five minutes.' He looks down at his watch, checking the time.

I laugh and relax a little, but my hurting muscles tense when Nat and Lizzy head my way, encouraging Charlie to join us. Nat brings a bottle of wine with her and pours four healthy glasses. She passes one to each of us.

Charlie is the one to toast. 'To true love.'

I shoot her a look, and she smiles.

'True love,' Lizzy echoes, her eyes flicking to Jason at the other end of the table, where all the boys, bar Jack, are gathered. Dad pulls out the playing cards and declares war.

'True love,' I say quietly, hearing Jack in the kitchen taking instructions from Mum.

'Whatever!' Nat snorts, rolling her eyes as she dives head first into her wine. 'So.' She places her fingers on the bottom of my wine glass and encourages me to drink. 'Tell us about this new bloke of yours.'

And just like that, I know they're not going to drown me in sympathy. They're not going to ask questions, dig for more information or make me feel like I'm under the spotlight. Instead, they're going to act like the nightmare last few months never happened. They're going to act like Jack and I are normal. Like we met under normal circumstances. Like there has been no misery and heartache. I give them thankful eyes, and they all smile in return.

Jack wanders in and places a platter of nibbles in the centre of the table, catching my eye as he sets it down just so. He smiles, and I have to force myself to swallow down the emotion that creeps up on me unexpectedly. 'He's perfect,' I say quietly. 'Handsome, kind, ambitious and encouraging.'

'Sounds like a dream,' Jack replies casually, attracting all the girls' attention.

'Hey!' Lizzy grabs an olive from the platter and chucks it at him. 'Girl talk. Scram!'

He holds his hands up in surrender and backs out, looking across to my dad as he goes. 'I believe that's six minutes' survival time . . . so far.'

'I have a Scotch ready when you need it, son,' Dad says flippantly, dealing the cards out to Jason and Micky.

My heart could burst. Normal. This is all normal. This is how I've wanted it to be from the moment I fell for Jack, but how it couldn't be. I wanted to share everything about the man I'd fallen for with my friends. I wanted to talk girlie about the kisses, the sex, the feelings. I wanted to tell Mum and Dad that I'd met someone who'd knocked me off my feet, and I wanted to do this. Share him with them. I wanted Mum to love him, to welcome him into her home. For him to be part of the family.

Beyond wanting Jack so desperately, I also wanted this.

Acceptance. Love. Normality.

'I understand now,' Lizzy says, pulling me from my reflections. I look at her in question, and she smiles, faintly but genuinely. 'Seeing you together, I understand. Everyone does.'

I nod, blinking back my tears, more thankful than I've ever been.

'How tired are you?' Jack asks as he pulls away from my parents' house and I wave my goodbye.

It's been a wonderful evening. I've laughed, I've soaked up the affection that Jack has showered me with and I've relished the fond looks that have been thrown his way by all of my friends and family. They get it. They understand. I let my head fall back and roll to the side so he's in my sights. 'I'm not tired at all.'

He smiles at the road. 'You're lying, but I'm not going to argue with you. There's somewhere I want to take you.'

'Then take me,' I tell him, once again happy to let him take charge. We drive back into the city, chatting about nothing in particular, and Jack parks up in a side street in central London. 'Where are we?'

He doesn't answer, getting me out of the car in silence. 'You okay to walk for a few minutes?'

'Yes. Where are we going?'

Again my question is ignored, and Jack starts walking us towards the main road up ahead. I remain quietly curious until he brings us to a stop on the pavement, turning to me. 'We're here,' he says quietly.

I frown and look up, quickly realising where *here* is. I lose my breath for only a moment. 'Where we met,' I murmur, looking through the windows into the bar.

'Back to the beginning.' Jack leads me in and heads straight for the exact spot on the bar where he had me bent over. So many memories, vivid and clear, power to the forefront of my mind. He helps me onto a bar stool, takes one up himself and faces me. 'Are you drunk?' he asks seriously, staring deeply into my eyes.

My smile must be cracking my face. I decide to play his game, just like I decided to play his game on that fateful night I met him. 'Not in the slightest.'

'Care to prove it?' His head tilts, and there's a small pout on his lips.

'Yes.' I nod decisively. 'Are you going to bend me over the bar?'

'Don't tempt me.' He grins, calling for the barman. 'Two tequilas, please.' He tosses a note on the wood, making sure he brushes my hand tactically as he withdraws, his grin widening when I inhale. I'd love to tempt him, have him manipulate my body to where he wants it. I'd withstand the pain it would certainly spike, but I know he won't indulge me that much. 'Let's play,' he murmurs, glancing up at me.

A rush of incredible, overwhelming happiness powers through me. 'What do I have to do?'

Jack takes the salt and my hand, licking the back with a firm, long stroke, looking up at me as he does. 'You taste good.'

'So I'm told,' I muse, watching as he sprinkles the salt. 'Do you lick every woman you meet in a bar?'

'There's only one woman I've ever licked, and ever will.'

'Lucky woman.'

'Lucky me,' he counters, bringing my hand to his mouth and lapping up the salt before knocking back his drink. He hums his pleasure, unable to hold his smile back when I let mine break free. 'There's one more tequila,' he says, placing my hand on the bar by the glass. 'And it's yours.'

'I see something I'd like far more than tequila.' I go off script, saying what I really wanted to say the night I met Jack Joseph.

'Then take it.' He sits back on his stool, folding his arms over his broad chest. I glance around the bustling bar. We're in public, out and about, in plain sight for everyone to see. And for the first time I don't have to worry about keeping my hands to myself. I don't have to worry about being seen with a man who I shouldn't be with. It's alien, and so very hard to wrap my head around. 'What are you waiting for?' Jack asks, breaking into my thoughts.

The truth is, I don't know. To wake up, maybe? I slip down from the stool with caution, and I can tell Jack struggles not to help me. His thighs part a little, inviting me in. I walk forward and take his arms, unfolding them from around his chest and directing them around my waist. He lets me guide his moves, putting myself between his legs and looking up at him. And I kiss him. In public, with passion, love and everything I feel for him that I've never been able to share with the world. This man is mine.

'You move fast,' he says into my mouth. 'I only bought you a drink, and now you're trying to get me into bed.'

I chuckle, pulling back and finding his grey eyes. Grey eyes that are exploding with sparkles. 'Take me home,' I whisper. I want him to put me in bed and lick me everywhere. I want him to kiss me, touch me, make love to me.

'Your wish is my command, baby.' He picks me up in the middle of the bar for all to see and strides out with me wrapped around him. But we don't make it to the car, only to the end of the street. I'm placed on my feet on the kerb. 'Wait there,' he orders gently, turning and checking the road for traffic before jogging across to the other side. When he arrives, he faces me, him on one side of the road, me on the other. A little sob escapes when I realise where we are and what he's doing, as cars pass between us. He's *really* taking us back to the start.

'You mentioned home,' he calls across to me, his grey eyes bright. 'Look in your back pocket.'

My forehead bunches as I feel my way to my bum, pulling out a piece of paper. Slowly unfolding it, I split my attention between Jack and whatever's in my hand, curious and cautious all at once. I scan the sheet which I quickly establish contains the details of . . .

'Land?' I ask, too quietly for Jack to hear from across the road. I look up and find him looking pensive. 'What is this?'

'Ours,' he calls. 'I bought it for us.'

I let my gaze fall back to the paper in my hand, my head twisting, making it impossible for me to absorb the information staring up at me.

'Just say yes,' Jack shouts.

I laugh. 'I don't know what I'm saying yes to.'

He rolls his eyes dramatically, dropping his head back to look to the sky, like I'm slow. Then he paces across the road. I yelp when he lifts me from my feet, even though he does it with the utmost care, and I gasp when he cages me in against the brick wall behind me. 'I love this wall,' he declares, all husky and low. It does my restraint no favours when he talks to me like that, especially when he's talking about *this* wall. This wall that's another part of our story, like the tequila, the bar, and the hotel just around the corner where we spent all night exploring each other, getting to know each other's bodies. Our hearts began to tangle tightly that night, so tightly nothing would ever pull us apart. 'You're saying yes to everything with me, Annie.' His lips hover a few millimetres from mine. 'I've bought that land for us. You are going to design our home and—'

'You are going to build it,' I breathe, his plan finally making a breakthrough in my mind.

'Preferably with lots of bedrooms so we can fill them with babies.'

'Oh my God.' I drop the paper and squeeze him hard.

'It's me and you, baby. The house, the kids, the life, everything. We'll have it all.'

'I only ever wanted you,' I admit, sinking my face into his neck. 'I can't believe I finally have you.'

'You more than have me, baby.' He holds me so strongly, his heart pounding against mine – our beats in sync, their rhythms perfectly matched, the powerful love weaving, tangling us tighter still. 'You possess me. You own me. You rule me,' he murmurs in my ear. 'You are everything to me, Annie Ryan. My pulse, my heartbeat, my breath. Everything.'

My vision clouds as the tears pool in my eyes. 'I'm ready.'

'That's good, because I paid the deposit yesterday.'

'No, you don't understand what I'm saying, Jack.' I wrestle myself free and grab his hands, fixing him with a determined stare. 'I'm ready.' I direct his touch to my stomach and watch as comprehension dawns on him. He shoots me a look, one that's a mixture of uncertainty and elation.

'You're ready?'

'Haven't we had too much of our precious time taken already?' I ask.

'Way too much,' he agrees, his face pained.

'Take me home, Jack,' I order, sounding as sure as I feel. 'Put me in bed, make love to me. Be gentle if you must, but please make love to me.'

He groans and deepens our kiss, gathering me up in his arms. His arms, the place where nothing can touch me. My sanctuary. My haven. My home.

I had an affair. I was *that* woman. I fell in love with a married man. It was wrong, and we both suffered for it. We have both lost something – a loss we will share forever. But we still have each other. Part of me feels robbed by whoever's up there in charge of the Fates for keeping Jack from me for too long. But we were always going to find each other, no matter what. No matter who tried to keep us apart. Even me and Jack ourselves. Nothing could stop it. Nothing could stop the connection that was so strong it sent our worlds into chaos.

Jack was never really forbidden. Because he was always mine. And I was always his. Even before we knew it. Even before we found each other.

But we found each other in the end. Yet this is not the end for us. This is just the beginning.

True love prevailed. The greatest love. *Our* love.

'I'll hold your hand if you hold mine,' he mumbles around my lips.

'I'll never let go.'

Acknowledgements

This one has been the toughest yet, and there's no doubt I could not have got to the finish line without my trusted support network, especially the following people:

My wonderful agent, Andy. Your input and guidance have been invaluable. Thank you from the bottom of my heart. Your obsession with *The Forbidden* and your faith in me made me truly believe that I could step out of my comfort zone and give this story to my readers.

To Beth at Grand Central, you took a chance on an unknown author in early 2013 with a little book called *This Man*. You told me then that you weren't in it for the short haul and that you were excited for my future. Eight novels later, your enthusiasm for my words has never wavered. Thank you so much for giving my stories a home at GCP. And, mostly, thank you for standing by your word. Here's to the long haul and many more words.

To my editor Stateside, Leah, and my editor here in the UK, Laura, you guys are pure gold. I can't imagine my writing process without both of you there to support me. You two have played a key role in me making *The Forbidden* what it is. I can't thank you enough for championing me and pushing me in what has been the hardest tale of passion that I've ever written. I couldn't have done it without you. All of you.

Loved

The Forbidden?

*Tweet Jodi @JodiEllenMalpas,
Facebook/JodiEllenMalpas and join her
newsletter to get her latest news
www.jodiellenmalpas.co.uk*

Find your next read ...

Addictive, dangerous, your guiltiest pleasure yet . . .

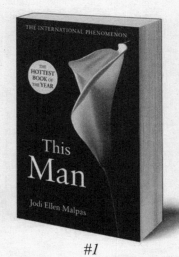

#1

#2

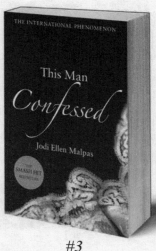

#3

Available Now

ONE NIGHT – *the hottest pulse-pounding trilogy . . .*

#1

#2

#3

Available Now

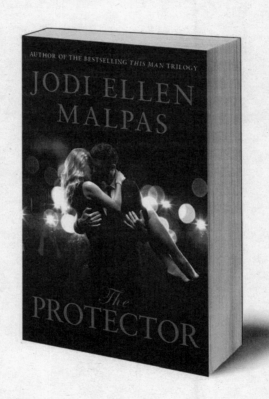